REAL
PLAYERS
NEVER
LOSE

MICALEA SMELTZER

Cover Design: Emily Wittig Designs

Cover Image: Regina Wamba

Editing: KBM Editing

Formatting: Micalea Smeltzer

REAL

PLAYERS

NEVER

LOSE

REAL
PLANETS
NEVER
LOSE

Real Players Never Lose

I've heard the whispers on campus of what a player Teddy McCallister is. Most girls on campus are vying to be *the one*, but guys like him don't settle down.

When he overhears that my tuition has been pulled and I'm going to basically be a college reject he makes me an offer I can't refuse.

Be his fake girlfriend until graduation so he can get his inheritance.

It seems simple enough. I need the money and he needs someone to make him look committed.
If one thing is certain, it's that I won't be falling for him.
But no one warned me about what happens when my fake boyfriends starts to fall for *me*.

ONE

Teddy

WINTER BREAK WAS A FUCKING FIASCO OF EPIC proportions.

I don't know why my dad thought a ski trip to Vale would make things better. I would've rather spent my break cooped up in the mega mansion like a prisoner than forced to pretend that we're one big happy family on vacation as we smiled and waved at cameras.

I couldn't even enjoy skiing like I normally would've.

But the McCallister family is nothing if not all about the appearances.

Gag me.

I open the door to my shared dorm with my friend

Jude. He's a junior and I'm a senior, but I pulled strings sophomore year so that we'd be roomed together. It helps when Daddy Dearest is a huge donor to the school you're attending.

It's a few days before the new semester starts. It took some convincing to get back early, but my mom was on my side. If it wasn't for her, I think I might've strangled my dad a long time ago. He's a controlling son of a bitch. He doesn't care about me or even her. The only thing that man loves is money and now he's using it to keep me in line.

If I don't do what he wants, he'll keep my inheritance from me.

My grandpa set it up so that I would receive it upon my college graduation. I think the old man was afraid I'd skip out on school if he didn't add that stipulation, and he was probably right.

But with my dad holding the reins now, it means I have to listen to him.

And sure, I've fucked around a lot—I'm a twenty-one-year-old red-blooded male. Of course, I like having sex and drinking in excess and partying until the sun comes up. It's college. Who doesn't do that shit?

But I got shit-faced over the summer and accidentally stole a yacht—I thought it was my family's—and after trashing the inside with a party I accidentally crashed it. My dad had enough after that and laid down the law.

My senior year is fucked because of his iron fist. Thank God I only have a few months left and then I'm done with this place, I get my inheritance, and I can bounce.

I have no idea what he'll do when he doesn't have his precious one and only child to continue on the family business and connections.

Jude's not back yet, so I have the place to myself which is an appreciated change. It was nice living with him before, when we could both enjoy women and booze, but watching him while I can't is a total annoyance. Sometimes I find myself questioning if I was really that bad.

Yes, yes I was.

Actually, I was worse, but that's a story for another day.

Jude and I have a shared space between our bedrooms that's big enough for a couch, TV, gaming system, and tiny kitchen. We're stuck sharing a bathroom too, which was weird for me at first when I came to college since I grew up in a house with seventeen bathrooms.

Yeah, *seventeen.*

I've never even taken a shit in all seventeen. Why anyone needs that many bathrooms is beyond me.

And at prep school we all had our own private quarters.

I set my suitcase on top of my unmade bed.

At the estate I grew up in, there would've been someone making sure my sheets were clean, bed was made, and whisking my suitcase away to unpack.

I won't lie, it was strange when I first came to school and realized I had to do shit myself. Even at the fancy

3

prep school I attended there was always someone picking up after me.

But now I like doing shit myself. Well, like is a strong word, but I guess I appreciate not being coddled twenty-four-seven. I'm not complaining. I know I'm privileged as fuck, but all I'm saying is it's not always what it's cracked up to be.

Having money doesn't mean things are constant rainbows and sunshine.

Sometimes it means you're merely a pawn and even a punching bag when need be. And you can never say a word or they'll end you.

A lump forms in my throat, and I swallow it down. I don't want to obsess over this. I'm typically a happy go lucky guy. I refuse to let things get to me. Especially anything involving my father.

I dump everything out of my suitcase, freshly cleaned by the maid at the penthouse we stayed in. I shove everything into drawers, not bothering to refold it, because what fucking difference does it make if it's folded or not when I pull it out to wear it?

With everything put away in less than five minutes, I stand in the middle of my room with my hands on my hips. It's quiet in here. Too quiet.

I turn on my Bose speaker and the annoying voice tells me it's now connected. I turn on my Get Pumped playlist and drop to the floor, banging out a set of sit ups, then push-ups, then burpees. Anything to keep my body moving.

I don't like idle time and I don't like silence.

Both of which I currently have in spades.

I work out until I'm covered in a light sweat, then hop in the shower. By the time I get out, towel wrapped around my waist, Jude's arrived.

I'm both glad for the company and irritated, because I know this place will be crawling with people soon. Jude wasn't always such a manwhore, but after his longtime girlfriend left him for another football player, he kind of lost his shit.

"'Sup, man!" He greets me with a wide grin. "How were the slopes?"

"Great." I scrub a towel over my scalp.

"That's all I get?" He scratches his jaw.

"Uh ... fantastic?"

He shakes his head. "You seem out of it, dude. You know what'll fix that?" He doesn't give me a chance to respond. "Beer and chicks."

"What do you have in mind?" I hope he doesn't pick up on the edge in my voice.

"Harvey's, what else?"

"Sure, why not." Harvey's is our usual haunt, and I could go for a beer or five. It won't be the typical crowd since most of my friends aren't back yet, but what does it matter? Besides, it'll keep people from hanging in our room and I can get out for a while. Even if I have to keep my hands to myself. Such a fucking tragedy. "When do you want to go?"

"Nine?"

"Perfect."

HARVEY'S IS NORMALLY PACKED from wall to wall, where even standing room is filled up. The bar is the go-to for most people on campus. But with students not required to be back until Sunday, people are using that time to their advantage.

Despite the small crowd and lack of most of our friends, Jude and I still take our usual U-shaped mega-booth in the back near the dancefloor.

It isn't long until guys and girls crowd the table and Jude pulls one of the girls, a busty blonde, onto his lap. A raven-haired beauty is talking up a storm to me, but I'm mostly ignoring her. She's fucking gorgeous—long hair, pert tits, and big lips I'd like to see wrapped around my cock—but I can't go there. One of my father's stipulations is no one-night-stands and since that's all I ever do I've had to give up sex entirely. It's been over six months and at this point I'm mostly numb to my baser desires, but when a chick is giving me the *fuck me* eyes it's tough.

"Are you even listening to me?"

"Uh…" I blink at the dark-haired beauty. "No." I don't even bother to lie.

Her brown eyes turn to slits. "Do you even remember my name?"

Again, *"No."*

She rolls her eyes. "Fiona was right, you really are an asshole." My cheek stings when she slaps it, sliding out of the booth and off to look for another victim. I don't even remember a girl named Fiona either, so I guess I really am an asshole.

I lived the first three years at Aldridge in a haze of booze, women, and marijuana. I'm not into the harder shit. But this year, I've had to stay alert ... well, mostly. I've had a few slips, but my friends reined me back in, knowing how important it is that I don't fuck up. Honestly, it fucking sucks seeing things through clear eyes. A lot of the glamour and appeal of college has faded, but I only have a few months left, and at least these will be filled with baseball, then I graduate, get my inheritance, and I can bounce.

I've spent my whole life being groomed to take over the family business—to schmooze the rich and famous, rub elbows with politicians, and dazzle royals. I never minded the idea of it, I'd been raised in this world, but I realize now I don't want to be like my dad. Cold and cruel, not caring who I hurt on the way to the top, even if it's my own child.

The McCallister family comes from *old* money. I can trace my family tree back for generations.

And when my friends ask what exactly my family does, I always either ignore them or find a way to change the subject. How do I explain that my family descended from a prominent Scottish royal, that there's a castle there still named after us, and that the wealth continues to grow from multiple businesses we own, to real estate, and even oil? The McCallister family has sought wealth like some people hunt Pokémon. Only one has led to a slippery moral compass.

I finish off my beer and lean over to Jude. Two girls are draped over him, clinging like long-limbed octopuses that don't dare let him loose from their grip lest he get picked up by other predators.

"Dude, you need a refill or anything? I gotta take a leak."

"Another." He mouths, pointing at his empty glass.

Sliding out of the booth, I go to the bathroom, hiding inside longer than necessary. For once, I'm not enjoying myself. It's not even because I'm trying to be on my best behavior, I'm just in a shit mood from being with my parents for weeks.

The whole thing was a fucking joke.

The only blessing is, by the time I got to be a sophomore in high school, my dad stopped using me as a human punching bag. The bruises have faded, but the trauma hasn't.

That was another blessing of going to school away from home. I didn't have to deal with *him*.

Lifting my shirt in the empty bathroom—*that's* how barren Harvey's is, that even the bathroom has no one in it —I look at the jagged scar on my abdomen. He slammed me into a wrought iron gate at a cousin's estate in Spain and one of the spikes on the end of it pierced my skin. I was only twelve and I thought I was going to die from the pain.

My dad had taken one look at my face, at the tears I was holding back, and screamed, *"Look what you've done now!"*

As if it was *my* fault, he pushed me.

As if anything in my childhood was my fault. Sure, he'd try to make me believe that, but I knew better.

I'd be lying if I said most of my rebellion hadn't been done to try to piss my old man off. I used to always try to keep him happy. If he was happy, there was less chance of him hurting me, but when I got big enough that he knew he couldn't push me around anymore, I used that to my advantage and did dumb shit.

But now, I need that inheritance if I have any chance of getting out for good.

Getting out never used to be a thought in my mind. I didn't think I *could*. But I realize now that the precious money waiting for me after I graduate can buy me my freedom.

Swinging the door open, I head over to the bar and order another beer for Jude and a glass of water for myself. Once I drink all of it, I'll allow myself to have one more beer before I call it a night.

Back at the table, I hand Jude his beer. "Dude, where'd you disappear to? You were gone forever. Find a girl to steal away with for a moment?"

"Sure," I mutter, sitting down with my pathetic water.

Jude's too absorbed in the girls at his side—a third having joined—for him to notice the sarcasm dripping from my voice.

A year ago, I would've been cheering him on. Fuck, a year ago I would've been covered in girls like he is. But now seeing him surrounded does nothing but irritate me and give me a mild headache, because I know they're bound to come back to the dorm with us, and I'll have to listen to their porn style level of fuckery for the entire night. Except, I finally got smart and utilize my noise canceling headphones. Don't know why it took so long for me remember them.

We hang at Harvey's for another two hours, before we pile into an Uber minivan, the three girls following Jude like he's God's gift to women.

I can't believe I'm even thinking this, but how the hell did I tolerate these girls and all their chittering? If I have to hear one of them breathily tell Jude how hot he is one more time I'm going to lose it.

Back in our dorm, I bid adieu to the four of them and lock myself in my room. I learned early on to lock my door unless I wanted a strange girl crawling into my bed. Whether on purpose or by accident, it doesn't matter, I'm not going to have that.

Lying in bed, arm curled around my head I look up at the glow in the dark dinosaurs I put on the side of my wall. They're cheap plastic things I bought at the local dollar tree, but they were another fuck you to my parents, because I was never allowed to have something so cheap looking in my bedroom growing up.

All about those fucking appearances again.

"WHO THE FUCK is banging pots and pans this early in the morning?" I bitch, throwing off my sheet and stumbling out of bed. I look at my phone, plugged in on my desk and see that it's after ten. "Okay, so not early in the morning."

I shove my hand in my boxers, giving my balls a scratch. The banging continues and I go to open my door but realize it's locked. Grumbling under my breath, I twist the lock and finally open it, stumbling into the living area.

"Oh, for fuck's sake," I cry, slapping a hand over my eyes at the three naked girls sprawled between the couch and floor. A multitude of condom wrappers litter the floor along with a used bottle of lube—and that's just what I was able to observe before shielding my eyes. Jude is nowhere to be seen, probably in his room. He doesn't hang around after he's had his fill.

But I realize if Jude's not here, and the three girls are still passed out—which, *how* with this banging—then it's not coming from inside the dorm, but outside.

More than likely it's someone on the same floor that's come to complain about Jude keeping them up last night. It wouldn't be the first time it's happened.

Ripping the door wide open, it's not a fellow student standing on the other side.

It's my father.

My.

Father.

"What are you doing here?" I blurt, rubbing my eyes in case I'm imagining things. I didn't drink much last night, but I sure as hell am hoping I'm absolutely plastered right now.

Unfortunately, rubbing my eyes doesn't work like shaking an Etch-A-Sketch to get rid of the image in front of me.

"I can't check on my son?" My father's silvery gray

eyes, so light it's like they were bleached, stare back at me with a challenging look. His thin lips are flat, not an ounce of humor on his face.

"You never have before. To what do I owe this pleasure?" I purposely keep the door open as little as possible to block him from the three naked girls, and landfill worthy number of used condoms.

God-fucking-dammit, Jude!

"I wanted to make sure you were settling back in well."

"You flew all the way from Vale less than twenty-four-hours after me, to make sure I'm settling in well?" I scoff, crossing my arms over my chest in disbelief. "Mom and you didn't even bother to bring me freshman year, so I apologize if I'm not buying your bullshit."

"Let me in."

Fuck no.

"Why should I?"

"Is there something you don't want me to find in here, son?"

"I have nothing to hide, but I'm beyond pretending that we have a good relationship. Look around, father, there are no cameras. There's no need to play pretend."

"You're right." His eyes flash, and it's only for the fact that I'm caught by surprise that he's able to shove me hard enough that I stumble back, he forces himself into the dorm.

Rage boils beneath the surface of his skin when he takes in the women on the couch and floor.

"What the fuck?!" He shouts, rushing me. He pushes

12

me into the refrigerator and it literally rocks from side to side. Somehow, none of the girls wake up at his outburst.

"Take your fucking hands off me," I warn, teeth gritted.

"You can't tell me what do." He's so pissed that his spit hits my face as he speaks.

This time I shove him back and then mockingly dust off my chest like I'm completely unaffected by him manhandling me. The thing about abuse is even when you're used to it, it still hurts — not only in a physical way, but soul deep, because you know a parent is supposed to protect you, not harm you.

"I warned you about this," he seethes, finger pointing toward the living area but eyes never leaving my face. His normally pale color is beet red, and a vein in his forehead pulses. I wonder what would happen if I poked that vein.

"This," I gesture to the girls, "isn't my mess. It's Jude. My roommate's. I know you don't know him, but he's quite the ladies man."

"I don't see your roommate, I see *you.*"

"Yeah, because he's shut up in his room nursing a hangover and a porn level of sex."

His hand strikes out, slapping me.

The man hasn't laid a hand on me in years, and in the span of less than five minutes he's pushed, shoved, and slapped me. That's how I know he's beyond pissed and reaching a murderous level of rage.

He claims he's angry because I'm not the perfect son, but we both know it's a lie. Even if I did and said everything he wanted, walked the straight and narrow, he would still hurt me because while he's already a rich powerful man, beating up his son makes him feel *invincible*.

"Do not put another fucking hand on me."

His eyes flash, that same look I've seen over the years that says *try me*. It promises a world of hurt and pain.

Think of your inheritance. This man holds the purse strings.

I curse my grandpa for croaking on me. He wasn't the best, but he was better than my old man.

"I warned you what would happen if you screwed up—"

"This isn't my fucking screw up." The urge to barrel down on him is strong, but I resist. *Think of the money. Think of the freedom.* "In fact," I find myself saying, a complete lie rolling off my tongue effortlessly, "I have a girlfriend, and unlike you, I believe in being faithful when I make a commitment."

"You don't have a girlfriend."

He's right, but I'm not cowing to him.

"I do."

"You never mentioned her the entire break."

"Because the three of us discuss my personal life extensively." Doubt fills his eyes and I capitalize on it. "It's new," I continue, rambling out my ass, "we'd only been together a month before break."

His lips purse, disbelief in his eyes. "Prove it."

"Huh?" I'm taken by surprise.

"Prove it," he repeats. "Bring this girlfriend to dinner with your mom and I at the estate next weekend."

"I can do that."

"If you're being honest with me, I'll forget … this." He

wrinkles his nose like he smells something sour, flicking his fingers at the naked girls.

"Erase it from your memory, because she's real."

"Mhmm," he hums doubtfully. "I'll see you next Saturday at seven PM."

He straightens his shirt, smoothing it free of wrinkles that aren't even there.

No other words are exchanged between us as he walks out the door. It clicks shut softly behind him. My dad might throw punches, but he's not the slamming doors type.

One of the girls lifts her head up, blinking open sleepy eyes. She's completely oblivious to her nakedness when she notices me in the kitchen.

"Did someone slam the door?"

I throw my hands up. It's not even noon and I'm done with this fucking day.

TWO

Vanessa

I GOT BACK TO CAMPUS LATER THAN I WANTED.

I certainly didn't expect to be breezing in on Monday, the day classes start again, but when you're doing what you can to hold the pieces of your family together when you're home, you do what you have to do.

Swiping my ID to get into my dorm, a loud buzzing sounds and it flashes red.

"What?" I mutter to myself.

I swipe it again and stare at my card.

"You have to be kidding me."

I'm tired from the all-night drive and wanted to shower and catch maybe two hours of sleep before my first class.

That won't be happening now.

Grumbling all the way to the opposite end of campus where the administration building is, I earn more than a few strange looks from my fellow students. I don't give a shit. I'm cranky and my pits stink and I'm also hangry. It's a lethal combination.

I storm into the building, reminding myself it's not the secretary's fault and I can't take my anger out on the poor unsuspecting soul. It's a glitch in the system more than likely, but I need my ID working so I can not only get into the dorm but grab a bite to eat.

Taking a deep breath, I steady myself before entering the office, plastering a smile on my face.

"Hi," I say in my politest tone to the secretary at the desk. "There seems to be something wrong with my ID." I hold out the flimsy piece of plastic to her. "I tried to get into the dorm, and it wasn't working."

"Hmm." She pushes bedazzled glasses up her nose. "That's strange."

She takes my card, turning it this way and that. She slides it through something that looks like a credit card swiper, a puzzled expression on her face.

The door opens behind me, bringing with it a hint of expensive cologne.

I don't turn to see who the newcomer is, but I feel the presence behind me like whoever it is commands attention from the very air of the room itself.

The secretary squints at my ID and starts typing on her computer.

"Oh," she whistles lowly, "honey."

It's not a good *"Oh, honey."* It's the kind of voice adults use when they're about to deliver devastating news.

Her hesitant eyes flicker to me. I hate the pity I find on her face.

"What's wrong?" My stomach sinks, waiting for the blow.

She clears her throat. "Sweetie, your term hasn't been paid, so technically you're not a student anymore."

My blood turns cold. "What do you mean?" Panic snakes through my veins.

What does she mean it hasn't been paid? I'm here on scholarship. Where did the money go? This is my senior year! I'm supposed to be graduating in a few months!

"It seems like your scholarship was pulled unexpectedly."

"Wha-? How? How does that even happen?"

"It can be for a number of reasons, sweetie." She winces, not meeting my eyes. "Unless it's paid in full by Friday, there's nothing we can do, and until it's paid you won't have access to your dorm."

"But all of my things are in there!" I protest. "I'm a senior! I need to graduate!"

I thought fainting dramatically only happened in movies, but I start to feel light-headed, swaying on my feet. Then again, the lack of food might have something to do with it.

"Like I said—"

"Yeah, yeah. I got it," I snap, my entire world crumbling around me.

There's no fucking way I'll be able to get the full

payment for my final semester. There's a reason I'm a scholarship student. Aldridge caters to the kids of the rich and famous, not people like me from backwoods Georgia who grew up with nothing.

Aldridge University was my chance to escape working at the local Piggly Wiggly or gas station like the rest of my family. Heart-stopping panic squeezes my chest, tears stinging my eyes, because that's exactly what's going to happen. I'm going to have to go back, and my sister can gloat all about how she knew I'd fail.

"Just look at you, you're not cut out for that life."

I wanted to have a career in communications and Aldridge was the biggest stepping stone to getting there, not only for my degree, but for the connections that I've built over the past three and a half years.

Now it's all being flushed away because for some insane reason my scholarship has been pulled without explanation.

"I never got a letter," I blurt at the lady. "No one notified me my scholarship had been pulled."

She clacks on her keyboard some more and tells me a date when the letter was mailed.

I close my eyes, thinking of the smug way my sister acted over the entire break.

She got the letter. She knew. She fucking knew and didn't say a word. She was probably buzzing with excitement, waiting for me to have to come back so she could wave the piece of paper in my face.

Blood or not, I hate that bitch.

"I see. Thank you for your help."

"I'm sorry," she says, and I think she truly means it. She narrows her eyes on whoever is behind me. "Teddy McCallister, have you lost your ID *again?* This is the fifth time this year!"

"Aw," the voice behind me cajoles, "Mrs. Jostin, it's senior year, I've gotta set a record."

Shaking myself free from where I'm frozen to the floor and blocking him, I turn around, and finally face the guy who's listened to the entire woes of my predicament.

Teddy McCallister.

Campus heartthrob. Player. Life of the party.

I've personally never met him, only heard of him and seen him around campus. Like always, I'm taken aback by his clear jungle-green eyes. They're bright and glittery emerald jewels. If it wasn't unfair enough for the guy to have the most beautiful eyes I've ever seen, they're also framed in the longest, thickest set of lashes. Not to mention, he's gorgeous. The kind of handsome that's somehow both classic and wholesome. Sharp brow, angular cheekbones, cut jaw. He's the epitome of hot. Stubble coats his cheeks, and his brown hair is unkempt in a purposeful way. He reminds me of a young Luke Perry. Rest in peace. Thanks to my mom I had a crush on the 90s heartthrob from a young age. I've watched the entire show at least ten times in completion.

He's studying me with astute eyes, but an easy-going smile. It's a weird combination and I stare back with a narrowed expression, wishing I could read his mind.

Mrs. Jostin clears her throat. "Teddy?"

I break eye contact first, and duck my head, shuffling out the door as quickly as I can.

Away from his scrutinizing green-eyed gaze, I inhale a breath, letting reality sink onto my shoulders.

What. The. Ever. Loving. Fuck. Am. I. Going. To. Do.

I've always been level-headed, excellent at keeping common sense in situations, being the voice of reason, but right now I feel nothing but blind panic. I waitress part-time to supplement what my scholarship doesn't cover, but it leaves little left for me to save, so what I do have in savings is only a few thousand dollars. It's basically pennies compared to a semester of tuition at this school, and I know there's no way I'll qualify for a loan.

I allow myself another full minute to freak out internally in the hallway before I force myself to leave. Outside, the cold crisp winter air slams into my face, reminding me how tired I am from my drive. Now, I don't even have a dorm to *sleep* in—one where all my stuff is, except what I packed for break.

The first tear falls, then right behind it an entire torrent.

Oh, God. How embarrassing?

There's a bench nearby and I scurry over to it, parking my ass so I can have my breakdown in relative privacy.

I dig through my purse, searching for a tissue. I find one at the bottom, but it's got a piece of gum rolled into it. Ugh.

My coat sleeve will have to do.

Sniffling, I wipe at my face, wracking my brain for some kind of solution.

I could always become a stripper. I mean, I'm far from skinny, definitely over-weight, but all girls are beautiful, and I have decent boobs. I don't think my stretch marks would scare the menfolk too badly.

But I can't dance.

Like at all.

Not one iota of rhythm in my body.

I blame my dad for that fact.

So yeah, stripping is out. I might be able to bartend at a strip club, the tips would probably be way better than my waitressing job at The Burger Palace. I don't like showing a lot of skin, it's personally not my thing, but I am not above showing off my boobs if it gets me the money I need.

But, and here's the kicker, it's not like I can pay over the course of the semester.

Nope, they want it all paid in full by the end of the week.

There is no hope for me.

I'm going to be a college dropout. Although, does it count as a dropout when you're forced into it?

The real kicker is Aldridge is rolling in the dough. They wouldn't even miss the money if they let me slip through, but we all know they're not going to do me any favors. Not some poor, pathetic scholar —

"Hey."

I look up at the sound of the voice, appalled someone has caught me crying — red-faced and splotchy. I must look halfway insane.

My horror is made worse when it's none other than Teddy McCallister.

Not only did he witness my complete and utter humiliation at being told my scholarship is *poof* gone, now he's found me crying my eyes out like I did when the news dropped in the middle of class that One Direction had broken up.

That was the third worst day of my life.

This obviously being the first now and the second I try not to think about.

"Oh, God," I mutter, embarrassed at my state. "Um." *Sniffle.* "Hi."

"Are you okay?"

"Peachy."

He squints. "It doesn't take a genius to see you're lying."

"What gave me away? Was it the tears, hysterical hiccupping, or red face?"

He grins. "All of the above."

I sigh, picking up my bag and standing. "Look, I'm fine."

I'm the furthest thing from my fine, but this is the last guy on campus I want witnessing my breakdown. I can cry from the comfort of my car, and I very well might be sleeping there too because I don't want to shell out what little money I have for a hotel.

"You don't look fine." He's amused. I guess to him my problems barely register on his radar. I've heard he comes from one of the wealthiest families in the *world*, not just the

United States. I can't even begin to fathom what it would be like to have that kind of money.

"I will be. Thanks for checking on me."

I start to walk away, but his voice calls me back. "Wait, don't go yet."

There's a slight desperation to his tone.

Turning back around, I give him a curious look. "Why not?"

He fidgets awkwardly, shoving his hands in his pockets. His nose scrunches and he finally blurts, "I think I can help you."

"Help me?"

"With your tuition. You said you're a senior, there's only one semester left—"

I hold up a hand to shut him up and surprisingly he presses his lips together. "How the hell do you think you're going to help me? It's a lot of money even for just one semester."

"Listen, I need a favor, a huge one. You help me, and I'll help you."

I look at him in disbelief. "What could you possibly need that's worth that much money? Do you even have that amount?" I know he comes from a wealthy family, but it doesn't mean the riches are his.

"I have enough. I don't get my inheritance until I graduate, but I have an account from my mom. It's got several hundred grand in it, that's more than enough to pay your tuition."

He says several hundred grand the way I'd say I have five bucks. Casually and unaffected.

I gulp. "I'm not blowing you for money."

He snorts. "Didn't ask you to, sweetheart."

"What would you want in exchange for paying for this semester?"

I can't believe I'm even entertaining this. Am I really this desperate?

Answer: yes, I am, in fact, this desperate.

"Look," he starts, then shakes his head. "You should sit down." He points to the bench. "We should sit down." Now he's stuttering, and it would be kind of adorable if I weren't so emotionally strung out.

"I like standing."

"Fine. Okay. Yeah, um." He runs his fingers through his hair. "Listen, I need a girlfriend, a fake girlfriend because I kind of lied to my dad—he's a real prick by the way—because he didn't believe me when I told him the truth, so the only way out of it was to convince him I have a girlfriend. Which he doesn't believe I have. So, he's challenged me to bring her home next weekend, so yeah, you would do me a real solid pretending to be my girlfriend. Knowing my dad, next weekend won't be good enough. There's no telling how long this relationship will last. It might even go as far as marriage and babies."

I don't think he takes a single breath in that long-winded rambling speech.

"I hope you're kidding about the marriage and baby part."

He pats his crotch. "I would never kid about future Teddy Juniors. Scratch that, I would never name a kid what my parents named me. Our kids can have their own names."

"I'm not having your babies."

He scoffs. "Why not?"

"This is insane." I cover my face with my hands, tears long since dried. Letting my hands fall, I level him with a look, one like my mom would give me as a warning that if I didn't stop whatever it was I was doing that I would regret it. "You, *you* are insane."

"Nah, babe, I'm perfectly sane. This is a rational decision. Mutually beneficial. You need your tuition paid, and I need a fake-girlfriend."

"That's a lot of money for a fake-girlfriend. You're popular. I'm sure you could find any lucky lady on campus that would do this for free."

"I'm sure I could, but you don't know me, and you don't seem to want me. I mean, you've already scoffed at the idea of having my children, when most would be more than glad. That makes you the perfect fit, because you won't get attached."

I snort, a totally and completely unladylike sound. "Yeah, you definitely don't have to worry about that."

"I'll go back in there right now," he points over his shoulder at the administration building, "and pay. Say the word."

"You're crazy," I gasp in disbelief.

"I promise you, I'm not. I'm completely rational."

"No sane person pays for another's tuition."

He shrugs. "It's not that much money."

I reel at his words, and realize that to him it's not, but I can't wrap my head around that. I count every cent, divvying it out and deciding if I have enough extra to treat myself to a coffee or order a new pair of leggings, but he's talking about nearly *forty-thousand* dollars for one semester of school like it's nothing. I can't relate to what it must feel like to throw money around willy-nilly.

I tuck a piece of hair behind my ear, his eyes following my movement.

"Say yes … I don't actually know your name." He scratches his brow. "That's bad. If you're going to be my fake-girlfriend I should know your name."

"I haven't agreed to anything and it's Vanessa."

"Vanessa," he swirls my name around his tongue like an expensive wine he's trying to identify the notes of, "you need me and I need you. This is a symbiotic relationship."

"It's *no* relationship."

"Please?" He pouts his bottom lip, clasping his hands beneath his chin. Dropping his hands, his eyes are nothing but serious. "I need you."

He doesn't need *me*. He could pick any girl on campus regardless of what he said. Many of them would be glad to do it just for the social ladder bump it would give them. Me? I couldn't care less about popularity.

It's on the tip of my tongue to tell him to let me think about it, but what do I have to think about? All I have to do is bat my eyes and pretend to be his girlfriend. My part in this is easy, not like giving up a huge chunk of change like he's planning on. Though he's as casual about it as someone buying a Big Mac at McDonalds.

"Yes."

27

His eyes turn to saucers, like he was expecting to have to do more convincing. "Yes?"

I nod, hoping I don't regret this decision. "Yep. You've got yourself a fake-girlfriend."

He holds his hand out to me to shake on it. His palm is rough, calloused, not at all what you'd expect from a rich kid like him. He plays baseball, so maybe that's why.

He finishes the handshake by pulling me into a tight hug, stealing all the oxygen from my lungs. He lets me go with a blinding white smile that he probably paid top dollar for.

"You're a life saver, Van."

"It's Vanessa."

He frowns. "Nah, as your fake-boyfriend I should call you by a nickname. It shows familiarity."

"All right, Ted."

His eyes narrow to slits. "No. I'm not a serial killer. I'm a cuddly bear. Teddy it is. Besides, Teddy is already a nickname."

"Fair point," I sigh, already wondering if I've made a horrible decision. It's not like I gave it very much thought, but what's a girl to do when she's desperate and an opportunity like this arises?

"We should exchange numbers."

"Right." I shake my head. "Of course."

This is hands down the weirdest encounter I've ever had, and I can't think straight.

"We should meet up tonight."

"For what?" I blurt.

He flicks his hair out of his eyes. "To get to know each

other rapid fire style. I told my dad I'd started dating someone a month before break, so we're supposed to have known each other almost two months now."

I blow out a breath. "That makes sense."

"I'll call you with the deets."

Deets? What person actually says deets?

"Sure. Okay."

"I'll have your tuition paid in a few hours. My class is starting soon, and I'll have to run by my dorm to get a check."

In a few hours my tuition will be covered, and I'll be able to graduate this spring like I should've been in the first place. I'm realizing what a divine blessing it is that Teddy walked in behind me today.

"What about a contract? Don't you want me to sign something saying I won't bail on you?"

"I suppose I should, but I don't want a paper trail. I feel like I can trust you, Van, and my gut is rarely wrong. Are you planning to flake out?"

"No," I scoff.

"Then perfect. No contract needed."

"This is insane." I rub my hands over my face.

"So, you've said." He grins. "See you tonight."

He winks at me and then he's jogging away, sliding behind the wheel of a blue Porsche.

What the hell have you gotten yourself into, Vanessa?

I'm in way over my head. That much is obvious.

THREE

Teddy

I PULL UP OUTSIDE A TRUCK STOP AROUND THIRTY minutes from Aldridge, since Vanessa suggested it would probably be smart for us to meet somewhere no one from school is likely to be, that way we can go over all the details people usually know about each other when they've been dating for a couple of months.

My car is going to stick out like a sore thumb here, but there's nothing I can do about it now.

I park the Porsche, shutting off the engine. A text from Vanessa says she's already inside.

I don't know what I was thinking, but when I heard about her predicament I *wanted* to help. For once I could do something decent with my family's money. Besides, I did need to track down a fake-girlfriend, and she seemed like the perfect candidate. I'm not sure why my instinct seemed to know I could trust her for this job, because I've never even seen the girl on campus before. But my gut is usually right about people.

I slip my sunglasses off and stick them in the cupholder.

Breezing into the truck stop, my stomach rumbles at the smell of the greasy food. Looking toward the booths, a hand raises and waves me over.

I grin as I walk over to Vanessa, lowering to kiss her cheek before I slide in across from her. She stiffens a little at the touch of my lips and I feel like a dick.

"Sorry," I say sheepishly. "I didn't mean to make you uncomfortable."

I've always been an affectionate person, and sometimes I forget that others aren't so keen on physical touch.

"It's okay." She tucks a wavy piece of dark brown hair behind her ear. "I need to get used to it."

Vanessa is beautiful, and I'm honestly questioning how I never noticed her before. Surely, we've had to cross paths at some point? In the dining hall? Coffee shop? A party? I guess campus is large enough that we might've missed each other, but—

"Are you hungry?" she asks me, jolting me from my thoughts.

"Starved."

She passes me a plastic menu that's sticky to the touch. Hopefully from disinfectant and not greasy fingers, but let's be honest it's definitely the latter.

31

She studies her own menu, her nose scrunched in an adorable way.

Adorable? Really, Teddy? You can't already be thinking your fake-girlfriend is adorable.

But obviously, this only makes sense if I *am* attracted to Vanessa. And I'd totally fuck her.

I'd be lying if I said I hadn't checked her out the moment I walked into the office and stood behind her. She's thick and curvy, with a nice ass, glossy hair, and soft voice that I could listen to all day. Then when she turned around, I got a good look at her face, and I was even more attracted than I was before. Blue eyes, Angelina Jolie-esque pouty lips, and big boobs.

I'm a simple man, give me some tits to look at and an ass to hold and I'm happy.

But, of course, women are off limits.

Unless they're of the girlfriend variety.

Well, the fake kind.

"Have you eaten here before?" I tap my fingers against the table. I've always had more energy than I knew what to do with.

"I used to work here."

"Oh?" I arch a brow, laying the menu flat on the table. "Where do you work now?"

She worries her bottom lip between her teeth. "The Burger Palace. I'm a waitress. I'm sure it's a far cry from the world you know."

There's an edge to her voice and I know what preconceived notions she probably has about someone like me.

I bite my tongue, so I don't say a word. She's not

wrong. I grew up with a silver spoon in my mouth, but what people forget is that silver can poison you.

Changing the subject, I say, "What would you recommend here?"

"Stay away from anything pasta. The steaks are okay, but if Julio still works here they're more likely to come out burned than anything else. The sandwiches are where it's at."

I turn to that part of the menu, finding names like *Dolly Parton's Boobs* and *Billy Ray's Mullet.*

"Hi, y'all. I'm Sheila. I'll be your waitress this afternoon. What can I get y'all to drink?"

"Lemonade." Vanessa smiles at her. "And I'm ready to order if he is."

"I'm ready."

"Okay." She smiles at me. It's an uneasy smile, one that I know stems from the fact that we don't know each other well yet, but we're going to have to work on it because if my dad sees her smile like that, he'll know something's up. "I'll have the Before He Cheats on wheat with fries."

"And for you?" The middle-aged waitress turns to me, pen poised against her pad of paper.

"Coke and the Luke Bryan's Jeans also with fries, please."

"I'll get this in and be right back with your drinks."

When the waitress is gone, Vanessa lets out a breath like she's been unconsciously holding it. She gives me an awkward smile, her eyes darting quickly from mine to different spots around the room and back again.

I'm amused and more than a little surprised. She was such a spitfire, but all that bravado is gone for now. I have a feeling it'll be back before I know it, and I'm more than looking forward to it. Our verbal sparring is a foreplay of a different type.

After our drinks are dropped off, I decide to get down to business.

I yank out the rumpled piece of paper from my pocket that I've been adding questions to over the past few days along with a pen I brought just for this occasion, because fuck if I ever normally have a pen on me.

"Favorite color?"

"Huh?" She looks at me like I'm speaking a foreign language.

"Favorite color?" I repeat. "As your interim fake-boyfriend I should know things about you and vice versa. That's why we're here."

"Right." She plays with the ends of her hair, and I make a mental note of that because it must be something she does when she's nervous. She meets my eyes, nose crinkling again. *Nose crinkle*, I scribble. "Um ... green." She cringes and I have no idea why. "And yours?"

"Orange."

"Orange?" she exclaims. "I don't think I've ever met anyone with the favorite color orange."

If I'm being honest, orange only became my favorite color when I was fourteen and overheard my father say it was the most appalling color known to man.

"Now you've met one. Favorite show?"

"*Gilmore Girls*—are you seriously taking notes?" She

eyes the paper on the table between us, marred with my chicken scratch.

"I mean, with my genius level IQ I'll more than likely remember everything you say, but better safe than sorry in case I need to study up. There's no telling what my father might ask either of us."

Her eyes widen. "Is he really a jerk?"

"Worse." I squint at my smudged writing. "Where's the weirdest place you've had sex?"

She blinks at me. "Pass. A lady never tells."

"Pssh," I scribble down *will find out later* beside that answer. "Mine is a church confessional. I'm not even Catholic but I did almost see God that day."

"You're kidding, right?"

"Why would I kid about that?"

She rubs at her forehead, puffing out a breath. No doubt she's questioning what she's gotten herself into with me. Frankly, I feel bad for dragging her into my mess. Vanessa seems kind, even a little shy. She's someone my dad will have far too much fun toying with, but I'll do everything I can to protect her, especially since she's doing me such a solid. I know she thinks it's nothing compared to me paying for her final semester, but having her help is priceless.

"Next question," I mutter, silently cursing my awful handwriting. It's surprising I wasn't forced to learn how to write neater. "Favorite food?"

"Cheeseburger."

I grin. "My kind of girl. That's my favorite."

"Can I ask you a question?" She bites her lip hesi-

35

tantly, eyeing the table.

"Sure. I'm an open book. Nothing's off limits."

She rolls her eyes, drawing random designs on the tabletop with her index finger. "Why me?"

She basically asked me the same thing the other day, and the truth is I don't know. She wasn't wrong when she said any girl would've been happy to volunteer, but when I heard her predicament it seemed like maybe we'd been placed in each other's paths. But I don't want to say that, or she might think I'm insane and I'm pretty sure she already thinks I'm halfway to crazy.

"Because." *Come on, Teddy, you can do better than that.*

"Because why?"

Her blue eyes are large and round, waiting eagerly for my answer, for some sort of explanation.

I sigh, running my fingers through my hair. "I don't know. My gut told me I could trust you, and my gut is almost always right."

"Huh."

"Here are your sandwiches." The waitress interrupts us to put our plates on the table.

Vanessa wasn't lying. The sandwiches look fucking fantastic, better than what I expected that's for sure. My stomach rumbles again, reminding me that the one skittle I found in my cupholder and ate earlier wasn't exactly the sustenance I need.

Neither of us say anything for a few minutes, eating in silence. I guess I'm not the only one that's hungry.

Once the monster in my stomach is sort of happy, I get back to my list of questions.

"Where were you born?"

"A little town called White Claw, Georgia. Go ahead, laugh at the name. It's where my family still lives."

My lips twitch but something tells me she'll want to throw something at me if I give into the full-blown laughter I'd like to have.

"Siblings?"

"One older sister who I'm pretty sure is the spawn of the Devil. That's it, thank God. What about you?"

"Born in Nashville and attended a boarding school in upstate New York. No siblings. Just me. They got their male heir on the first try and didn't bother with a spare."

She blinks at me, probably trying to decide whether or not I'm serious, which I am.

Picking up a fry, she swirls it in ketchup and uses it to point at my list before she pops it in her mouth. "What else you got on there?"

"Have you ever been arrested?"

"Nope. You?"

"Um..." I press my lips together. "Yes. But you don't need the details."

"Murder?"

"No."

"Rape?" She narrows her eyes.

"God no!" I rear back, offended. "Never."

"Just tell me, then. Otherwise, I'm going to keep imagining terrible scenarios."

I clear my throat, looking away. "Grand larceny."

"Grand larceny?" She spits out a bite of food in surprise.

"It was an *accident*."

She blinks. Blinks again. Mouth agape.

"How does one *accidentally* commit grand larceny?"

"By being shit-faced drunk and thinking you're throwing a party on your parents' yacht, only to crash said yacht, then realize it is in fact *not* your family's."

"Your family owns a freaking yacht?"

"And a private jet. More cars than anyone possibly needs. As well as estates all over the world."

"You say that like it disgusts you."

"Don't get me wrong, I've enjoyed the fringe benefits, but *things* don't make up for the lack of a real family."

"Oh." She plays with hair again. I notice chipped red polish on the ends of her nails. "That's really kind of..."

"Pathetic for me to complain about? I know. I'm lucky that I've never had to worry about money."

"Actually," she frowns, my eyes zeroing in on her full pillowy lips, "I was going to say it's sad."

I pick up a fry, tearing it into three separate pieces. "Poor little rich boy, right?"

She rolls her eyes. "Now you're just fishing for sympathy. Economic status doesn't guarantee happiness. Horrible people just exist."

"Aka, money doesn't buy happiness?"

Her lips twitch into a *real* smile and I count that as a total victory. "Let's move on to other questions."

"Good idea." I clear my throat. "Are you on birth control?"

She chokes on a bite of food. That question isn't actually on my list, I'm just an ass and wanted to see her reaction.

"How is that any of your business?"

"If we decide to fornicate, obviously."

She snorts, wiping her mouth on a napkin. "You did not just use the word *fornicate*."

"What would you prefer? Knocking boots? Bumpin' uglies? A bit of the old in and out? The no-pants dance? Or, my personal favorite," I grin triumphantly as her face reddens, "slime the banana."

"You … you…" She flounders at a loss for words.

"Are very fuckable, I know."

"No, no!" She wags a finger at me. "That was not what I was going to say. And there will be no sex happening between us," she swings that same finger back and forth from her to me, "because this relationship is entirely fake, need I remind you."

I rub my jaw. "Can you seriously look at this face and not want to fuck me?"

Her eyes threaten to bug out of her head. "I'm leaving." She wipes her mouth with a napkin and reaches for her wallet. "Thanks for paying my tuition, and I owe you one, but this isn't it."

"Whoa, whoa, whoa," I chant, placing my hand over hers. She gives me a death glare and I quickly pull my hand back. "I was kidding, I'm sorry. I have a weird sense of humor. I'd tell you I'll work on it, but there's no changing me at this point. Please, Van, I need you."

I slap my hands together in a prayer position, holding them beneath my chin. My lower lip pouts out.

She stares at me, perhaps weighing my sincerity, before she sighs and puts her wallet back in her bag. "Fine, but no joking about having sex with me. It makes me feel like a prostitute." She shudders. "Not that there's anything wrong with that, if that's what you want to do, you do you girl, but that ain't me."

I try not to grin. I don't think Vanessa is aware of how amusing and unassumingly funny she is.

"I'll do my best. Unfortunately, many of my jokes are sexual in nature. Take it with a grain of salt." She looks like she's ready to reach across the table and slap me, so I decide to quickly change the subject. "Next question, when's your birthday? As your boyfriend, I should know your birthday."

"Fake," she reminds me unnecessarily, "and it's June twenty-fourth. I'm a Cancer, since I figure that question is probably on your list too."

"March third," I answer for myself, "and Pisces." Pursing my lips, I look over my questions. "What's your favorite cookie?"

"How is that important?"

"Because I like to bake cookies, naturally I'd know your favorite by now."

"Oh." She plays with a strand of her hair, wrapping it around her index finger. "Snickerdoodle."

"Same." I grin. "Look at us, we have so much in common."

"Mhmm," she hums doubtfully.

"What about hobbies?"

She frowns, a fry hovering halfway to her mouth.

"Between school and work I don't really have time for hobbies. I used to garden with my mom."

"Interesting." I make a note on my paper. "Mine is baseball and obviously baking."

"You weren't kidding about the cookies, were you?"

I scoff. "I would never kid about baked goods."

She pulls her hair over one shoulder. "This fake relationship ... exactly how far are we taking this? Like am I just supposed to pretend in front of your parents or?" She waits for me to elaborate.

"We need to keep up the charade with my friends and on campus. I'll tell them that we started going out before break and decided to make it official."

"So ... the whole campus is going to think I'm dating you?"

"Is that a problem?" I scratch my head.

"It's just you're popular and I'm not."

"So?"

"Teddy," she scoffs. "We come from completely different worlds. Both on and off campus."

"Again, *so?* I know you don't know me well, yet, but you will, and I don't give a shit what other people think of me or who I'm with, even if it's not real. People are always going to talk. But that doesn't mean you have to listen."

Her lips thin. "You have a good point."

I tap my forehead. "It's not entirely air up here." Consulting my list again, I ask, "What are you studying?"

Her lips twitch like she's trying not to laugh. "You're taking this really serious, aren't you? And it's communications."

41

"I have to, there's no telling what my dad will ask about you. I need to be prepared. What do you plan to do with a communications degree?"

"I'd like to get into public relations in some way." Leaning over the table, she whisper-hisses, "Why do I feel like you're interrogating me for a job position, not getting to know me?"

"Sorry." I give her a sheepish smile, feeling my ears turn red. "I don't really know exactly how else to do this and I've never even had a real girlfriend—"

"Hold up." She literally raises a hand, silencing me. "You've never had a girlfriend?"

I snort. "No. I went to an all-boys school growing up and don't get me wrong, we all found ways to meet up with girls, but I didn't date. After I came here I…" I flounder, trying to find the right words but not wanting to stick my foot in my mouth in front of her.

"Whored around?" she supplies, arching a fluffy dark brow.

I snap my fingers. "Exactly. Though," I put a hand to my chest, "I've been on my best behavior this year. Mostly because of Father Dearest, but—"

"Has anyone ever told you that you're an over sharer?"

"Once or twice?" I grin and her blue eyes light up with amusement.

She shakes her head, pushing her plate to the side. "What's your major then?"

"Business. The plan was always to take over my family business, but…" I trail off, shaking my head. "I'd rather go out on my own. A lone wolf you might say." Then, because I'm me and can't help myself, I let out a howl.

"Teddy," she hisses, trying to climb her way across the table to slap a hand over my mouth.

I stop howling, instead laughing. "You should see your face, Van."

Red-faced, she looks around at the truckers staring at us. "I hate you."

"No, you don't."

She covers her face with her hands. "You love embarrassing me, don't you?"

"I do that with everyone." I give a shrug, stealing a fry from her plate since I ate all of mine.

"How are you still hungry?" she scoffs.

"I'm a growing boy."

She shakes her head, flabbergasted. "You're something else."

"Anyway, tomorrow I think we should make our relationship campus official."

"Campus official?" She raises a brow. "What does that mean?"

Her voice has gone high and squeaky. I don't think she's even noticed the octave change. I knew when I proposed this whole idea to her that she wasn't the kind of girl who coveted popularity. I don't know how exactly I knew; I just did. Maybe it's because while she checked me out in the office, and obviously recognized me, she didn't give me flirty eyes or try to get me to notice her or even slip me her number like so many girls do.

I was instantly intrigued, especially since I needed to find someone to fit my girlfriend role.

"We'll go to Harvey's tomorrow night with my friends. I'll introduce you. We'll hang out." I shrug, and then add the part I know she won't like. "Obviously we'll have to hold hands and kiss."

"What?" She blanches. "No. No way." She swings her hands back and forth. "I'm not doing that."

I arch a brow. "Ah, but you've already agreed to it. I mean, being my fake-girlfriend implies that there will be hand holding and kissing, maybe the occasional boob grab or ass smack."

Her lips part and she knows I'm not wrong.

"Right." She nods along. "But no boob or butt touching." Biting her lip, she says hesitantly, "I've never been to Harvey's. What should I wear?"

She's joking, right? She's been at Aldridge since freshman year and never been to Harvey's? Blasphemy!

"How have you never been to Harvey's? I-It's like a rite of passage!"

She tugs on her hair. "Because I've been busy studying, working, and frankly just getting by. I know that someone like you probably can't relate to that, but —"

"Listen, I understand having to work and I study too, mind you, it's not like grades are handed to me. I *am* smart." My tone is a bit brash, but it's a sore subject for me. I know I'm a jokester and I don't take life too seriously, but I hate when people assume that automatically means I'm dumb.

"Oh." She pales. "I didn't mean it like that. I'm sorry if it came across that way."

I wiggle my fingers, erasing her concern. "Sorry, it's a sore subject. Anyway, my point is surely you've still had time to go out."

She winces. "I'm just not that person, Teddy. I'd rather stay in than go out."

I feel like there's more to it, something she's not telling me, but I don't push it.

Plowing on, I say, "I'll pick you up tomorrow at eight. Harvey's is casual. If you have cowboy boots, even better, but it's not required." I wink, trying to lighten the mood. "And remember," my voice drops to a serious tone, "you have to pretend to like me."

FOUR

Vanessa

I HAVEN'T GONE ON A DATE SINCE MY JUNIOR YEAR OF high school and that was an epic disaster. My date got food poisoning and threw up all over me and the interior of his car. I still shudder at the memories.

While I've lacked in the dating department, I have had some hookups in the past few years. After all, I'm not a nun and a lady has needs.

But right now, standing in front of my closet filled mostly with jeans, casual shirts, sweaters, and an overabundance of hoodies, I'm wishing I would've prepared better with at least *one* date ready outfit in my arsenal.

I'm sure my roommate Danika has a plethora of date clothes, not that any of her stuff would come close to fitting me, and frankly I wouldn't want to wear it if it did. Our styles are a world apart.

Speaking of the devil, or in this case, thinking it, the main door to our suite opens. Danika breezes in, bringing with her the cloying scent of her vanilla perfume. Her bright red dyed hair practically glows as she passes by my open door.

She looks like she's on a mission, so I'm startled when she backpedals and eyes me curiously where I stand in a robe, curlers in my hair, juggling three different shirts. Well, not literally juggling, but—

"What are you doing?" Her tone is skeptical.

"I ... have a..." *deep breath.* "Date. I have a date. With my boyfriend. A man. Who is my boyfriend. My manfriend if you will."

She presses her lips together, trying not to laugh. "I didn't know you had a boyfriend." She doesn't sound accusing, curious more than anything.

"I-It's new. Started just before winter break."

"Huh." She rolls her tongue around her mouth. "Can't decide what to wear?" Leaning against the doorway she takes in the mess of my room, where I've drug out practically every item of clothing I own.

"Yeah." There's no point in lying since the truth is obvious.

"Mind if I help?" She hesitates on the threshold.

Danika and I have never really been friends. We became dormmates last year, thrown together when my previous roommate graduated, and she requested a new one. But we're not enemies either. We're just two very different people and that's okay.

"Go for it." I drop the shirts in my hands to the bed with the others. "Obviously I'm not having any luck."

She kicks her shoes off outside the door, and walks in. "You should definitely wear those jeans that make your ass look like a million bucks."

I rear back in surprise at her compliment. The sad truth is it's rare as a bigger girl to get compliments from a skinny girl. Thank God I've never valued my confidence on others' perceived notion of me. It might sound dumb to some people, but I start every morning by reminding myself that I'm smart, worthy, and beautiful inside and out. It was something necessary when growing up with a narcissist for a sister who loved tearing me down in petty ways. The biggest FU I gave her was when I stopped caring about what she said. It took away any and all power she had over me.

"Um, which ones?" I typically pay so little attention to what I wear that I have no clue which jeans she's referring to.

"The light wash ones with the rips in the knees." She purses her lips, setting down a plain black t-shirt. She reaches for a red shirt, quickly discarding it as well. "Do you have anything that shows a little skin?"

I look down at my big chest. "When you have tits like mine, even full coverage tends to look indecent."

Once, in high school, I got sent to the principal's office for wearing a turtleneck. I had no idea those could be seen as scandalous.

"Mmm," she hums, staring at my boobs. "Good point, but you want to show a little skin."

"I do?"

She stares at me like I've lost my mind. "You said this guy is your boyfriend, don't you want to entice him?"

My cheeks redden. I realize that yeah, if this was a real relationship and not the monstrosity it's bound to turn out to be, that I would be trying to tease him. "Um, yeah," I mutter. "I suppose I should show a little skin."

She taps her lip, thinking, her finger shooting into the air dramatically in an *aha* movement. "I have just the thing." She runs over to her room before I can tell her that I doubt anything she has will even cover my left tit.

While she's gone, I find the pair of jeans she was talking about and yank them out of my drawer and slip off the pair of black leggings I've been wearing.

I'm wiggling the jeans up my ass when Danika returns. "Try this." She passes me a black scarf looking garment. I take it from her and realize that it's a short sleeve wrap top.

I fully expect it not to work, because that's how it goes when I try to borrow clothes, but surprisingly it's a perfect fit. The top wraps around, holding my chest in and covering my bra so no part of it peeks through. It also does a good job of covering most of my stomach while leaving little slivers of skin to tantalize.

"You're so hot," Danika says approvingly. "Your boyfriend is going to take you straight to his bed, forget going out."

"You think?" Not that I'll be going anywhere near

Teddy's no doubt STD infested bed, but knowing I look good enough for the possibility makes me feel nice.

"For sure." She nods approvingly.

"Thank you for your help." I mean it whole-heartedly. We're not besties by a longshot, but this feels like one of those quintessential girl bonding moments.

She goes back to her room and I clean up the disaster that is mine.

Glancing at the time, I curse myself for letting it get away from me and quickly take out the curlers, brushing and fluffing my hair so that it falls in more natural looking loose waves. There's no time for a full face of makeup, so I do as much as I can in the little time I have. I finish off the look with a bold red lip so that it looks like I tried harder than I actually have.

Wiping away a smear of mascara from beneath my eye, I pick up my phone to text Teddy to let him know I'll meet him outside.

He replies back almost instantly.

Teddy: I'm already here.

I blanch, groaning when there's a knock on the door.

"Ooh!" Danika squeals from her room. "Is that your man?" She appears in my doorway, an eager smile on her face. I think she's more excited about this date than I am.

He paid your tuition, I remind myself. *This is the least you can do.*

"Yes," I grit out between my teeth. *"Unfortunately."* The last is muffled under my breath with no way for her to hear it.

Grabbing up my phone, I stick it in my pocket. My

ID, credit card, and everything else important I might need is stuffed into the sticky wallet on the back of my phone. Those things probably have an official name, not that I'd ever remember it.

Before I swing the door open, I remind myself that I have to *act* like a girlfriend which means showing affection and being excited to be in his presence.

Teddy stands at the door, a few girls in the hall staring at him with open-mouthed expressions. Their gazes swing to me, waiting to see if he's there for me or someone else.

Bringing his hand out from behind his back, he offers me a single pale pink daisy.

"For me?" I stare at the flower with surprise, my hand outstretched and hovering, unsure if I should take it.

He grins. "Obviously. You *are* my girlfriend."

One of the girls lingering in the hallway gasps. I take the daisy from him, sniffing it. I don't know why I even do that. I always find most flowers lacking any sort of smell.

"Thank you." I give him a tiny smile. "Babe," I add belatedly, cringing at my awkwardness.

He chuckles. "You're welcome." He gives a long dramatic pause, rocking back on his heels. "Babe."

Turning around, planning to put the flower in some water, I squeak when I come face to face with Danika. She looks dumbfounded. Her eyes flicker back and forth from the man standing in the doorway to me. Teddy continues to smile, completely unbothered, but I start to feel a tad uncomfortable.

"Do you know Teddy?" I ask, trying to keep my voice light and not betray my burning curiosity.

She shakes her head. "No. Sorry. Here, let me take that so you can go." She reaches for the flower and I hand it to her. "Have a good time, lovebirds."

She ushers me outside and into the waiting arms of my … *boyfriend*.

Because from this moment on I have to erase the *f-word* from my brain because for all intents and purposes, this is now real.

He leans in, giving me a peck on the cheek. Naturally, my face betrays me when I cringe with awkwardness, but Teddy, who never takes anything too seriously merely gives a slight laugh.

"Relax," he murmurs, hand resting against my lower back. "At least act like you like me."

A laugh bursts free of my lips and I *do* relax. I'll give the guy credit, he's surprisingly easy to be around.

"Have a good evening, ladies." He gives the girls lingering in the hall a gentlemanly tip of his head.

When we get into the elevator, I expect him to remove his hand from my back and step away, but instead he surprises me by clasping our hands together. I look down at our joined fingers with a mystified expression.

Clearing his throat, he says, "Remember, you have to pretend to like me."

"Right." A light-sweat has broken out across my skin, and I know I have to be turning an unattractive shade of tomato red. "Uh … how did we meet again?"

We texted last night and randomly throughout the day, trying to build our love story, and now when it counts, I'm blanking.

The doors slide open and Teddy tugs me along since my legs are barely working. Outside, his sports car sits parked diagonally across three spots. I can't help but roll my eyes at the arrogance of it.

People stare at us as we walk to the car and I hate that a part of me worries that they're wondering what Teddy's doing with me.

I've worked so hard on my confidence and self-esteem and been doing a lot better. But in moments that old insecurity likes to rear its ugly head.

I stuff down that self-doubting and anxiousness to a back part of my mind.

Teddy opens the passenger door for me, and I mutter a soft, "Thank you," as I crouch down to get inside the low-lying car.

Sliding into the car and letting the engine purr to life, he finally answers my question now that we're alone again. "We met when I went to The Burger Palace. You were my waitress, wooed by my indelible charm. We spent the evening talking and the rest is history."

"And your friends are going to buy this?" Doubt fills my tone.

Even Teddy looks a little unsure. "They will."

"You should've picked someone who's a better actress." I play with a piece of loose fringe on my knee. "I'm never going to be able to pull this off."

Surprise zings through my body when Teddy's hand lands on top of mine. He laces our fingers together, a half-smile quirking his lips. "I didn't want another girl. I chose you."

I inhale a shaky breath. It's on the tip of my tongue to say something *yet again* about how any girl on campus would've jumped at the chance, but he's right. He chose me—going as far as to pay my tuition in exchange, which let's be honest isn't a fair trade at all.

I make a silent vow to myself that this will be the last time I say anything about it to him.

I agreed to his terms and we're in this together until the end of the school year when we both graduate. He'll get his inheritance and I'll get my diploma.

"What's your go-to karaoke song?" he asks, changing the subject.

I don't know whether this is more of his getting to know each other questions or he's simply trying to distract me.

"'The Real Slim Shady.'"

"Eminem?" He glances at me briefly in shock before his eyes are back on the road.

"What? I can't like Eminem?"

"Nah, it's not that." He grins, driving with his left hand, the other still holding on to mine. It really shouldn't be so sexy, him driving one-handed, but I think maybe my hormones are in overdrive and anything could make me hot and bothered right now. "You just don't look like a rap girl."

"I don't look like a rap girl?" I scoff, stifling a snort. "What do I look like then?"

"I don't know, the One Direction boy bander type."

"Hey," I protest, angling my body in his direction, making him tighten his hold on me. "Don't diss One

54

Direction, and I'm perfectly capable of loving both. What song would you choose?"

"Shania Twain's 'Man! I Feel Like A Woman!'"

I press my lips together, but a snicker still slips through. "I would not have guessed that."

"I like to keep people on their toes."

"That you do." It's quiet for a few minutes before I voice a question of my own. "I know you play baseball, but I have no idea what position you play."

"Shortstop." I look over to find him smiling from ear to ear, green eyes glinting with amusement.

"What? Why are you smirking at me?"

"You know I play baseball."

I roll my eyes. "Don't act so cocky. You're popular. I might not be Ms. Social Butterfly, but I do hear things."

"And what have you heard about me?" He flicks his blinker on. "If it's the twelve-inch rumor it's not *that* big. Don't get me wrong, it's still plenty big, but —"

"Teddy?"

"Yes?"

"Are you talking about your penis size?"

"Yes." He smirks, parking near the front of the bar. "It's ten, in case you're wondering. And yes, I measured."

My jaw drops and I yank my hand out of his. "I didn't need that information!"

"It's big, sure, but not *too* big. Just right, if you ask me. At least, no one has ever complained before."

"I'm getting out of this car right now."

"Wait." He glares at me when I reach for my door. "I'll open the door for you."

"Why?" I give him a speculative look.

"I've never been a real boyfriend before, but if I was, I'd always open doors for you, so that's what I'm doing."

"Oh."

"I *can* be a gentleman." He leans close to me, and I hold my breath, unsure of what's about to happen. "Ten," he mouths.

"Oh my God." I shove him back by the shoulders. "You're so gross."

He cackles the entire time he gets out of the car, crossing in front of it, and as promised, opens the door for me. I step out, shaking my head.

He wraps an arm around my waist, pulling me into his side. He presses his lips to the shell of my ear, sending a shiver down my spine.

"Showtime," he murmurs.

Stepping into the bar, I resist the urge to slam my hands over my ears because it's so damn loud. I've heard Danika mention she was coming to Harvey's before, even extended an invitation my way a few times but stopped after I always said no.

"You *like* this place?" I shout to be heard, holding on tightly to Teddy so I don't get lost in the crowd.

"Yeah, it's the best." He steers me toward the back and my heart races because I know the moment he stops it's time to put my game face on.

When I see the big table he's leading me to, my heels dig into the concrete floor. "Oh no, no, no. I can't do this," I practically whine.

He leans down to my ear again. "It'll be fine. Trust me."

Trust him? *Trust him?* Is he insane?

Trusting him is what got me into this whole fiasco in the first place.

We reach the table, all eyes on us, and there's no turning back.

"Guys," Teddy's voice booms to be heard above the din, "this is my girlfriend Vanessa. Vanessa, this is ... everybody." Before I can panic even more over not knowing their names, he starts pointing and rattling them out. "That dude with the black baseball cap that looks like he's plotting murder is Mascen. Beside him with the glasses is his girlfriend Rory." The girl in question smiles and gives me a tiny wave. "That guy there with a furrow in his brow is Cole. I call him Dad." He points to what might be the most gorgeous guy I've ever seen. You know, besides my boyfriend. "And on his left is his girlfriend Zoey. Also known as Mom."

The pretty girl with curly hair and warm brown eyes smiles, shaking her head. "And we call him our pet dog."

I snort, trying to cover it by rubbing my hand under my nose.

Teddy continues on like nothing happened. I think it must take a lot to faze him, but clearly his father gets under his skin.

"The dude with two girls that I have no idea the names of hanging all over him is my roommate Jude." Looking at the guy in question, muscular and tall even sitting down, with thick dark brown hair and a stubbled jaw, blue eyes shadowed by heavy brows, I decide that all of Teddy's friends are gorgeous. "On the end there is Cree." The pale-skinned guy with wavy, nearly black hair, and icy blue eyes, lifts his hand in a wave. "No idea who the girl is."

"My name is Janessa. We hooked up last year. Did you forget?"

Cree scoots away from the girl and she glares while Teddy shrugs. "I don't remember most girls, sweetheart."

Her jaw drops and she glares at me like I was the one who insulted her. "What's so memorable about *her?*"

My blood goes cold.

"Way more than you," is all he says, squeezing my hand like he's silently telling me *I've got your back.*

The girl ends up leaving with a huff, and the others scoot down to make room for us, while Teddy points out two other guys to me. Daire and Murray. No idea if I'll be able to remember all these names, but I'll try my best.

"You hungry? Thirsty? What do you want to drink?" Teddy passes me a menu, nuzzling my neck when he does.

"Um I'll have a margarita." I feel like such a basic bitch for ordering one, but they're my favorite, and I haven't had one in way too long because I can't waste my money on frivolous things.

"Sure thing, babe. What about food? I'm going to get a burger." He plays with a strand of my hair, wrapping the dark curl around his finger. Leaning in, he glides his nose over the column of my neck, and I gasp. I feel him grin as he pulls away.

I read over the menu, only giving it a cursory look, and ask for the vegetarian sliders.

Teddy slides out of the booth to go place our order at the bar, leaving me all alone with his friends. Panic begins to unfurl inside me.

"So," Zoey turns to me, "you and Teddy, huh?"

She sounds curious and amused.

"Me and Teddy," I echo, nodding my head a bit too vigorously.

Cole leans around his girlfriend and I find my breath catching at how hot he is. "I always knew someone would steal his heart one day. He said you guys met just before break but didn't say where."

"Oh, um," I tuck a piece of hair behind my ear wracking my brain for the agreed upon tale, "I work at The Burger Palace, so that's where. He came in and sat in my section. He was very tenacious, wouldn't take no for an answer, and now here we are." I give a tiny shrug, like that it explains it all.

Zoey laughs, bumping my shoulder with hers. "That sounds like Teddy. He's like a dog with a bone." Sobering, she adds, "He's sweet and deserves someone who likes him for ... well, *him*."

"He's a good guy." I spot him weaving through the crowd, my margarita and his beer in each hand.

Sitting back down, he slides my drink in front of me. "Here you go, babe." He kisses my cheek and I jolt, startled by his easy affection.

I've never been a touchy-feely person, but he obviously is. I'm going to have to get used to it, so I don't look like I'm crawling out of my skin every time he touches me. Plus, since this is supposed to look real to everyone, touching and kissing need to be involved.

"Thanks." I wrap my hand around the glass, taking a sip of the alcohol. It's not too strong, which I prefer, but it should give me a nice, pleasant buzz. It'll help me get through this night and that's all that really matters.

Teddy leans into me, his nose grazing my cheek. We look like two lovers whispering sweet nothings as I curl into him so we're in our own private cocoon.

"Can you at least *try* to look like you're not having a stroke and actually enjoy my presence?" He doesn't sound pissed, more like amused.

"Sorry. I'll do better."

He gives me a reassuring smile. Inhaling a deep breath, I plaster a smile on my face.

"How did you and Cole meet?" I ask Zoey. She seems nice, and even a little quiet like myself.

Her fingers clasp around a bottle of root beer—an interesting choice for a bar.

"Teddy actually introduced us when I needed a place to live and Cole needed a roommate."

"Look at you." I grin at Teddy. "I didn't know you were such a matchmaker."

"What can I say?" He tips a bottle of Zombie Dust in my direction. "I'm a real romantic at heart." He throws his arm around my shoulders, tugging me impossibly closer until I'm practically in his lap. His warm lips touch the side of my forehead, my eyes fluttering closed. An embarrassing happy sigh passes, unbidden, through my lips.

My eyes fly open, and I look at Teddy to see if he heard, and if the shit-eating grin he's wearing is any indication, then he definitely did.

Thankfully, I'm saved from saying something that might mortify myself further when the waitress drops off our food.

Teddy digs into his burger like he hasn't eaten all day.

"Are you a junior?" Zoey asks me and I smile appreciatively at her effort to carry on the conversation.

"No, I'm a senior."

"Ah, so you're graduating with these guys then." She indicates Cole, the guy named Mascen I haven't spoken to yet, and Teddy. "The rest of us are juniors. What are you studying?"

"Communications." I pick up one of the sliders and take a bite before I continue. "I want to get into public relations. Or at least that's the plan."

"Have you and Teddy had classes together before?"

I glance at my boyfriend for the moment. He looks a little lost at the question and I frown. "Yeah, we have. We shared a class last semester for communications theory and two last year."

Teddy looks at me in surprise, and I know he doesn't remember me at all. If he's worried I'm offended, I'm not. The classes are huge and it's impossible to know everyone in class. If Teddy wasn't so popular on campus, I wouldn't have been aware of him, and I only ever really saw him in passing because we never sat in the same sections.

"Do you have any together this semester?" She picks at the sticker on her bottle.

"No, not this time."

I feel Teddy staring intently at the side of my face.

"Aw, that's too bad." Zoey frowns. "Especially now that you guys are together."

"It's truly a Greek tragedy." I don't mean to be sarcastic, but sometimes it just slips out.

I've barely finished eating when Teddy grips my hand, tugging me out of the booth.

"Let's dance."

"I don't dance," I grumble, trying to extricate myself from his hold.

He ignores me, sweeping me onto the middle of the dancefloor. 'Funny' by Zedd plays loudly through the speakers. Hand on my waist, Teddy yanks me against his body until we're practically flush. My breath catches at the intensity in his forest green eyes.

"How is it possible we had classes together and I only just noticed you?" I feel the rumbled vibrations of his voice against me.

I shrug. "I don't stick out in a crowd. Classes are big and we were never put in a group together for an assignment, so how would you notice me?"

His Adam's apple bobs. "I should have."

I look away, the intensity in his gaze doing something strange to me.

"It's really not a big deal."

He grabs my chin, tipping my head up. "It is to me."

My breath catches, brows furrowing in puzzlement. "Why?"

His lips turn down, not quite a frown, more like he's

62

trying to puzzle something out. "Because I should have," he settles on.

I look at him like he's crazy, but I don't say anything because frankly my brain seems to have emptied of words.

"Why did you want to dance?"

"Why wouldn't I want to dance with my beautiful girlfriend?" He counters and I feel my face flush. He guides my body easily. I'm a puppet in his arms.

"I like your friends," I admit. "They seem cool. Zoey's really nice."

"They feel more like my family." He lowers his head, rubbing his nose against mine in an Eskimo kiss.

My hold on him tightens at his words and the melancholy tone of his voice. I don't know the details of Teddy's family life, but I know enough that it's not good, and honestly, I'm a tiny bit afraid of what I might be walking into when I have dinner this weekend with his parents. I'll have to put my game face on, because that's the whole point of our arrangement.

"You're lucky to have them, then."

"I know." His lips form a smile, but I see the pain behind his eyes because the people who *are* his family aren't the way they should be.

My relationship with my sister is a cesspool of fuckery, but I have a good one with my parents. I can't imagine if all my immediate familial relationships were strained.

Teddy holds me tighter against him and I find myself tilting my head back to take him in. He's studying my face, like he's searching for an answer to a question I don't even know.

Lowering his head, he sweeps his lips along my neck. Reaching my ear, he says, "I'm going to kiss you."

"W-What?" I stutter, my voice not holding its usual power because he's put me under his spell.

"People are watching." Another sweep of his lips. "You *are* my girlfriend. People expect us to kiss."

He's right.

I know it, and his smirk tells me he knows it.

I give the tiniest nod, but it's all the invitation he needs as his lips capture mine. It feels like my soul is being stolen from my body, his kiss intense and not at all what I expected. He waits for my lips to part and then his tongue sweeps inside.

Claiming.

He's staking claim to me.

Fake, I remind myself. *This isn't real.*

But God, it feels so real. I find my body bowing into his and he holds me upright. I think we've stopped dancing, but I can't bring myself to care.

He ends the kiss suddenly and it's like ice water has been poured down my spine. He grins, cocky as ever. He *knows* he affected me.

"Can we go out again tomorrow?"

"W-What?" I stutter, my brain lagging from the kiss and unable to process what he asked.

"Can we go out again tomorrow?" he repeats, smirking, his green eyes sparkling. "I want to make sure we know each other thoroughly before this weekend."

I don't know how we went from kissing to this, but I

roll with it, acting as if it didn't have any sort of effect on me, because frankly, it *shouldn't*.

"I have to work tomorrow."

"What if I came by after practice? I could order dinner and ask you questions when you have time to check on me." He winks. "I'm a handful, so you'll have to check on me a lot."

I bite my lip, unsure if I want the distraction that is Teddy to come to my work, but he has a point. We need to know each other inside and out before this weekend.

"Okay, that should be fine."

"Good." His arms tighten around me and I inhale the woodsy fragrance of his cologne clinging to his shirt. "Thank you again for doing this."

"Stop thanking me. Let's be real, you've done me a far bigger favor than the one I'm doing you."

He shakes his head. "Stop saying that. It was just some money."

"That's easy for you to say when money isn't an issue in your life."

His lips downturn. "That's not what I meant. And money might not be an issue for me, but it doesn't mean my life is perfect."

That haunted look I notice from time to time shadows his eyes. An ache fills my belly. I feel bad for what I implied.

"I'm sorry. I know money isn't everything."

"No, it's not." His voice grows deeper.

The song we started dancing to has moved into another and we keep moving around the dancefloor.

When we make it back to the table my skin is damp with a layer of sweat. Teddy's grown quiet, seemingly lost in his head. From the looks the others shoot in his direction I take it this is unusual, and I feel responsible for it.

I end up downing another margarita and then a third before Teddy grabs my hand and says he's taking me home.

"I don't wanna go back to the dorms," I slur, trying to pull my fingers free of his. "I'm having fun. I want another drink." I look back toward the bar, waving goodbye to Zoey in the process.

"If you have another drink, you'll hate me tomorrow, and we have classes."

"Shit." He's right. I totally forgot.

Outside, I inhale the fresh night air, letting the cold seep into my lungs. It sobers me a tiny bit, and I don't protest anymore, getting inside the car when he opens the passenger door.

We don't say anything on the drive back. I lay my head against the cool, passenger side window, fighting to keep my eyelids open.

Teddy parks outside Connell Hall where my dorm is located and shuts off the engine.

"You don't need to come up with me," I say, reaching for the door handle of the car. "I'm fine."

He rolls his eyes playfully at me, a smile on his lips. "Just because I'm your fake-boyfriend doesn't mean I'm not going to treat you like I'm a real one."

I narrow my eyes on him. "I'm not having sex with you."

He chuckles. "You say that now."

"And I mean it."

He shakes his head, trying to hide his amusement. I think he likes our banter.

"Don't even think about opening that door," he warns me, slipping out of the car.

My brows furrow in confusion, thinking *what door?* When he opens the car door I'm leaning against, I realize he meant that one. Whoops.

I slump outside and with Spiderman-like reflexes he catches me before I tumble onto the pavement. "Whoa, Van. I didn't know you were such a lightweight."

"I don't go out, remember?" I remind him. "And I'm *not* drunk."

Comfortably buzzed? Yes. But not drunk.

I get my feet under me and stand beside the car, leaning most of my weight against Teddy, and he acts as if I weigh nothing.

"Come on, let's get you in your bed."

I pass him my card into the dorm, wincing when I relive that moment in my head when it didn't work. God, what a disaster things would've been if the man at my side hadn't come to my rescue.

Who would've thought that Teddy McCallister—campus player and all around goofball—would be my knight in shining armor, my savior.

Teddy holds onto me in the elevator, my eyes heavy with the need to sleep. I'm not a fun drunk, I'm a sleepy drunk.

Wait, I'm not drunk. I'm NOT.

The elevator opens on my floor and it's quiet at this hour. He helps me into my dorm and Danika must still be up because I hear him say something to her before my legs are swept out from under me and my head rests against his warm solid chest. His heart pounds against my ear. *Ba-dum, ba-dum, ba-dum.*

"Ba-dum? What's ba-dum?" He sets me down on my bed and starts taking off my shoes, letting them drop to the floor.

"Did I say that out loud?"

"Mhmm," he hums, appraising me with hands on his hips.

"It's the sound of your heart."

"I'm not sure my heart should be saying *ba-dum.* Maybe I should have it checked out by a cardiologist." He sounds amused.

"Maybe." I roll over, gathering my hands beneath my head.

Warm, rough fingers brush strands of my hair off the side of my face, tucking them behind my ear. "I'd offer to put your pajamas on for you, but I don't want to get slapped."

I mutter something, but I'm not sure it's even English.

He laughs, and there's the lightest press of something against my temple — *his fingers? His lips?*

"See you tomorrow, Van."

Tomorrow.

Because Teddy McCallister is now in my life.

I fall asleep, still feeling the imprint of his lips on mine. Not even the alcohol could erase the feeling.

FIVE

Teddy

I WAKE UP TO ZOEY'S SCREECH. SLAMMING MY HANDS over my ears, I groan, "Mom, stop screaming."

Her hand covers her heart, eyes threatening to bug out of her head. "You have *got* to stop sneaking in here. Give us the key back."

Cole pops around the corner, lips pursed when he finds me on the couch in my boxers. "Dude, how many times have we told you this has to stop?"

"Where else am I supposed to go? My dorm is basically a twenty-four-seven revolving door of pussy thanks to Jude. The guy would be better off seeing a therapist like a normal person."

"Do *you* see a therapist?" Cole crosses his arms over his chest in challenge.

"Of course. I video chat Phil once a week. Cool guy. He recently got hair plugs, though, and it looks hella weird, but good for him. I'm sure it'll be great when they grow in fully."

Cole looks at me like I've lost my mind. "I can never tell if you're being serious or bullshitting me."

"'And that's one secret I'll never tell. You know you love me—'"

He holds up a hand. "Are you re-watching *Gossip Girl* again?"

"Chuck Bass is bae."

He rubs his face. "Take a shower and put your clothes on."

"Come on, Dad. I wanted some more sleep."

"We," he wags a finger between Zoey and him, "have class, so you can't stay here."

I roll my eyes. "I'll lock up on my way out."

"Nuh-huh." He shakes his head forcefully. "You leave when we leave."

"Fine," I grumble, rolling off the couch. Scratching my stomach, I bend over and scoop up my pile of clothes. "I'll go take that shower now."

"Mhmm." Cole watches me through narrowed eyes. "You do that. That was some kiss you and Vanessa had last night," he taunts after me.

I stop halfway down the hall to react, looking back to find him walking over to Zoey in the kitchen. He wraps his arms around her from behind, and she giggles when he kisses her neck. I would never admit it to anyone, I'm a man and I have my pride, but I'm envious of their love. It's so easy, and natural. It's nothing like the cold and clinical 'love' I grew up around that I now realize was never love at all, but the word used as a weapon.

I think of the kiss, how Vanessa's body felt clasped against mine, and swallow thickly. I can't think about it — can't allow myself to go there with my thoughts.

Locking myself in the bathroom, I clean up and put last night's clothes on. They smell like stale beer and cheese from Harvey's, but I'll swing by my dorm and change before I go to class.

I'm going to have to do something about Jude bringing so many girls back to our room. I hate to cramp the dude's style, but I need to be able to sleep and also not get crucified by my father for someone else's mistakes. I already make enough of my own.

The most ironic part of it all is my dad changed his mind about me living off campus with Cole because he thought there was a higher chance of there being girls and parties.

It worked out for Cole and Zoey, though. He needed a roommate, she needed a place to live, and in the end they fell in love with each other.

Leaving the bathroom, my stomach rumbles at the smell of bacon and eggs.

"Mom, please tell me you made breakfast for me, too."

Zoey rolls her eyes, setting out three plates. "I would never leave you out, T."

I hug her side and kiss her cheek, getting swatted on the back of my head from Cole.

"Don't touch my girl like that."

"Come on, man. I didn't mean anything by it, and you know it."

I can't help it that I'm a touchy person. I blame it on the lack of affection I had growing up. Now I'm trying to make up for it.

Cole grumbles something unintelligible around his mouthful of food. I sit down beside him, Zoey on his other side, and dig in.

"This is great, thanks, Z."

"Thank Cole. He does most of the cooking."

"Thanks, Dad. I'm honored you didn't leave me out of breakfast."

He sighs, looking to the heavens for answers. "Can I please have your key back now? You don't even live here."

I pretend to think for a second. "No."

"I'm changing the locks," he mutters.

"You can't."

"I'll ask the landlord."

We both know he won't. "Okay, Dad."

———

I'M tired as fuck after baseball practice, my muscles aching and sore. Sure, I work out regularly on my own, but Coach has been putting us through the wringer, and it's showing in the way I can hardly move.

I pop a couple of Aleve before I pack up my stuff and head out, muttering goodbye as I go. I ignore the strange looks from Mascen and Murray. I'm too tired to worry about it, and I need to get over to The Burger Palace to see Vanessa.

I hope to God we can fool my parents this weekend, but my gut tells me that one dinner isn't going to be enough to satisfy my father. The prick will enjoy dragging this out and making me sweat.

Getting into my car outside the practice facility, I shoot her a text, letting her know I'm on my way. I'm not sure if she'll even have time to check her phone while she's working, but if she does get the chance, at least she'll know.

I've never been to The Burger Palace before. It's a diner outside of town, and I don't usually go anywhere except Harvey's. I've never even been to the fancy Italian restaurant that Mascen's girlfriend Rory works at.

Twenty minutes later I'm parking in the lot outside of the diner, cringing at the state of most of the vehicles there and praying nothing happens to mine while I'm inside.

Grabbing my backpack off the passenger seat—I figured I could get some studying in during the times I can't talk to Vanessa—I groan from the pain in my right shoulder. I'm going to have to ice it when I get back to the dorm.

And fuck, I can't forget to have a conversation with Jude about the girl situation.

Walking into the diner, the smell of greasy cheeseburgers and salty fries hits my nostrils. After practice, the last thing I should be eating is this kind of food, but man, it smells amazing.

I look around for Vanessa and spot her taking an

order. She must feel my eyes on her, because she looks over jolting a little in surprise. Maybe she didn't think I was serious about showing. With the end of her pen, she indicates a booth for me to sit at.

Shrugging my backpack off, I dig out my laptop and my business management textbook. I still can't figure out why we have to keep wasting money on physical textbooks when the internet exists.

A few minutes later Vanessa swings by my table, a dark curl trying to escape her hair-clip.

"Hi." Her voice is soft, and I can sense the underlying awkwardness there that needs to disappear before this weekend. She can be awkward with my parents, since she'll be meeting them for the first time, but not me. It'll be a dead giveaway that this is a farce. "Here's a menu." She sets it on the table beside my computer. "You want anything to drink?"

"Water's fine."

"Okay," she jerks her head in a nod, "I get a break in an hour, but I'll check on you as much as I can."

"Thanks." I smile at her, sliding the menu closer to me.

She walks away and my eyes zero in on her full, round ass. A light-yellow dress hugs each and every one of her curves.

My dick stirs in my pants and I grind my teeth together. I cannot afford to be getting boners over my fake girlfriend. I've been good this year, stayed celibate since July, and I don't need to screw things up now.

Vanessa comes back a moment later with my water in a red plastic cup with *Coca-Cola* scrawled on the side.

"First question of the evening," I start before she can run away from me, "what's your favorite candy?"

"You know those blue and white shark gummies?" I nod my head, recalling it. "Those are my favorite. I haven't had them in years, though. What about you?"

"Skittles. The orange one in particular."

"Interesting. I have to get back…" She points over her shoulder. "Unless you know what you want?"

"A Caesar salad with grilled chicken. Dressing on the side."

Her nose wrinkles. "That's it? I thought guys like you would eat way more than a salad."

"Believe me, I'd love to, but practice kicked my ass, and I'll get sick if I eat too much."

She bites her lip, blue eyes darting away from me. "Right. I'll put that in." She turns on her heel and walks over to the open kitchen area, hollering my order into the back.

While Vanessa tends to her tables I focus on my schoolwork. Contrary to popular belief I actually like school. I've always enjoyed learning new things and expanding my knowledge. I think one of the things that sucks the most when it comes to my father is knowing I've put in the work to take over everything our family name stands for, and I'd be good at it, but I don't want it at the expense it would cost me.

I won't sell my soul, and that's what he expects me to do.

Getting my hands on my inheritance will secure me a stable future even if I decided to never work, which isn't what I want. I might be planning to walk away from my family's fortune and dynasty, but I fully intend on building my own.

It's not long before Vanessa is bringing my salad, and she's about to dart away before I can ask another question, but I gently grab her wrist between my fingers, tugging her to stay.

She purses her lips, eyeing me like an unruly child. It's not the first time I've gotten that look in my twenty-one years, but it is the first time it's turned me on.

"If you could go anywhere in the world where would you go?"

It wasn't the question I planned, but maybe it's because she looks so desperate to flee, ready to be anywhere but here, that makes me ask.

She shrugs her wrist out of my hold, and for a second, I think she's going to actually run away from me, but then she says, "Paris."

"Why?" It's another question, but she doesn't call me on it.

"It looks so beautiful and rich with history. The lights. The flowers. The architecture. Just ... everything." A wistful smile touches her lips. "There's a street artist there too, anonymous, of course, and I like that he—or she— leaves behind something beautiful that makes a statement but washes away in the rain."

"What? Like chalk art?"

"I'm not sure how they do it." She gives a shrug, seeming to forget that a moment ago she was trying to run from me. "But I love it. Each piece is unique and well thought out, but it's not permanent, and that feels like such a reflection of life itself." She seems to come back into herself and says, "Where would you go?"

"I've been to a lot of places most only dream of seeing, but I've never been to Egypt so that's where I would go. I want to see the Pyramids."

"Why?" Now she's the one asking another question and it makes me smile.

"The history is remarkable and there's so much we still don't know. To say I've been there feels like I've been *this close*," I hold up my thumb and forefinger a teeny bit apart, "to something bigger than anyone alive today can even begin to comprehend."

Her dark blue eyes narrow on me in a speculative way. "You're different than I thought."

I grin back at her. "Stick around long enough, Van, and you'll learn that I'm full of surprises."

———

LESS THAN AN HOUR LATER, Vanessa slides into the booth across from me, letting out a sigh of relief the moment her ass touches the cracking vinyl seat. She lets her hair down, fluffing the dark strands. A burger and fries sit on a plate in front of her, but she eyes it like she'd rather be eating cardboard. It looks good, better than my salad at least, but I'm sure if I worked here and served burgers all evening, I wouldn't want it either.

She picks up a fry, stares at it for a solid three seconds, and then chews the end of it.

"So," she finishes the whole fry, "what other questions do you have for me? Credit score? Pretty sure that's like zilch. Favorite animal? Dogs—particularly pugs. If I don't own a pug named Penny one day, I'm suing. Favorite book? *Little Women*. Um..." She taps her bottom lip. "Favorite movie? *Titanic*. RIP Leo DiCaprio." She does the sign of the cross, oblivious to my grinning face across from her. "Did I miss anything?"

"I think I've got a few more here." I point to my trusty list.

She sighs. "Should've known. You keep adding to it don't you?" She takes a bite of her burger, groaning in anger when the tomato flies out the bottom and splatters on the plate.

"Perhaps. Do you have any questions for me?"

She tilts her head to the side. "Why baseball?"

"What do you mean?"

She swirls a fry in ketchup. "It seems like most guys like you would go for football. It *is* the most popular sport in the United States."

"Guys like me?"

"You know, hot. Popular."

A grin overcomes me. "You think I'm hot?"

She huffs, rolling her eyes. "You know you're hot."

"Oh, I know it, but me knowing it and you saying you think I am are two completely different things."

She rolls her eyes again. "You're the kind of guy who kisses his reflection, aren't you?"

"Absolutely. Gotta show myself I care, you know? But don't worry, you give me the chance and I'll show you how well I can worship you instead." She chokes on a sip of water, spraying it across the table so I get pelted in the face. I dry myself with a napkin. "I can make you do that other places too."

"Oh my God!" she shrieks, throwing the lemon from her glass at my head.

It lands in my hair. Pointing to it, I say, "Look, I have a tiara."

"Nothing fazes you, I swear," she grumbles, glaring at her burger.

"Not really, but to answer your question, I chose baseball because of my grandpa. He played in his youth and when I was little it was something we bonded over. I happened to be really good at it, and now here we are."

"What was his name?"

"Next question."

"What?" She pales. "Why is that off limits?"

"Because it's my father's name and my name too."

"So, Theodore then?"

I grin, chuckling. "Teddy's not short for Theodore in my case."

Her nose scrunches as she thinks. "Then what is it short for?"

I pick up my water glass. "I'm not telling, sweetheart. I'll never live it down."

"Is it really that bad?"

I think for a second. "Yeah."

"Hmm ... if it's not Theodore, Edward then?"

"Nah, babe. I don't sparkle in the sunlight. I'm a real man."

"Thomas, maybe?"

"Big fat no."

"Fine," she blows out a breath, "I give up for now, but I'm going to figure this out."

"No, you're not."

"Your cockiness will be your downfall, McCallister."

"Ooh," I lean closer to her across the table so there's little space separating us, "keep talking dirty to me."

She shakes her head. "You're ... I don't know what you are exactly, but it's something."

I chuckle, leaning back into the booth. "Got any other questions for me?"

She bites her lip, thinking. Her lips are a soft pink color without the use of any sort of lip product. I find myself thinking about her lips. How they felt against mine, what it was like, and especially what she'd look like with them wrapped around my cock.

"Are you even listening to me?"

I jerk back into myself. "Uh ... w-what did you say?"

She heaves a sigh, her breasts straining against that tight yellow uniform. *"Men,"* she mutters. "I *asked* you what your biggest fear is?"

"Failure," I blurt without a thought. "Honestly, that's what I've been most of my life, but I don't want to be that guy anymore. I want to do more. Be more. Make a difference."

"Hmm," she hums quietly, taking another bite of her burger.

"What?"

"That's just not the answer I expected."

"What did you expect?"

"I don't know, striking out with a girl?" She smiles, joking.

Shaking my head, I push the shaggy strands of hair out of my eyes. "Babe, I never strike out. When I have my sights set on something I never, ever lose."

"That so?"

"Yes," I say with absolute certainty.

But as she gathers up her plate and walks off so she can get back to work, I think I might've met the one girl who has the capability of ending me.

SIX

Vanessa

"IS IT TRUE YOU'RE DATING TEDDY MCCALLISTER?"

I look up at the girl sliding out a chair across from me in the library. It screeches on the hardwood floor before she plops her butt on it. I don't recognize her at all, but she clearly knows who I am. This is what I get for 'dating' a campus heartthrob. The worst part is girls have been trying to cage him for years and now they think I've done the impossible.

Dark glossy hair spills over her shoulders and her lips are painted in a bright red lipstick I'd love to wear but would be too afraid I couldn't pull it off to ever try.

"Uh…" I look back and forth from my textbook to my new table guest, a little peeved about having my study time interrupted. "Yeah?"

Shit, it's not supposed to sound like a question.

"You sound like you're not sure, does that mean it's a rumor?"

"No, we're together. Like a couple. He comes over and we make out and have sex and stuff. Totally couple things. He sends flowers too."

Oh my God kill me now!

"Oh." She frowns. "Okay. Is it like ... serious?"

My lips part. "Are you really asking me if my boyfriend and I are committed?"

"Well, I mean, yeah. Teddy doesn't date. It's a little surprising is all."

"Why exactly is it surprising?" I close my textbook, crossing my arms on the table ready to challenge her.

She gives a tiny shrug. "Like I said, he doesn't date and lots of girls have tried, believe me." Obviously, she's one of them. "Everyone knows he's worth a lot and wants to secure the position."

"What position is that exactly?"

She doesn't answer with words, instead she lifts her left hand, rubbing her ring finger.

I roll my eyes. "Teddy is a person. He's just a guy. He's not cattle for sale."

"Oh, honey." She shakes her head like I'm so pitiful and stupid. "It's sweet that you think so." She gives a tiny shrug. "While you might've been able to secure the girl-friend position first, it doesn't mean you're here to stay." She stands up from the table, tugging down her itty-bitty miniskirt. It's way too cold to be wearing something like that this time of year, but to each their own.

I watch her walk away, disappearing between the tall ancient stacks of books.

My study vibes are ruined now, so I pack up my computer — a secondhand monstrosity that I swear weighs twenty pounds — and textbooks, to head back to my dorm.

Stepping outside into the chilly air, I zip up my coat and pull out my wooly pink mittens from my pockets, slipping them onto my hands.

I know for most it isn't even that cold, but growing up in the south, this is practically Antarctica to me.

Before I go back to the dorm, I decide to grab a coffee. At least it'll help warm me up. I reach out for the door, but a hand beats me to it.

"There you are, babe." Lips connect with my chilled cheek, and I jolt at the unexpected touch.

My eyes dart up to Teddy's bright green ones. "You have got to stop sneaking up on me like that. It freaks me out," I hiss under my breath as he follows me into the line.

He looks at me in confusion. "I was calling your name. You didn't hear me?"

"Oh." My face falls. "You were?"

"Yeah. I tried to flag you down."

I take off my mittens, rubbing my suddenly warm face from the heat of embarrassment. "Sorry, I was distracted."

"Why?" He cocks his head to the side, seeming the tiniest bit worried. The genuine concern does something to my heart.

"One of your groupies cornered me in the library."

"Groupies?" He chuckles, shoving his hands into the pockets of his jeans. He's wearing a light brown beanie, dark strands of his hair poking out from beneath, and a gray sweatshirt clings to his muscular form.

"That's what I'm calling her. She's gunning for the position."

"What position?"

"Forget girlfriend, she wants to skip straight to wife."

"Ah." He leans back on his heels. "She's threatened by you. Did you catch her name?"

"Didn't ask." I adjust my backpack straps, my shoulders already aching from the weight as we move up in line. "Have you slept with everyone on this campus, though?" I hiss under my breath, my words laced with a venom I don't expect.

He thinks about it—seriously stands there and contemplates his answer. "Not everyone. I mean, I haven't slept with you."

It's the silent *yet* that has me lightly smacking his arm with the back of my hand. Teddy laughs uproariously, causing more than a few people to look in our direction. When they notice it's Teddy, they shake their heads and go back to their business.

"I won't be sleeping with you." I stare straight ahead at the menu board even though I always order the exact same thing.

"Who said anything about sleeping?" he counters, the side of his arm brushing mine. The guy has zero awareness of personal space. "The things I'd like to do with you don't include sleeping."

If I wasn't indebted to this dude, I'd be out the door now and I'd never look back. But the fact of the matter is,

I'm in this for the long haul after what he did for me, so that means dealing with his crude sense of humor.

"You're incorrigible."

"It's true since I'd like to be *in*side of you."

"Oh my God." I pinch the bridge of my nose. "How have you made it this long without someone punching you in the face?"

"I haven't. That has happened on occasion." A dark look steals over his face, and he clears his throat.

It's finally time for me to place my order and I force a cheery smile at the girl working the counter who's staring open mouthed at me and ... my boyfriend. *Right*.

Apparently, I need to get used to these looks.

"It's true, you do have a girlfriend?" She gapes at him, eyes wide as saucers.

I bump him out of my way with my hip and say, "Yes, Teddy McCallister and I, Vanessa Hughes, are dating. We go on dates. We kiss. We have lots and lots of hot sweaty sex. Now, can I please get a medium coffee with almond milk. And sweetums, what do you want?"

Poor Teddy is doing everything he can not to burst into uncontrollable laughter, which of course in turn makes my own lips twitch with barely contained amusement.

"I'll have a frozen caramel swirl. Medium as well."

"It's cold out!" I admonish.

"So?" He shrugs. "I want a frozen coffee. Let me live my life ... *snookums*."

I try to pass my card over to the girl, but he shoves my hand out of the way and gives her cash, telling her to keep the change. He puts his hand on the small of my waist, ushering me over to the 'Wait Here' counter.

"Sweetums, huh?" He whispers near my ear, his lips tickling my skin.

"Snookums?" I counter, hoping he didn't notice the shiver that skated down my spine. What was that about anyway? My body needs to get itself under control. I cannot afford to be attracted to my fake-boyfriend.

"Hey," he raises his hands innocently, "I was just following your lead."

Our order is up, and he passes me my cup before taking his own. He follows me outside and takes my hand. My first instinct is to pull it away, but of course that would raise suspicion.

I allow myself to relax, getting used to feeling of his hand around mine.

We walk in silence for less than a minute when he asks, "What was that about anyway? The kissing and that we have a lot of hot sweaty sex? Not that I wouldn't love to have such sex with you, but you keep turning me down."

I sigh, blowing out a breath that fogs the cold air. "I'm just a little peeved after running into your groupie in the library. I was trying to study and then she came along asking if I was actually dating you since so many others have tried to lock you down and were unsuccessful, and then she implied that I'm basically paving the way for the next person whom you'll wife up."

"And you got jealous?" he surmises, a smirk teasing his lips when they wrap around his lime green straw.

My lips pop open. "I'm not jealous. I have nothing to be jealous about. It's just that…"

"That?" he prompts, a dark brown arching.

I stop walking and he does too, his palm warm in mine since I didn't bother putting my mittens back on. "Look," I toe the ground, my boot shoving a rock off the cobblestone pathway, "I don't like people treating me like I'm replaceable and nothing special or like they're waiting to push me off some sort of first place podium I didn't even claim. I know what people are thinking about us."

Teddy's forehead wrinkles with confusion, his fingers flexing against mine. "I don't know what you mean?"

I sigh, biting down on my bottom lip as I try to hold back tears. I don't like showing this vulnerable side of myself. I've worked so hard to grow and move past thinking of myself as the big girl and that it somehow makes me lesser, because it doesn't. But certain situations bring out those nagging doubts that I've buried but haven't fully killed.

Sucking in my cheeks, I twist my lips back and forth. "They're looking at you—the hot sport's player, the ladies man, the big guy on campus, and then they see me— average looking, overweight, normal me, and they're wondering what the hell the two of us are doing together and even though this isn't real between us, it's still the reality."

Teddy looks like I've stung him. "But … no. You're beautiful, gorgeous." Sincerity rings in his voice, the truth of his words reflecting in his eyes too, and my heart tugs at that, softening inside my chest.

He's nothing like I ever expected.

"You know who everyone on campus thinks is worthy of you? Some Instagram model wannabe and that's not me. It'll never be me. I come from a poor family. I've worked my ass off to get here and yeah, I'm not horrible looking, but I'm not who all these people envision you with and that will work against me. Again, I know this is fake, but the hurt from the judgement? That's real."

He looks at a loss for words and I feel bad for laying all of this on him, but it's true. We're the only two people on campus who know what this is.

"I'm in this with you," I remind him. "I'm not going anywhere. I keep my promises. But this is only the beginning."

His jaw flexes. "I can ... I can protect you. I'll—"

My eyes close and I exhale a sigh. "Teddy. It's so sweet that you think you can, but you're not a god. You can't control an entire campus." Extricating my fingers from his, I add, "Don't worry. I'm a big girl. I'll get over it. Besides, it's on me to learn to control my feelings."

And get over the past, I think to myself.

"Vanessa!" he calls when I walk away. He jogs after me, tugging on the sleeve of my puffy coat. "There's something you're not telling me. What's going on?"

I glance down at the ground, surprised by how intuitive he is. It's so much easier to look at those worn stones than his worried face. "When I was in high school, the most popular guy in school started taking notice of me. I was so flattered. He was a senior and I was a freshman. He played football and was the guy all the girls wanted, and I couldn't believe he wanted me. It was all a lie, an elaborate one where the rug was yanked out from under me at the homecoming football game when…" Tears fall from my eyes at the horrible memories. "When my own sister revealed that he was *her* boyfriend and she'd put him up to seducing me just so she could mock me about thinking he'd actually liked me." I shake my head, unable to meet Teddy's horrified gaze. "She still doesn't know I lost my virginity to him." I huff out a tragic, humorless laugh. "He wasn't supposed to go that far, I guess." I shrug. "Let's just say, I'm a little extra sensitive to people thinking I don't belong with the popular guy. I've been through that, and they were right, because it was all a lie, and here we are again." I wave a hand at him. "At least this time I'm a willing participant."

He swallows thickly, his Adam's apple bobbing. "Van, I'm so sorry that happened to you."

"Yeah, me too." I wipe away a tear, burying those memories down again. I don't want to relive that time period, the horror and embarrassment I felt. "Seriously, don't worry. I'm okay. I'm in this."

This time, when I walk away, he doesn't chase after me.

SEVEN

Teddy

"WHAT ARE YOU DOING?" JUDE ASKS FROM THE doorway of my room when he finds me aggressively typing on my computer.

"Looking for this fucker I want to murder," I utter through clenched teeth.

After I searched Vanessa's name online, it was easy enough to find her old high school. Now, I'm going through the online yearbooks, looking for the guy who fucked her over. Her sister too for that matter.

No one ever deserves to be treated like she was.

"Uh…" Jude hesitates, wiping a towel over his damp head. "I can't tell if you're serious or not."

"Well, maybe not murder, but I might send a glitter bomb. Or shit. Can't you mail poop to people you hate?"

"What the fuck is going on?" He steps further into my room, and I finally look up.

"Dude, why's your cock out? I thought you had pants on."

"I just got out of the shower. Stop acting like you don't see wagging dicks in the locker room all the time."

"Doesn't mean I need to see yours," I mutter, scrolling through photos.

"Fine, fine. I'll go put pants on."

He walks away and I call after him, "Would it be appropriate to send a potato that says, 'Get Fucked'?"

He comes back in thankfully wearing a pair of jeans. "Ted, give me more information than that."

"Don't call me Ted. I ain't Bundy."

Jude chuckles. He likes riling me up. The problem is I'm already livid. After I fill him in on what happened to Vanessa, he's as pissed as me. Jude might be a manwhore but he doesn't talk shit about women or treat them like it.

"Fuck, grab Mascen, that dude has enough hatred to fuel an entire country, and let's pay this asshole a visit."

We both peer at the senior photo of the smug fucker. Tristan Samuels.

I flick over to the photo of Vanessa's sister. The slender cheerleader who played an unforgiveable prank on her sister. Fuck, I don't think it can even be called a prank. It's a flat out hate crime against her own flesh and blood. I scroll to the freshman section, my heart jerking when I find Vanessa, her smiling braces covered teeth staring back at me, blue eyes behind a pair of red glasses. She looked so happy, so innocent, and those two fuckers hurt her. I knew she was trying to brush it off like it wasn't a big deal, but the pain in her eyes said everything she wouldn't.

"Do you think we can be back by morning?"

I'm dead ass serious.

"The three of us can take turns driving and sleeping."

I wet my lips with my tongue. "Let's do it."

My normally easy-going personality has gone out the window. All I want is to see those two people realize that the shit you do has consequences. Vanessa deserves better than to be treated in such a horrible way, and I'm absolutely fuming over the fact that the bastard had the audacity to take her virginity too.

"You call Mascen and get him on board and I'm going to pack my shit."

He's only taken a few steps when I say, "Thanks, Jude."

"That's what friends are for."

———

"Listen, all I'm saying is you need to let me know if I need to have a lawyer on call." Mascen pumps gas into his Land Rover. We decided to take it since it had the most room. It wasn't like the three of us were going to fit in my sportscar. I was a tad surprised when Mascen agreed readily, but after I explained the situation, like Jude, he was livid too. Cole will probably be mad we left him out, but I'm not about to drag him into this mess in case we get arrested. It's not likely, but the three of us have the money to bail ourselves out. Cole's a scholarship student, so he can't risk his status.

"I'm not going to get arrested," I scoff like the idea is preposterous despite the fact that this is the very concern that's kept me from inviting Cole along. Mascen eyes me like he doubts that. "I'm not. I just want to talk to the guy."

And her sister who I found out is married to the fucker. Like Jesus Christ, Vanessa can't escape the psychopaths.

"Talk with your mouth?" He mimes moving his hand like a mouth. "Or with your fists?" He forms one.

"I haven't decided yet."

The gas pump dings, and he finishes up, hopping in the SUV and finding all the snacks and drinks I raided from the convenience store. He doesn't say anything, merely shakes his head with a huff and shoves everything in the back with Jude.

"Treat my snacks with some respect. At least give them a little kiss on the cheek before you smack their ass and send them on their way."

Mascen snickers, slipping sunglasses on to shield his eyes from the setting sun.

He cranks up the music and grins as he pulls onto the highway. "Let's get in some trouble, boys."

EIGHT

Vanessa

THERE'S ONLY A DAY LEFT UNTIL DINNER WITH TEDDY'S parents. This week has gone by in a blink, and suddenly as I'm standing here in my dirty yellow work uniform, I realize that I have nothing appropriate to wear. At least nothing nice and expensive that people like his parents would expect me wear.

I hate to say it, but I think I'm going to have to dig into my savings for something. Maybe I can convince Danika to go shopping with me. I'd rather not have to brave stores on my own when I have no real sense of style or idea of how to put pieces together.

The bell above the front door chimes, and on instinct I glance over to see who's entered the diner. I recognize him instantly from the cut of his shoulders, even clothed in a warm winter coat. A school baseball cap is pulled low over his eyes as he walks over to the same table he sat at earlier in the week.

I haven't talked to him in two days, not since I confessed what my sister and her then-boyfriend, now husband, did to me. I'm not sure if I disgusted him or —

"Excuse me, can we get some napkins?" One of my tables flags me down, and I realize I've been standing there staring for way too long.

I grab up some extra napkins and pass them out. Filling up a cup with water, I bring it to Teddy and set it in front of him. "If you want something else to drink let me know." He looks up and I gasp. "What happened to you?" There's a small cut on his lip, a faint bruise around his eye, and when I look at his hands resting on the table, I see that his knuckles are cracked.

"Would you believe me if I said the other guy looks way worse? Because it's true. I told him he could get one punch in, and as a man of my word I let him."

"What did you do?" I start racking my brain for any hint I might've heard on campus of Teddy getting into a fight, but there was nothing.

"Vanessa," my boss calls, "order's up."

I sigh, knowing I'm going to have to wait to interrogate Teddy further. Grabbing the order for one of my tables I drop it off and freshen up their drinks.

"Do you want anything to eat?" I ask Teddy when I swing back by his table.

"The Caesar salad with chicken like last time."

I put his order in, check my tables, and then return to

him. "What did you do?" I ask again, leaning against the side of the table.

Those piercing green eyes of his glimmer with an intensity that nearly rocks me backwards and somehow I know, *I know*, before he even opens his mouth.

"You didn't seriously think you'd tell me what that prick did to you and I'd just stand idly by and do nothing?" My lips part. "Come on, Van. I'm not that kind of guy."

"How did you even find him?" I blanch, clutching my order pad to my chest.

He sighs, removing his hat and running his fingers through his hair. "It wasn't that hard once I found the online yearbook."

"I ... I can't believe you did that."

"Believe it, babe. Mascen and Jude helped too. Tristan isn't looking too good right now." And if there was any doubt in my mind that he might be making it up, they're erased with the mention of Tristan's name. His eyes hold mine, somber when he says, "I hope you know that you never deserved to be treated and used like that. You didn't do anything wrong."

I look away, unable to handle the intensity in his gaze. "You don't know that," I mutter, toeing the ground.

"No one deserves that, and I might've only just met you, but I know that. It's taken care of now. He'll never even look at you again. I also had some choice words for your sister, sorry about that. Actually, scratch that," he makes a noise like a record scratching, "I'm not sorry at all. She deserved it."

"I can't believe you—they—that all of you did that … for *me*." My voice cracks embarrassingly, and I press my lips together to hold back tears.

Teddy laces his fingers together on the table, and my eyes once again go to the bruises marring his normally flawless skin. "I'd do anything for the people that I care about. That includes you now."

"R-Right," I stutter. I toss a thumb over my shoulder. "I … um … I'm going to check and see if your salad is ready."

I dash away, wiping a tear from my cheek that I hope he didn't see. I don't need anyone to fight my battles for me, but that doesn't mean this isn't the nicest thing anyone has ever done for me.

Teddy's salad is done, and my boss tells me when I finish my current tables I can go on break. Most of them are almost ready to leave, so Teddy isn't quite done eating when I sit down with a B.L.T.

"Can I ask you another question?"

My lips tick with a smile. "Don't you always?"

He chuckles, a glimmer in his eyes that gives me a glimpse of what a mischievous little boy he must've been. "What's something you should know how to do by now but can't?"

I have to think for a few minutes before I answer. "I can't swim," I admit shyly, looking at my plate. "That's definitely something I should know how to do by now. What about you?"

He answers without hesitation. "I can't ride a bike."

"What?" I gasp. "But that's like ... a rite of passage as a child."

"Not for me." He lifts his water glass, chugging down the rest of it. "Please, don't take this the wrong way. I know I have many things to be grateful for but growing up all I wanted was a normal life." He gives a humorless chuckle, looking at the wall to his left and the neon sign of a burger with a crown. "I guess that makes me sound so incredibly selfish."

I don't know what makes me do it, but I reach across the table and place my hand on top of his, rubbing my fingers over his injured knuckles. "Teddy," his name is a soft exhale, and his forest green eyes shoot to mine, "I've only known you a short time, but even I can tell that you're the least selfish person I've ever met."

"You think so?"

I rub my lips together, thinking of how he paid my tuition, how he drove all the way to my hometown with his friends to defend my honor.

"No, Teddy. I *know* so."

NINE

Teddy

Smoothing my hands down my light blue oxford, stiff from the dry cleaners, I inhale a shaky breath and then knock a few raps on Vanessa's door. Nerves zip through my body, wondering if we can truly pull off this dinner with my parents.

They live near Nashville, so we'll have an hour drive each way, but at least on the way there it'll give me time to prepare. I'm going to be dragging Vanessa into the lion's den, and I'm terrified she's going to get gnawed on like a juicy piece of meat.

I hear a snicker over my shoulder, feel eyes on me from some of the other residents on this floor. I turn, putting on a charming smile and wave at the group of girls before I knock again.

The door opens this time, and her roommate stands there with narrowed, shrewd eyes like she's sizing me up. "She's almost ready. You can wait on the couch."

She lets me in, quickly closing the door. No doubt the chicks out there were trying to get a peek inside.

"Danika, right?"

"Mhmm," she hums, crossing arms over her chest. The gesture pushes her breasts up, and I quickly divert my gaze. Fake relationship or not, I'm not going to be checking out Vanessa's roommate when she's a room away. "What are your intentions with her?"

"Um." I blink a few times, taken off guard. "Excuse me?"

She puts her hands on her hips, her angular face framed by black hair. "Listen, Vanessa and I aren't best friends. We're kind of complete opposites, but she's a nice girl and I like her. I don't want to see her get hurt by some douchebag popular guy, okay? She deserves more than that, so all I'm saying is if you plan on hurting her, just leave. You've never dated before, but I did some asking around and apparently you haven't been as loosey-goosey this year—"

"Loosey-goosey?" I mouth.

"I'm not done," she plows right over me. "Vanessa isn't the kind of girl you use for some quick fun. Don't hurt her. I know how to get rid of a body."

I swallow, eyeing her warily. "Um ... you're kind of scary."

She grins. "Good."

The door to Van's room opens and she steps out. Her

dark hair is curled, hanging past her breasts, and she wears more makeup than her usual. The dress she chose is a pale pink with long sleeves and ends past her knees. A black coat is slung over her arm and she holds a pair of heels in her hands.

"Do I look okay?" she asks me hesitantly. "I was trying to keep it modest, and to be honest, that's kind of hard with big boobs like mine and oh my God now I'm rambling. But I wanted to look nice to meet your parents and—"

"You're always gorgeous," I tell her honestly, "but damn you look beautiful tonight."

Her cheeks pinken.

"You're meeting his parents?" Danika asks in surprise.

Vanessa's eyes dart between her roommate and me. She bends, slipping her shoes on. "Yeah, why?"

"No reason. You two kids have fun." She gives a little wave and shuts her bedroom door behind her.

"That was weird. Have you slept with her?"

I put a hand to my chest. "I swear to you, I have not fucked your roommate. She's just protective of you."

"Of me? Why?" She gives Danika's closed door a baffled glance.

I shrug. "Beats me." I take her coat from her and hold it open so she can slip her arms inside. "But we have to get going. We're going to hit traffic."

"Right," she sighs. I don't know what makes me do it, but I lean in and kiss the corner of her mouth. It's the closest I've gotten to her lips since Harvey's. She freezes, blue eyes darting up to mine. "W-What was that for?"

Taking a step back, I shove my hands into the pockets of my dress pants. "No reason other than I wanted to."

She touches the skin I just kissed and lets her fingers drop. "Right." Her cheeks turn a lovely shade of pink and I can't help but wonder if she's thinking of what that real kiss was like. "I guess I need to get used to that, huh?"

"Well, it will look weird if I don't kiss my girlfriend. Everyone knows I'm a hands-on kind of guy."

Her shoulders lift with an inhale, and she grabs a purse I didn't even notice. "I guess we better go, huh?"

"Time to face the firing squad." I groan like I'm in physical pain at the thought alone.

Wide, panicked blue eyes meet mine. "Is it really going to be that bad?"

I place a hand on her lower waist. "You have no idea, babe."

—————

"HOLY FUCKING SHIT! This is where you grew up?"

She eyes the Grecian manor home that's sorely out of style with the typical Nashville homes and mansions. But that's my father for you. He wanted something that threw wealth in people's faces as soon as they rounded the long driveway and the house came into view.

"I mean, yeah, when I was here. I was mostly at my boarding school, so this doesn't really feel like my child-hood home the way I'm sure other people feel about where they grew up."

Her full lips turn down into a frown. "That's really kind of sad."

My grip on the steering wheel tightens as I continue up the long drive. "It's all I knew."

For a long time, I didn't realize life could be any different. Not until I came to Aldridge and saw that not all families are like mine.

"My hands are so sweaty." She goes to wipe her hands on her dress, but I quickly grab them, stopping her. "What are you doing?"

"Just hold my hand in yours. We can both have sweaty hands."

She throws her head back and laughs, the sound light and mystical, so carefree despite her nerves.

"That's ... unexpectedly sweet of you."

"I have my charms."

I pull around to the back of the house and park in front of the massive garage that actually extends underground and houses my father's antique car collection.

"Are there any last-minute things I should know before we go in?"

"I think we've covered most of it. Even if we'd started dating when I told my dad, there would be plenty of things we'd still be learning about each other."

"Fake."

"Huh?" I look over at her in confusion.

"If we'd started *fake*-dating when you told him."

I shake my head. "Right."

She looks down at my hand in hers, rubbing her thumb gently over my injured knuckles. "I still can't believe you went all the way to Georgia just to deck Tristan in the face."

"It wasn't a big deal."

She straightens, her eyes steady on mine. "It was, Teddy. No one..." She chokes up a bit. "No one has ever done anything like that for me. I've never had someone to defend me."

"Well," I clear my throat, "now you have me."

She releases my hand and glides her fingers through her hair before undoing her seatbelt. I can feel her trying to put up walls and it's fucking annoying. Can't we at least be friends?

"Let's get this over with," I grumble, opening my car door.

I hurry around the side and open her door before she can. A tiny smile dances on her lips as she steps out. Closing it, I lock up the car even though it's unnecessary. No one that isn't expected stands a chance of getting onto this property.

Taking Vanessa's hand, I lead her over to a side door and enter a code.

"This place is a like a compound," she mutters.

"You have no idea."

She looks around in awe and maybe a little horror as I lead her through the mansion.

Shiny marble floors. Rows and rows of columns. Massive chandeliers. We pass room after room, her eyes growing rounder. I wonder if it looks as ostentatious to her as it does me. My mom isn't as bad as my father, but she's still all about the show and flashing their wealth in the faces of others. Growing up, I loved everything money could buy, until I got old enough to realize it can't buy you things of real value.

"Have you ever gotten lost in here?" she whispers under her breath.

"Yes," I admit, laughing a little at how absurd it is.

You should grow up in a home, not a museum, but that's all this is.

"Did you ever have any pets?"

I snort. "And have muddy paws running amok in this place? Absolutely not. But like I said, I was at school most of the time and during the summers we traveled. Even for most holidays we weren't here."

"That's…"

"Sad?" I supply.

She looks up at me with a melancholy expression. "I was going to say depressing, so yeah, same thing. I can't imagine growing up with such coldness."

"It's all I know." My voice is a little gruff, my throat clogged with emotion. "Besides, it doesn't matter. I have my friends. I have you."

"Y-Yeah," she stutters, that flicker in her eyes like she's not sure if I'm being serious or just playing a part. It shows how much she still doesn't know me yet, because I have a hard time being anything other than real.

We get closer to the formal living room where I know my parents will be waiting. A staff member gives me a head nod as he walks past and Vanessa gasps.

"Yes," I sigh heavily, "we have full-time staff."

"I swear this place is as big as Disney World." She

looks around and around trying to take it all in, my grip on her hand tightening because whether she knows it or not, she's my lifeline right now. Not because she's playing the part of my fake-girl, but her presence is a soothing balm to having to deal with my father.

"It's pretty big," I mutter in agreement.

She hasn't even seen anything but the maze of halls. There's an indoor pool. Two outdoor pools. A tennis and basketball court. A guest house that's the size of a regular house. There's even a bowling alley in the basement.

My dad's deep voice booms as we round the next hall, my grip on Vanessa's hand tight enough to cut off circulation, but if it's bothering her, she doesn't say.

"My parents are very formal," I hurriedly whisper under my breath. "Just refer to them as Mr. and Mrs. McCallister."

She tugs on my hand, urging me to stop in the hallway. I tuck her against a column, using my body to shield her from staff walking by and my parents if they'd happen to leave the living room.

A jolt runs through me when she places her hands on my cheeks. "We're in this together. You and me. Right?" I jerk my head in a nod. "Good." She leans up on her tiptoes, still not tall enough in her heels to reach my ear. "I've got you."

I swallow thickly when she falls back to her regular height, her eyes holding mine captive. She sees how much I hate being here, how much I don't want to do this or put her through this, and she's still got my back.

I don't know what fucking miracle sent her my way but I'm eternally grateful for it.

Raising her hand to my lips, I place a gentle kiss to her knuckles, not missing the tiny gasp that catches in her throat.

"Teddy, we know you're here!" My father calls out in that commanding voice of his, the one that demands that you do what he wants and do it now.

A staff member gives a tiny whimper as she runs by even though he's not shouting at her.

For now.

I've never brought anyone here. Not my friends and certainly not a girl since I've never dated. But Vanessa is about to face the lion's den with me, and I *know* she thinks the favor she's doing pales to the money I shelled out for her school payment, but she's wrong.

I count to three, and then the two of us walk into the massive formal living room. There's a grand fireplace that's the center focal point of the room and my father paces in front of it, a glass of brandy gripped loosely between his fingers.

"There you are. Took you long enough."

"Yes, well, it's been a while. I got lost in the halls," I snap, sarcasm dripping from my words.

My mom stands from the couch, her dress rippling around her long legs as she glides toward us. "Ah, it's so nice to meet you. I'm Lenora, Teddy's mother. My son lacks manners and didn't tell us your name."

She takes my mom's offered hand and says, "I'm

Vanessa. It's really nice to meet you. Teddy speaks highly of you both."

Across the room my father makes some sort of noise that's too dignified to be called a snort, but close enough, and downs his brandy. "I highly doubt that. Teddy doesn't think too fondly of us."

My mom frowns, and I feel a tug of guilt. She's not perfect, but she's not him, and I don't like hurting her.

My father crosses the room in a few long strides.

"It's nice to meet you Mr. McCallister." Vanessa extends her hand to him and he looks down at it as if it's a wild snake, ready to strike.

"I'd say 'likewise' but considering my son has never brought home a woman before and just so happened to conveniently announce he had a girlfriend when I caught three naked women in his room, you'll find that I'm a little lacking in the believability department. My son doesn't do monogamy, especially not with someone so…" He looks her up and down. "Inferior and lacking in good breeding."

Good breeding? For fuck's sake.

I snarl, my lips pulling back from my teeth. "Don't talk to her like that."

"Hmm," he hums, his eyes glassy. It's obvious he's already a few drinks deep. "Are there some feelings in that heart of yours? Ones that don't revolve around chasing tail and getting into as much trouble as possible?"

Vanessa squeezes my hand and when I look down at her I find that her shoulders are straight and there's a fire in her eyes. She refuses to be affected by anything my father says, and while I'm grateful for that, it doesn't lessen the anger I feel because he has no right to spew his hateful shit.

Cocking my head to the side, I level him with a challenging look. "I learned from the best," I tell him. "After all, I was only six when I first caught your secretary with her legs in the air on your desk."

My mom squeaks, her hand flying to her chest. She's not surprised by my confession. She's well aware of my father's multiple affairs and tolerates them because it means she doesn't have to deal with his unwanted advances and can go on spending the family money. Sometimes I wonder how she ever tolerated him long enough to make me.

A muscle in my father's jaw clenches, his knuckles white against his glass. He lifts it, downing the rest of the amber colored liquid. In a hushed whisper he grinds out, "You ungrateful little bastard—"

"Dinner is served."

"Ah," my mom jumps on the welcome distraction, "dinner. Let's eat."

Vanessa and I follow them into the dining room, sitting at the custom twenty-foot table. Every single thing in this mansion is larger than life, all for show.

The first course is set in front of us, and I inconspicuously use my pinky to point to the correct fork when I see Vanessa's panic-stricken expression.

Silence reigns around us. My mom is probably scared to broach a conversation, my father is still recovering from our verbal sparring. Vanessa, by some miracle, doesn't look like she's ready to flee out the front door. Not that she'd even be able to find it since it's so easy to take a wrong turn in this place.

Dinner is almost over, we're waiting for dessert, when my father speaks again.

"How is it that you two met?" I open my mouth to answer, but he silences me with a glare. "I'm asking her. Surely she can speak for herself."

I don't think I've ever wanted to punch the arrogant son of a bitch more in my entire life. Vanessa might be here playing the part of my girlfriend, but I still feel protective of her and the last thing I want is for him to cut her down.

Vanessa clears her throat, her hands clasped loosely in her lap.

"I work at a restaurant, and Teddy came in for lunch one day. That's how we met."

My father pounces like a lion on its prey. "A waitress, I presume?"

"Y-Yes?" She stutters out her answer like a question.

His eyes swing to me, a glass of wine clasped in his one hand. He swirls it lazily as he stares me down. "A waitress." He clucks his tongue. "You'll find any way to defy us, won't you? Does she know what we're worth? Girls like her are only looking for one thing, you know."

"And what exactly is it you think I'm looking for?" Vanessa asks through clenched teeth.

Something flashes in his cold gray eyes. The challenge. He likes the fight in her. Sick bastard. My hands clench into fists beneath the table. I want to deck him in the face, but that small voice in the back of my mind reminds me that I have to be on my best behavior. I can't risk anything until I have my inheritance. While it's in his control I'm helpless.

With a calculated smirk his gaze moves from me to her. "Money, darling. It's all people like you are after." He swings back to me, swirling his wine in the glass. "You are using protection, aren't you? The last thing we need is an unplanned pregnancy, though I'm sure that's what she'd like to secure a sizeable payout."

Vanessa sits up straight, ready for a fight. "I don't appreciate what you're implying, sir." The fact she manages to tack on sir in an attempt to sound respectful nearly makes me break out into laughter. "Need I remind you, I've only met you tonight, and you've barely spoken to me, mostly just spewed ridiculous rhetoric when you don't even know me, nor have made an attempt to know me, so excuse me if I refuse to feel offended by what you *think* you know about me. Because, again sir, since it seems to beg repeating; you don't know me."

Silence.

I don't think I've ever seen my father speechless, but Vanessa eloquently put him in his place. This is the moment when I'd break out into a slow clap if I didn't know it would land me in hot water.

My father stares her down, his face growing redder and redder by the second.

"Ah, dessert!" My mom finally speaks up as one of the staff carries in plates of crème brûlée. It's my favorite, and I know my mom probably asked specifically for it to be prepared. I appreciate the gesture, but the last thing I want is dessert.

"Looks great, Mom," I say as if she was the one who made it, when I'm not sure she's ever cooked a day in her life. When I was a small boy it was our cook Maggie who taught me how to bake. "But I really think we should get going."

"What?" she blanches, spoon poised above the caramelized sugar surface. "No, please stay. Enjoy dessert and then we can —"

"You're staying for dessert." My father's firm tone allows no room for argument.

Beneath the table, Vanessa's hand finds my knee. She rests it there lightly in a reassuring way, silently telling me we can get through this.

"Fine, we'll stay," I grit out, resting my left hand atop hers and wrapping my fingers into hers.

I don't let her hand go the entire time I eat my crème brûlée. My favorite dessert tastes like cardboard as I count down the seconds until we can get the hell out of there.

After the dishes are cleared, my father stands, undoing the button on his suit jacket. "I have some things to attend to in my office. I expect to see you both here next Saturday for dinner as well. In fact, why don't we make this a regular thing since it was so … enjoyable."

My mouth parts, and before I can utter a word, he's gone. My shoulders cave in on themselves.

Yes, I roped Vanessa into playing the part of my fake girlfriend for the rest of the school year. I figured on the rare occasions I had to see my parents I'd bring her along, and on campus she'd keep other girls from breathing down my neck. But the last thing I ever expected was for my father to request *weekly* dinners.

I look across the table at my mom, noticing her stricken expression when he leaves the room.

"Mom," I say, drawing her attention. "We need to get back to campus."

"Oh, yes, of course."

She stands from the table and I hug her, holding her a little extra tight.

"It was nice meeting you, Vanessa." She surprises me when she moves in to hug her.

Vanessa appears just as shocked but returns the gesture. "It was nice to meet you too, Mrs. McCallister."

"I told you," she smiles gently at her, "call me Lenora. Be careful on the road, dear." She pats my shoulder. "Let me know you get in safe."

She strides from the room, leaving behind the heavy floral scent of her perfume.

It's finally just Vanessa and me again, and my shoulders sag in relief.

Taking her hand, I say, "Let's get out of here."

She doesn't protest as I drag her through the maze of halls back to the side entrance we came through. No words are exchanged between us until we're in the car and I'm speeding down the driveway.

"I'm so sorry, Van." I shake my head.

"You're sorry?" She glances at me with a mystified expression.

I snort, gripping the wheel so tight I know I'm cutting off the circulation in my hands.

"Of course, I'm sorry. Sorry you had to witness that. Sorry he talked to you like that. It's unacceptable and then for him to have the audacity to demand weekly dinners. No." I shake my head adamantly. "It's not okay."

She places her hand on my tense knee. "You don't need to apologize on his behalf. Besides, I'm the one who's truly sorry. God, Teddy, no one should grow up with a parent like that. Your mom doesn't seem horrible, but she doesn't stick up for you, and I could never let someone talk to my child like that." I don't think she even realizes it, but she rubs calming circles around my knee. "I see now why you needed my help."

I chuckle humorlessly. "I feel bad for dragging you into this mess." Jerking the car off the side of the road Vanessa squeals in surprise as rocks kick up around the car. I slam it in park and shove my fingers through my hair. "It's a fucked-up situation."

"Hey." She tugs on my right arm, pulling it loose from where I'm trying to yank my hair out. "Hey," she repeats, taking my face between her hands and forcing me to look at her fully. "Did I ask for Tristan and my sister to do what they did to me?"

I scoff. "Fuck no. They were sick and twisted—"

"Exactly," she says in that same calm tone like she's consoling a child. "You didn't ask to be born into your family. You didn't ask to be treated like that, and you stuck up for me when you didn't have to. I haven't known you long, but it's obvious you try to carry the weight of the world on your shoulders. I'm telling you that you don't have to. I see now why you want to secure your inheritance." She looks down, biting her lip. "I thought at first it was a greed thing, wanting as much money as you can get your hands on, but…"

I place my hand over top hers on my cheek. "I just want to get away."

"I'm in this with you."

Because she feels indebted to me.

"You don't have to do this."

I know our whole agreement was so I would look like I have my shit together to my dad. A girlfriend makes me look like I'm taking life seriously and settling down from my wild ways, but fuck, I didn't think he'd treat her so poorly. So, yeah, I'm giving her an out.

She rolls her eyes. "You're not getting rid of me that easily, and we're not letting your dad win either." She snorts and lets her hands fall from my face. I'm forced to let go of her, and I miss the warmth of her hand beneath mine.

What the hell is happening to me?

I can't go catching feelings like some goddamn virus and definitely not for the girl already pretending to be mine.

Oh shit.

"What is it?" Vanessa probably senses the internal panic raging through my body.

"Nothing," I mutter, glancing out the rearview mirror before I pull back onto the road. "It's nothing."

TEN

Vanessa

I PICK AT A DRY TURKEY SANDWICH FROM ALDRIDGE'S dining hall. It's after one, so it's quieter in here than usual and I use it as an opportunity to work on a paper I have due next week for my Communications Theory class. Honestly it might be the worst class I've ever taken.

Ignoring the stares from people I don't know, I get a paragraph written before I'm interrupted by a text message.

Teddy: Where are you?
Me: The dining hall.
Teddy: Be there in a few.

It's Wednesday, days after the fiasco of a dinner with his parents, and I can tell he's still tense from it, which saddens me because he's known for being such a happy go lucky kind of guy. It's awful that anyone, especially his own parent, can suck the happiness out of him.

The whispers start up, and I stiffen a little in response, knowing he's entered the building.

I know we're early into this arrangement, but I'm not sure I'll ever get used to the attention he draws from everyone. After what happened to me with Tristan, I didn't put much stock into the popular crowd and never understood why people acted as if they were gods and not the normal mortals that they are. It's even weirder now that I'm associated with that crowd through Teddy.

His shadow falls over the table I secured in a corner, and I jolt when he bends, kissing my cheek. Affection seems to come so easy to him, which surprises me considering his upbringing.

"Hey," he says, a little breathless like perhaps he jogged from wherever he'd been when he texted me. He drops a baggy onto the table before he pulls out the chair across from me and plops into it. His hair is the tiniest bit windblown, his cheeks red from the crisp air.

"What's this?" I pick up the baggy of cookies. "Are these snickerdoodles?"

"I was stress baking." He sets his backpack in the chair beside him. "And you said they're your favorite, so…" He gestures lazily at the bag clasped in my hands.

"So, you made me cookies?"

"Um…" I swear his cheeks get even redder. "Yes."

"Hmm," I hum and take one out, biting into it. "Oh my God. Teddy." Cookie crumbles from my mouth onto the table. "These are delicious."

He grins from ear to ear, his whole face lighting up. "You like them?"

"Um, like?" I look from the cookie in my hand to the bag. "I fucking love them."

"Good." He sits back in the chair. He eyes my dry turkey sandwich. "You know what," he slams his hands down on the table suddenly, startling me, "I'm going to get something to eat. You've gotta have something better than that. This place has way better stuff than the prepackaged shit at the front."

I don't have a chance to tell him I opt for those because it costs less than the others, because he's already walking away.

"He's so hot." A girl at a nearby table gushes to her friend.

She blushes when she catches my gaze, ducking her head to face the table.

"It's okay." I smile at her before glancing over my shoulder at Teddy in line and sue me, but I do ogle his ass for a second. "I get it. He's hot. Look all you want but no touching."

She laughs lightly and leans closer to my table. "How did you two meet?"

I give her the same spiel we came up with that we've been telling everyone.

"Aw." She clutches her chest, positively swooning. "That's so cute. I wish something like that would happen to me."

"It will," I assure her. "One day. We all deserve our great love."

The words burn my tongue, because I know she thinks Teddy is my great love I'm talking about.

He returns to the table and sets down two trays, his eyes roaming from me to the girls I was speaking to and back. A mischievous smile dances across his lips, and I have no warning before he's lowering his head, and instead of his typical kiss on my cheek, or the one that grazes the corner of my mouth, he goes full on.

He hasn't kissed me like this since Harvey's, and I squeak in surprise since I wasn't expecting that, but the high-pitched sound quickly lowers to a moan. My body responds to his like he's a conductor and I'm the orchestra. His tongue slides past my lips, and I taste a hint of coffee on his tongue. At some point his hand slides around the back of my neck, holding me in place, and damn if it isn't the sexiest thing a man has ever done when kissing me.

Suddenly it's over, and I feel cold from the lack of his touch.

Clearing his throat, he sits back down like nothing ever happened and his tongue wasn't just in my mouth, and slides the one tray nearer to me. "Try it."

"What is that?" I ask in shock, not because it looks terrible but because it looks like something you'd find in a gourmet restaurant.

"Steak frites."

"You rich pricks," I mutter, but I say it with a smile so he knows I'm joking.

I push my mostly uneaten turkey sandwich out of the way and dig in.

"You like it?" He inquires a minute later.

"It's delicious."

"Here." He shoves his hand in his pocket and yanks out a card. He passes it to me, and I see that it's his student ID. "Use it any time you want something."

"Um ... Teddy, you kind of need this."

He shrugs. "I'll tell Mrs. Jostin I lost it like usual."

I snort. "How does that poor woman deal with you?"

I eye the card on the table, my teeth digging into my bottom lip because I realize Teddy actually knew why I had chosen my pathetic turkey sandwich, but he played dumb about it to not make me feel bad, and now he's offering me his student ID so I can get whatever I want and not have to worry about the cost. He plays the dumb jock role well, but Teddy McCallister is the furthest thing from stupid.

"Ah, she loves me. She just pretends to be irritated by my presence."

"Yeah," I suppress a smile as I grab his card and slip it in my backpack, "I'm sure it's all pretend."

I don't plan on using his card, but I know how he is, and if I don't accept it, he'll just keep harping on it until I give in anyway.

Teddy glances at the girls at the table near us and waves. I guess they haven't taken their eyes off of us. I've done surprisingly well ignoring the unwanted attention I've gained since becoming his temporary girlfriend. Since my freak-out where I confessed about my freshman year of high school it's like a weight has been lifted off my shoulders, one I didn't know I'd been carrying around all these years.

It's one thing to deal with trauma, it's another to let it go.

Thanks to Teddy, I've finally let it go.

"There's going to be a party at Cree's place this Friday. I want you to go."

I wrinkle my nose at his request. Parties are not my thing, but I'm not working so there's no reason for me to refuse. Plus, it's part of my duties.

"Sure, who's Cree again?" I wrack my brain, filtering through my mental images of all his friends I've met. "Dark hair?"

"Yeah. He plays ice hockey. He was the one sitting at the other end across from us at Harvey's."

"Mhmm," I hum my agreement, even though for the life of me I can't remember him.

"You'll get used to everyone eventually," he promises.

I wish I felt as confident as he does about it. Teddy seems to know everyone on campus and be friends with at least half of them.

"Wait," his brow furrows as if something has just occurred to him, "don't you have some friends I should meet? I mean, I *am* your boyfriend."

I look down at the table, brushing a crumb onto the shiny tile floor. "You've already met Danika and she's the closest thing I have to a friend."

"That's ... that's *it*?"

He's obviously horrified by my lack of friendships.

"It's not that I'm opposed to friendship," I defend,

playing with the ends of my hair, "I'm just so busy. I have classes and studying, work, there's not enough time for anything else."

"But ... you make time for me."

I give a small laugh. "Teddy, I don't think people make time for you. You just appear."

He ponders my reply. "This is true."

I study the side of his face when he looks away, the elegant shape of his profile. The slope of his nose and pout of his lips and something heavy sinks into my stomach because I'm only beginning to know this guy, and reeling from his sudden appearance, but what am I going to do when he's gone?

ELEVEN

Teddy

"DUDE, WHY ARE THERE SO MANY FUCKING COOKIES IN here?" Jude swipes one from a plate and pops it in his mouth. "Not that I'm complaining," he spews cookie as he speaks, "but I'm going to end up gaining ten pounds, and it's going to be hard to explain."

He rubs his rock-hard abs and me being me, I lift my apron to show off my own since I'm shirtless beneath it.

And yeah, I wear an apron when I cook. A really fucking manly one.

Okay, so maybe it's blue and white polka dots with a white frilly lace, but since I'm the one wearing it, I make it manly. Besides, Maggie got it for me, and I'll never ever get rid of it.

"I'm stressed," I grumble, turning away from him to pull out another batch from the oven.

When I'm stressed, I bake. It's the only thing that seems to bring me any sort of peace when I'm in a certain mood. Right now, I have way too many things weighing heavily on my mind. Baseball, graduation looming, my father, and now Vanessa and the fact that I think I'm catching feelings.

I've never had feelings for a girl beyond lust.

But in the short time of getting to know Vanessa I find myself *wanting* to be around her and spend more time with her. She's cool, and feisty, and fucking gorgeous. Sure, I think about what it'd be like to have sex with her, but it's more than that, and it terrifies me.

He picks up another cookie and sniffs it before shoving the whole thing in his mouth. "You're going to have to start handing these out on campus to get rid of them."

I don't tell him, but I have been.

"Are you gonna be at Cree's tonight?"

It's a dumb question, of course he will be, but I'd like to move the convo away from my cookies.

"Fuck yeah, man." He swipes another cookie and saunters back to his room. "I'm not going to miss out on a good time." The door closes behind him and I whip off my apron, hanging it on the plastic hook beside the fridge.

I throw the cookies that are already cooled into a plastic baggy and leave the rest sitting out. I'll need to pick up Vanessa soon, so I hop in the shower. I don't want to smell like baked goods. At least tonight will be casual and fun, not like this weekend's dinner. I can't believe my father has roped us into this, but at the same time this is exactly the kind of shit he likes to pull. I swear the fucker gets off on making people as uncomfortable as possible.

Changing into a pair of jeans and a long sleeve t-shirt, I stuff my feet into a pair of boots, and slip on a jacket. I know some guys get off on not bothering with a coat in the cold so they can be like Queen Elsa and say the cold never bothered them anyway, but that's not me. It's fucking freezing, and I'm putting on something warm.

I shoot a text to Vanessa that I'm leaving my dorm and then holler the same to Jude, who calls back that he's leaving later.

I walk over to Vanessa's dorm, flashing a smile at the girl who lets me in. She bats her eyes back and my smile disappears. I don't want her getting the wrong idea.

Instead of waiting for the elevator, I take the stairs up to her floor and knock on the door when I arrive. For once there aren't any girls lingering in the halls.

Vanessa opens the door and steps out.

I can't help myself when I look her up and down. She's wearing a pair of fitted jeans that hug her legs and accentuate her hips. I want nothing more than to grab her and pull her into me, to kiss her like I did in the dining hall. Fuck, that kiss has been living in my head rent free since then. I did it because I wanted to know if it would be as good as I thought it'd be.

It was better.

But then, I had the cover of our fellow student body to

play into the 'show'. Now, there's no one, so if I kiss her it'll be suspicious, and it's way too soon to be telling my fake-girlfriend that I think I might be catching real feelings.

I shove those thoughts out of my head, putting on a carefree smile and tossing an arm around her shoulders. "Are you excited to party tonight, Van?"

She scrunches her nose. "Not particularly."

"Aw, don't be like that. You're going to love it."

"I DON'T LIKE IT," Vanessa announces as soon as we walk into the door. She grabs onto the side of my arm, sticking to me like glue. The lights are dimmed, a song by ILLE-NIUM blasting from several Bluetooth speakers stationed throughout the house.

"We only need to stay a little while."

"I can't believe this is how I'm spending my night off." I feel a tad bad for dragging her out when she puts it like that, but I need to make frequent public appearances with her to establish our narrative and keep the girls on campus from leeching onto me.

"I'll make it up to you."

"How?" She looks doubtful.

"Somehow." I lead her back to the kitchen where the drinks always are. "You want anything?" I go to the fridge where I stashed my Zombie Dust earlier in the day since I was driving by.

"Yeah, give me whatever you're having."

I pop the top on both and pass one to her, clinking our glasses together. "Bottoms up."

She scrunches her nose like a bunny and takes a sip. Her lips turn down and she chokes out, "That's delicious."

I throw my head back in laughter. "Don't lie to me, Van."

"I don't like beer."

I lean my hip against the counter, looking her up and down. My teeth dig into my bottom lip as I fight to say the things I want to, because I know I'd send her running screaming into the other direction. My dick stirs in my jeans at my overwhelming attraction to her.

"What do you like?" I hope to fuck my voice doesn't sound as high to her as it did to me.

"Margaritas."

I tip the bottle to my lips, her eyes following my movements. "Guess I'll have to take you back to Harvey's then."

She doesn't reply, instead she's looking around at all the people crowded into the kitchen. Taking another sip of beer, she cringes and glares at the bottle.

Chuckling, I take the bottle from her and put it back in the fridge.

"Let's dance."

Her eyes threaten to bug out of her head. "I hate dancing." Her eyes dart around like she's afraid all these people here will be judging her.

"We're at a party, Van. *Let go*," I urge her. Holding out a hand, I plead, "Trust me. You had fun dancing with me at Harvey's, didn't you?"

Her eyes flicker back and forth from my outstretched hand to my own eyes, and I see the hesitation in hers. My stomach drops because I don't know if the hesitation is from truly not wanting to dance or if she's thinking of how last time I ended up kissing her.

I take another gulp of beer and stick it in the fridge beside hers. "We're doing this."

I don't give her a chance to overthink it or protest before I take her hand and lead her out of the kitchen.

It's not the song playing, but a couple of guys are yell-singing Harry Styles' Sweet Creature at Cree.

"What are they doing?" Vanessa eyes the rowdy hockey players surrounding Cree who's standing in the corner of the room with a drink.

"Ah, it's a thing they do a lot with him."

"Why?" she asks, crinkling her nose again. I'm not sure she's aware she does it and it's one of those things I find endearingly adorable about her.

"His name's Cree." I shrug like that explains it all, because to me it does.

"I'm still not following."

"Oh, the guys on the hockey team call him Creature because of his name."

I put my hands on her hips, and she stiffens for a second. Exhaling a breath, she loosens a small bit.

"Relax," I murmur in her ear, "dancing is supposed to be fun."

Blue eyes, dark as the ocean, stare back at me. "I'm sure it is, if you have rhythm."

I chuckle, my fingers splaying onto her ass as I

encourage her to move to the same beat. "You've got rhythm. Believe me." Her cheeks pinken at my words, and she starts to tense up again. She looks around the room, anywhere but at me. "Get outta that pretty head of yours."

Her eyes dart back to mine, determination glinting there. Her arms wind around my neck, and I don't know what comes over her, but she lets go of whatever was holding her back and really starts to dance. I move with her, getting lost in the music, in the feel of our bodies.

I've always loved dancing, which isn't something I readily admit to. Baseball is fun, and I do love it, but it's hard work and long hours of practice. Dancing is a way to express myself. Sure, I'm no professional and not any good, but that doesn't matter, and it's what I want Vanessa to realize. You don't have to be good at something to enjoy it.

Vanessa licks her full pink lips, and my eyes track the movement helplessly. I swallow thickly, cursing myself for being affected by every little thing she does. The thing about this girl is she's sexy as fuck and doesn't even know it. She's not trying to turn me on like so many other girls have in the past.

She turns around, shimmying her ass against my crotch, and I bite back a groan.

"Van," I say in a low, warning growl.

She stiffens when she notices my rock-hard erection. Looking over her shoulder at me, her eyes are filled with surprise. "Is that for me?"

I wrap my hand around her neck, holding her in place so she can't look away from me.

"You know it is."

Her lips lift into a coy smile. "I probably shouldn't like that." Her voice drops to a low murmur, "But I do."

Fuck.

My hands tighten on her hips. "Van," I growl her name in warning, and she gives a small laugh, spinning back around to face me.

"You know," she giggles, rubbing her fingers against the back of my neck, "I think you're right. Dancing isn't so bad."

"Don't toy with me." I narrow my eyes on her.

She laughs, standing up on her tiptoes so she can reach my ear. "But it's so fun." She drags a finger down my chest, her eyes following the trail she makes. "We can't go there, though. I won't … I won't do that."

I lower my head like I'm going to kiss her, and she gasps, but I move from her lips to the crook of her neck. "Are you sure about that?"

Startled eyes dart to mine and then her arms slacken around me as she moves away. I silently curse myself for saying that. I didn't mean it. I know nothing like that can happen between us. I need her too much to ruin our arrangement just because I want to fuck her. But sometimes I can't help the things I say.

"Come on," I reach for her hand, "I'm sorry. That was a dick thing to say."

She glowers at me, and despite being nearly a foot shorter than me I somehow feel like I'm being scolded and put in my place.

"Yeah, it was." That blue-eyed glare holds me prisoner

in the center of the room. Other couples continue to dance but shoot us annoyed glances for standing in place. "That shit might work with other girls, but not me. I know ... I know what this arrangement is, and it's not real," she whispers the last under her breath so no one else can hear, but I'm able to read her lips. "I won't allow myself to be used. Never again."

"Fuck," I curse, looking away from her when I realize what she's reminded of. In my lust induced haze it didn't even cross my mind. "I would never do that to you. I swear it."

She looks me solidly in the eyes and after an appraising moment, nods. "You're right, you wouldn't. Underneath all the cocky things you say, you're a good guy, Teddy, but please, stop talking about getting me in bed. I'm..." She pauses and gestures to my suddenly tight jeans. "Flattered, and yeah, you're hot, but this," she wags a finger between us, "isn't for that, and I won't blur the lines."

I guess I should be glad one of us is sensible, but instead it strikes me that maybe she's not as attracted to me as I am her.

"I'll stop making sexual comments."

She frowns, almost like that's not what she wants, but all she says is, "Good."

"Can we dance again?" I offer my hand like a gentleman in a period piece. "I'll keep my mouth shut, but him," I look pointedly at my crotch, "I can't help."

She giggles at that, biting her lip before she looks

away. She seems to be coming to terms with something and then takes my hand.

Dancing with her is nice, more than nice, but I remind myself I can't go there with her. I've managed to stay celibate this long. Less than four more months longer won't kill me.

I think.

"Why does Cree throw these parties?" she asks, looking over at the guy who's sitting on the couch looking bored out of his mind while a girl leans over, boobs in his face, trying to get his attention. He pointedly ignores her chest, unlike me who wouldn't be able to not ogle a nice pair of tits.

"Beats me." I shrug. "Because he's off campus, I guess."

"Maybe," she hedges, "but he looks miserable."

She's not wrong. "I don't really question other people about their motives," I admit sheepishly. "I figure if something is my business, they'll let me know."

"You don't get curious about things?"

A pit forms in my stomach. I don't know how much I want or should share with her.

"At an early age I learned not to ask questions, or…"

"Or?" she prompts, when my gaze drifts away, my jaw clenches tight.

"It was either ask questions and get beaten or stay silent and unhurt." Her gasp is loud enough to be heard over the music, earning us more than a few stares. Forget dancing. Gripping her hand, I lead her out of the room and back to the kitchen, where I grab my drink — I'm going to need it if we're having this conversation — and then lead her upstairs. I check Murray's room and find it empty, so I pull her inside and lock the door behind us. She looks around uneasily and I feel even more like shit than I did before. "I brought you in here for privacy for this conversation, not so I could fuck you."

"Right." She stares at the bed like maybe she *is* wondering what it'd be like if I did.

"Look, no one knows about my dad. No one," I repeat, sitting down in Murray's desk chair. The desk is piled with empty snack bags and water bottles. Dude needs to clean his room.

She looks at me in surprise. "Surely your friends — "

I shake my head and she frowns. "I've never told a soul. Until you."

She walks over hesitantly, like I'm a cornered animal she's wary of spooking. "Why not?" She sits on the floor in front of me, crisscrossing her legs. Her hand lands on my knee, her touch tentative but comforting nonetheless.

"Because it felt weak."

"Weak?" She rears back in surprise.

"I know that sounds dumb, but it's true. I didn't want anyone to think I was pathetic or even worse, that I deserved it."

Her tiny gasp sounds incredibly loud in the otherwise silent room. "Teddy," her tone is soft, pleading with me. "No one, definitely not your friends, would ever think that. When did it start?"

"I don't really remember." I give a humorless laugh. "Young, I know that much. It started with spanking if I did anything remotely out of line, then moved to punches, but always in places where no one would see. Thankfully, I was away a lot at school, but summers, holidays … he always found something I did horribly wrong and needed punishing for."

"God, Teddy."

"Sometimes he *did* visit me at boarding school just to remind me of what would happen if I didn't stay in line."

I see the pain in her eyes, and I curse myself for letting her in on my terrible secret. I don't want her to have to carry this burden too.

"I'm sorry," I touch her cheek, rubbing my thumb over her smooth skin, "I shouldn't have told you."

Her eyes widen with surprise. "Yes, you should have. I'm glad you did. It helps me understand you better and your dynamic with your parents." She pauses, biting her lip. "Does your mom know?"

"She has to. He's never done it in front of her, but I think she knows."

"And she never stopped it?" Vanessa looks horrified on my behalf. Taking my hand from her cheek, I place it on top of hers on my knee. She immediately wraps her fingers into mine and it makes me feel ridiculously centered and at peace to feel her touch.

"I'm pretty sure he hits her too. I mean, he's an emotionally and verbally abusive asshole anyway. I don't ever want to be like him, Van," I admit my biggest fear. "I don't want to be that kind of father. How could I ever hit my own kid?"

I picture my own child in the distant future and there's

no way I could ever raise a hand against them. I'd take my own life before I'd do that.

With her free hand she touches her fingertips to the line of my jaw. "You won't."

"How do you know?"

"Because you wouldn't have that fear otherwise. You're not him. You're you. You are your own person. You define your way."

"*Fuck.*" Actual tears sting my eyes. "You have no idea how badly I needed to hear that."

She gives me a watery smile, and I realize she's nearly about to cry too. "It's the truth."

I bend down, my nose grazing hers. "I really want to kiss you right now," I confess. "Not for show, not because anyone is watching. I want to kiss you for me. Because I want to."

She surprises me by nodding eagerly like she wants this as badly as I do.

Bending down from where I sit, I cup her jaw in one hand tilting her lips up to meet mine. She makes a tiny noise the moment our lips touch. I didn't know I could literally be brought to my knees by kissing a girl, but I find myself slipping from the chair and kneeling above her cross-legged position.

Her lips part and I use the opportunity to deepen the kiss.

She arches into me, her breasts pushing into my chest. The urge to run my hands over her body is strong, but I hold her cheeks instead, forcing myself not to take this further. Not after the talk we had earlier.

A kiss has always been a means to an end for me, to get to the fun stuff—you know, sex. But knowing that's not where this is headed makes it all the sweeter and more intense.

This is a kiss that *matters*, and I feel a pull in my stomach, one that's telling me I'm fucked when it comes to this girl.

I force myself to pull away, knowing I'll get carried away if I don't stop this. Her surprised blue eyes stare deep into mine as she raises trembling fingers to her kiss swollen lips.

Yeah, baby, my gaze tells her, *I'm the last man you're ever going to kiss*.

TWELVE

Vanessa

THE WEEKS PASS IN A BLUR, MY TIME IS NOW SPENT going to class, studying, working, and hanging out with Teddy. The most surprising part is how often we hang out because we *want* to and not because we have to.

I've had more dinners with his parents, most of them spent in silence except for the times his father makes some cutting remark geared at Teddy. Usually aimed at how he's not good enough, or his past mistakes, or in my opinion the worst of all is when he all but says that Teddy's stupid.

People like that shouldn't have the ability to procreate. Not when there are couples out here desperate for a child and either unable to conceive or adopt. Sometimes it's downright laughable how fucked the world can be.

Sliding into the booth that I now think of as Teddy's, I pick up a fry and munch on the end of it. "What are you thinking so seriously about?" I reach across and poke the wrinkle forming between his brows. He looks up from his phone with a startled expression like he didn't hear me sit down. "Not hungry?" I eye his Caesar salad that normally he's devoured by now, starving from finishing his practice.

"Sorry." He runs his fingers through his thick brown hair, sticking it up wildly in the front. "I got distracted."

"Hey, it's okay. You still have to tip me anyway," I joke.

He grins, my favorite sly boyish smile of his. "*Just* the tip?"

I swat at him and he laughs, ducking away from my hand. "What's going on though?" I chew on another fry. I've been on my feet for several hours already at The Burger Palace and my feet are crying in relief at finally being able to sit down.

"Um…" He scratches at the scruff on his cheeks. "Valentine's is coming up."

"Fuck." I scrunch my nose. "It is?"

"Yeah." He pokes at a piece of chicken with his fork. "I'm trying to plan something for you."

I lean close to him and lower my voice, "You remember this isn't real, right? You don't have to do anything."

That wrinkle returns. "Fake or not, I'm doing something for you for Valentine's Day."

"For the love of all that is holy, please don't take me to a fancy restaurant."

His eyes grow large. "Well, *shit*." He scoops up his phone and makes a call while I shrink into the booth. "Hey," he says when someone picks up, "that reservation I made for McCallister, cancel that. Yeah. Yep. Mhmm. Thanks." He hangs up. "Pretend you didn't see that."

"I'm so sorry," I blurt. "I didn't know you—"

He holds up a hand to silence me. "Don't be sorry. I'm glad you said something. I'd rather do something you'd like and honestly, I hate fancy restaurants too. You know I've never had a girlfriend before, fake or not." He gives an awkward shrug. "I'm kind of learning all new things here."

"Well, every girl is different, and I like things simple," I admit, taking the tomato off my sandwich. Our cook knows I hate them and now puts them on everything just to spite me. One time I got home and found a slice in a baggy stuffed into my backpack. "I'd be happy sitting in the car eating fast-food or taking a walk through a park. Ooh, or even going to the animal shelter and walking the dogs and petting the kitties." I light up at the idea.

"Interesting," he muses, finally eating his dinner. He taps the side of his head. "Keep going, I'm taking notes."

"I actually haven't given it much thought before. I've never had a boyfriend either, at least not one that's real." I snort, thinking about the irony that I was in a fake rela-tionship my freshman year of high school—unbeknownst to me of course—and now history is repeating itself for my senior year of college. At least this time I'm in on the secret.

"Look at us," he wags a finger between us, "we're

learning together. Now come on, Van, I'm sure you've got something more for me."

I sigh, twisting my lips back and forth. "Fine, I have to admit that while it's corny I've always seen those cheap stuffed animals and candy chocolate hearts and been a little jealous that I didn't have a guy to buy me any." Picking up a fry, I break it in half, mortified at myself for admitting that. "What about you?" I counter, desperate to shuck the attention from myself and onto him.

"What about me?" He scratches at his eyebrow.

"What would you want to do for your ideal Valentine's day?"

"Honestly, everything you've said sounds really nice. I guess because of the way I grew up I've been taught to think of most things from a showy standpoint and not a sentimental one, but now that I think about it, just hanging out with the girl I care about, watching some movies and eating pizza, making love to her after..." His gaze drifts away, lost in his thoughts. "Yeah," he nods after a moment, "that sounds nice."

"There's a lot to be said for keeping things simple," I muse, staring at my sandwich. "Not everything has to be some grand event. I think when you're with someone you really care about it doesn't matter what you're doing as long as you're together." Drifting back to myself, I give him a sheepish smile. "Seriously, though, this isn't ... we aren't ... what I mean is, I don't expect you to do or get me anything for Valentine's."

"Van?"

"Yes?"

"Shut up."

I chuckle. "Right, okay."

He rests his arms on the table and leans closer to me. I notice every fleck of gold in the depths of his forest green eyes. It's unfair for a guy to be blessed with such beautiful colored eyes, and if that wasn't enough, they're framed by the longest, thickest curled lashes I've ever seen.

"You should know by now, I do what I want, and if that means doing something special for my fake-girlfriend on Valentine's Day, I damn well will."

"Has anyone ever told you that you're kind of a strange guy? I mean that in a good way, but—"

He sweeps his fingers through the air. "A time or two. Now," he clears his throat, his lips pursed as he levels me with a look like he's a prosecutor and I'm a witness on the stand, "I have to add to your fake-girlfriend duties." I must make some sort of face because he chuckles and adds, "I swear it's not that bad."

"What do you need?"

"Baseball season is starting, and I want you in the stands cheering me on."

"Oh," I sigh in relief, grateful it's not something that involves his parents. His mom isn't so bad, in fact she's kind of sweet, and I can see she loves Teddy, but his dad? I thought he was bad the first time I met him, but after Teddy told me about the abuse, I have absolutely no tolerance for the man. "That could be fun."

He chuckles. "It's definitely not dinner with my parents."

It's like he can read my thoughts sometimes. I don't

know if it's that they're so obvious on my face or he's just that intuitive.

"And thank God for that."

He laughs fully this time and I'm glad that despite the shit he's had to endure, Teddy still has a sense of humor. He's never let the serious stuff weigh too heavily on him, and I haven't told him, but I envy him for that. After what my sister and Tristan pulled, I definitely let it eat away at me and affect who I was as a person for a long time.

"Ugh," I groan, looking at the time on my phone. "I need to get back to work."

He frowns at his half-eaten salad and pushes the bowl away. "Forget this shit. I'm sick of it. Bring me a chocolate milkshake. I promise to tip real good. Nice and slow."

I roll my eyes as I stand, gathering my stuff. "How on earth did you con me into this again?"

"Simple." He leans back in the booth with a smirk. I feel a tingle in my pussy from that dangerous smile and curse my treacherous body for thinking we can go there. I won't toe that line with him. "We needed each other."

He's not wrong, and it's beginning to scare me the more I realize how close we've grown, because the end of this arrangement should be a clean break, but I'm not sure it will be, and I'm terrified of the fallout. I've had my world obliterated before. I'm not sure I can handle a second time.

It's a reminder to hold my heart close.

I can't fall for my fake-boyfriend. That's trouble with a capital T.

THIRTEEN

Teddy

PUTTING TOGETHER AN ENTIRE EXTRAVAGANZA FOR Valentine's Day for a girl who isn't even actually my girl-friend is probably the most insane thing I've ever done, but also something that's brought me a joy I don't even want to begin to think about.

Is it possible that me, the player who was always looking for my next one-night stand, actually likes—*gasp*—monogamy. The most ironic part of all being that I'm not even actually getting any ass.

Oh, how the tables have turned.

This morning I had a bouquet of flowers delivered to her, a bunch of random looking wildflowers if I had to guess. Not roses. Roses make me think of stuffy old ladies.

I also had breakfast sent to her—French toast from a local diner.

Parking outside her dorm, I start to panic, thinking about how I've gone way overboard.

I just … fuck. I want to make this special for her and me, even if this whole relationship is a farce, it's the most serious thing I've *ever* had in my life, and I want to treat her right.

I think aliens have kidnapped my body. Please, for the love of God, I hope they don't use an anal probe. I know it's been a while, but I'd prefer to be the one doing the pegging, not being pegged, please and thank you, weird green aliens.

"Get yourself together," I mutter to myself, gripping the steering wheel so tight I'm cutting off circulation.

Releasing it, I lean back in the seat and shoot Vanessa a text that I'm coming up. Sliding my phone back in my pocket, I eye the giant stuffed pink octopus with hearts I picked up at the drugstore along with the box of chocolates.

My phone buzzes as I get out of the car, and I'm not surprised to find the usual text from her insisting she'll come down.

I never listen, and she never stops trying. It's honestly amusing how stubborn we both are.

I head into the building, slipping in behind a group of girls. They giggle, batting their eyes. I flash them my winning smile and tip my head before I jog up the steps. Stepping onto Van's floor, I spot her waiting for the elevator and grin. I walk carefully, silently over to her and stop beside her.

"I told you I was coming."

"Ah!" she screams, flailing. "Don't do that!" She swats at me. "You could've given me a heart attack."

"Come on, now, have some faith. I need to keep you alive after all."

She shakes her head, her breathing irregular as we step onto the elevator and head down.

"I still think this is dumb," she mutters, crossing her arms. She's dressed casually, like I told her to after her confession that an elaborate evening was the last thing she wanted. But with her arms crossed beneath her chest, I can't help but admire the swell of her breasts in the cut of her v-neck shirt. She's wearing a jacket over top, and jeans with sneakers.

"You know," I pretend to pick dirt from beneath my blunt fingernails, "it'd be nice if my girlfriend would at least pretend to like to spend time with me."

She rolls her eyes, fighting a smile. *"Fake*—meaning all of this is unnecessary. Seriously. You could've ignored the day all together."

"Well, too bad. I'm not doing that."

The door dings and I reach for her hand before they slide open. She stiffens for a second, but relaxes, putting on her game face when she sees the girls waiting to get on.

I'd be lying if I said a part of me didn't feel a little hurt over that fact—that she can put on an act so easily in the face of others, but when it's just the two of us, she balks at the idea of intimacy.

Because this isn't real, my conscience taunts. *She's only doing what you should be — what you* asked *for.*

I lead her outside and open the passenger door for her. She releases my hand and slips inside, those dark blue eyes flickering upward with a smile as she places the stuffed octopus and chocolate in her lap. But of course, it's not a thank you that comes out of her mouth. No, she always has to surprise me. "Your car is so low to the ground my ass touches the asphalt. Is it worth having a car this fancy to get ass burn?"

I throw my head back and laugh, not having expected that at all to leave her mouth.

Leaning against the open car door, I cock my head to the side. "What kind of vehicle would you prefer, dear?"

She looks around the spotless interior — I have it detailed regularly. Eyes gliding back to me she clears her throat, her nose wiggling. "One not so … flashy. You know what they say about men and their flashy cars or too big trucks?"

"What's that?" I inquire, already knowing where she's going with this and eating it up like an ice cream sundae.

"They have small penises," she whisper-hisses, flaring those blue eyes innocently.

I wet my lips with my tongue, smirking. "Trust me, babe. There's nothing little about me, and definitely not my cock."

A gasp flies out of her throat, her cheeks turning red, and I relish in my ability to render her speechless. I close the door and walk around the front of my car, slipping inside. Starting it up, the engine purrs like an exotic feline, and I grin as I turn my head to look at her.

"Maybe if you're a good girl I'll let you play with it."

"With w-what?" she stutters, eyes wide. "Your dick?"

I laugh again, a fully-body belly laugh. God, this girl.

"The car, princess. Why would I be talking about my cock?"

Her cheeks grow even redder, and I chuckle as I drive away.

———

"YOU SERIOUSLY BROUGHT me to an animal shelter?" Her voice kicks up in pitch as I park outside the brick building.

"Hey, it was your idea," I remind her.

"I know. I guess I didn't expect you to actually bring me to one."

That pink octopus is still clutched firmly in her arms, and she keeps sniffing the top of its head.

"Are we going to go in or sit here?"

She nods eagerly, eyes lighting up. "Go in."

"I'll get the door," I remind her, stepping out of the car and going around to open hers.

I offer her my hand and she takes it, leaving the octopus behind on the passenger seat.

Inside the building I wave at Mary, the lady who runs the shelter. I stopped by earlier to make sure it was okay for us to come and wrote out a donation check—not because I had to, but because I wanted to.

"What first?" I ask Vanessa. This is her day after all.

She rubs her hands together giddily. "Kitties."

I chuckle, holding on tighter to her hand. There are

separate areas for the cats and dogs, so I lead her through the correct doorway. Immediately, she drags me along to the first metal crate, crooning at the glowering cat inside who looks like he'd rather slit our throats than listen to her baby talk.

The notecard beside his crate says his name is Mittens.

"Such a sweet name for such a beastly looking creature," I muse, staring into his yellow green eyes. He hisses at me and I rear back. "Bastard," I chuckle, while Vanessa giggles at me.

She peers into every cage, speaking to each cat, before we move on to the dog room and she repeats the same process. We each take a dog for a walk and then play with them in a fenced in area attached to the shelter.

When we're finished and heading back to my car, Vanessa's cheeks glow with excitement as she beams up at me.

"This was amazing. Thank you."

I nearly piss myself when she perches on her tiptoes and presses a quick kiss to my cheek.

"It was your idea," I remind her, opening the passenger door.

She turns, staring at me so intently I start to squirm beneath the scrutiny. "Yeah, but you're the one who listened."

She crouches down and picks up the octopus, sitting with it in her lap again. Before I close the door, she looks at me with a smile. "What's next?"

"I DON'T HAVE any other Valentine's to compare this to, but ... it'll be hard for this one to ever be topped." Vanessa gives me a slow, careful smile when I park outside her dorm. I see the hint of sadness in her eyes, the reminder that I've done all of this, and we're not even actually together.

I feel a sting in my gut at her words, because one day in the future some other guy will be doing this for her, and it *will* be for real.

"I'm glad you liked it." I rest my hands on the steering wheel, ignoring the temptation to take her face in my hands and kiss her like I did that night at Cree's place.

"You know," she tucks a strand of dark hair behind her ear, "I'm beginning to think you're not the player everyone says you are."

I throw my head back and laugh. "Oh, trust me, I was worse than what they say but people change and maybe..." I pause, gathering my thoughts. "I don't know. As much of a prick as my father is, I think maybe these months of strict orders have done me some good. I mean, at least I'm thinking with the right head for once." I tap the side of my forehead.

She laughs. "Whatever it takes, I guess. But Teddy?"

"Mhmm?" I hum, leaning in closer to her, drawn in by her sweet scent of citrus and something vaguely flowery.

"You're really not so bad."

I'm shocked when she leans over the center console, brushing her lips lightly against mine. It's not a kiss, I don't know what it is, but before I can beg for more, she's slipping out of the car with her stuffed octopus tucked under her arm and the chocolates clasped in her hands.

She looks back at me with a wink and I shake my head, fighting a smile.

She didn't let me get the door.

Damn temptress knew what she was doing.

FOURTEEN

Vanessa

MY LAPTOP SITS OPEN IN FRONT OF ME, AND I STARE AT that stupid blinking cursor, willing words to come to my brain. I have a paper due in three days for my marketing strategies class, and I haven't even started it yet.

Love that for me.

My favorite brown and orange plaid blanket is wrapped around my shoulders, but even it can't bring me comfort right now. I'm too stressed for that. I push my blue-light glasses up my nose and pout my lips.

Music, that's what I need. I slip off my bed and scurry over to the corner of my room where I set up my record player, putting on the Fine Line album from Harry Styles.

I'm about to waddle back to my bed when Danika appears in my doorway. She's dressed in a sleek pair of black jeans and a lacy mesh long sleeve top over a black bralette. It's a sleek and sexy outfit, a far cry from the sweatpants and oversized Britney Spears shirt I wear beneath the blanket.

"I'm about to head out."

"Um ... okay?" It comes out as a question because it's not like Danika to give me a heads up she's leaving. She just comes and goes as she pleases, answering to no one but herself.

She brushes her curled maroon-red hair over her shoulder. "Are you and Teddy serious?"

My brows furrow at her seemingly random question. "Yeah?" I curse myself over the fact that it comes out as a question.

"Look, I know it's none of my business but just be careful with him."

I narrow my eyes on her. "Have you had sex with Teddy?"

I've asked Teddy himself and he denied it, and while I don't think he's a liar, you never know. He could've forgotten.

"Oh, ew. No." She makes a face. "But I know plenty of guys like him, and it's rare for them to do the whole relationship thing. I want you to be careful. I know we're not exactly friends." She gives a tiny, humorless laugh. "That's my fault. I'm not very good at the whole friends thing. But I don't want to see you get hurt."

I feel this sudden tug, this urge to tell her everything about my arrangement with the campus player, but I don't because I know how important it is to keep this secret.

"I'm being careful," I promise.

She nods, her lips twitching into a thoughtful smile. "Okay." She starts to turn to leave but pauses. "Even though we're not exactly friends, I'm here for you any time you need me."

"Thanks." I mean it, too.

She lingers in the doorway a moment longer before she dips her head in a nod and leaves.

I settle back on my bed, curling my legs beneath me and making sure my blanket is wrapped firmly around my shoulders. Sure, it'd probably be easier to slip a sweatshirt on, but I've always loved the feeling of comfort when I'm swaddled in a blanket.

I manage to get a few sentences typed out before I'm interrupted by a knock on the door.

"What the hell?" I grumble, shucking my blanket off.

I swear if it's Tiffany in the room next to ours, out of shampoo again, she's *not* getting mine. I lent her my holy grail shampoo that costs me like thirty-bucks, and she never gave it back. Since I hate confrontation, I never asked for it either.

Swinging the door open, it's not Tiffany on the other side.

There's a jolt in my heart, and my hand automatically flies up to the spot like I'm trying to rub away a soreness. But that's not what it is. No, it's the fact that my stupid treacherous heart is *excited* by the image of Teddy standing before me. He's wearing a backwards baseball cap, loose gym shorts despite the cold, and an Aldridge U sweatshirt.

His hair curls beneath the ball cap and his green eyes sparkle like he's happy to see me.

Honestly, it's unfair how guys can toss on a basic backwards cap and their hotness level goes up, but a girl wears one and it's because we didn't wash our hair.

He holds up a greasy brown bag, another smaller one tucked behind it. "I brought dinner." He lifts a plastic baggy in his other hand. "And dessert."

My lips threaten to smile at the freshly baked cookies. "Stress baking again?"

"You have no idea," he grumbles. "You gonna let me in or not, girlfriend?"

"Oh, right." I step aside and allow him entry into my dorm room.

I realize it's the first time it's been just the two of us here and we've always been leaving, never staying, and now I can't help but wonder what it looks like from his eyes.

It has the standard furnishing every suite has with a couch and two chairs in the main area, as well as a bookcase, and a small table with two chairs. As far as decorating goes, neither Danika or I have done much beyond a gray and white rug and a few pink throw pillows. I spent more time decorating my room since that's where I spend most of my time.

I know it would be safer to stay out here with him. It's less personal, doesn't reflect so much of *me*, and there's also no bed—just the idea of Teddy lounging on my bed might send me into a tailspin—but I know I don't want to stay out here. It's not where I'm comfortable.

Flicking the fingers on my right hand, I motion for him to follow me into my room.

He looks around as I ease the door closed, purposely leaving it cracked. He smirks when he notices.

"Nice digs." He eyes the white macrame dream catcher above my bed. "Did you make that?"

I snort a laugh. "Um, no. I bought it at Urban Outfitters because I'm a basic bitch."

He chuckles, toeing off his sneakers. "Where do you want me to put these?" He raises the bags again.

"We can eat on the bed."

"Cool." He sits down on the end, my laptop beside his hip. I pick it up, moving it to my desk before I sit beside him.

"What'd you get?"

"Five Guys. They're my favorite, but I don't get it often." He lifts the bottom of his sweatshirt, showing off his impressive abdominals. He smirks, smoothing the fabric back down. "I didn't know what you like on your burger, so I asked for all their toppings on the side."

My eyes widen. "What?"

"I didn't want to mess it up. Don't worry, I gave them a nice tip for the trouble."

"You're—"

"Hot, amazing, awesome, one of a kind, a perfect catch? Yeah, I know." He pulls out a foil wrapped burger and passes it to me, then hands me the smaller bag that I assume has all the condiments and toppings. "There's plenty of fries in the bag too. They always give so many."

"Thank you. You didn't have to do this."

He rolls his eyes, unwrapping his own burger. "I think it's time you realize I only do things I want to."

He stares into my eyes, and I get lost in that endless sea of green and gold. My brain, unbidden, goes back to the house party, to his confession about his father and the kiss we shared.

Clearing my throat, I go to work assembling my burger.

A minute, maybe longer, passes in silence when he clears his throat and confesses, "My dad is requesting our presence at a function this weekend."

"What kind of function?" I eye him warily.

Once again, I wonder why he chose me for this impossible task. I'm not the type of girl someone like his father would be pleased to have his son with—not with their status. I'm poor, from the wrong side of the tracks. I have to work. I drive a clunker of a car. But for some reason Teddy chose me that day and I know he saw that I was in need, but he didn't *have* to help me.

I guess, beneath that gorgeous face, the flirty banter, and player ways, maybe Teddy McCallister has a heart of gold.

No, in these weeks I've gotten to know him I realize 'maybe' is an injustice. Teddy is a good person. A little wild, and cocky of course, but at his core he's a kind and caring person.

"Are you thinking about me naked? Because you have this serious look on your face. I promise you, it's way bigger in reality, and yes, it'll fit. I have lube."

I grab a pillow off my bed and smack him with it while he breaks into riotous laughter.

"You're such a pig."

"And you made me get mustard on your bed." He points to the yellow blop on my white bedspread.

"It's okay, you can afford the dry-cleaning bill."

He cackles with amusement. "I've never met someone who keeps up with my wit so easily. It's refreshing."

"What can I say? It's a gift." I don't tell him that I'm not like this with anyone else, but with him, it's like all the walls I've built to protect myself don't exist at all. With his easy and accepting personality I've never felt the need to be anything but me. "You didn't answer my question."

"About what?" He stuffs a handful of fries into his mouth. Such a caveman.

"What kind of function this is exactly?"

He rolls his eyes, stifling a snort. "Some fancy shmancy schmoozefest brunch thing at my family's country club."

I process his words and ask carefully, "When you say your family's country club do you mean you're members or that you own it?"

He stares at his half-eaten burger like it holds all the answers in the world. He clears his throat and mutters, "We own it."

"What else do you own?" I inquire curiously.

"If I listed everything out, we'd be here for days."

"Wow. That's…"

"Horrifying?"

"I mean … kind of. Cool too, I guess."

"The mega wealthy like to put their hands in everything. Their influence is far and wide."

"You don't seem to want that life."

"I used to," he admits honestly. "It was all I knew, what I was raised for, but last year was a wake-up call." His brows lower, shadowing his eyes. "I thought I was untouchable because of my family's name, money, influence ... and that's true, but consequences exist for a reason, and I was skirting away from them all, and I realized if I continued down the path I was on, I was going to end up exactly like my father, and he's the *last* person on the planet I want to be like. I want to have a good heart, to be known for my kindness. One day I want to be a good husband and father. And money, it doesn't buy those things. It can buy comfort, stability, but the saying is true; it doesn't bring you happiness."

I think about all the shit I've been through in my life, how money would've made things easier, but overall I'd say I've been happy and loved. Looking into Teddy's lonely gaze I know I wouldn't switch places. I'd take my poor wallet with a rich heart over the reverse any day.

Our eyes hold, and I realize that while Teddy is an outgoing, fun guy who is always making people laugh, there are shadows that cling to him, haunt him. On the surface he seems like your typical college guy, and maybe that's who he truly was once, but that's not the guy I've gotten to know.

I'm suddenly thankful for our deal, not just because he saved my ass, but because I think maybe I've made a life-long friend out of it. I can't imagine him never being in my life after this.

"What made you come here?" I blurt suddenly. I wave my hand to the food spread between us. "Why'd you bring dinner?"

He wipes the corner of his mouth free of ketchup. "Because I wanted to. I could've gone to Cole's, I do love to bug the shit out of him, or even Mascen, and I could've pestered Jude to hang out, but ... it was you I wanted to be with."

His brows furrow, eyes narrowed at his own statement like he's surprised by the revelation.

"Huh," I muse, fighting an amused smile. "If I didn't know any better, I'd say you like me."

Teddy clears his throat, the faintest stain of pink on his cheeks. He picks up the plastic bag and holds it out to me. An offering or a distraction, I don't know. "Cookie?"

FIFTEEN

Teddy

VANESSA: WHY WAS THERE A KNOCK ON MY DOOR AND when I opened it there was a bag of clothes from NORDSTROM sitting there?

I can tell from her capitalization of the store that she's ticked off, but...

Me: It's just some clothes for brunch tomorrow. You can pick what you want and return the rest or keep them all. I don't care.

Vanessa: I don't need you to shop for me.

I sigh from inside my car where I haven't even pulled away from her dorm yet.

Me: I know you don't, but I figured chicks like clothes, and it would make it easier for you.

I'm not making any sense, but I don't want to tell her that

I did it because I can see the worry on her face every time I pick her up. Worry that her clothes aren't good enough for my parents, that *she's* not enough. I mean, it's always possible I've made a grave assumption, but I've seen the way she plays uncomfortably with her clothes in their presence, eyeing the ones on her body and then the ones they wear.

Vanessa: I can pick out my own clothes, Theodore.

Me: Still not my name no matter how many times you try to act like it is. A smile of amusement plays on my lips.

Me: Take them all back. I don't care.

And I don't. I don't give a shit what Vanessa wears, but I just want her to feel comfortable, well as much as she can in the presence of my father.

She doesn't reply right away so I pull away from her dorm and drive to Mascen's townhome, parking in the driveway.

Somehow, even after swearing I'd never do it again, I agreed to run with him.

I think I agreed just because of his endless taunting of telling me I've gotten slow in my old age. As if I'm *old*. The fucker is jealous because clearly, I'm the better looking one of the two of us.

Getting out, I close the door to my car and lock up when another text from Vanessa finally comes through.

Vanessa: You've already done enough for me with my tuition. Anything else is too much.

I stare at the message for a moment before I type out my reply.

Me: Nothing is too much. Keep the clothes. Please.

I don't wait to see if she replies. After tightening my shoelaces, I ring the doorbell and wait for Mascen to join me.

He steps out, ready to go, wearing his usual dick-headed smirk.

"Ready?" He arches a brow.

"Prepare to get your ass whooped."

He chuckles. "It's cute you think you can keep up with me."

If you'd told me this morning I'd be puking my guts up in a bush after Mascen pushed me into a ten mile run, I wouldn't have shown up. The bastard knows too as he cackles from the light post he leans against.

"Told you that you needed to start running with me. This is pathetic."

"We play baseball," I groan. "I need to know how to sprint, not run long distances."

"It helps with endurance." He claps a hand on my back, laughing when I get sick again.

There's absolutely nothing left in my stomach, and if he thinks I'm actually going to make a routine of this he's wrong.

"You're worse than Coach."

"Someone has to toughen you up," he taunts, using the bench nearby to stretch his legs.

"I'm plenty tough." I wipe my mouth with the back of my hand, hating the taste of bile on my tongue but there's nothing I can do about it at the moment.

He finishes stretching and we walk the last few blocks back to his townhome.

"See you later." I unlock my car, heading for the driver's side.

"Whoa, whoa, not so fast," he chants after me, and I glance over my shoulder at him. He leans his hip against the back of my car, and I narrow my eyes at the spot where his flesh meets metal.

"Get your grubby body away from my car."

He rolls his eyes at my dramatics. "All I want to say is, don't be a pussy and give up after today. Meet me at the park tomorrow morning at five."

"No."

"Yes."

"You better mean five in the evening," I warn, eyes narrowed to slits.

He laughs uproariously, stroking his fingers lovingly against the cobalt blue paint of my car. "That's real cute, Theodore."

"Not Theodore," I taunt. "I've been telling all of you that since freshman year."

"Whatever," he guffaws, walking toward the garage. "See you in the morning."

"No, you won't because I'm not coming."

He laughs and laughs and he's still laughing when I get in my car and back away.

Stupid bastard knows I'll show up, because I hate letting people down.

I SMOOTH my navy-blue tie down against my dry cleaned pale blue oxford and then slip my arms into my dark blue suit jacket. I'm sure my father will scoff at the varying shades of blue in my attire, but I don't give a fuck.

Making sure my suit and everything is perfectly in place, not a hair on my head sticking in a wrong direction, I step out of my room, already prepared for Jude's reaction.

He leans back on the sofa, a game playing in the background on the TV, and starts laughing as soon as he lays eyes on me.

Arms up, I spin in a circle, giving him every angle. "All right, all right. Get it out now."

"Where the hell are you going?" He rubs a hand over his heavily stubbled jaw. The guy looks like he hasn't seen a razor in at least a week.

I reach down and swipe a bottle of *my* Zombie Dust from the table in front of the couch and drain it, leveling him with a glare while I do. "Don't touch my beer," I warn.

It's an empty threat. He steals my beer all the time, and I never do anything about it. It's annoying, sure, but there are worse things in the world. Doesn't mean I don't like fucking with him.

"You didn't answer." He glides his fingers through his brown hair, waiting for me to reply.

"Some stupid brunch at the country club my parents own."

"Sounds like hell."

"Hell would be more fun and certainly warmer."

He chuckles, already focused on the TV again. "Good luck with that."

I'll need more than luck, but I don't say that to him.

Straightening my collar, I send a text to Vanessa that I'm on my way to her dorm.

When I pull up, this time she's waiting out front, having beaten me to meeting her at her door.

I park and hop out before she has a chance to reach the passenger door, opening it smoothly for her and taking a deep, dramatic bow. "For milady."

She rolls her eyes playfully at me and pushes her hand against my shoulder in a lighthearted gesture as she lowers into the car. She's wearing one of the dresses I bought her—well, I had a personal stylist pull them after I described what I felt like Vanessa liked most and vetoed anything I knew she wouldn't like. The green and white dress hugs her body, emphasizing her assets, and I have to silently chant to myself not to stare at her tits.

All the months of celibacy might be catching up to me, because my dick stirs to life, straining against my pants.

"What should I expect today?" She voices as soon as I'm behind the wheel.

I blow out a breath, putting the car in reverse. "Honestly, I don't know. I'm assuming this is a fundraiser of some sort, so mostly it'll be my father parading me—and now you—around while he bullshits about what a great son I am and how close we are. My mom will consume enough mimosas that by the time brunch is actually served, she'll be completely wasted." I take a breath, feeling the weight and strain in my shoulders from the burden of being a part of my own family. "Everyone there will be ridiculously wealthy. You'll probably see a few well-known musicians, politicians, and who the hell knows who else might show." I give a shrug, merging onto the highway.

When I glace at Vanessa, she's staring at me open-mouthed. I notice for the first time that her hair is pinned up in a bun, a few hairs framing her face.

"What?" I ask, paying attention to the road, slamming my hand onto my horn when a driver tries to cut me off.

"Is my girl Taylor Swift going to be there?"

I snort. "Doubtful. Most of the musicians are the old type."

"What a tragedy." She looks out the passenger window.

It's quiet for a few minutes between us, but I can't stand the silence for a full hour, so I rack my brain for more questions to ask her.

"Is there any sort of stuffed animal or blanket or some-thing you've had since you were a baby?"

Out of the corner of my eye, I notice her head whip in my direction at the random question. Body relaxing into the leather seat, she sighs, "No. You?"

I rub my lips with my right hand, trying to hide a smile. "A blanket actually. It looks more like a rag now than a blanket."

She laughs lightly. "And where is it?"

"My dorm, of course."

Even though I'm not looking at her, I can feel her surprise.

"You're nothing like I expected," she murmurs, so softly I'm not sure she meant for me to hear. It's not like she hasn't said it before, though.

"What did you expect, darling?" I ask anyway, amusement coloring my tone.

She shakes her head, looking down at her hands. "An overly cocky, jerk more interested in himself than anything else."

"*Ouch.*" I fake a wince.

"You asked," she reminds me.

"That I did," I sigh, tightening my grip on the wheel. "I think I used to be exactly what you expected." The admission comes out a bit forlornly. "I mean, I was never purposely arrogant or rude to people, but I definitely thought I was untouchable."

It takes me by surprise when her hand lands gently on my knee. There's nothing sexual about the touch. She's not gliding her fingers tauntingly or sliding them up my thigh. She's only trying to comfort me, and I think for the first time in my life I realize that small gestures like that mean more than a quick fuck.

"What was it like going to a boarding school?" I don't know whether she's trying to distract me from wherever she thinks my brain has gone or is genuinely curious.

"Not so bad. It meant I got to be away from my dad."

"I know sorry doesn't change anything, but I am sorry you have a parent like that."

"We all get bad cards dealt to us now and then. He's one of mine." Wanting to change the topic from my dad, especially since I'll have to spend the entire afternoon in his presence, I say to her, "Tell me something I don't know about you yet."

Her hand shifts on my knee. "Well, speaking of cards, I can do card tricks."

"What?" I blurt in surprise.

"Nothing super fancy, don't get too excited. But some basic slights of hand are my specialty."

"I'm still impressed. You'll have to show me."

Conversation reaches a lull as we reach the Nashville limits; no doubt, like me, she's thinking about what we'll be subjected to when we arrive.

Turning off the highway, I take the familiar stretch of road and turn into the club. The gates open automatically thanks to the tag in my car that it scans. I take the winding road slowly, that way I can glance at Vanessa from time to time and take in her reaction.

The sprawling white plantation style building comes into view and her mouth drops in awe.

"It's beautiful."

"Beautiful, but like a lot of beautiful things it's cold and empty on the inside."

She bites her lip. "That's not always true."

I snort, my knuckles turning white around the wheel with the knowledge that I'm minutes away from facing my father. "Prove me wrong. Give me an example."

I'm not prepared for her soft exhale of, "You."

I nearly swerve off the road. "What?"

She blushes, fiddling with the bottom of her dress. "You're beautiful, Teddy, inside and out. There's nothing cold or empty about you. I hope you know that."

My brain doesn't seem capable of processing what she said.

"Teddy?"

"Mhmm?" I mumble, hoping she can't hear the catch in my voice.

"Are you okay?"

"As okay as I can be with what we're facing."

She looks at me doubtfully but doesn't pester as we pull beneath the archway, and one of the valets steps forward.

"Welcome, Mr. McCallister," the young guy says as he swings my door open.

It doesn't matter how many times I ask them to call me Teddy here, I'm always Mr. McCallister.

I slip out of the car, adjusting my clothes so everything lays correctly and then cross the front of the car, opening Vanessa's door for her and offering a hand.

Tucking her hand into my elbow, we walk into the building, and I tip my head in greeting at some of the people we pass.

"Do you know where we're going?" she whispers under her breath, eyes wide as she takes in the club.

"Of course."

I lead her to the restaurant area of the country club, and she stiffens when she sees how many are gathered. The smell of money practically permeates the air, and Vanessa's fingers tremble against my elbow as eyes turn to us.

My parents are in the middle of the room, speaking to a group of people, some of which I recognize.

"Relax," I murmur to Vanessa as we approach them. "All of them can smell fear like a shark with blood in the water."

Her fingers squeeze my elbow, and I can tell she wants to run, but she squares her shoulders, lifting her chin in a defiant way and fuck if it doesn't make me want to push her against a wall and kiss her until she can't remember her own fucking name.

"Teddy." My mom smiles when she spots us, encouraging us forward. "And Vanessa. So lovely to see you." She kisses each of my cheeks and does the same with Van.

I don't say anything, because if I did it'd be about how I was forced here by my sperm donor at her side.

"It's nice to see you again, Mrs. McCallister."

"I told you, call me Lenora, dear." Turning to the woman at her side, she says, "Marcia, meet Vanessa. This is Teddy's lovely girlfriend."

"Oh, a girlfriend." Marcia smiles, taking Vanessa's hand. Giving a fake hyena-like cackle, she turns that smile to me and places a hand on my arm. I instantly stiffen. "There was a time when I thought you might settle down with my Olive."

"Olive?" Vanessa repeats, eyes skating between the woman and me. "Is that like your dog?"

I snort, quickly covering it with a cough, but not before I can avoid my father's death glare. I know not for one second does Vanessa believe she's talking about a dog, but if it isn't the sassiest comeback I've ever heard.

If Marcia's face wasn't permanently frozen from

plastic surgery, I'm positive her glare would be of seismic proportions.

"Olive, is my daughter, dear. She grew up with Teddy."

"You named your child Olive?" Vanessa cackles. "I feel sorry for her."

Marcia turns red, and before something can happen that neither of us wants to be a part of or witness, I tug Vanessa toward the drink table.

"That was incredible," I say low enough for only her to hear, purposely brushing my lips over her cheek as I do.

She frowns. "I hope I didn't cause you too much trouble with what I said."

"If it does, it was worth it, I promise you that." I place an order for our drinks, and grin at her. "You know what's even funnier?" She arches a brow in wait. "She has a dog named Ashley."

Vanessa throws her head back and laughs. "Wow."

"I know." I tip my head in thanks when the bartender passes me our drinks. "Have you ever had a mimosa before?" She shakes her head. "It's champagne and orange juice. It won't get you drunk, but it'll help ease the nightmare of this."

She looks around the large, mostly white room. There's an entire wall of windows overlooking the golf course and lake in the distance. Even I have to admit this place is nice, but I'd still prefer hanging out in Harvey's to this.

With our drinks in hand, we return to my parents' table where they're now seated, Marcia nowhere in sight.

My father narrows his eyes on Vanessa, lips thinned, but he holds back on whatever cutting remarks are currently rattling in his brain. That's one saving grace of being in public. He has to put on a show.

"What occasion are we celebrating?" I ask, pulling out a chair for Vanessa.

His lips twitch but he doesn't reply. It's my mom who says, "Ralph Woolford—I think you know him—has decided to run for governor. This is in his honor to show our support and raise funds."

"Ah." I jerk my head in a nod. "How much did it cost a head to get into this brunch?"

"That's not important," my father bites out, hand clasped around a glass of what I'd guess is bourbon.

I exchange a look with Vanessa. I'm already plotting our escape.

"How's school?" My mom asks, directing the question to each of us.

"Dandy," I respond, smiling when I see the vein in my dad's forehead pulse. God, I fucking love messing with him in public and forcing him to keep wearing his mask.

"Good. Excited to graduate."

"I'm sure, I'm sure," she chants, picking up her glass of champagne. "What are your plans after graduating?"

Before Vanessa has a chance to answer my father cuts in with, "Don't pretend to care what she has planned. She won't be a part of our lives long enough for it to matter."

Beneath the table my hands fist, nails digging into my palms. Almost immediately Vanessa's hand is overtop my right one, providing a much-needed sense of calm.

He goes to take a drink as Vanessa replies with, "I don't know about that. I mean, Teddy and I were planning for a wedding by the end of the summer, and I do so hope to be pregnant by this time next year. We want to be young parents."

Bourbon sprays across the table, hitting me and the man to my left.

"Pregnant?"

"Not yet, of course," Vanessa sips daintily at her mimosa. "But soon enough. Do you want to be called grandpa?"

My mom dabs at my father's white shirt with a napkin and he shoves her off, storming for the restrooms if I had to hazard a guess.

"Well," she sighs, setting the soiled napkin on the table. "Personally, I do think I'd prefer something a little more creative than grandma."

———

AFTER BRUNCH, I sneak the two of us out a backdoor and show Vanessa around the grounds. The sun glints off her dark hair, showing strands of red and blonde sprinkled throughout the brunette.

She's looking at the garden like she's never seen anything so beautiful, but I have, and it's her.

Spinning back to me, her cheeks glow with happiness. "This is amazing. It's like something out of a fantasy novel."

Wisteria hangs above her, framing her in its purple

halo. I shove my hands in my pockets, watching her as she spins around, her dress lifting around her ankles. The smile on her face brings one to my own.

I sense a presence behind me and look over my shoulder. My spine stiffens, and I stand taller at the sight of my father.

Vanessa has her back to me, sniffing a flower. "Van," I call softly. She turns, her cheeks glowing with happiness. That happiness dims when she notices the man behind me. "I need to speak with my dad. I'll be right back."

"Are you sure?"

I feel a traitorous tug in my chest, knowing this girl would play buffer between my father and me if I asked.

"Positive."

Hesitation contorts her features, but she nods, turning back to the flowers.

Shoving my hands in my pockets, I brace myself for the inevitable altercation.

My father turns, a silent command to follow. We step into a shadowy alcove off of the garden.

"What the fuck kind of game are you playing, son?" His eyes are glowing with barely leashed anger, nostrils flaring.

"First off, I'm not playing a game." I step back, not because I'm afraid, but because I don't have to take him glowering right in my face. "Secondly, you lost the privilege of calling me *son* the first time you ever laid a hand on me."

His face turns a mottled red. "Watch your mouth."

I bite my tongue, reminding myself I have to make it to

graduation. I can't afford to lose my shit prematurely. He smirks when I don't have a comeback for him.

"You are not planning to marry that girl."

"Is that a question or?"

"It's a goddamn statement you little prick." He looks near to busting a vein in his forehead. "You will not be marrying someone like that, and definitely not having children with them."

"Someone. Like. What."

"*Beneath us.*"

I laugh incredulously. "You really think that your last name and bank account make you some sort of god." I shake my head at the ridiculousness of it.

"Need I remind you, you share the same last name, *son*, and that bank account has kept you very happy." He straightens the lapels of his jacket. "Keep your girlfriend for now, Teddy. Have your fun. Play your games. But remember, I play games too, and I not only call the shots," his voice lowers, and he leans into me, his alcohol laced breath falling over me, "I always win."

When he's out of sight, I kick at the bench nearby, cursing under my breath.

Hate is a strong word, but there's no better one to describe how I feel about my father.

SIXTEEN

Vanessa

I KNOCK ON THE DOOR TO TEDDY'S DORM ROOM AND
rock back on my heels. My bag is cradled to my chest, my
fingers fiddling with a patch I ironed onto it. I can't help
but feel extremely awkward standing here. The dry erase
board on the door says, "My dick is bigger than Teddy's."
With a crudely drawn penis. Someone else has come along
and adorned the little guy with a curly fro that I think is
meant to be pubic hair, a mustache, and a quote bubble
that says, *Bonjour!*

I knock again and yelp when the door swings open.

His roommate towers above me. He's even taller than
Teddy, and I have to crane my neck back to take all of
him in.

"Hi," I squeak.

His brown hair is shaggy, but coiffed back in an artfully messy way. Heavy scruff covers angular cheekbones and dark bushy brows arch over warm brown eyes.

He would be entirely intimidating if it wasn't for the wide smile he boasts.

"Ah, hey, Vanessa. Teddy mentioned you were coming over to watch a movie."

He insisted I needed to start making regular appearances at his dorm or Jude would start to get suspicious. So here I am. Overnight bag and all—yeah, he said this had to be a sleepover, but his ass *will* be sleeping on the floor.

Jude closes the door and turns to me, his grin growing impossibly larger. His hands go to his narrow hips, and I feel my face heat with nerves. I never seem to know what to say to people that I don't know well, and knowing that he went with Teddy all the way to where I grew up—

"Thank you," I blurt.

His brows furrow deeply. "Uh ... for getting the door? Sure. You're welcome."

"No, not that." I shake my head, frustrated with my awkwardness. "Thank you for ... for what you did with Teddy. I..." I look down at my scuffed ratty pair of Sperry's. I got them second-hand from a thrift shop and they belong in the trash, but I can't seem to part with them. Forcing myself to meet his eyes, I say, "Thank you for what you did with Tristan."

"Ah, shit. You don't have to thank me for that. Sounds like that prick deserved to be taught a lesson." His voice lowers and he adds, "I gotta admit, it was interesting seeing Teddy lose his shit like that. He's such a chill guy, but he's crazy fucking protective of the ones he cares about."

"He cares about me?" The words tumble from my lips before I can stop them.

He gives me a puzzled look. "I would hope so. I mean, you're his girlfriend."

"Right." I give a tiny laugh, covering my face with my hands. "Where is he anyway?"

"Shower." He tosses his thumb toward the bathroom. "You can hang out here or his room if you want."

"Oh, I'll uh just go to his room."

Jude points me to the right room, and I give him a smile of thanks as I drop my bag on the floor.

I spin around in a circle, taking in his room uninterrupted while I have the chance.

There's the stereotypical Sports Illustrated calendar hanging on his door, but beyond that it's nothing like I expected. The bed, gray and white bed covers and sheets, is neatly made. His desk is clutter free, with only his laptop, a notebook, and pen on top. There is a pair of jeans over the back of the desk chair and that's the only 'dirty' thing about this room. I expected clothes all over the place, most likely unwashed, his bed a mess, and trash piling on the floor.

It's such a contrast to his chaotic personality.

Sitting on his bed, I reach over and trace my fingers over dinosaur stickers adhered to his wall.

The bathroom door opens outside of the room, and

nothing prepares me for the sight of a damp Teddy in only a single white towel.

Sweet baby Jesus, give me strength to resist this man.

Droplets of water cling to his impressive pectorals and abs, sluicing down and getting lost in the terry cloth towel. There's a scar on his abdomen, jagged and what some might call ugly, but I find it fascinating. Scars have always drawn me in. The way I see it, they tell a story.

His brown hair is black with wetness, and green eyes are sparkling with barely withheld laughter when he catches me staring.

"Hey, Van." His voice is practically a purr.

He closes the door behind him, and I ease off the bed. "I'll step outside so you can change."

He grins, that cocky adorable smile that makes my gut dip. "You're my girlfriend. This isn't anything you haven't seen before."

"Wh—" Before I can get the question out, he drops the towel, so it pools on the floor around his ankles. "Oh my God." I slap a hand over my eyes, but not before I get a full look at his penis. His very large, surprisingly nice-looking penis. But Jesus Christ, if it's that big when he's flaccid, I can't even imagine when he's hard. There's a small four-leaf clover tattoo in the dip of his V that no one would ever see unless ... well, unless he's naked.

Teddy chuckles, the sound warm and laced with humor. "It's just a penis, Van."

"That's not a penis!" I shriek. "That's a battering ram!" I drop my hand, not thinking, this time getting a shot of his perfect ass before he fully pulls up his sweatpants.

No. Fucking. Boxers.

He turns, his grin even bigger than before. "So, you're saying it's big?"

I blanch, lips parting. Crossing my arms over my chest, I stick my chin in the air. "No, no. That's not what I meant. It's not big. It's average. Small even. It's the Volkswagen Beetle of penises."

He throws his head back and laughs. "Oh, baby, it's so cute when you lie to me."

My hands fist at my sides. "Don't, *oh baby*, me."

"Why not?"

I ignore his question. "And what the hell did you mean by having seen your penis before. Unless you're having some weird ass sex dreams, I have not seen your penis."

He chuckles, pulling out his desk chair and running the towel over his damp hair. "I didn't mean in the literal sense. But since you're pretending to be my girlfriend, it's safe to assume Jude thinks we've had sex, and he'd get suspicious if you left the room."

"Yes! But you didn't need to just whip it out like that."

"I didn't whip it out. I took my towel off. My cock is kind of attached to my body in case you hadn't noticed."

"Oh, I noticed."

"I know you did." God, I want to wipe that smug smile off his face. "And no, I don't have weird sex dreams about you. Just normal ones."

My jaw drops. "You, sir," I point a finger at him, "need to stop that."

He throws his head back and laughs uproariously.

"Why are you laughing?" I demand, hands on my hips.

"I can't exactly control my dreams, Van."

I frown. He's right, of course, but I still can't tell if he's fucking with me or not. I decide to drop the conversation.

"What are we watching?"

"No, idea." He picks up the jeans from the chair and puts them away. "You can decide. Remote's there." He points beside his bed.

I reluctantly pick it up and turn the TV on as he putters around his room, straightening things that are already neat and tidy. He hasn't bothered to put a shirt on, and dammit if the sight of all that rippling muscle isn't distracting as fuck.

Clearing my throat, I force myself to focus on the task at hand. After logging into my Prime Video, I go to the section with everything I've bought and bring up season one of *Beverly Hills, 90210.*

"Any boyfriend of mine, fake or not, needs to be well-versed in my favorite show. Plus, you remind me of Luke Perry."

Teddy arches a brow. "I remind you of a 90s heartthrob?"

"You know who Luke Perry is?" I counter.

He chuckles and my nipples tighten in response to the husky sound. My body refuses to catch up with my brain on how I can't be attracted to him.

He rolls his eyes playfully. "I know I'm a beauty, but there are brains here too." He taps the side of his head. "Yes, I know he is." He proceeds to start fluffing the pillows. "Do you care if I order pizza?"

"No." I stand awkwardly in the center of his room, hands in my back pockets. "Pizza is always good."

"Cool." He picks up his phone and his eyes scan my body. "You should change into something more comfortable. I'd suggest the nude, but I have a feeling you won't go for it."

"You'd be correct." I purse my lips, totally giving him a mom-glare. "I wouldn't mind changing," I admit, picking up my bag. I clear my throat. "You can leave."

A slow grin spreads over his face, sticky and sweet. "Are you sure you want me to leave, babe?"

I swallow past the lump in my throat.

No.

"Yes."

He smirks as he heads for the door but pauses when he reaches me, the scent of his body wash — woodsy and masculine — clinging to his skin. "I'll leave, but just know that your eyes gave me a very different answer than your mouth." He wets his lips with his tongue. "I'd like to see you use your mouth for far more ... *pleasurable* things than lies."

The bastard doesn't give me a chance to respond before he slips out the door, closing it soundly behind him.

I quickly flick the lock before he decides to barge back in and find me half-naked. Pulling out my favorite pair of sleep pants with little cherries on them, a jog bra — with boobs as big as mine I'm not about to free-boob it in the presence of Teddy and Jude — and a tank top. I change as quickly as possible and stuff my backpack under his desk.

Opening the door back up, I poke my head outside the

bedroom. Jude is reclined on the couch, but it's almost comical how small he makes the couch appear. It's not big to begin with, but with his height and musculature it looks more like a chair.

Teddy leans against the counter in the kitchen, smiling when my gaze finally lands on him.

"Pizza is ordered. You want a drink?"

I tiptoe out of his room, my heart racing with nerves. It feels … intimate to be hanging out in his space like this. Sure, he's been to my dorm, but I was doing homework. We weren't going to watch a show together and spend the night.

"Um, whatcha got in there?" I bite my lip as he opens the fridge.

"Zombie Dust, some blue Gatorade, orange juice, water, Mike's Hard Lemonade, uh…" He squats down, moving things around. "A random ass Juicy Juice no idea why the fuck that's in there. Some Coke—the drinking kind, not the nose candy one."

I try not to laugh; it only encourages him. "I'll have the Coke."

He grabs a can and passes it to me, taking a water for himself.

"Come on, babe," he smirks when I bristle at the endearment, "let's watch your show." He places his hand low on my waist, fingers rubbing idly against the skin exposed between my bottoms and tank top.

The touch sends a shiver up my spine, but I have to not pull away.

I feel like this entire night is going to consist of me,

constantly telling myself *don't be suspicious*, since we need to Jude to believe this relationship. I feel bad for deceiving his friends, but Teddy seems to think it's necessary.

Settling on his bed, I cross my legs and hit play on the first episode of season one. The bed dips with Teddy's weight as he settles beside me. "Do you want a blanket?"

"N-No," I stutter. There's no way I could be cold, not with him so close and the heat of his body practically like a furnace. No, I won't be needing a blanket—not unless it's to smother the flames of my stupid desire.

"Why do you seem so nervous?" He grins at me, clearly delighted that he has some sort of effect on me. "If you want to jump my bones, all you have to do is ask? Or don't ask, just jump me."

I narrow my eyes on him. "I thought you were going to keep the sexual innuendos to yourself from now on."

"I've tried and failed." He fluffs the pillow behind him, getting comfier.

"Try again," I bite out.

"I mean, I'll do my best, but anyone that knows me would think it was suspicious if I wasn't my usual vulgar self with you."

I exhale heavily. He always has to have a freaking point and it's annoying. "Just ... try to keep them to a minimum."

"Do they make you uncomfortable?" He sits up, suddenly serious. His easy smile vanishes.

I rub a hand over my face. "Not ... not uncomfortable. Just..." I search for the right words. "I know what this is and what it isn't, and when you make comments like that, it confuses me." I relax a little, satisfied with my answer.

"Look." He rubs his stubbled jaw. "I know this isn't real, and you don't actually want to have sex with me." His green eyes flicker over my face like they're searching for something. "But my attraction to you? That *is* real."

I think I stop breathing. My heart might even stop beating.

My fake-boyfriend, one of the hottest guys on campus, is admitting to being attracted to me?

I know I'm not ugly, that's not where my surprise comes from, but in the back of my mind I assumed Teddy chose me to play this role because he *wasn't* attracted to me and there would be no chance of him fucking up things further. I've chocked a lot of his innuendos up to this point as just him being his usual flirty self—not that he was genuinely interested in me in that way.

The problem with this relationship being a farce is that the lines are blurred between what's for show and what's reality, and it's confusing.

"Are you okay?" He snaps his fingers in front of his face. "Do I need to perform CPR? I took a class in middle school, but I think I remember the gist. But then again, if I put my mouth on yours, your heart might stop all together from the pure perfection of my lips."

"Get out of here with your nonsense." I swat playfully at his shoulder. He flinches before my hand makes the light contact with his shoulder, and I instantly cover my face to hide my mortification. Dropping them, I gasp, "Teddy, I'm so sorry."

He worries his tongue against his cheek. "No, I'm sorry. I knew you weren't going to hurt me but I—"

"You don't have to explain." My hands flutter around him, wanting to make this better, but I don't know how.

It doesn't matter that I was only being silly with him. He's been abused by his father his whole life, a reaction like his is understandable.

He grabs my flailing hands, tugging me closer until I'm in his lap. "It's okay, Van. I swear it."

Tears prick my eyes, not for myself, but for *him* because no one should endure what he has. "I'm sorry."

He cups my cheeks, rubbing his thumbs against my skin in soothing circles. "It's okay. I'm okay. Sometimes I can't help it when I'm caught off guard."

A tear drops from my lashes onto my cheek, and I gasp when he darts forward, licking it away.

"D-Did you *lick* my tear?"

He smiles shamelessly. "Yes."

"God, you're so—"

"Wonderful, amazing, out of this world?" He rubs his nose against mine. "I know."

"Weird. I was going for weird." I slip off his lap, settling onto his bed once more. I take a breath, getting my emotions in check. "Now watch the show."

He chuckles, adjusting the pillow behind his back. "I like it when you're bossy."

"Forget weird, you are seriously disturbed."

Of course, my statement doesn't faze him a bit.

A little bit later he gets a notification on his phone and goes to meet the pizza guy at the dorm entrance. I pause the show while I wait, once again looking around his room. Sure, I'm being nosy, but I can't help it. I feel like the things a person keeps in their personal space says a lot about them.

On the corkboard above his desk, he's tacked up a few positive quotes that surprise me to see. There are some of those instant photos scattered around too. One with him and Zoey, another with Mascen, Cole, and him. There's a third of Jude and Cree wearing those oversized glasses you get at a place like the Dollar Store. The only other photo is one of him and his mom when he's probably only three or so. She holds him on her hip, smiling broadly at her little boy.

That one makes me sad, because I feel like genuine smiles like that were probably hard to come by in his childhood. No matter how his dad is, it's clear his mother truly loves him.

"Snooping?"

"Ah!" I grab my chest, jumping back a foot from the desk to glare at Jude in the doorway. He sips one of the Gatorades. "Don't do that!"

"I'm not the one being nosy."

"I'm not," I protest. "I'm *looking*, besides this is clearly in view; it's not like I opened a drawer."

"That was next, I'm sure."

It was.

He flashes an amused smile and steps further into the room. "Oh, shit I love this show." He points at the paused screen.

"You do?"

He shrugs. "My mom played reruns all the time. I kind of got sucked in. It's addicting."

The door into the suite opens and Teddy growls his displeasure when he sees Jude in his room. "You better not be hitting on my girl."

Jude rolls his eyes. "I'm not slimy enough to go after my friend's girl. I *do* have standards."

Teddy snickers. "Prove it."

"Mind if I hang?" Jude asks. "I was just telling Vanessa I love this show."

Teddy eyes his friend curiously. "I learn something new about you all the time. I don't care, though. It's up to Vanessa."

"What can I say?" Jude takes the pizza boxes out of Teddy's hands and sits down on the bed without waiting for confirmation. "I'm full of surprises."

Teddy turns to me, eyes glimmering with amusement. "You want me to kick him out?"

"No, it's fine."

Teddy sits down on the opposite side of his bed which forces me to be in the middle. The bed isn't that big, so I end up with each guy plastered against my side. I start the show back up as Jude cracks open the top box.

"Ew, veggie pizza."

"Don't knock it." I snag the box of my pizza from him. "I love it."

"It has *mushrooms* on it." He shudders dramatically.

"That one's mine," Teddy protests, reaching across me to try to confiscate the other box from Jude.

"No takie backsies." Jude holds on tightly to the box.

"I didn't give it to you. You stole them."

"Share with your girlfriend."

"I want my pepperoni pizza."

Jude pulls out a slice, the cheese melty and gooey. "Mmm, delicious."

"If Vanessa wasn't between us right now, I would tackle you."

I roll my eyes and swipe a slice of the pepperoni and hand it to Teddy. "Stop whining."

"Thanks, babe." He swoops in, kissing my cheek.

"You're welcome, snookums."

Jude snorts so hard that pizza sauce shoots out of his mouth from the bite he took. "Snookums," he cackles. "What else do you call him?"

Teddy smirks, waiting.

"Mmm," I hum, thinking. "He likes it when I call him Daddy."

Teddy drops his bottle of water, wetting his lap. "Shit!" He curses, scooping it up and swiping at his very damp sweatpants that now cling even more to the shape of his dick.

Jude leans forward, grinning at Teddy. "I should've known."

Teddy rolls his eyes. "I hate you guys."

Jude holds his fist out to me, and I hit mine against it.

Quiet settles between us as we eat and watch the show. If someone had told me that at some point, I'd be sitting in Teddy McCallister's room hanging out with him and Jude, I would've laughed in their face, but the world works in mysterious ways.

Just like my brain.

Because as I sit there between the two guys, their body heat radiating around me, my thoughts drift in a direction I've never ever allowed them to go before.

Of me knelt between two men, them worshipping my body and making every pleasure come to life.

I squirm uncomfortably from the pulsing between my thighs.

"Are you okay?" Teddy whispers in my ear. I give a shaky nod. "You're wiggling a lot."

"I'm fine," I squeak, my voice dangerously high-pitched.

"I feel like you're lying."

"Well, I'm not," I clip out, my tone short.

"Shush, I'm watching this." Jude flaps a hand in our direction in a gesture to shut up.

Teddy scoffs at Jude's bossy tone.

After three more episodes, Jude heads to his bedroom, and I excuse myself to use the bathroom and brush my teeth as I ready myself to go to sleep.

I've tried not to focus on the fact that I'm staying the night with Teddy, but now there's no escaping it.

I stare at my reflection in the bathroom mirror—a bathroom, that while messier than Teddy's bedroom, doesn't boast pee on the floor or toothpaste stains in the sink.

Gripping the porcelain, I stare into my too-wide blue eyes.

"Get a grip. This isn't a big deal. Stop making it into one. All you're doing is sleeping."

"Are you talking to someone in there?"

I squeal at the sound of Teddy's voice on the other side of the door.

"N-No."

"So, you're talking to yourself then? Because you were definitely talking."

"Leave me alone."

"I need to brush my teeth."

"You can wait."

"No, I can't."

I swing open the door and glare up at him. "Why are you so annoying?"

"It's part of my charm." He brushes past me and grabs a lime green toothbrush off the sink, adding a dollop of toothpaste and then wetting it.

It's way too small in the bathroom for both him and me, his body touching mine every time he moves. Crossing my arms over my chest, I say, "Everyone knows you wet the toothbrush *then* put the toothpaste on."

He grins around the white suds in his mouth. Spitting first, he replies, "There is no wrong way. You just like to argue with me."

"Do not."

"Do too."

"Is this foreplay for you guys? Do I need to wear headphones tonight?"

I spin around and collide with Jude's bare chest— literally slam my forehead into his hard pectoral muscle. "Ow." I rub my forehead, his big hands on my upper arms to steady me.

"Take your hands off my girlfriend," Teddy growls behind me. He sounds legitimately pissed off and territorial.

Jude gives a lopsided grin as he lifts his hands in the air. "Headphones it is."

He disappears from the doorway, and I swing back to face Teddy. He's so close in the tightly enclosed space that I have to tilt my head all the way back to even look at his face.

"Possessive, much?"

There's a hot, delicious spark in his eyes. He gives a low chuckle that has my nipples tightening against my shirt. He looks down, smirking when he notices the way my body reacts to him.

"Of what's mine?" His voice has deepened and dammit if the sound of it doesn't turn me on even more. "Hell yeah, baby."

"I-I'm not yours."

"Keep telling yourself that." Jerking his head toward his bedroom he says, "Get settled. I'll be there in a second."

"Don't tell me what to do," I snap, but then because I'm an idiot, I do what he asked.

I reason that I was planning on going to his room anyway.

Pulling back the bed covers I slip beneath the sheets. They smell freshly washed, and I narrow my eyes in suspicion that maybe Teddy's room isn't normally this clean.

Teddy returns to his room a few minutes later, closing the door behind him and grinning when he finds me laying in his bed with my stuffed octopus he got me for Valentine's.

"Well, if this isn't precious."

I roll my eyes. "Shut up."

He laughs, clapping his hands together. "Let's get this show going."

My brows furrow. "You want to watch more?"

He laughs, scratching his smooth muscular stomach. "No, the one we're going to put on."

"What are you talking about?" I'm beyond confused and feeling more than a little stupid that I have no idea what he's talking about.

"We have to make Jude think we're having sex."

"Uh…" I gape at him. "How do we do that?"

"The way I see it, we have two choices. We could do it the old-fashioned way and actually have sex. Preferably I vote for this option."

"What's the second one?" I grind out between my teeth, ready to hurl my octopus at his smiling face.

He shrugs, moving over to the bed. "We fake it."

"What?"

"You know, bounce on the bed, some fake-moaning—maybe I'll even slap your ass if you're a bad girl."

This time I do throw the octopus and he laughs, catching it easily.

Right. Baseball player.

He moves over to the bed, placing his hands on the mattress. He's so close to me that I could count every individual eyelash if I wanted.

"Be nice to him." He hands the octopus back to me. "He doesn't deserve to have your anger taken out on him."

"Then don't make me mad."

"But it's so fun. Seriously, though," he motions for me to scoot, "Jude will think it's weird if we don't have sex."

"You have got to be kidding," I grumble.

"Bet."

I rub a hand over my face. "What do you want me to do?"

He doesn't answer, instead, he grabs me and swings my body over his so that I'm straddling him.

"I like this view."

"I should slap you." I glower down at the too-hot-for-his-own-good player beneath me.

He wets his lips, flashing a crooked smile. "You just cried over barely swatting me. We both know you won't slap me."

"I hate you." I go to climb off him, but his big hands settle on my upper thighs, his thumbs settling dangerously close to an area I shouldn't want him anywhere near. Narrowing my eyes, I ask, "What are you doing?"

"Having fake-sex with my fake-girlfriend. Or at least trying to." He leans up, capturing my earlobe between his teeth and I gasp. "Come on, Van. Help me out."

"I didn't know when I agreed to this that fake-sex was involved too."

"Just play along." He doesn't give me a chance to say another word before he starts moving his hips under me, the bed squeaking loudly beneath us.

Embarrassment pinkens my cheeks, and I cover my face. "I can't do this," I hiss. "This is mortifying."

He stops moving and pulls my hands away from my face. "Yes, you can. Do you want Jude to think we're crocheting in here?"

I giggle. "Do you even know how to crochet?"

"God no, but I do know how to do this."

He rolls his hips again, and this time I moan and there's nothing fake about it.

"Just like that." He smirks, entirely too pleased with himself.

My hands settle on his bare chest. "Don't do that."

"Do what?" He bats his eyes innocently like a dramatic damsel in distress. "This?"

The jerk does it again, and I can't help the moan of pleasure that leaves me. Wicked, cruel, hard-headed, rich, *bastard*.

I open my mouth to tell him to go to hell, that I'll jump on his fucking bed and make weird noises if that's what it takes, but this isn't necessary. Then his hands tighten on my thighs, fingers digging in with delicious pressure that not even the cotton of my pajama bottoms can shelter me from. Wetness pools in my core, my body always so quick to betray my mind. Another moan passes between my lips, and this time I'm the one rolling my hips against him.

More. I need more.

I rock faster, logic fleeing from my brain and hiding around the corner.

He sits up, pressing a kiss to my neck.

"Say my name, babe. Say it loud. I want everyone on this fucking floor to know you belong to me."

Jesus. Fucking. Christ.

We're faking this. There is no penis in the vagina action. He's not even technically touching me, but I can feel the hard ridge of his cock through our thin pajamas — the one I called Volkswagen Beetle sized but is more like monster truck — and damn if that isn't enough to turn me on even more.

Now would be a good time for logical, take-no-bullshit-Vanessa, to make her return and ask him who the hell he thinks he's talking to trying to tell me shit.

But lust-addled Vanessa *likes* the bossy tone in his voice.

Even strong women like to be bossed around from time to time.

I grab onto the hair on the back of his head, yanking him away from my neck. His eyes are glazed, and I'm sure mine look very much the same. It took no time for me to go from bitching at him to practically putty in his arms. Stupid hormones.

"Don't tell me what to do," I force myself to say, but the breathlessness in my voice betrays me.

He gives a slow lazy grin, trying to lean in and kiss me, but I don't let him get close enough. "You like it. Don't even try to deny it."

I do like it, and that enrages me.

I open my mouth to argue — it's what I'm best at — but he grabs the back of my neck and pulls my mouth to his. His eyes look surprised a millisecond before our lips touch, and I think maybe he didn't plan on kissing me, but the moment we do neither of us tries to stop what happens next.

He kisses me deeply, tongue tangling with mine in a tantalizing way.

I've been kissed plenty of times, but none of them stack up against what Teddy can do.

He doesn't just kiss, he fucks with his mouth.

My hands end up on his face, his stubble rubbing my palms, while his end up on my ass, grinding me into his erection.

He bites down on my bottom lip, then soothes the hurt with his tongue.

Soon, he has his wish, and I'm crying out his name, practically shouting it as I orgasm. He groans, fingers tightening on my ass until I'm certain there will be bruises left behind in the shape of his fingerprints. Wetness coats my inner thighs—combined with both of our pleasures.

Teddy's lips are swollen, his eyes glossy with desire as we start to come down from our high.

I open my mouth, searching for words, but then on the other side of the suite Jude yells out, "Encore!" and I bury my face in the crook of Teddy's shoulder, realizing silence is my best friend right now.

SEVENTEEN

Teddy

PRACTICE WAS BRUTAL, AND I'M NOT MY USUAL SELF AS I step out of the showers and walk up to the lockers.

"What the fuck is wrong with you?" Mascen asks, dropping his towel and yanking on his pants.

"Nothing." I start changing my clothes.

Not only was practice rough, but I can't stop thinking about the other night with Vanessa. I didn't intend for things to happen the way they did—sure, I needed to make it seem like we were having sex otherwise Jude would figure out something was up—but I thought we'd just make a bunch of porno-esque fake moans, get the bed rocking, and call it a night.

But the second I pulled her onto my lap all rational thought went flying out the window. She looked like a fucking goddess above me, felt like one too. And if it was that mind-blowing and I wasn't even inside her ... *fuck.*

Mascen yanks on his shirt, giving me *what the fuck, dude* look.

"What?" I ask innocently.

"It smells like crap in here from all the bullshit you're spewing."

I snort, zipping up my hoodie. "That's just Murray's balls."

"Hey!" Murray slaps his towel against my side. "Why are you bringing me into your lover's spat?"

"Are you having relationship trouble with Vanessa?" Mascen asks, suddenly serious.

"No," I snort, staring into my locker, using it to shield me from his scrutiny.

How can I possibly begin to explain to my best friend, that me, the eternal bachelor, one and done Teddy, is developing *real* feelings for his very fake girlfriend? Oh, right, I can't tell him anything because I'm not about to confess now what I've done.

Mascen slams his locker closed, shouldering his backpack. "You don't want to talk? Fine. Don't fucking talk. I don't much like words anyway. I'll see you at six in the morning for a run."

"No, you won't!" I yell after his retreating figure.

He gives me the finger over his shoulder. "Yes, I will or, I'll be at your dorm dragging you out of bed, don't think I won't."

The locker room door slams shut behind him with those parting words.

Murray looks confused as fuck as he tugs on his shirt. "What the fuck is going on?"

I don't reply, I shut my locker and get the hell out of there.

———————

NORMALLY I WOULD HEAD to The Burger Palace after practice. Not today. I just don't have it in me to face Vanessa. Especially not when my thoughts are a tangled jumbled mess.

Instead, I drive over to Cole and Zoey's apartment. For half a second, I think about knocking, but then I'm like nah why start that now?

I wish I had because as soon as I let myself in, I'm met with the sight of Cole's bare ass with Zoey bent over the counter.

"My eyes!" I shout, slapping a hand over them. "Mom! Dad! Stop that!"

I hear their shouts and curses as I swiftly turn around and slam the door shut behind me. I start down the stairs and hurry to my car when steps sound behind me.

"Teddy, I swear to God if you don't give me the fucking key right now, I'm calling the cops on you. Don't test me."

I turn around to Cole glowering at me, hand outstretched. He's tossed on his jeans but didn't even bother to button them to come after me.

I don't even fight him as I finally, after more than six months, relinquish the key to the apartment I never got to live in. After walking in on that ... yeah, I don't want that to happen again.

"Why are you even here?" he asks suspiciously, crossing his arms over his chest.

Clenching my hands at my sides, I look away.

"Teddy, it's not like you to beat around the bush, and I know you well enough that I can tell there's something on your mind."

Grinding my teeth together, I shove my fingers through my hair. "It's Vanessa, okay."

He narrows his eyes. "Please tell me you didn't do something stupid and cheat on her?"

I rear back in shock. "Fuck no, what do you take me for?" He gives me *the look* and I sigh. "Right, yeah, I know."

"What's the problem then?"

"I just have so many feelings," I blurt, and immediately wish I could take the words back because I feel like a fool.

Cole presses his lips together, trying not to laugh. "Have you never had feelings before, bro?"

I roll my eyes. "Not like these."

He chuckles, rubbing his jaw. "Zoey's decent by now. Come on up."

"Are you seriously inviting me inside after I just saw you and your girlfriend fucking?"

He narrows his eyes on me, and I have a feeling he'd punch if he could. "Do you want my help or not?"

"Fine," I grumble, following him back up the stairs and into the apartment.

"Please tell me you got the key," Zoey bursts out as soon as we step inside.

Cole holds it up triumphantly. "Yep."

To me, Zoey points like a mother scolding her child — there's a reason I call her mom. "Don't you ever do anything like that ever again. I hope you're good and truly scarred. You deserve it."

With those parting words, she flounces out of the room, and the bedroom door shuts behind her.

Cole walks over to the refrigerator and offers me a small bottle of orange juice and takes a root beer for himself.

"Sit down and start talking."

I gulp down half of the orange juice before laying down on the couch like I'm in a therapist's office.

Then I start spilling my guts to Cole.

"Hold up," he says from where he sits on the coffee table beside me, "you're telling me you suckered this poor girl into being your pretend girlfriend and now you've fallen for her?"

"I didn't sucker her," I defend. "I *asked*, there's a difference, Dad. And I haven't fallen for her ... yet, but I think I might be falling. It's more than I've ever felt for a girl before. Normally I just want to pump and dump, but I haven't even slept with her and I want..."

"You want?" He prompts.

"I want *her*, for real. I want what we have already, the friendship and banter, but more. I want the kisses and touches to be real too. What's wrong with me?"

He grins slowly, his teeth blindingly white. "Looks to me like the player has lost."

"Lost?" I snort. "Me, Teddy McCallister, *never* loses. The game changed, that's all."

He rubs a hand over his jaw. "So, what are you going to do about it?"

"I haven't figured that out yet."

He lets out an exasperated sigh. "You might want to figure that out."

Rising from the couch, I say, "Don't tell anyone about the fake-relationship crap. I don't want them to know."

"I won't say a word."

"Not even Zoey."

He doesn't have a chance to reply because she peeks her head around from the hall. "I heard everything anyway."

"Dammit, Zoey," I grumble, shaking my head. "You can't tell anyone either."

"My lips are sealed," she promises. Sitting on the end of the couch, she gives me an amused look.

"What? I know you want to say something else."

She laughs, exchanging a look with Cole—and I feel fucking pathetic that I feel a tug in my heart because I want that.

Me.

Teddy McCallister.

Who has never had, nor wanted a girlfriend.

Never pictured myself married or any of that shit.

Suddenly wants those looks where you say everything

without opening your mouth. I want to cuddle, have inside jokes, hold hands, the whole fucking shebang.

Maybe I was abducted by aliens and my brain has been scrambled?

If that's the case, then little green dudes, could you please return me to my normal state?

I feel a tingle down my spine with that thought, because I don't *want* to go back to that.

"I just find it amusing you asked Vanessa, a girl you'd never met before, to do this for you when any girl on campus would've been happy to do it for you. No questions asked. No favors. Nada."

I rub my fingers over my jaw, my stubble thicker than normal. Coach is going to give me hell if I don't shave it soon. Even though she didn't ask me a question, I say, "I don't know. My gut seemed to know she was the one I needed."

"Interesting," she muses.

"Don't be cryptic, Mom," I snap, and Cole glares at me.

"Don't talk to my girl in that tone."

Zoey snickers. "I can handle him, babe."

He gives her a heated look. "I know you can."

"Oh, ew. Don't make sex eyes in front of your child. I'm leaving now."

Before I make it to the door, Zoey says, "We should have a movie night, and you bring Vanessa."

I pause, sighing. "I'll think about it."

Then I slip out the door and down to my car.

EIGHTEEN

Vanessa

I HAVEN'T SEEN TEDDY SINCE OUR SLEEPOVER. AFTER
we both got off from freaking *dry humping*, we cleaned up
and went to bed without saying another word.

He even slept on the floor without protest.

The next morning, he took me to breakfast, but barely
spoke which was very un-Teddy-like.

And since then, it's been only text messages, so color
me surprised when there's a knock on my door Friday
morning just before I'm about to head to class.

He stands there without his trademark smirk, looking
surprisingly awkward and unsure of himself.

I narrow my eyes in suspicion.

"What's up?" I ask hesitantly.

Why does my fake-boyfriend look like he's about to break up with me for real?

Despite his somberness, his eyes are zeroed in on my chest. The long-sleeve black shirt I yanked out of the drawer this morning is a little snug and definitely accentuates the girls. Clearing my throat, he jerks his head up at being caught and finally there's a tiny grin from him.

"Hey." His voice is deeper than normal, like it hasn't been long since he woke up.

"Hey? I reply questioningly. "I was about to leave for class."

"I won't be long. I just wanted to drop this off."

From behind his back, he pulls out a shirt and two tickets.

"What's this?" I take it from him hesitantly. The fabric of the t-shirt is super soft like it's been well-loved and washed many times.

"Tickets for you to come to my game."

"There's two," I point out.

His green eyes shine with amusement. "I thought you might want to ask Danika."

"Oh ... that was nice of you. And the shirt?"

"It's one of my baseball shirts. It has my number on the back. I want you to wear it."

I bite my lip, leaning against the open doorway. "Are you sure you want me to come?"

His brows furrow. "Of course. Why wouldn't I?"

"You've been avoiding me this week."

He doesn't even deny it. "I've been busy, that's all." I

don't believe him for a second. "And had a lot on my mind." Running his fingers through his hair, he blows out a breath, "I *want* you to come. Okay?"

"Okay," I repeat. "I'll be there then."

He smiles. "Good." He lingers awkwardly in the doorway. "Are you leaving now?"

"I was grabbing my bag when you knocked."

"Cool. I'll walk you to class then."

I eye him warily. "Are you breaking up with me?"

"What?" He gasps. "Fuck no."

I cross my arms over my chest, and his eyes once again drop to the swells of my breasts. "You're acting weird."

"I'm a weird guy, Van." He forces his eyes up. "You should be used to it." He cracks a smile.

"I haven't seen you since last weekend, and now you show up at my dorm with a shirt and tickets to your game, and you really have nothing else to say?"

"Oh." He holds up a finger. "That reminds me. I brought you cookies." He takes off his backpack and digs through it, procuring a baggy filled with— "They're oatmeal. I know snickerdoodle is your favorite, but I made oatmeal this time."

"Um, thanks," I take the baggy from him. "Do you ever bake anything besides cookies?" I ask curiously.

"Cookies are my favorite to make, but I can do cakes —can't decorate worth a shit, though—cheesecake, donuts," he starts ticking them of on his fingers, "brownies, and fudge."

"Who taught you how to bake?"

He gets a wistful look. "The cook we had growing up. Her name was Maggie."

"Was?"

He clears his throat, shouldering his backpack. "She passed a few years ago."

"I'm sorry."

He shrugs. "Can I walk you to class now?"

Rolling my eyes, I huff a sigh. "You're not going to leave until I agree, are you?"

"Nope." He grins from ear to ear.

"Just hold on."

I leave him at the door, not bothering to invite him inside. Dropping off the shirt and tickets in my room, I grab my bag and meet back up with him.

He takes my hand before I can even close the door behind me.

"Come on, girlfriend," he declares, swinging our arms.

"So, you're going to ignore the fact that you've been MIA this week?" We take the elevator down and he doesn't let go of my hand, humming the entire time. "Teddy," I prompt.

"I texted you," he mutters, holding open the door for me, "it's not like I was radio silent. I've been busy."

"With what?"

"Studying and…"

"And?"

"And *stuff*."

Irritation bubbles inside me, but I dam it down because he doesn't owe me an explanation. If we were an actual couple there's no way I would let him get away with this, but we're not, so I let it drop and don't speak a single word on our walk across campus.

Instead, I look around at the old buildings, the ivy clinging to their exteriors. Wrought iron benches dot the pathways, some with students sitting on them.

Like always when I'm on campus with Teddy people look and stare, the shock of Teddy being in a relationship still not having faded almost three months later.

He drops me off outside my public speaking class with a peck on the lips and another plea for me to come to his game.

I don't enter my class right away, instead watching his retreating figure. A few girls give him lustful gazes as he walks by, but he ignores them. He keeps moving forward, and instead of the joyful, cocky walk he normally boasts, he's slightly bent forward, shoulders curled inward, like the weight of the world is upon him.

"I'VE NEVER BEEN to a baseball game," Danika says, gripping a bag of popcorn in one hand and a Coke in the other as we find our seats—damn good ones right at the front.

"Me either." I follow behind her, plopping into my seat and smiling hesitantly at the guy beside me who gives me a dirty look.

Well, then.

"All I know about baseball is that there's a bat and they hit a ball," she continues, earning a glare from the guy beside me.

"Then why are you guys here?" he drawls, sending major *go away* vibes.

Danika leans around me, plastering him with a glare that makes most cower. "Because her boyfriend plays, not that it's any of your business."

The guy looks me over, sneering. "And who's your boyfriend?"

His tone is doubtful and downright rude.

"None of your fucking business," I snap, and he chuckles, muttering something to his friend. More than likely he's saying something about me being a liar. Well, whatever. He wishes I cared what he thought.

I take a sip of my lemonade, wincing from the overly tart sour flavor. Should've gone with the Coke.

Danika notes my expression and laughs. "I told you so."

"Yeah, yeah, yeah," I chant, setting the drink in the cupholder.

"Want me to grab you something else?"

"It's not a big deal," I promise, pulling my hair off my neck and tying it with a band. It's not even that warm out, just the barest hint that spring is around the corner, but I'm so nervous I've worked up a sweat. I hope to God I don't get pit stains in Teddy's shirt. Talk about embarrassing.

Danika stands, already pulling out cash from her pocket. "What do you want?"

I bite my lip. "Coke."

"I'll be right back." She shimmies down the aisle again, my seatmate ogling her ass.

I stare at him until he notices me, and the guy gives me an unabashed smirk. "Your friend has a nice ass."

My skin prickles at his tone. "You have a nice face…" He grins at the supposed compliment. "When it's squished beneath my tires."

"Bitch," he mutters.

"Sexist pig."

My phone buzzes and I'm surprised to see a text from Teddy. I figured I wouldn't hear from him until after the game.

Teddy: Did you make it?

Me: Already in my seat.

Teddy: Everything good?

Me: For the most part.

Teddy: What does that mean?

Me: The guy beside me is kind of a dick.

Me: Don't worry. I can handle him.

He doesn't reply and I figure he's been distracted by a pre-game pep-talk or whatever it is that goes on before a game.

"Who'd you say is your boyfriend again?"

I eye the dickhead beside me. "I didn't."

"Right," he chortles. "Because he's probably not even real."

"Yes, my boyfriend is imaginary because I'm five." I shake my head incredulously. I can't handle the idiocy of some people.

"No sane guy would deal with your bitchy attitude."

I glower at him. "I'm not the one who started off with

rude comments. I thought sports were supposed to bring people together, but clearly I was wrong."

"Dude," his friend mutters on his other side, "shut up."

His friend's words have no effect. "I just don't understand why *girls* even come to these games. Girls don't like sports. You never know anything about them, and you're just here to chase players."

"Hey!" A girl protests behind me. "I'll have you know my dad took me to games all the time, and I happen to love the *sport* not the guys who play it."

Clearly the guy beside me, probably a freshman based on his baby face, was raised in a sexist household.

"Leave," commands a deep, no-nonsense voice. Shivers skate down my spine because I *know* that voice.

I look over my shoulder to find Teddy towering over us, his shadow long behind him. His face is intense, scarily so. Not that I'm afraid of him, because I'm not, but there's this intensity that tells no one to cross him.

"I said, leave," he repeats to the guy beside me.

I don't look to see the guy's reaction. I'm too busy taking in Teddy in his uniform. Sure, I knew what they looked like, but I never mentally prepared myself for seeing Teddy in one, and Jesus Christ it clings to his long muscular body like a second skin. I know if he turned around, I would get an incredible view of his ass.

Not that I want to look at his ass.

Because I don't.

That would be weird.

"What the fuck, man? I'm not leaving."

"Are you being a jerk to my girl?" My heart dips at his *my girl* comment, and I silently curse myself. I have got to get my feelings in check and remind myself none of this is real.

"I don't even know your girl."

Teddy gives an exasperated sigh. "She's right beside you." The guy gulps audibly. "She's here for me, not to listen to you spew whatever bullshit is coming out of your mouth. Don't make me repeat myself again."

I expect the guy to argue further, but he gets up without protest and leaves this time.

"Am I cool to stay?" The other guy, his friend I assume, asks. "I told him to stop being a dick."

Teddy defers to me. "Was he bothering you too?" I shake my head. "You can stay … for now." He looks me over, as if he expects to find some sort of physical injury when really it's just my irritation burning under my skin. "You good?"

"I'm good."

He grins. "Cheer for me, babe."

I expect him to run off, but of course not.

This is Teddy, and we need to be even more public with our relationship, so he swoops down and grabs my face gently between his palms, kissing me in a way that's not decent for the public.

"Just a preview for later." He winks and I swear a girl starts crying nearby.

I watch him leave, heading back to wherever he came from.

Danika returns a minute later, passing me a Coke. She

notices the empty spot beside me and the way the eyes of people in the stands keep straying to me. "What'd I miss?"

"You don't want to know." I sip the soda, suddenly completely parched.

"Whatever you say." She looks out in the field with a tiny smile as players are announced. "Play ball!"

NINETEEN

Teddy

VANESSA'S HAND IS WARM IN MINE AS I LEAD HER through the off-campus house located in Frat Row. We're celebrating our first winning game, and I'm riding high from the victory.

Something else that has me worked up is Vanessa in my shirt. She wanted to change after the game, but I refused. I like seeing my name on her too much, and the way the fabric stretches across her tits is fucking magnificent. Seriously. It makes my mouth water.

She had every right to question me this morning.

I *have* been avoiding seeing her in person. Texts are easy, because I don't have to look at her, be around and feel ... *things*. Things I've never felt before. Last weekend made me realize that while I'm attracted to Vanessa on a physical level, it goes much deeper than that, and it fucking terrifies me.

I've never really dated or had an official girlfriend. I don't know how to do *this*, and I don't know how to tell her fuck this fake-relationship, I want it to be real, because something tells me she won't be as keen on the idea as I am.

And rejection?

That's not something I'm used to at all.

So, for now, I have to hold my tongue. I can't risk sending her running for the hills. Not when I do still need her to uphold her end of the bargain when it comes to my parents.

"Ugh, this music is awful," she remarks, wrinkling her nose at the dub-step. "Who listens to this shit?"

"Frat boys," I reply, gripping her hand tightly as bodies press against us. "Smithy!" I call out to one of the frat guys I know, and he pulls me into a one-armed hug. "What's up?"

"Nothing much, man. Nothing much. I've got your zombie shit in the basement fridge. I put a Post-It on it for no one to take it, but you know how it is, so no promises it's still there." His gaze moves over to Vanessa at my side, looking her up and down with a gleam in his eyes I don't like. "Who's this fine lady?" He licks his lips like she's some juicy morsel I've brought forth in offering.

"This is my girl, Vanessa." My tone is possessive, and I don't care in the least. Smithy and I have shared a few classes, that's how we've gotten to know each other, but he's not a good enough friend for me to think twice before decking him in the face if he keeps leering at Vanessa.

"Your girl, huh?" He eyes her, ignoring me.

"Yeah, my girl. So stop looking at her like that."

He chuckles, finally looking at me. "You're a possessive bastard, aren't you? Maybe when she's done with you, she'd like to get to know me."

"Smithy," I warn.

"I can speak for myself, thank you very much." Vanessa lets go of my hand, shoving her body in front of mine so she can stare down Smithy. "Bold of you to assume I'd be interested."

Smithy throws his head back and laughs, then wags a finger at me. "I like her."

He picks up his beer and disappears into the crowd.

I pull Vanessa back by her hips and turn her around. "It's hot when you get all bossy."

She rolls her eyes. "You're such a raging horndog you probably get hot and bothered watching a worm wiggle."

I snort, pressing my lips together so I don't dissolve into full-blown hysterics. "A worm?"

"It was the first thing that popped into my brain. It's weird in there sometimes."

"Seems like it."

"Are your friends here?"

"Some of the team will be, but Mascen is probably celebrating with Rory and Cole doesn't really like parties, so I'm sure he's home with Zoey."

Wow, my best friends are really wifed up—well, basically—and that's ... weird. Don't get me wrong, I'm happy for them, but it sucks being the odd man out. I look over at Vanessa, and think to myself *at least I have her*, but I don't. Not really. Not in the way I want.

"Shouldn't we go to the basement so you can get your weird zombie beer?"

"Don't diss my Zombie Dust, woman."

I reach for her hand, and she slides hers into mine, giving me a shy smile.

We push our way through the throng of bodies. It's got to be a fire hazard with how many people are crammed into the house, but campus always overlooks these parties. I guess they figure that college kids will be college kids and let the cops deal with us if it gets that out of hand.

Down in the basement, it's less crowded, and I feel Vanessa relax a tiny amount.

"Want to play some pool?" I ask her, pausing at the fridge to dig out a beer. Blessedly, they're still there untouched.

When I look over my shoulder at her she's grinning. "Only if you want me to smoke your ass."

I grin back, letting go of her hand so I can pop the cap. "I do love a challenge."

"Oh, I know," she laughs.

Over at the pool table I greet the guys there, William, a frat brother of Smithy's, De'Andre a beefy football player, and Daire one of my good buddies who's a hockey player.

"Hey, guys." I greet all of them with a hand smack. "Mind if we join? My girl here says she can kick my ass."

The guys chuckle in amusement, Daire the first one to

speak. "Absolutely, this I've got to see." He passes his pool cue to Van. "You guys go on and do a one-on-one. We'll observe."

If Vanessa is bothered by the idea of the three of them watching, she doesn't show it.

Vanessa bites her lip, trying to tame her smile. "You're going down, pretty boy."

"OH! SHE SMOKED YOU AGAIN!" Jude chortles, smacking me on my shoulder.

Him and some other guys showed up during our first game and have been hanging around ever since, watching me get my ass handed to me.

I don't mind, because it means I get to check out Vanessa's exquisite ass any time she bends over the pool table.

"Yeah, yeah, yeah," I chant, lining up my next shot.

The ball should go right in the pockets, it's perfectly set up, but just as I'm about to hit the ball, Vanessa laughs at something one of the guys says and I'm distracted, completely missing it.

Her laugh deepens when she sees I flubbed again. "Looks like I need to give you some lessons."

"Where *did* you learn to play so well?"

She bites her lip, wiggling her ass as she bends over the table. The worst part is I know she's not doing it on purpose to entice me, but it doesn't mean it isn't working.

"Would you believe me if I told you there was a club at

my high school? After..." She cuts herself off, but gives me a look and I know exactly what she was about to say. "I needed a distraction and the guys in the club were funny and never judged me. I still talk to a few of them even now."

And now I'm fucking jealous over dudes I don't even know the name of.

Cole told me once that when I fell, I'd fall hard and fast for a girl. I laughed in his face, but the joke is on me.

"Any of them attend school here?" I ask casually, and Jude shakes his head knowing there's nothing innocent about my question.

"No." She hits the ball, and it smacks another one, the two of them shooting in opposite directions and somehow both ending up in the pockets.

Cheers ring out among the guys gathered around. The girls sneer, irritated by the lack of attention for themselves.

Vanessa smirks at me. "Tired of having your ass whooped, pretty boy?"

I smirk, rubbing a hand over my jaw. "You think I'm pretty?"

She rolls her eyes, lining up her next shot and calls the net.

I'm not surprised when she beats me again easily.

"My turn," Jude declares, stepping around me.

"That's *my girl*," I warn, my voice dropping.

He looks over his shoulder at me with a curious smile. "Dude, chill. It's only pool."

Except this is Jude, and he fucks practically anything

that moves. He might be one of my closest friends after Mascen and Cole, but that doesn't mean I won't whoop his ass if he looks at Vanessa the wrong way.

"Jealousy is cute on you, sweetie." She pats my stubbled jaw as she passes by me. I sigh. There's no winning with this girl. "You can be my cheerleader."

"Sure, where are my pom poms?"

"I don't have any pom poms," Daire pipes up, his eyes glazed from whatever is in his solo cup, "but I have this." The idiot pulls a tissue out of his pocket.

"Ew, dude. I don't want to wave around your used tissue. That shit is nasty."

"Wave your dick around!" Someone else yells out from the crowd, a couple of girls chime in with agreement.

Vanessa suppresses her laughter but points at me in warning. "Don't even think about shaking your dick in my face."

I wet my lips with my tongue. "Babe, that's not what you were saying the other night."

She turns red as the crowd rings out in a chorus of *ohs*. "Get me a drink," she demands.

"Yes, milady." I bow deeply.

Melting into the crowd, I make my way over to the fridge, grabbing a fresh beer for myself and one for Van.

Getting back through the group takes a ridiculous amount of the time, since no one wants to give up precious space. Eventually I manage and approach the table to find Vanessa already beating Jude's ass, which makes me feel infinitely better—not that I care about losing to a girl, I don't, but what I don't want is to deal with Jude's ribbing if he wins.

Passing Vanessa the beer, she gives me a grateful smile and takes a sip before lining up for her next play.

Fuck, I love watching the way she concentrates. She's taking this seriously, but then so is Jude. They're game takes longer than the ones between Vanessa and me— probably because I kept fucking up checking out Vanessa's ass every five seconds, not to mention her tits.

Her game with Jude wraps up, with her winning, and everyone groans when I announce we're leaving. More than one person—all guys—stop Vanessa on her way out, making her promise to play them next time. I growl in annoyance. I can't help that I'm a jealous fucker.

I keep my hand on hers all the way to my car, opening the passenger door so she can get in.

Once I'm behind the wheel she turns to me with a smile. "That was actually fun."

"I'm glad you enjoyed yourself." And I mean it. I don't like the fact that most of the things I take Vanessa to are things she hates. I want her to *want* to do things with me. I'm treading in dangerous territory, I know.

As she's buckling her seatbelt, she asks, "Do you mind stopping and getting something to eat? I'm starving."

"Me too," I admit, maneuvering around the badly parked vehicles. "What do you have in mind?"

"Anything but The Burger Palace," she pleads.

I chuckle. "I've got an idea."

"MMM, PANCAKES," she hums as the plate is set before her in the twenty-four-hour diner.

"I've never seen someone so excited about pancakes before," I quip, nodding my head in thanks at the waitress when she sets my plate of eggs and sausage in front of me, along with a strawberry milkshake.

She stares at me, dumbfounded. "Pancakes are the superior breakfast food and one should always be excited when basking in their presence." I shake my head at her, fighting a smile. She pulls her dark hair back and off her neck, securing it with an elastic band. "God, all this hair makes me so hot. I keep thinking about cutting it to my shoulders, but then never do."

"Don't cut it," I blurt, practically begging.

She looks at me wide-eyed. "Why the hell not?"

I shrug innocently. "You're beautiful either way, but I love your hair."

She points her fork at me, a piece of pancake speared on the end. "Why should I do what you say?"

I smirk at her, leaning across the table. "Just admit you like arguing with me. Is this your version of foreplay? Please, tell me you're getting wet right now."

Her mouth falls open, and she flings the piece of pancake off her fork so it pelts me in the forehead. "I can't take you anywhere," she admonishes. "Stop making every-thing sexual."

I pick the food off my face and put it on the table. "I can't help it when you like fighting with me, and your cheeks get all flushed, and you look hot and bothered."

Pressing her lips together, she stares down at her plate

for a moment and then says, "I won't be cutting my hair. But not because of what you said. I like my hair, and I know I'd regret all my life choices if I cut it all off."

"You're kind of dramatic. Has anyone ever told you that?"

"Me?" She blinks at me like I've caught her off guard. "What about you?"

"I *know* I'm dramatic," I admit. "But don't tell anyone else I said that."

She digs into her food, ignoring me for the moment.

I do the same, hungrier than I realized. I didn't eat anything except a protein bar after the game and before the party.

"What's your plan after graduation?," I fucking hate silence. Sure, with Vanessa it's surprisingly comfortable, but I'd still rather be talking. Silence lets my mind wander too much, where I dwell on things better left forgotten.

She sips on her milkshake—chocolate—humming at the flavor. "Ideally, I'd love to move to New York City and get a job at a PR firm. More than likely, I'll have to intern somewhere back home, which isn't ideal, but you do what you have to do. What about you? Where do you want to go?"

"I'm not sure." Pushing the eggs around my plate, I think about what I say next. "Once I come into my inheritance, I can go wherever I want. Do whatever I want. I could even give myself time before I figure things out. I know I want to start my own business, but that's as far as I've gotten."

"You should do something with baking." The response rolls off her tongue without a second thought.

"Like what?"

"I don't know." She wipes her mouth with a paper napkin, crumbling it up when she's done and setting it by her plate. "What about a food truck? Those are popular."

I don't know why, but I laugh at the idea of me driving around a food truck selling baked goods, but then I sober because it's not a bad idea. Not at all. "Hmm, you have a point."

"I do?" She sounds surprised that I agree. I guess I can't blame her since I did laugh at first.

"I enjoy baking and being around people. A food truck could be fun. Not that it would be easy, but I think I'd like it."

She bites her lip, her blue eyes serious when they meet mine. "Whatever you do, you should love it, Teddy. You deserve to be happy just as much as anyone else."

TWENTY

Vanessa

I'M ALREADY RUNNING LATE FOR CLASS, BUT THAT doesn't stop me from stopping at the coffee shop for a much-needed caffeine fix. Luckily, Professor Franklin doesn't pay attention to anything that isn't right in front of his face, so chances are I can slip in unnoticed.

Yanking open the door, I suppress my urge to groan out loud at the sight of the long line.

If I was smart, I would turn around and leave.

But, coffee.

While standing in line, I dig my wallet out of my backpack, so I don't have to do it when I get to the register. After placing my order, I step to the side, leaning against the exposed brick wall out of the way of other people. People never used to notice me, but now I feel the stares and wish I could sink into the wall and disappear.

"He's going to get tired of you, you know?"

I'm not paying attention, and it doesn't click in my brain right away that the words are meant for me.

"I'm talking to you," the voice snaps, closer to me than before, and this time I do pay attention.

A petite blonde, her hair slicked back in a ponytail, with pert breasts highlighted by her tight top glares at me like I kicked her puppy. Which I would never. Puppies are precious.

"Um ... can I help you?"

She rolls her eyes, letting out a haughty sigh. "You're dating Teddy, I was just saying he's going to get tired of you. You're not his type."

I snort at her declaration. Sure, her rude words sting, but I won't let it get to me. "Yeah, that's why he's dating me and not you."

Her full lips part in indignation. Her wrist flicks and I don't have time to move before her iced coffee is sailing out of the cup and all over me.

The cold stings my skin, ice and coffee dripping off my body.

"Bitch," she hisses—but from where I'm standing, I'm not the one spewing hate or throwing drinks at people, so she seriously needs to redefine her definition of the word.

"What the fuck?" I recognize the voice and the girl in front of me pales, not bothering to stick around. "Shit. Are you okay?" A big hand loops around my wrist and turns me around, taking in the coffee staining my sweater.

"I'm fine," I grit my teeth, holding back tears of embarrassment.

"What was that about?" Jude looks around for the girl who's already fled out the door.

"She was trying to stake her territory." I pick a piece

of ice off my sweater and drop it on the floor. "I'm so sorry about this," I apologize to the worker who comes over to clean up the mess.

"Wasn't your fault." She flashes a tired smile, blushing when she notices Jude.

My name is called out for my order and he points. "Yours?" I nod and he goes and grabs it. With my coffee in his hand, he takes my elbow and leads me outside.

"Where are we going?" My tone is a rough demand as the beefy football player pulls me along.

"I'm not letting you walk around campus in a coffee-soaked shirt. That's not cool."

I don't point out that I could always go back to my dorm and change, because it's all the way on the other side of campus and I hadn't planned on it anyway. I'm already late so I would've toughed it out in my wet shirt.

He opens the door to a building and sets my coffee and his backpack on the floor, rummaging inside. He produces an Aldridge U football sweatshirt and passes it to me.

"Thank you." I take it gratefully. We're in a low traffic area, where not a single soul has passed us yet, so I turn my back to him and slip out of the sweater and pull his sweatshirt over me. It smells like his cologne and is super soft like he's washed it a million times. Balling up my shirt I stuff it in my bag. Facing him, I lift my chin. "Could we maybe keep this between us?"

He stares at me like I've grown another head. "You don't want Teddy to know?" I bite my lip, shaking my head wordlessly. "Why the hell not?"

I look away, down the brightly lit hall fighting the stinging in my eyes. "Because it's just not that important."

"Vanessa—"

"Thank you, again," I hurry to say, "but I'm going to be late to class."

He calls after me, but it's too late. I'm already out the door.

I don't go to class.

TWENTY-ONE

Teddy

WALKING INTO THE OFF-CAMPUS BAR, IT'S SURPRISINGLY subdued for a Wednesday evening. Occasionally the guys and I frequent the out of the way bar, so we can catch up and shoot the shit without everyone breathing down our necks at Harvey's.

Mascen, Cole, Cree, and Jude are already seated at the bar, and I walk over to join them.

"Hey." Sliding out the stool, I sit down, my body nearly folding in on itself. I'm fucking exhausted after a simple phone call from my dad—I say simple, because it was his typical B.S. and nothing out of the ordinary. "Thanks for this."

There's already a Zombie Dust waiting for me, and I take a couple of gulps letting the alcohol hit my system.

"Saw your girl today," Jude starts, and I look over at my friend questioning the tone in his voice. "Some girl threw coffee at her."

"What?" I instantly bristle, ready to go on the defensive.

He sips at a Fat Tire, then rubs his lips together. "She didn't want me to tell you."

"Why the hell not?" I demand, ready to get the fuck out of there and find her.

Fuck, I wish I'd known. I would've been there in a heartbeat. Vanessa doesn't deserve to have to deal with this shit because of me.

"Maybe it has something to do with her not being your real girlfriend."

My mouth falls open and I struggle to find words. Jude sounds pissed, which he has every right to be since I've been lying, but I'm angry too.

"You told them?" I swing a hand at Cole.

"We're your friends." Mascen glares at me. "You've been running with me practically every morning and haven't said one fucking word about this scam you're living."

I slam a hand down on the shiny wood countertop. The bartender glances over in concern and goes back to polishing a glass.

"Did you also tell them that I want my fake-girlfriend to be my real-girlfriend?" I'm ready to jump across the guys to punch Cole on the end.

"No." Cole grins proudly. "I knew they wouldn't believe me. They had to hear it from you."

Beside me, some of the fight goes out of Jude. "You really like her?"

"I do." My voice is steady, sure.

"Good. She's a great girl."

I narrow my eyes on him. "You're not interested in my girl, are you?"

He chuckles. "Come on, Teddy. You know I'm not ready to be shackled." He angles his stool closer in my direction. "I am curious, what were you guys doing in your room that night? Did you actually have sex because it sure as hell sounded like it."

"No." And if he thinks I'm going to give any more detail than that, he's wrong.

"You're awfully quiet." My words are directed at Cree who hasn't said one word since I showed up.

"I'm just here for the free beer. Mascen said you were paying." I growl at that, giving Mascen the finger. "Seriously, dude, I can't believe you felt you had to get a fake-girlfriend to deal with your dad *and* lie to us about it. We would've never judged you for it, as long as you didn't use her." He narrows his eyes on me, his normally easy-going smile dropping. Cree has a younger sister and a protective streak a mile long because of it.

"I would never use Vanessa." The thought alone makes me sick.

Something in my voice must convince him, because he nods, "Good," and turns his attention back to his beer.

"Why did you think you couldn't tell us this was fake?" Mascen's the one that voices the question, but with the way all the guys turn to me I know they want the answer too.

Sipping my beer, I weigh my words before I speak. "Because that requires telling the whole truth."

Jude gives me a funny look, brows furrowed. "What the fuck does that mean?"

I rub my jaw, not sure where to even begin.

I guess the best place is to start at the beginning, so that's what I do.

―――――――――

BY THE TIME I finish telling my friends all about my father and the abuse, they all look horrified. Which is a reasonable reaction, but it's part of the reason I've always kept my mouth shut—to avoid those looks, the pity.

"Listen, don't say anything, okay?" I practically beg, feeling like a pathetic fuck. "It's just ... part of my life. One, I want to put permanently in my past after graduation like so many other things." I'm rambling now, but I don't care.

"Fuck, man." Jude claps me on the shoulder. "You don't think we'd judge you for something like this, do you?"

I wrap my hands around my beer, staring at the bottle instead of my friends. "Look," I begin, clearing my throat, "I know I haven't always been the best guy or made the best choices—"

"Whoa, whoa. I'm going to stop you right there." This time it's Cree who pipes in. "So what if you've had a little too much fun at times? That doesn't justify *anything* your father has ever done to you." I peel at the label on the bottle. "You know that, right?"

Fuck. I feel the telltale burning of tears behind my eyes. "I don't know what I know anymore," I admit, wetting my lips with my tongue. "I do know my father's a royal prick, and I also know I care about Vanessa."

"So, what are you going to do about it?" There's a challenge in Mascen's eyes.

"Yeah," Cole begins, "I've never known you to be one to sit back. You always take what you want."

The problem is I can't *take* Vanessa. I have to show her I'm serious, that I want her, that I care.

Standing, I slap a hundred-dollar bill on the table. It's more than enough to cover this first round. If they want more, it's on them.

"I have to prove it to her." Pointing at each of them, I warn, "Don't let her know that you guys know. I don't want her to feel embarrassed or some shit."

I don't wait for their reply, I'm already headed out.

———————

DANIKA OPENS the door giving me a disgusted look. I have no idea what's crawled up her ass or why she seems to despise me.

"I assume you're the reason she's been crying off and on tonight."

It's not a question, but I treat it as one anyway. "No, but I know why."

I bristle just thinking about what Jude told me. Vanessa is too good, too kind, to deal with petty ass bullshit from girls who think they're better than her when in reality they're nowhere close to the kind of woman she is.

Danika sucks her cheeks in and seems to be debating about whether or not to let me inside.

"This wasn't my fault," I promise her.

She steps back. "Don't make me regret this." Her eyes glint with warning, and I have the feeling she's the kind of girl who would know how to get rid of my body and not leave a trace behind.

I don't give her a response, instead heading right back to Vanessa's room and opening the door. It's dim inside except for those twinkle Christmas lights hung behind her bed. Her record player is going in the corner of the room, playing a Taylor Swift album.

"Van?" I tiptoe into her room, closing the door behind me. "Why didn't you call me?"

"Because," she sniffles, only the top of her dark head visible beneath the mountain of blankets, "it's not your problem, and I'm stupid for being upset about it."

I crouch down at the head of her bed, gently peeling back the layers of covers until her pretty blue eyes and pert nose become visible. "If something upsets you, your feelings are valid. Don't negate them by using words like stupid."

She gives a soft sniffle. "I don't like letting other people's opinions affect how I feel about myself, but ... I got embarrassed. I ... assume Jude told you everything?"

"Most of it."

236

"It was in front of the entire coffee shop." Her lower lip trembles, and I'm torn between wanting to kiss her and my desire to hunt down the girl that hurt her. "In the moment, I didn't even think about what had happened. I was so shocked. But after, when Jude took me away and gave me his sweatshirt, that's when it set in, and I just ... I'm not used to this attention." She wipes away a tear, her face still mostly covered by the blankets. "People staring, muttering, making up stories about me—hating me on the grounds that I'm with you, and it's not fair, and I'm just ... tired." She finishes her speech with a sigh.

My cheeks hollow when I suck them in, realizing I have no words to make this better. I can't wave a magic wand and have it all go away. The people on campus are still going to do and say what they want.

"Scoot over." I kick my boots off, lifting my shirt over my head.

"What?"

"I'm comforting my girl." My fingers go to my belt buckle and she shrieks.

"By getting *naked*?"

I chuckle. "Do you *want* me naked? Because I'm more than happy to accommodate you by also removing my boxers."

"No, no!" she cries, the covers stirring. "Leave them on."

"Ah, yes, wouldn't want to scare you with my monster truck of a penis."

"I said Volkswagen Beetle," she harrumphs.

I tug off my jeans, leaving them in a pile on the floor.

"That's what your mouth said, but your eyes said something else." She opens her mouth argue, but I don't give her a chance to voice it. "I'm not here to talk about my penis, as nice looking as he is. I'm here for you."

I climb over her body and tug some of the covers away so I can join her beneath them.

"What. Are. You. Doing." She tries to hold onto the blankets.

"Getting cozy. I want blankets too. You can't have them all."

"You are so annoying—"

"Annoyingly awesome? I know, right?"

"Ugh!"

I finally manage to make it beneath the blankets and tentatively reach for her body. If she doesn't want me to hold her, I won't push it, but man I'll feel better if she'll let me. When she's in my arms I know she's safe and cared for.

Thankfully, she wiggles her body against mine and allows me to fold myself around her. I sigh in relief when I'm fully spooning her, my breath pulses against her neck, and she gives a small giggle. It's good to hear.

"You didn't have to come here." She curls her neck against my bicep so she can look behind her at me.

"I know I didn't. I wanted to."

She exhales a shaky breath, rolling over fully to face me. Her fingers tentatively rub my jaw, tracing over the stubble there.

"You're nothing like I thought you were." Her voice is

a soft murmur, and her words ... they mean more than she'll ever comprehend.

"I'm nothing like I thought I was either."

She reaches out, and I hold my breath, afraid any movement might spook her. With her index finger she touches my lips, tracing over the shape of them.

"You being here shouldn't make me feel better, but it does."

She looks impossibly vulnerable with the admission and my heart tugs.

"I'm glad I'm here, baby." I kiss the top of her head.

"Can we put on *Beverly Hills, 90210*?"

I chuckle, rubbing my fingers over the soft skin of her shoulder. Everything about her is soft to my hard. If she was anyone else, I'd put the moves on her right now, shoot my best shot, but she's not just anyone; she's *the one*. She's special, and that means I have to be patient. Even if my dick is aching to be inside her.

"Anything you want." I'd agree to just about anything to cheer her up. "Want me to order food?"

"No, that's okay." She sits up and grabs her remote, turning the TV on. Looking back at me, her blue eyes shine brightly with something I can't decipher. She doesn't speak right away, but when she does her words pierce my heart.

"I'm sorry your father doesn't see what a wonderful, smart, kind human being you are. But I do."

I don't say it out loud, but her opinion of me is all that matters.

TWENTY-TWO

Vanessa

THE DOOR TO TEDDY'S DORM SLAMS OPEN AND JUDE stomps in carrying with him the scent of stale beer, cigarettes, and sex. Collectively, Teddy and I look over at the football player as he shuts the door, kicks off his boots, and promptly takes his shirt off, revealing a scratched up back and hickeys covering various spots on his torso.

He looks over, wide-eyed, as if only seeming to realize the room isn't empty.

"Busy night?" Teddy quips, arching his brow in a look that looks all too much like a father scolding his unruly child.

"Something like that." He reaches for his belt. "Hey, Vanessa."

"Dude, don't start stripping here." Teddy slams a hand over my eyes.

I giggle, trying to pry his hand away. "Wait, I want to see the show!"

Both guys laugh and Teddy drops his hand.

Unfortunately, Jude is still wearing pants. He walks over to us, placing his hands on the back of the couch, glaring at the TV. "You guys have been watching it without me." The accusation rings in his voice.

"Sorry, dude." Teddy doesn't sound sorry at all.

"I'm going to shower, and then I'm watching too."

"Maybe we don't want you to," I quip.

Jude chuckles. "Of course, you want me to. I'm way more fun than this pathetic ass." He claps Teddy on the shoulder, heading to the bathroom.

"You better shower. You smell like a fucking brothel." Teddy plugs his nose.

Jude flips him the bird, shutting the door behind him.

"You want another drink?" Teddy hops up from the couch, picking up trash that's piled on the table.

"Sure." I pass him my empty can of Coke.

With the show paused for the moment, I stand up and stretch my legs. I figured with it being Friday night, Teddy would want to make an appearance at a party or Harvey's, but he said he was worn out from school and practice all week and just wanted to chill for the evening and asked if I wanted to hang out and continue with our watch of *Beverly Hills, 90210*. He won't admit it, but he's obsessed.

When I turn around to face the kitchen area, Teddy is

standing there with orange juice and another can of soda for me.

"You're beautiful."

"Huh?" His statement catches me off guard, seeming so out of the blue.

"You're beautiful," he repeats, like he feels it needs to be said again.

I look down at my worn sweatpants and oversized t-shirt with a Georgia peach on the breast pocket. My hair is up in a messy bun, there's not a lick of makeup on my face. I am the poster girl of IDGAF.

"Seriously?" I'm completely stupefied. Teddy sets down the drinks on the counter. His eyes flare as he crosses the short distance between us. "Teddy?"

He cups my face in his hands and kisses me. I'm surprised at first, not having expected it.

I'm even more shocked by the fact that we've shared more intimate, *real* kisses than ones put on for show.

Hands still tenderly cupping my face, he glides his lips over to my ear sending a shiver down my spine in the process. "When will you realize that you are the most captivating woman I've ever laid eyes on?"

I swallow, a lump suddenly blocking my throat. "You can't say things like that."

"Why the hell not?" He's not angry, instead amused.

"Because we're not a couple."

He presses a kiss to the shell of my ear. "I want us to be."

I stiffen in his arms. "That's not what this is."

His eyes narrow. "But it could be."

"But it's not." I step back, putting some distance between us. I can't think clearly when he's *right there*. I wrap my arms around myself like some sort of mockery of a security blanket. "I know what this is and what's it's not —and it's *not* a relationship, Teddy. It's a transaction. You paid for my school and now I'm doing you a favor. That's it." Hurt flashes in his eyes, and my stomach rolls. I don't mean to hurt him, but it's the truth. Yes, I'm attracted to him, way more than I'd like to be, but we wouldn't be *anything* if I wasn't here to play a part, so that's what I'm going to do. He only wants me because I'm around all the time—so that's what I tell him. "You wouldn't be interested in me if I wasn't here. I'm accessible. Easy."

His nostrils flare. "That's what you think? Jesus, Van. It's like you don't know me at all." He runs his fingers angrily through his hair, mussing it. "Yes, I never noticed you before, and I'm sorry for that. I had a stick up my ass, and I was shitting my life away being a goddamn playboy for no good reason other than that's all I thought I was worth. I realize now I'm more than that, fuck *you've* helped me realize that."

"I don't know where the lines got blurred between us, but they have been for a while, and I think it's time that I remind us both of them before I get hurt."

He laughs incredulously. "Before *you* get hurt?" He waves a hand between us. "Right now, it looks like *I'm* the one being hurt."

I shake my head. "Like I said, we both know you wouldn't be interested in me like this if I wasn't here. It's just a fact. We run in different circles and are from two very different backgrounds. Our lives should've never intersected. It was pure happenstance that it did."

His jaw ticks, but he doesn't get a chance to say anything because the bathroom door opens and Jude steps out, freshly showered and wearing a pair of low hanging basketball shorts.

"Oh, good, you paused it." He walks past me, giving me a chin dip in greeting. "I want popcorn, what about you guys?" He shuffles past Teddy, rummaging through a cabinet. Turning back with a box in hand, he gives us a funny look. "Were you guys fighting?"

"No!" We shout simultaneously.

Teddy picks up the drinks and passes me the Coke.

Taking a steadying breath, I paste my game face on and take my place on the couch beside him.

A few minutes later Jude joins us, sitting on the floor with his back against the couch. The show is back on, but I can't pay attention—not when Teddy's body is coiled with tension beside me.

My words hurt him, but I didn't mean to. Sometimes I need to learn to keep my big fat mouth closed.

Tentatively, I reach out with my pinky gently touching the tip against the side of his own finger. He doesn't react at first, but then he loops our fingers together and I breathe a sigh of relief and allow my body to relax.

At some point I must drift off to sleep, because I'm only half-aware when I hear Teddy murmur, "No, I've got her." He picks me up from the couch, and I must mumble something about being too heavy because his lips brush my cheek. "No, you're not. You're perfect."

A moment later he places me on his bed and tugs the covers up to my chin. They smell of his woodsy scent, and I inhale it like an addict. Fuck, what's wrong with me.

He pulls away, and I reach out lightning fast, grabbing his wrist. His skin is warm, the hair scattered across his arm rough against my palm.

"I didn't mean to hurt you." I don't know what's made my tongue so loose, like I downed a truth serum, but there's been no alcohol involved. He crouches down in front of me, so we're eye level, extracting his wrist from my hold. He glides the tips of his fingers over the curve of my cheek.

"I'm a big boy, Van." His eyes dart to my lips and then away. "My feelings may be hurt, but I'll get over it."

"We're not right for each other. You see that too ... don't you?"

He stands up, gazing down at me with an intensity that sends a shiver down my spine.

"No," he says simply and walks out his bedroom door.

TWENTY-THREE

Teddy

I DIDN'T THROW UP AT ANY POINT DURING MY RUN WITH
Mascen this morning, which I take as a win—even if it
still feels like my lungs are on fire with every breath I
take.

He didn't push me to talk either, which I appreciated.
That's the great thing about Mascen. Dude hates talking,
so even when he knows you've got a lot on your mind, he
doesn't push you to speak.

After the run, I went back to my dorm to get ready for
this evening—aka another torturous dinner with my
parents.

"You're looking snazzy." Jude looks up from his phone
when I exit my room.

"Only the best for the 'rents," I mutter, making sure my belt is centered and my tie is knotted perfectly.

"Fuck, I'm glad my family isn't like that."

Jude comes from a wealthy family too, but from the way they act, you wouldn't know it. His mom is the CEO of a major retail company, while his dad stayed home with him and his brother and sister growing up. Any time I've met them, they're dressed normally—not the constant black-tie affair my parents aim for—and incredibly kind, not full of themselves at all.

"Maybe they can adopt me," I remark, grabbing an orange juice bottle from the fridge. "Are your parents looking to add an almost twenty-two-year-old to their family?"

"I'll inquire on your behalf," he quips, kicking his feet up on the coffee table. "Speaking of," he cranes his neck so he can see me, "what are we doing for your birthday?"

"Nothing," I growl quickly and forcefully, hoping to shut down future inquiries with the one word.

"Ah, come on," he cajoles, swinging an arm out, "we have to do something."

"No, we don't."

Last year, I woke up wreaking of alcohol with some other unknown substance coursing through my veins and two naked chicks in a hotel bed.

"Come on, dude. You only turn twenty-two once." He starts humming the Taylor Swift song. "I'm sure Cree won't mind if we have it at his place."

"I'd rather hang out with Vanessa."

And I would. Despite the fact she continues to remind

me we're not actually together, she's quickly become one of my favorite people. A night in binge watching her favorite show and eating some pizza or whatever sounds way more enjoyable than a party.

What the fuck is happening? Who am I?

I think I might need a lobotomy because clearly, I've lost my sanity.

"Bring Vanessa," he reasons easily.

"I don't want a party." I comb my fingers through my hair, ignoring the pit in my stomach that forms every time I have to engage with my parents.

"What if we go away for a weekend," he continues, undeterred. "A bunch of us guys and girls. It could be fun."

"Maybe." I scrub my hand down my face. "I have to go."

"Great, I'll find a place and get it booked."

"That's not what I—"

"La, la, la," the douche ignores me.

I don't have time to argue with him, though. I'm already running late.

By the time my Porsche screeches to a stop in front of Vanessa's dorm, she's already stubbornly waiting outside —to prevent me from coming up to get her—looking hot as fuck in a blue wrap dress that comes down to her knees, with long sleeves. It's not scandalous in any way, but blood rushes to my dick despite that fact, because this girl turns me on like no other.

I take a deep breath, thinking about baby turtles and

other random shit that doesn't involve peeling that dress off of her, and hop out to open the door for her.

"I can get the door," she protests, her dark hair curling around her breasts.

I lean in, the scent of her perfume. "Citrus and flowers," I murmur.

"Huh?"

"Nothing," I mutter, embarrassed I said that out loud. "And we've been over this, Van. I know you're capable of getting your own door, but *I* want to, because it makes me feel good to serve you."

She gives a soft laugh, pausing before she gets in the car. "Serve me, huh?"

She has no idea how much I'd love to serve and worship her. "Y-Yeah," I clear my throat.

Saying no more, she sits down, and I close the door.

Taking a deep breath, I straighten my tie. It's going to be a long ass night.

———————

"You're awfully quiet this evening, son." My father cuts into his steak, bringing the rare bite to his lips. He pauses there, arching a brow as he waits for me to comment.

"A lot on my mind," I say in a clear tone, despite the fact I want nothing more than to grumble at him.

There's a twitch at the corner of his mouth, that tiny piece of steak hovering inches away from his thin lips. "You're not failing, are you?"

It takes everything in me not to roll my eyes and snap at him. "No."

He finally sticks the bite in his mouth. Chews. Slowly. Drawing it out. His eyes slide to Vanessa, sizing her up. "She's not pregnant, is she?"

She stiffens beside me, shoulders straight. "*She* is sitting right here," Vanessa speaks before I can, "and no, I'm not pregnant. I'm sorry to disappoint you, since I know you're so desperate for grandchildren, and no doubt will be a fluffy bear of a grandfather, but alas, the red river is still running strong and true."

I have to press my lips together to keep from laughing. Even my mom looks like she's struggling not to chuckle. She presses her napkin to her mouth to hide the twitch in her lips.

My father's face turns an unsettling shade of red. "Watch your mouth, girl."

"Why?" She blinks innocently at him, and I fucking love how she doesn't cower to him. She was intimidated initially but not anymore. "What are you going to do about it?"

His eyes bulge, the vein in his forehead near bursting. While a part of me wants nothing more than to laugh, the other part of me prickles in fear.

I wonder what people would think if they knew that I was a grown man and still absolutely terrified of my father.

Before he has a chance to respond there's a crash of thunder so loud it somehow manages to penetrate the thick walls of the mansion. My mom startles, her fork clattering to her plate and the same hand flying up to press against her chest.

"Oh, my—was that thunder? I'd swear rain wasn't in the forecast. Mae!" She calls out for one of the staff who immediately comes scurrying. "Is there a storm?"

"Yes, ma'am. Looks like it won't be stopping until early morning. There are flood warnings."

"Floods?" My mom pales. "Oh, Teddy. Vanessa. You must stay the night. You can't be driving back to campus in this." Both Vanessa and I protest vehemently, neither of us wanting to be stuck here over night, but she won't take no for an answer. "It's not safe. I would never forgive myself if you two were in an accident. Mae will prepare your room for you and don't worry Vanessa, you'll stay with Teddy, I'm not under any illusions that you two are waiting for marriage." She winks at Vanessa who looks like she'd rather die than spend the night in my old room.

"Mom, I'm sure it's really not that bad." Unfortunately for me I've barely finished speaking when there's another loud clap.

Fucking hell.

She purses her lips and dips her chin at the same time, and I know we're not getting out of here tonight.

Across the table my father throws down his napkin, gets up, and leaves the room.

―――――

"I CAN'T BELIEVE THIS." Vanessa crosses her arms, eyes roaming around my room.

"Trust me," I eye the king-size bed, "I'm not happy about it either."

Sharing a bed with Vanessa? That's something I'll never complain about it. But doing it inside my childhood prison? Fuck no.

She frowns, letting her arms drop from beneath her breasts—breasts that I was most definitely *not* checking out. "I'm sorry," she murmurs softly, "I'm sure this is even worse for you."

I shrug, moving toward the bed that's already turned back with pillows fluffed like you'd find in any five-star hotel.

"It is what it is." My tone is lacking any sort of care or enthusiasm. If I didn't know my mom would be hurt if we snuck out and drove home in the storm, I'd do it in a heartbeat. "I'll sleep on the couch." Reaching for the pillow, I go to move it to full size sectional couch in the corner of my room in front of a fireplace with a flat screen TV.

She purses her lips and exhales. "Don't be silly, this bed is massive. Just stay on your side. Besides, what if your mom pokes her head in in the night? Can't have her thinking we're fighting." She rubs her hand over her face, and I notice the dark circles under her eyes. Once more she looks around my room with a frown.

"What is it?" I know something is on her mind.

Biting her lip, she says, "Did they have your room redone when you moved out?"

My brows furrow. "No?" For some odd reason it leaves my mouth like a question.

"It's always looked like this?"

"I mean..." I pause, looking around and trying to see what she sees. 'Crème' walls as my mother called the color, dark wide plank hardwood floors layered with more 'crème' rugs, large windows with thick curtains so no light is let in come morning, paintings of fields and flowers and other random shit I don't give a fuck about, and furniture all in varying shades of that blasted 'crème' color again, the only spot of color—if it can be called that—is the pale blue bed coverings. It's a feminine room, that's for damn sure, but it's not like my say ever really mattered since my time here was always limited. "Yeah," I finish.

Sadness clouds her face. "There's nothing *you* here."

"Nope," I agree, no sense in arguing with her since it's pretty fucking obvious. "This isn't my home, Van. It never has been and never will be."

My grandparents' manor was far more of a home than this one ever was. My grandpa, though a serious business-man, was always kind to me and made me feel special. It often made me wonder how my father was his son, because the two seemed so vastly different.

I startle when her cool fingers touch my stubbled cheek. "You deserve more than this." I know she's talking about more than the room. "You matter, Teddy. You're important."

I bite my tongue so I don't tell her that if that was true, she wouldn't already be trying to erase me from her life before our agreement is even up.

"Go ahead and shower." I nod to the bathroom. "I'll grab you some clothes to sleep in."

"Are you sure?"

I nod, already walking away from her. I need space, not from her, just from this place, but I'm fucking stuck so pacing will have to do.

The bathroom door clicks shut softly behind her, and I let out a world weary sigh. I fucking hate being in this house. Dinners are bad enough, but an entire night?

Searching through my drawers, I find most empty which isn't much of a shocker, but eventually I manage to scrounge up an old shirt from my prep school that'll work as a sleep shirt for Vanessa and a pair of sweatpants for me.

I knock and open the bathroom door to set the shirt on the counter and nearly lose my shit on the spot. The glass shower enclosure is fogged up, I can't see anything but her silhouette, but that doesn't mean anything to my dick which is suddenly so hard I don't think there's any blood left anywhere else in my body.

I should turn around promptly and leave, but I've never been too smart when it comes to these kinds of decisions.

She tilts her head back beneath the spray of water, and I'm forced to bite back a groan. I palm myself over my pants, tilting my head back. My body feels hot and achy, my clothes too tight.

Fuck, fuck, *fuck*. I have to get out of here.

I take a step out of the room and ease the door shut behind me. Leaning my back against it I take several breaths to calm the erratic pace of my heart while flooding my mind with thoughts that will get rid of my erection, or at least make it less noticeable until it's my turn to shower and I can take care of business.

Sitting on the side of the bed, I do my best to wait patiently for Vanessa to finish up. The second the door opens, though, I lose all cool and fly past her and slam the door shut behind me.

"Someone's gotta take a shit real bad." I hear her remark through the door.

I'd much rather that be my problem than the fact that if I don't blow a load soon, I'm pretty sure my balls will shrivel up and fall off. That's not something I want to risk.

The bathroom is still steamy from her shower, a small section of condensation on the mirror wiped away. It smells of soap, but obviously it's not Vanessa's normal scent and I instantly dislike it. It's too stuffy smelling. Like champagne and roses and other shit no one actually cares about.

Turning the shower on, I strip down in record speed and step beneath the spray, taking my dick in my hand. I'm aching and harder than I've ever been in my life. I'd like to think all these months of celibacy play into that fact, but I know it'd be a lie. It's Vanessa. She gets me so fucking hard, unlike anyone else.

It doesn't take me long until I'm coming, hand braced against the marble tile to hold me upright. My whole body shudders, and I struggle to remain standing. Once I've caught my breath, I race to wash up and get out, only to realize I've forgotten my sweatpants.

Fucking figures.

I brush my teeth thanks to the other fresh toothbrush laid out wrapped in plastic beside the one Vanessa already opened and used. Once my teeth have been aggressively brushed, I open the bathroom door to find Vanessa already lying in bed on her side, facing away from the bathroom. She sits up at the sound of the door opening and looks relieved to see me which fills my chest with a stupid sort of pride. I feel like a grade school kid when the only thought in my brain is *she likes me.*

"Lose your pants?"

Don't do it, Teddy. Don't do it.

"I know you like seeing me naked." I drop the towel.

Her jaw drops, eyes bulging as she ogles my cock— *Jesus Christ I'm going to be hard all over again*—and slaps a hand over her eyes. "Put that thing away! It's a weapon!"

I laugh, a true deep belly laugh, and grab my sweatpants from where I left them on a chair. Yanking them on I find that they're a tad short—more than a tad actually, but will have to work.

"The weapon has been sheathed."

She hesitantly lets her fingers drop. "What if I whipped my boobs out all willy nilly like you with your actual willie!"

"Then I'd be a happy man," I quip, slipping into bed on the opposite from her.

She lets out a groan and rolls away from me to face the opposite side. "Men."

I chuckle, pushing a button on the remote that brings up a hidden TV in the foot of the bed. Vanessa sits up once more, mouth parted in shock. "There's a TV in your fucking bed?" Before I can respond, she points to the living area of the room. "*And* there? You live in excess."

"I didn't decorate the room." The *obviously* hangs in the air. "But it doesn't mean I won't enjoy the finer things."

Vanessa rubs her lips together, seeming to contemplate something. "Can we watch *Beverly Hills, 90210?*"

"Anything for my girl," I blurt, reddening at how easily I said that. Vanessa, thankfully, ignores me.

I log in and put the show on where we left off, and Vanessa somehow manages to burrow further into the blankets, looking like some sort of little woodland creature in a nest.

"Comfy?"

She gives a small giggle in reply that I take as a yes.

The show starts and we're both silenced, and somehow, despite being locked in my prison once more, I manage to actually fall asleep.

A HEAD IS TUCKED beneath my chin, a thick tuft of curly hair tickling my nose and soft breaths gusting against my neck. It should be the most uncomfortable position, but I find myself not wanting to move and grinning to myself instead. If Vanessa woke up right now and found herself octopused around me, she'd be horrified, but somehow in her sleep, she sought my body out for comfort in the night, and in my unconscious state, I still managed to open my arms to comfort her.

Nuzzling my nose against her freshly washed hair, I

inhale the scent that's not her normal one. I never used to think much about relationships and what came with them, not the easy stuff or the hard stuff, or even the little things in between like cuddling. But with my arms wrapped around Vanessa right now, I find that I like cuddling more than I ever thought I would.

I allow myself a few precious moments longer before I slide out of the bed, careful not to wake her. Taking soft steps across the room, I shut the door behind me quietly and take a piss before I brush my teeth. My clothes from yesterday are where I left them, and I go ahead and change into them, glad to be rid of the too-short sweatpants.

I expect Vanessa to be up when I reenter the room, but she's still snoozing away with her arms now wrapped around my pillow and one leg thrown on top of the covers. I chuckle to myself, amused. I scribble a note, letting her know I'll be back. The last thing I want is her leaving the room without me and getting lost. That's exactly the kind of ammunition my father *doesn't* need.

I allow myself a few more seconds to look at her peaceful sleeping face, pink lips slightly parted with light breaths. She looks so at ease and content.

Forcing myself away, I shut the door behind me and go in search of coffee. At least I don't have to run with Mascen this morning. Thank Lord Disick for that.

Down to the kitchen I go, and my luck must be good because I don't run into either of my parents along the way, and I know neither will be in here. Sometimes I wonder if either of them set foot in a kitchen even when they were children.

"Hey, Constance," I say to one of the cooks. If I had to hazard a guess, I'd say it looks like she's making some sort of scone.

"Mr. Teddy." She smiles big and wide. "Good to see you. I didn't know you were here."

"Liar," I joke, heading to the coffee pot shared by the staff. "You're all a bunch of gossips, and I'm sure these weekly dinners have been a big topic of conversation."

"They have," she chortles, cutting into the dough. Across from her, Roger, another cook, merely shakes his head.

"So, what are you all saying?" I reach for a coffee mug and pour myself a cup, dumping in a mountain of cream and sugar. I need the fucking sweetness today. I fix a cup for Vanessa too, all the while waiting for an answer. Turning to Constance with the mugs in hand, I arch a brow prompting her to finally reply.

She wipes flour covered fingers on a rag and gives me a smile. "The girl ... she is good for you. Just what you need. Your father..." She says no more, we both know she doesn't need to.

"It's good to see you, Constance." I drop a kiss on her cheek before I head for the swinging door.

She laughs behind me. "Ever the charmer, Mr. Teddy."

When I return to the bedroom, Vanessa is beginning to stir. She groans, stretching her arms above her head. "What time is it?"

"Almost eight."

"Ugh." She sits up, rubbing her temples. "I feel like I'm getting a migraine. How the hell do you *wake up* with one of those?"

"Take this, maybe it'll help." I hold out the mug to her —plain white and lacking any sort of personality, of course—and she takes it with a grateful smile.

"Bless you, kind sir." Pushing her unruly hair from her eyes, she stifles a yawn. After a hearty sip of coffee and a moan that goes straight to my groin, she asks, "When can we blow this popsicle stand?"

I sit down on the chair in the corner of the room, putting distance between us before I do something stupid like kiss her.

"After breakfast." I know if we sneak out before then it will lead to an argument I don't want to deal with. "Constance is making scones," I say enticingly when she gives me a sour look.

Stifling another yawn, she says, "I'm not sure I'm ready to face your father after dinner last night."

"I never want to face my father."

Her lips downturn. "You should never have to be in the same room as your abuser. That's not fair."

I take a couple of gulps of coffee before replying. "He's my father. It's not like I have a choice."

She swipes her tongue over her lips, ridding them of a drop of coffee. "That's not fair."

I stand up, heading over to one of the large windows and pushing the button to open the blinds. "I know it isn't, but what am I going to do about it? He's my father." Shoving my fingers through my hair, I swallow the rest of my coffee. "That's why you're helping me, remember? I have to get my inheritance, so I never have to deal with his bullshit ever again."

She clutches the sheets in her empty hand, her knuckles turning white with the force of her grip. I can see the sympathy in her eyes, but I'm thankful that she doesn't voice it. It's not something I want to hear, because *she's* not the one who needs to apologize. Not that I ever expect to hear an *'I'm sorry'* ever leave my father's mouth.

Taking another sip of coffee, she places the mug on the night table and slips from the bed. I try not to ogle her ass in a pair of blue striped panties poking out from beneath my old t-shirt, but it's a colossal failure. By some miracle she doesn't notice my gaze burning a hole into her ass and says she's going to get ready, the door to the bathroom closing behind her.

Downing the rest of my coffee I hope the sugar hits my system fast.

Too short of a time later, Vanessa emerges from the bathroom ready to face the breakfast gauntlet.

She doesn't complain when I take her hand and hold on tightly as we take the main staircase to the downstairs. When we reach the bottom, she gives me a reassuring squeeze and a small smile.

All my stress is for nothing because when we step into the dining room, the only person waiting for us is my mother.

The audible sigh of relief that comes out of my chest is embarrassing, but Vanessa doesn't comment on it.

My mom smiles, her eyes glimmering with absolute

delight at our clasped hands. I lean into Van, placing a kiss on her cheek before I pull out the chair for her to sit down.

"You two look well-rested," my mom comments, setting aside her iPad where she reads the morning paper. "You had a good night, I take it?"

Surprisingly, I did—but I credit sharing a bed with Vanessa to that miracle.

"It was ... fine," I admit reluctantly.

"The bed was very ... comfy." Vanessa follows up behind me.

We exchange a look, both of us fighting laughter at our lack of enthusiasm. My mom doesn't let it deter her.

"Glad to hear it." She claps her hands with a smile. "Now eat up, there's plenty."

I grab the pitcher of freshly squeezed orange juice and pour myself a glass and then one for Vanessa. With the glasses filled, I then pile eggs, bacon, French Toast, scones, and even a waffle onto our plates. Vanessa eyes the absurd amount of food and I shrug in response. "Try a little of everything. Constance is an amazing cook."

She shoots a tiny smile my way, then turns her attention to my mom. "Breakfast looks amazing. Thank you." Her eyes stray to the door, and I know she's looking for the same thing I've been.

"Where's Dad?"

"He left early for the office. There was an emergency."

My shoulders sag with relief. Beneath the table, Vanessa's fingers give my knee a gentle squeeze. I reach for her fingers, but she's pulled her hand back before I can.

We've almost finished eating breakfast, and I'm ready to get the fuck out of here when my mom drops a bomb on me.

Setting her cup of hot tea down on the table, she laces her fingers together leveling me with a look that I know means I won't like what she's about to say.

"Your father and I have planned a trip to Greece over spring break. We expect both of you to come of course." She smiles at Vanessa. "Do you have a passport, dear?"

Vanessa pauses with a bite of French toast halfway to her mouth. "Uh ... yeah. I was supposed to go on a trip to England my senior year of high school. It didn't happen, but I got the passport and everything anyway," she rambles adorably.

"Good, that's excellent. You'll love Greece."

Vanessa looks at me like she's waiting for me to say something, maybe to argue that we won't be going, but I can't. It's pointless. I know I won't win any kind of argument, so there's no point in starting one.

Gulping down the last of my orange juice, I mutter, "Sounds great."

TWENTY-FOUR

Vanessa

UNDER NORMAL CIRCUMSTANCES, I'D BE ECSTATIC AT the prospect of going to Greece. But visiting the beautiful historic country with Teddy's parents? No fucking thank you.

Really, I shouldn't complain about the free trip, and his mom isn't all bad, but the two of us alone with his parents for our entire spring break in a whole different country sounds like a recipe for disaster. At dinner, his dad looked like he couldn't decide who he'd rather have dead, Teddy or me.

Stepping out of the kitchen with an order, my heart skips a beat when I see Teddy sitting at his usual table. Or what had been, since he hasn't been stopping by The Burger Palace as much.

Dropping off the meals, I check if the customers need anything else before I circle over to Teddy.

"Happy to see me?"

I realize the smile hasn't left my face. "It's such a nice day, that's all."

"Yeah, it's beautiful," he remarks sarcastically, motioning toward the rain falling outside. His own smile never falls from his face. Leaning in conspiratorially, he drops his voice, "It's okay to admit you like me, Van. I'm very lovable. And fuckable." Leaning back in the booth, arm draped over the back he waits for my comeback with an eagerness that should probably irk me but instead I feel in places I shouldn't.

"Don't make me spit in your salad, McCallister." I narrow my eyes on the too-good-looking-for-his-own-good man in front of me.

"It's not like we haven't swapped spit before."

He grins in triumph at the sight of red staining my cheeks. "Just give me your order."

"Jude and Mascen are coming. I'll wait for them."

I tap my finger against my thigh. "Okay."

I start to leave but he calls me back with a question. "When do you get off?"

"Another hour." It's a short day for me today, which is nice because I need the break, but on the other hand I could do with the extra tips I'll miss out on.

"Good." He drums his fingers on the table. "I have plans for you."

I narrow my eyes. "I don't like your tone."

265

The smile he gives me doesn't ease my concerns any. "You worry too much, Van. It's going to be fine."

Ten minutes later, the two other guys have joined him, and they speak animatedly—well Jude and Teddy do, Mascen sits beside Jude with a sullen expression like he'd rather be anywhere else. But I get the impression from Mascen that that's just him.

"Hey, guys." I smile and give each of them a small wave. "What can I get you to drink?"

"Sweet tea for me, darlin'." Jude tosses me a wink and then groans, so I have a feeling Teddy has kicked him beneath the table.

"Water," Mascen replies gruffly.

"Orange juice."

"Orange juice?" I arch a brow at Teddy. "Seriously?"

"What can I say? It's my fave."

"If you know what you want to eat, I can get that in, too."

The guys rattle off their orders, and I go back to the kitchen to put it in and grab their drinks. When I get back to the table, I find the guys arguing, not loudly or obviously to most, but maybe because I've gotten to know Teddy pretty well in the nearly three months we've been doing this, I can tell from the tense set of his shoulders and the way his lips barely move as he speaks that he's mad about something.

"What's going on?" I ask hesitantly, setting down the cups and eyeing the three of them as I wait for an explanation.

They all look over at me and Jude grins. "Just trying

to explain to your boyfriend why a trip up to the mountains for his birthday is absolutely necessary."

My lips downturn in concern. "You don't want to do anything for your birthday?"

I panic, wracking my brain for when he mentioned his birthday to me. I know he told me the date, but...

"We've already booked the place," Mascen says in a gruff tone. "You're going."

I ignore Mascen, still looking at Teddy for an explanation. "I don't want the attention."

"Since when?" Jude guffaws. "Your birthday has always been a huge deal."

"That was before I fucked up." Teddy slams a fist on the table. "Don't you guys get that?"

Jude opens his mouth to speak, but Mascen stares him down and gets him to shut up. "It'll be a lowkey weekend. Just me, Rory, Cole, Zoey, Jude, Cree, Murray, and of course, Vanessa."

Jude slaps Mascen on the shoulder. "No single chicks? That's not cool."

"I think you can last a weekend without getting your dick wet."

Jude grumbles something under his breath and gulps down some sweet tea.

"I'm not sure my parents will be cool with me missing our weekly dinner." Teddy looks sick and stressed at the very thought, and my stomach dips. I hate that anything to do with his father fills him with so much dread.

Mascen's eyes narrow across the table at Teddy. Unfortunately for me, I can't stay and chat because I have to finish out my shift. Hopefully they can argue it amongst themselves and figure it out.

Forty-five minutes later, I'm sliding into the passenger seat of the Porsche since Teddy refuses to let me follow in my own car to wherever he's taking me. His easy smile is back, but his eyes are still a tad troubled.

"What did you get figured out with your friends?" I pull the seatbelt across my chest and snap it into place.

He pulls out of The Burger Palace, turning in the opposite direction of the one that will take us back toward campus.

"We're going away this weekend," he sighs, running his fingers through his hair, mouth tight with irritation.

"You don't want to go." It's a statement, not a question.

A few minutes pass in silence before he answers. "It's not that I don't want to go, it's just…" His eyes narrow, and he glances at me. "Are you comfortable playing this game all weekend?"

"I'm going to be doing it with your parents all spring break." I blanch at my word choice. "Not doing *it*, but you know, faking it—pretending."

Teddy chuckles, and the grip around my heart eases the tiniest bit because it's a normal, carefree type of laugh. "So, you're cool with it, then?"

I shrug. "This is why you paid off my tuition."

"Right." His shoulders sag, and I have the feeling I've said the completely wrong thing. I bite my lip, holding my hands tightly in my lap. I hate feeling awkward and out of place, but I have no idea what to say to make this better. I didn't think I said anything *bad*, but I can tell he doesn't see it that way. His fingers tap against the wheel in a way that I know he's irritated, and the worst part is I know it's with me. "There's something in the back for you." His voice jars me after long minutes of awkward silence.

I turn around, finding a shopping bag sitting upright in the back. Picking it up, I set it in my lap. "Should I open it now?"

"Might as well."

Apprehensively, I remove the contents of the bag, my brows furrowing in confusion at the bundle of fabric. "A swimsuit?" I hold up the high waisted light blue bottoms with white daisies on them. "I told you I can't swim."

"I remember." He throws the car into park, and I look at the building in front of us to find that it's a gym. "That's why we're here."

"At a gym?"

"They have a pool." He unsnaps the seatbelt, looking at me expectantly. "We're going to Greece in a few weeks. You have to know how to swim."

I clutch the swimsuit to my chest. "No, I don't. I don't have to get in the water. I like the land just fine. You know, rocks, trees, squirrels. Do they have squirrels in Greece? I—never mind—don't answer that because it's not important since I don't need to be in the water."

"We're going to be on a yacht for a week in the ocean. Forgive me if I'd feel better if you knew how to swim. Not that I won't have you strapped in a life vest, because believe me I will, but you need to know the basics of swimming."

I look out the side of the passenger window, fear

crawling up my spine with sticky fingers. "It scares me," I admit slowly, each of my words seeming to take an extra-long time to come out of my mouth.

Warm fingers grip my chin, urging me to face his too knowing green eyes. "I'll be with you. Do you think I'd let anything happen to you?"

No. I know he wouldn't. I hate admitting it to myself, but with Teddy, I feel safer than I have with anyone else.

"I feel stupid that I'm twenty-one, and I don't know how to swim."

He chuckles. "Remember, I don't know how to ride a bike." I giggle at that, the vice around my heart lessening a smidge. "I'm not expecting you to turn into an Olympic swimmer overnight. It's going to take a few lessons, and honestly, I just want you to learn the basics."

"Okay."

"Okay?" He waits for me to agree again, and I know, without a doubt, if I told him I didn't think I could do this, he would turn the car around and take me back to The Burger Palace.

I nod, setting the bathing suit in my lap and trying to smooth out the wrinkles my monster grip put into the fabric. "You won't let go of me, right?"

His eyes warm. "Never."

───────

I TIPTOE out of the locker room and over to swimming pool that's separate from the gym—though the row of girls on the elliptical machines have a clear view through the glass, thankfully they seemed more engrossed with a rerun of *Friends* playing on the TVs than the pool.

Teddy sits on the edge of the pool in a pair of light blue board shorts, his tan freckled shoulders on full display. I hate that there's a part of me that wants to dive right into his arms and let those wide shoulders close around me, protecting me from anything and everything.

I do my best to reinforce the steel bars around my heart. It's one thing to like Teddy, it's another to fall for him, especially when he's made it clear he has real feelings. I can't risk this ... risk *us*.

I clear my throat, alerting him to my entrance, and he turns around. Vibrant green eyes rake over my body from head to toe and back up again. A shiver courses down my spine. Normally if someone looked at me so intensely, I'd feel embarrassed by the scrutiny. I'd worry about the stretch marks on my thighs, stomach, and arms. The cellulite on my legs and ass. My less than perky boobs. But the raw desire in his eyes makes me feel like the goddess I truly am in body and soul, because nothing about me is a flaw, and Teddy knows that.

"Nice color," he murmurs, looking at the tips of my toes painted a vibrant hot pink.

"Thanks." I wiggle them and take a measured step forward, closer to the pool.

Teddy's hand closes around my ankle and he dips his head, indicating I should sit down beside him.

"We'll take this slow. Start by putting your feet in the water."

I do as he says, watching my pink painted toes and then my feet and legs glide into the water.

"It's warm!"

He laughs, brushing my hair off my shoulder. "Did you think it would be cold?"

"Yes," I admit shyly.

"They keep it heated," he explains evenly, not trying to make me feel bad for not knowing.

"Is a teacher going to ... um ... show me the ropes?"

He grins, eyes wrinkling at the corners. My breath catches in my chest at the sight of it.

You can't do this to me heart, you can't fall for Teddy McCallister. Anyone but him.

Because I know deep down Teddy would have the capability of breaking me in a way not even Tristan did. There would be a part of me I'd never get back.

"You're looking at him," he says, and it takes me a second to remember what I asked.

"Oh."

He drops into the pool, standing easily. The water barely touches his hips. "Now come on," he encourages, "you have to actually get in the water to learn."

I bite my lip, fear zipping through my veins.

Closing my eyes, I take the plunge.

TWENTY-FIVE

Teddy

I GLIDE MY PORSCHE BEHIND MASCEN'S SUV AND Jude's truck. Cole and Zoey are riding with Mascen and Rory while Cree and Murray are with Jude. They promise me it's going to be 'quite the weekend,' and I hope to fuck they're wrong.

Beside me, Vanessa is quiet, looking out the car window at the scenery as the car climbs the incline up the mountain to the 'cabin' Mascen booked. I'm sure Vanessa is expecting an actual small cabin, but I know Mascen, and this will be anything but tiny.

"My ears keep popping," she says after minutes of silence.

"Mine too. Want some gum?" I point to where there's a pack in front of the cup holders. She grabs the pack and takes a piece, popping it into her mouth. She takes another piece and extends it to me. "Thanks."

"You seem like you don't want to do this."

"It's not that I don't want to, but things feel different now. *I'm* different now."

"They're in front of us. You could always turn around, and we can do something else for your birthday. I won't tell."

"They'd never let me live it down."

"You know," she continues, "since your birthday isn't actually until Wednesday, we should do something else on the day of."

I'm surprised by her suggestion but try not to show it. "Like what?"

"I'm not sure. Whatever you want."

I open my mouth but close it before I blurt out that all I'd like is to do her. I don't think that will score me any points. "I'll think about it," I say instead.

"Oh." She sounds saddened by my response.

Keeping my eyes on the road, I curse. "Shit, I didn't mean it that way. I meant, yes, I want to do something with you, but I'll have to think about what that is."

"We don't *have* to do anything. I know this isn't real."

If I wasn't driving, I'd squeeze my eyes shut from the pain that simple sentence causes me. "Right," I utter, and neither of us says a single word for the rest of the drive.

THE 'CABIN' turns out to be a two-story luxury home, high in the mountains a few hours from Nashville. Vanessa practically presses her nose to the side of the glass to get a closer look.

"Wow, this place is gorgeous."

I park behind the others in the circular drive. Above the front door is a massive balloon arch thing with blue, green, and gray balloons and off to the side are large cut out letters that spell out Happy Birthday, Teddy. I have to admit, it does make me feel good that my friends wanted to celebrate my birthday. Most of my birthdays growing up were ignored and only celebrated if it was convenient to my parents to put together something that didn't remotely resemble a birthday party and was more of an excuse to have a gathering with their friends.

An uncontrollable smile touches my lips, and Vanessa turns slowly toward me, smiling herself. "Your friends really love you."

"Yeah, they do." I hope my voice sounds choked up only to me, but the way her eyes shimmer, I think she notices.

Climbing out of the car, I'm immediately mauled by Rory and Zoey and a chorus of, 'Happy birthday' and 'we love you' and 'this weekend is going to be the best ever.'

Vanessa hangs back, her fingers wringing together nervously like she doesn't want to interrupt. "Get over here," I tell her. Sure, things got a little awkward on the drive, but I don't like her feeling out of place with my friends. They're her friends now, too. She walks over to my side, and I wrap an arm around her, tugging her against me. "There's my girl." I press my lips to the top of her head.

"You're way better at this than I am," she says softly enough that no one else will overhear.

I don't bother responding. Pressing another kiss to the side of her head, because I can, I let go and say, "I'm going to get our bags."

She gives me a tiny, forced smile and moves over to stand with Zoey and Rory.

"This is great, man." Murray steps up beside me with his duffle bag slung over his shoulder as I bend into the trunk to grab my bag and Vanessa's. "Thanks for having me."

I chuckle. "This shin-dig wasn't my idea, but I'm glad you're here too. All of you."

He gives me a lopsided smile and smacks his hand on my shoulder before loping toward the door. "Someone give me a beer and let me in that hot tub."

Mascen walks over to me, shaking his head. "I'm going to regret inviting that dickhead aren't I?" he jokes, an actual smile on his lips. He looks, dare I say, relaxed. "You and Vanessa have the master, birthday boy." He looks over his shoulder at the girls, then lowers his voice to me, "How's it going with her?"

I look back at her, glossy dark hair hanging down to her breasts, blue eyes wide with excitement now, and her lips upturned into a smile. "She's insisting on keeping things ... professional."

Mascen tosses his head back, laughing in a way I rarely see him do. "Oh, man, it's awesome seeing you this fucked up over a girl."

Cole joins us, having overhead Mascen and laughs too.

"I always knew when this one fell it'd be a big deal. Who would've thought he'd fall for the one girl impervious to his charms?"

"Leave me alone," I grumble, grabbing the bags and practically sprinting into the house to get away from their cajoling.

Straight up the stairs I go, running into Jude and Cree in the hallway coming out of whatever bedrooms they chose. The master is at the end of the hall. I put our bags on the bench in front of the bed and take a moment to catch my breath—not because I'm out of shape or anything, I can handle two bags and some stairs, but because I need to brace myself for an entire weekend with Vanessa and my friends. They all know that we're not a real couple, but Vanessa doesn't know that they do, and since they know I actually like her for real I have a feeling they'll be busting my balls the whole time we're here.

It's safe to say I'm going to need a drink and stat.

I hope someone got my Zombie Dust. I am the birthday boy after all.

Turning to head out of the room, I find Vanessa standing in the doorway taking in the big room.

"This place is fancy. I mean, it's not as ostentatious as your parents' house, but this is way bigger than any place I've ever stayed at. This must cost a pretty penny, not that I'm judging, I'm just—" I chuckle, pressing a finger to her lips to quiet her. When my finger drops, her cheeks are flushed. "Sorry, I ramble when I'm nervous."

"I've noticed." I can't help myself when I brush my

nose against hers. A shiver skates down her spine. "Do *I* make you nervous?"

Her eyes close, a shuddery breath wracking her body. "No," she lies.

I grin. "Sure, I don't." Taking her hand, I blow out a breath because as much as I want to stay right here with her, I know we need to join the others. "We better see what everyone is up to."

Her fingers curl into mine reflexively. "Right."

Downstairs we find everyone spread through the open concept kitchen and living area. A row of windows behind the sectional in the living room has a view of the woods and surrounding mountains. There's a large deck with the hot tub Murray's excited about.

"For the birthday boy." Jude holds out a Zombie Dust.

"Thanks, dude." I take it gratefully, taking a drink.

"What about you, milady?" He turns his attention to Vanessa wearing his most charming smile and 'I want to fuck you' eyes.

"Don't look at my girl like that," I threaten.

He laughs. "Why don't you just pee around her?"

"Oh, ew." Vanessa's makes a disgusted face like she smells something sour. "Please, don't go getting any ideas."

"No to golden showers, got it. I'm taking notes here, babe."

She mock gags. "Please never ever utter those words again." She extracts her hand from mine. "I'll get my own drink, but thanks, Jude."

She joins the others in the kitchen, laughing at something Zoey says and my chest eases a bit, glad that she's already getting more comfortable.

"You've got it so fucking bad for her." Jude laughs at my side, smiling in amusement. "I still can't believe you guys pretended to have sex in your room for my benefit. Are you sure it was fake, because it sounded pretty fucking real?"

"Trust me," I take a gulp of beer, "it was fake. I haven't had sex since the summer." Jude spits beer on me. I level him with a glare. "Really, dude?"

"Summer was practically a year ago. That's ... that's forever. How's your dick holding up?"

"I don't want to talk about my dick."

"That bad, then?"

"Yeah." I go to take another drink and realize I've already downed the whole thing. I don't want to get shit-faced, so I don't make a move to get another one yet.

Feet pound down the steps, and I look over my shoulder, snorting at the vision of Murray in a speedo, swim cap, and goggles. "Hot tub time." He rubs his hands together.

"You need all that for the hot tub?" Cree cackles from the kitchen, shaking his head.

Murray sweeps a hand over himself. "Don't knock my style."

Then he strides right out the door, the Australian not at all bothered by our howling laughter.

"Jesus," Jude snorts, "if this wasn't my first drink, I'd be positive I was drunk." Returning to our early conversation, despite the fact I was hoping he'd drop it, he asks,

"Do you think this weekend will make a difference for you two?"

My eyes stray to Vanessa in the kitchen, she pops a grape in her mouth and says something to Cree. Jealousy stirs in my stomach, but I know it's stupid. Cree would never make a move on Vanessa knowing how I feel.

"I doubt it," I admit, and the honesty in my own words burns me from the inside out. As much as I want more, she doesn't, and I wouldn't push her to give more than she wants to.

Jude sends me a pitying look that makes me want to catch fire on the spot. I don't want anyone's pity. I'm a big boy. Rejection sucks, but I can handle it.

Unable to help myself, my gaze strays to the kitchen again where Vanessa tosses her head back and laughs.

"Do you ever think you'll have a serious relationship again?"

Jude scrubs a hand over his stubbled face, thinking about his answer. "Yes, one day. I enjoyed being in a relationship, but I got real fucking hurt and why not have some fun while I can? Being broken-hearted sucks, but I'm not jaded enough to think I won't find happiness with someone else. I think it'll be a long time, though, before I want to settle down."

"So, you don't think I'm crazy?"

He gives me a puzzled look. "No, man. When you know, you fucking know, and I see the way you look at her. If you're certain she's the girl for you, don't give up. You'll regret it if you do."

"Thanks for the advice." I mean it, too.

Grabbing a fresh beer, I take Vanessa's hand and pull her away from the others.

She can assume that every touch, glance, and kiss is fake, but I know, and so do my friends that I'm trying to convince her that this is for keeps.

TWENTY-SIX

Vanessa

My damp hair hangs like a curtain around my face, dripping onto the cotton of my over-sized t-shirt. I'm exhausted after a full day spent hiking and exploring the area around the cabin—although, calling this place a cabin is a joke. It's large and posh, with gleaming hardwood floors, chandeliers, and a massive stone fireplace in the center of the family room. I have no idea what Mascen paid for this place for just two nights, but it has to have been expensive. We head back to school tomorrow afternoon, and while I originally thought I'd be clamoring to leave, I've actually enjoyed myself, and I love Teddy's friends. You can tell they all get along and care for each other like a family of bandits who've chosen to build a life together.

Opening the bathroom door, I find Teddy already in bed. His long legs are stretched out on the mattress, crossed one over top of the other. He's still on his iPad like he was when I went to shower, going over notes from his coach.

I wish I could say sharing a bed with Teddy felt weird, but it's annoyingly easy, and I'm worried I'm going to have a hard time sleeping without him when I return to my dorm.

He looks up from the iPad, eyes roaming over me. They narrow on my tangled hair and the brush in my hand.

"I forgot my detangler."

Teddy sets the iPad off to the side while I rummage through my bag for the bottle I need.

"Bring it here," he commands when I have it in hand.

"What?" I blink owlishly at him.

That sweet, perfect grin, the one I wish didn't make my stomach tilt, flashes at me as he spreads his leg and points at the space between them.

"Come sit and I'll brush your hair."

"Y-You're going to brush my hair?" I stutter, stunned.

He shrugs. "Sure, why not."

I walk over to him with careful, measured steps like I'm approaching a wild animal with caution. I pass the detangler and brush to him, pointing at the bottle. "I only put a dime size amount in my hair."

"Okay."

Heart racing, I seat myself between his spread legs. Desire pools low in my belly, and I curse my body for reacting to him. I need to be stronger than this. He's just a guy.

He squirts some of the detangler onto his hands and works it into the long strands of my hair, his long fingers working the product through it with ease. I practically purr at the first stroke of the brush. He's gentle, careful not to pull at any of the knots. He takes his time, working them out, infinitely more patient than I tend to be.

"That feels so good," I practically moan when he works his fingers into the back of my neck.

"You like that, huh?" His chest vibrates against me, and I gasp when his lips caress the side of my neck.

No. "Yes." Trying to move my thoughts out of dangerous territory, I say, "My mom used to brush my hair to help me go to sleep."

"Did your parents know about Tristan?"

I stiffen at his question, old feelings churning inside me. "Not in the way you mean, but they found out later on."

"Did they punish your sister?"

"She was grounded, but beyond that what could they do?"

"And now?"

I blow out a breath, hating that my heart still stings with pain after all this time. "And now, in their eyes it was a silly teenage mistake, and we all need to be grown ups and move on."

Teddy lets out a sound behind me that can only be described as an angry growl. "You should never have to speak or even look at her ever again."

"I used to think after I graduated, I would just go back home, but I don't want that anymore." I haven't said this out loud to anyone, barely even let myself think about it. "Maybe I'll go to a city. I've always wanted to live in Brooklyn. I don't care if it's in a place the size of a closet."

"I think you should." He resumes rubbing my neck. "You can do anything you want."

"You think so?"

"You're a go-getter. Anyone can see that. If you set your mind to something, I know you'll go above and beyond to make it happen."

For some reason Teddy's faith in me means everything. Maybe because he's lived such a privileged life and I haven't, that if he sees something in me, then surely it must be there.

"You don't think I'm crazy?"

"Never." The one-word rings with truth. "There." He sets the brush down on the bed, the fingers of his other hand leaving my neck.

"Thank you." I slide off the mattress, gathering my things, and pretend not to notice when he tries to discreetly adjust himself.

Teddy gets off the bed, stretching his arms above his head. His muscles move beneath his skin, tantalizing me.

Stop staring at the man's abs, Vanessa. You're drooling!

Thoroughly stretched, he yanks the covers back on his side of the bed and climbs beneath them.

"Are you coming to bed?" he asks, after I've been standing for too long staring at him.

"Um ... yeah, right." I shake myself free of my stupor

and join him in bed, trying not to think about the fact that I woke up this morning clinging to him like he was the bed itself and that there was *drool* on his shoulder.

When I'm lying beneath the covers, he turns the lights off and rolls over to face me.

"What are you thinking about?"

"Nothing."

He chuckles, the sound sending a shiver down my spine in the dark. "When someone says they're thinking about nothing, it actually means they're thinking about everything."

"Or maybe they're thinking about too much and it feels like nothing because they can't pick one thought."

"Possibly." His teeth are bright white in the darkness when he smiles. "Are you thinking about me?" I don't reply and this makes his smile grow. "You are."

"I didn't answer."

"Silence is an answer." I jolt when his fingers glide over my hip. "Is this okay?"

"Y-Yes."

"Your skin is so soft."

"I can't think straight when you touch me." I curse myself for letting the truth slip out.

"I can't think straight when you're in the same room as me."

My breath is too loud in the otherwise quiet room. I feel like my walls crumble all too easily around Teddy. He's so easy to like, to care about, that I forget logic.

I fake a yawn. "I'm really sleepy," I lie.

The way he tenses I know he's aware of my evasion. "Goodnight, Van."

"Night, Teddy."

I WAKE BEFORE TEDDY, slipping from the bed carefully so he won't notice my absence. Slipping on a bra—no way am I free-boobing it around all his friends with these massive things—I meet everyone in the kitchen to prepare a birthday cake as well as breakfast.

The cake is simple—a boxed funfetti one—but we make two layers, trying to at least give the appearance of something nicer. Sure, we could've bought a cake, but I was the one that insisted we make it instead. I know it'll mean more to Teddy that way.

With the cake in the oven, we start on preparing a breakfast of pancakes, bacon, hashbrowns, eggs, and toast. For some reason I expected the guys not to help, but all of them join in and seem to be having fun. Cree and Murray are the ones I've hung around the least in the past and I find that Cree is quiet with an intensity about him, but a kind personality, and Murray is practically an equal counterpart to Teddy—a wild, loose cannon but you can't help sensing there's more beneath the surface.

We've just finished icing the cake and sloppily spelling out *Happy Birthday Not-Theodore* on the cake in bright red gel-like icing when Rory hushes us, and we hear the footsteps.

I stand in front of the island, unable to rid myself of the goofy smile on my face.

Teddy yawns, stretching his arms above his head. He hasn't turned and noticed us yet, but when he does his green eyes swim with emotion that he tries to keep at bay, and he can't stop the smile that breaks over his face.

"Happy birthday!" We all chorus and then break out in a sloppy, very out of tune rendition of the song.

"You guys." Two words, but you can *feel* the emotion. He crosses the space, coming to me first. Placing his hands on my hips, he presses his forehead to mine. "You did this for me?"

I try to nod but it's hard with his big head against mine. "We all did. We —"

"We love you, dude," Jude finishes for me, coming in for a group hug. Soon, everyone's piling on, and Teddy and I are buried beneath the mass of bodies.

When they disperse and it's Teddy and I alone in our bubble once more, his eyes seem to say to me, *This is what family is supposed to be.*

TWENTY-SEVEN

Teddy

"I TOLD YOU, WE DON'T HAVE TO DO ANYTHING FOR MY actual birthday."

Vanessa pouts at me, bottom lip jutted out in mock hurt. "Just because we already celebrated, doesn't mean we're not going to do it again." She towels off outside the pool, having come a long way with her swimming. She can tread the water easily now and float, which makes me feel loads better with our trip to Greece around the corner. I'm exhausted after a full day of classes where the professors are laying it on thick leading up to break, baseball practice, and then coming to the gym for Van's swim lesson.

"Can we celebrate by hanging out in my room and watching *Beverly Hills, 90210*?"

She grins at me, tossing the towel around her shoulders. Her hair hangs in a wet curtain that she keeps shoving out of her way. "I knew you were obsessed."

"Yeah, yeah." I wave her off.

"Is that really all you want to do?"

Surprisingly, it is. I don't want to find an on or off campus party, which is crazy because I love parties; I don't want a fancy dinner at some restaurant, I just want to hang with my girl.

She's not your girl, I remind my stubborn ass self.

Drying my hair, I try to hide my smile when I notice her checking out my abs. Me being me, I can't keep my mouth shut. "Like what you see?" I rub a hand over the muscles I work out hard for and eat right to keep. She turns a bright shade of red and fumbles with her sports watch. "And yes," I say, letting her off easy, "that's all I want to do."

We head to the separate locker rooms to shower off the chlorine and change into our street clothes. I finish first and wait near the women's room on a bench.

"Hi." I look up from my phone at the sound of the voice.

"Hello?" I reply hesitantly, eyeing the gorgeous blonde in front of me skeptically. I used to would've been all over it when a girl this hot approached me—big boobs, golden tan skin, blue eyes, and a body she clearly works hard for but now she's not doing it for me. Why? Because I had to go and catch feelings.

She smiles, pointing over her shoulder. "My friends dared me to come over and talk to you."

Right about now old Teddy would've plastered on his

signature cocky smile and said how I was flattered, new Teddy just says, "Oh?"

"I think you're hot and you seem cool—" *I seem cool? She doesn't even know me.* "—so if you ever want to meet up here's my number." She holds out a ripped piece of paper.

I don't move to take it from her, and her smile falters a bit. "I have a girlfriend," I explain. I don't want to be rude; it takes balls for a chick to approach a guy, but I'm not about to take that from her.

Her smile falters. "Oh, I'm sorry. I didn't know." She turns to walk away, but quickly swings back around. "Take it anyway, you know, in case you and the girlfriend don't work out."

I stare at her in shock. *What the fuck? Who says that shit?*

"Nah." Again, I don't take it from her, and it hangs limply from her fingers. "I know I have a good thing, and I won't let her get away from me that easy. When you meet someone that's your heart—not steals it, but it's like your heart beats beside theirs—you don't throw it away for someone random. Good things are hard to come by. You cherish them and nurture them. You grow from them, and you definitely don't take numbers from girls you don't even know the name of."

There's a gasp behind me and I turn, finding Vanessa standing there with tears shining in her eyes. For a second, I think I've done or said something wrong or that she's just shown up and hasn't heard a word I've said and actually thinks I'd take this girl's number, but then she dives down, tackling me into a hug on the bench.

A second later her hands are on my cheeks and she's kissing me.

Shock freezes me to the spot, and I don't move. I don't think she's ever initiated a kiss with me before, I've always been the one to make the first move. But right now, she kisses me like it's the most natural thing in the world. I thaw from my frozen position, my right hand gliding up her cheek to the back of her neck, holding her possessively against me. Her lips taste slightly like strawberry, and I bet she put on Chapstick before coming out here since she's been complaining about the chlorine drying her skin.

Someone in the gym whistles, and I curse them because the second Vanessa hears it, she pulls away from me. I move both hands to her cheeks, keeping her from pulling too far away.

Both of us are slightly out of breath. My eyes drop to her lips, pinker than normal and slightly swollen.

"That was some kiss, Van." Her cheeks turn the prettiest shade of pink, and she tries to duck her head, hiding those pretty blue eyes from me, but I won't let her. "Don't be embarrassed, my wish came true."

"W-What wish?" Her tongue swipes out to moisten her lips.

Leaning in, I brush my mouth against her ears. "The one I made when I blew out my birthday candles on Sunday. I wished for a kiss from you on my actual birthday."

"I don't think you're supposed to tell people your wish."

I chuckle, smiling at her in a way I've rarely smiled at others. "That's so it'll come true, mine already did, so I think I'm safe. I won't say no to more kisses, though."

She clears her throat, and I let my hands drop. "I think we should go now." Her eyes dart to the gym where I'm sure some people still watch. No idea where the blonde scattered off to, and I don't give a shit.

"Sounds like a plan."

AFTER THE KISS, I fully expected Vanessa to weasel out of spending more time with me this evening, but she surprises me by insisting on buying dinner—she refuses to let me pay—and we go back to my room.

Jude isn't in, and we settle in my room putting on the show I've quickly gotten sucked into. Sure, it's over the top and ridiculous and the acting isn't the best, but I can't seem to stop watching it. I won't admit it to her, but it's kind of addicting.

Since I have to be careful with what I eat, I opted for grilled chicken and a double serving of broccoli. Would I love to have the steak and cheese sub Vanessa ordered? Ab-so-fucking-lutely. But I know I'll regret it tomorrow morning on my run with Mascen. Dude's fucking obsessed with his cardio, and I still hate it with a burning passion.

Vanessa spreads the food out on my bed while I get the TV on and the show brought up where we left off. I hate to admit it, but I'm going to be sad when we finish.

We eat in silence, focusing on the show. At least she's focused on it, but my brain can't stop going back to that spontaneous kiss at the gym. I want to taste her lips again, but I know I have to stop pushing and let her come to me, if that's what she wants.

"I can't believe he died," she muses, breaking me from my thoughts.

"What the fuck, Van? No spoilers."

She tosses her head back and laughs. I find myself studying the smooth column of her throat. I never knew someone's throat could be sexy but hers is.

"It's not a spoiler." She shakes her head in mock-shame at me. "Luke Perry died of a stroke a few years ago."

"The one you think I look like?" I hope I sound as horrified as I feel.

"Yeah." She frowns so deeply that a wrinkle forms in her brow. "It's so sad. I mean, he was pretty young to have a stroke like that. Tragic." She shakes her head sadly, eyes glued to the television.

"A-Are you crying?"

She glares at me, but there's definitely a tear leaking from the corner of her eye. I swipe it away with a brush of my thumb.

"I'm extra emotional today, leave me alone."

I can't help but laugh. "Why are you so emotional?"

The glare she levels me with makes me feel like I must be the biggest idiot on Earth. "I'm on my period, Teddy!"

I toss my hands up innocently. "Sorry I asked."

"You should be." She tosses a piece of lettuce at me that fell from her sandwich.

I chuckle, lying back on my bed and crossing my arms behind my head. After a while, Vanessa lies down beside me, putting her head on my chest. She does it without hesitation, and I feel like a pathetic bastard that such a simple thing fills me with so much happiness.

She wiggles closer to me, tossing her leg overtop mine, and the next thing I know, she's fallen asleep. It feels like a big deal, her trusting me enough to fall asleep in my arms. I brush my lips over her forehead in a gentle caress and reach over, turning the light off beside the bed.

As I start to fall asleep, I realize that I would give anything, hand over every dollar promised to me, grovel on my knees, whatever was needed, to keep her.

TWENTY-EIGHT

Vanessa

SOMEHOW, I BLINK, AND SUDDENLY, IT'S TIME TO LEAVE for Greece. By some miracle, Teddy and I are flying over together and meeting his parents there. I think I'm as relieved as he is not to have to endure a flight with his father. Even still, my nerves are frayed. I've never actually been on a plane, and with a flight this long, I'm worried about how I'll handle it.

Danika left last night with a group of her friends to go to some beach in Florida. She said which one she was going to, but I was only half-listening because I was busy freaking out over every last detail and wondering if, despite Teddy's swim lessons I might drown.

All my bags sit by the door, waiting for Teddy to arrive. Our flight is at ten this morning, and he told me he'd pick me up at eight-thirty, which means he should be knocking on my door any—

Sure enough, there he is.

I swing the door open, hoping my freak out isn't obvious, but the way his lips twitch I'd say I've failed.

"Ready?"

"As I'll ever be."

"You know," his eyes scan the floor and my mountain of luggage, "I didn't take you for an over packer."

I punch him lightly in the arm. "I wasn't sure what I'd need."

His lips twitch with a smile. "I can tell."

I bite my lip, eyeing them. "Okay," I concede, "I did go a tad overboard."

"It's fine," he chuckles, reaching down and shouldering my backpack, adding a duffle bag to his shoulder and then grabs the handle of the largest piece of wheeled luggage.

I scoop up the rest and follow him out to his car. Somehow we manage to fit all of my shit beside and around his.

I don't know how things are typically done at an airport but I find it strange when we pull up to a side entrance and get out of the car. Someone immediately comes out the door and gets our bags onto a trolley and another takes Teddy's car.

"Where—" I start to ask where they're taking his car and our things, but he's already taking my hand and guiding me inside.

"Hello, Mr. McCallister," a lady greets, dressed primly in a navy pencil skirt and matching top. "Right this way."

We're quickly escorted through private security, our bags are checked, and the next thing I know we're being taken outside onto the tarmac and led to a large jet.

"This isn't normal, is it?" I whisper under my breath to Teddy, not wanting the well-dressed lady leading us to the plane to hear my stupidity.

He laughs. "To me it is, but no it's not." He gives my hand a reassuring squeeze, and I lean into him. When we get to the stairs leading onto the plane, he motions for me to go first.

I start up them and turn back to look at him. "You just want to look at my ass, don't you?"

He grins like a little boy caught with his hand in the cookie jar. "You know me well."

I shake my head but continue the trek into the plane.

"Champagne, Ms. Hughes?" The stewardess holds a tray with two glasses on it.

"Uh ... sure." She smiles as I take the glass. Moving into the cabin, I wait for Teddy, overwhelmed by the empty plane and all the seat choices.

Teddy's right behind me and my body relaxes when I feel the warm press of his hand against my lower back. In his other hand he clasps the other champagne flute. "Take your pick, darlin'," he drawls, allowing me to pick where we sit.

"No, you." I don't like the pressure of having to choose.

"All right." He steps around me and picks a place. "You want the window seat or?"

"Not window." I shake my head vehemently. The idea

of watching the world rush away from me at super speed isn't appealing.

He doesn't laugh at my fear, instead he takes the seat, and I plant my butt in the one beside him. Despite not caring for champagne, I drink the entire glass in one swallow, the bubbles dancing down my throat to my belly.

Teddy eyes me with a raised brow. "You good?"

"Absolutely."

SUFFICE TO SAY, I was not good.

In fact, I was absolutely terrified. I'd been nervous to get on a plane for the first time, but I honestly thought I'd be fine. But no, I hate it. I immediately start to feel dizzy and sick, despite this being what I'm certain is the smoothest flight known to man. I think the sickness is coming from my fear, not the flight, but logic is lost on me.

I whimper, practically climbing into Teddy's lap as soon as we're allowed to take our belts off.

"Van," he murmurs my name in a soothing voice, stroking his fingers through my hair. "What can I do to help?"

My fingers tighten in the soft fabric of his shirt. "Don't let me go. That'll help."

He doesn't laugh. He doesn't mock me. He holds me tighter, and I'll forever be appreciative of that fact. I'm also thankful we're on a private jet, not for the luxury of it but because it means no one else, except for the staff, witnesses my breakdown.

Still slowly gliding his fingers through my hair, Teddy begins to tell me random stories about himself and his friends, trying to distract me from my mental spiral.

At some point I manage to extract myself from the monkey hold I had on him and situate myself back in my seat. But I keep a tight hold on his hand while working to breathe in through my mouth and out through my nose.

My eyes are closed, but I sense the presence of someone else and then the stewardess whispers something to Teddy. I'm so lost in my spiral that my brain can't process what either of them says, but a few minutes later I startle when a cool rag is pressed to my forehead, and I blink my eyes open.

"How are you feeling?"

"Like I might throw up." I close my eyes at the admission, partly because the room started spinning again and from embarrassment.

"You're not going to throw up."

"You say that now, but you won't be laughing when it ends up in your lap." I stifle a whimper. "I thought flying would be fun."

"You'll get used to it."

I hate to tell him, but I don't think that's true. Don't want to dash his dreams, however.

"Maybe it would help if I laid down."

"There's a bed in the back."

I crack one eye open. "A bed? In a plane?

"I mean, if you weren't sick, we could join the mile high club easy." I can't manage to smile, but I am amused. "But the bed is for actual sleeping—don't get me wrong,

I'm sure fornication has taken place in it since it's used by many associates, but when you're on a long flight to other countries, a bed is a much more preferable option to sleep in than a chair, though these do recline," he rambles.

"Why didn't you lead with that?"

"Want me to lower it for you?"

"Please." He lets it down slowly to not make me feel even worse than I already do. "Thank you. I'm the worst travel companion ever."

"Trust me," the leather groans as he wiggles in his seat, "you're not the worst."

"How so?"

"Well," he coughs in a nervous way, "you haven't hit me yet."

"God, Teddy. I'm sorry."

"Don't be."

"You deserve more than you've been given."

He sighs beside me, the kind that sounds sad and desperate for something better. I wish I could be the person who gives that to him, but I don't think I am.

TWENTY-NINE

Teddy

VANESSA EVENTUALLY GOT OVER HER FLIGHT SICKNESS, but not until the second half of the trip when we were an hour away from touching down in Greece.

Her cheeks are flushed with color and her eyes are a clear crystal blue when we load into the waiting car that will take us to the boat dock where we'll board the yacht.

I'm trying not to think about the entire week that'll be spent on a boat with my parents. It's a mega yacht, but there are still only so many places I can hide from my father.

Vanessa spends the car ride glued to the window and drooling over the scenery. I'm so fucking pathetic that the look of awe on her face makes me hard. I need to get laid, but until I graduate, or until Vanessa realizes my feelings are real and that she wants me too, I'm stuck with my hand.

"Look at this place." Her nose is practically plastered to the glass. "Are you seeing this?"

"Oh, I'm seeing it. It's beautiful." My gaze doesn't stray from her. She's the only view that matters to me.

Fuck, I'm whipped, and I'm not even in an actual relationship. Someone give me a beer and a cigar so I can feel more manly.

The car takes us to a private dock where Vanessa is stunned to learn we have to take a boat to the yacht.

"We're riding a boat to an even bigger boat? This is incredible!"

I feel hungover from the flights, but Vanessa seems to be full of energy. Maybe it's the excitement of being in a new place.

Her hair blows in the wind created by the boat as we speed across the water to the yacht anchored farther out. Her smile is easy, sunglasses perched on her narrow nose. She looks more carefree and happier than I've ever seen her. Even if we have to endure this trip with my parents, I plan on making it an unforgettable experience for her.

"Wait, *that's* the yacht?" She gapes as we approach. "That thing is huge? You seriously crashed one of these?" She gives me an incredulous look.

Fighting a smile, I shrug. "I was drunk, and there might've been other substances involved."

"Other substances?"

"Look, I'm not proud of most of the shit I've done, so yes, I used drugs occasionally. I've never been an addict, and I've been clean since last summer. I mean, you've seen me, I don't even get drunk anymore. Sure, I drink, but not enough for it to be a problem."

"You know," she begins, and I'm totally expecting a reaming, "you're cute when you ramble. Your ears go all red."

"No, they don't."

She throws her head back and laughs, low and throaty, and fuck if it isn't turning me on. I have to face it, everything she does turns me on. Pulling her phone from the pocket of the shorts she changed into before landing, she snaps a picture and turns the screen to face me.

My stupid ears, are in fact, red.

"Well, guess you're right."

"I'm always right." She pushes dark, windswept hair from her face as the boat slows. "Are you ready for this?" Sadness touches her eyes as she appraises me, searching for any signs that I'm about to lose my shit.

"I'm never ready to deal with my parents."

VANESSA and I are escorted to our room by a staff member, to which she hisses under her breath, "Your parents even have staff on their fancy schmancy boat. I mean, of course they do." Then when we reach the room, she lightly punches my stomach and gasps, "This room is bigger than my entire house back home and it's on a fucking *boat*."

"Yacht," I correct. "If my dad hears you call it a boat, he'll have words."

She rolls her eyes, sitting on the bed and bouncing to test the mattress. "Let him. I can handle him. Any man that beats a child is a weak, pathetic excuse for a human being."

I have to force a swallow past the emotion clogging my throat. I don't normally get like this, but Vanessa is the first person in my life to know about my father, know and believe me and actively rebuke him. My mom knows, of course she does, how could she not? He's never hit me in her presence, but I don't understand how a mother doesn't know these sorts of things.

Vanessa lays back on the bed, gazing up the ceiling with a million tiny LED lights custom set to match the night sky and constellations. "Growing up, did you ever think about killing him?" I freeze at her question. She lifts her head and I see that she's seriously expecting an answer. "Be honest. I'm not judging."

"Yes." I push the answer past my lips. I sit down beside her and then lie back so we're both gazing at the artificial night sky. "I've imagined a million and one ways."

"Tell me about one."

I turn my head her way. "Seriously?"

"Absolutely." Her face is right there, full lips a breath from mine. If I wasn't afraid of scaring her away, I'd place my hand on her cheek and lean in until my lips were pillowed on hers. But I can't make the first move, not in here at least where it's private. In the public I can show her affection, and that's the cruelest trick of all.

"I hate to disappoint you, most of them aren't very creative."

"Surely, there's one that is." There's humor in her tone.

"Well, there was one." I start to laugh. "I think I was about twelve, and I'd just received a vicious beating, and I was hiding out in the yard when I saw a hot air balloon in the sky and I thought about being in one and just ... pushing him."

"Did it make you feel better thinking about it?"

"No." It's an honest answer. "It always made me feel sick when I thought about killing him. It made me think I was no better than him."

Vanessa's warm hand grips mine on him. "I promise you, you could never be your father."

I close my eyes, relief flooding through my veins. It feels way too good to hear her say that. "You have no idea how much I fear turning into him." I've voiced this to her before, but it doesn't change the fact that the terror still exists. Just because I can't imagine laying a hand on my own child, doesn't mean I'm not capable of it like he is.

She rolls to her side, and I reluctantly meet her look. I hate being vulnerable. It fucking sucks laying yourself bare to someone. Reaching with her finger, she traces the shape of my lips and then glides the tip of that same finger down the bridge of my nose. I feel cold when her touch disappears.

"No one with as beautiful a heart as you could ever do such a thing. Besides, the fact that you have that fear already tells me you'd ever hit your own child. You want kids then?"

I grin at her slight change in topic. "Yeah. You?"

"Mhmm," she hums, rolling onto her back again.

"How many?"

"Four."

"Four?" She sits up so fast I'm surprised she doesn't get whiplash.

I laugh at her disbelief. "Why is that so hard to believe?"

"Four is a lot."

"Maybe it's because I'm an only child that I always saw myself with a whole football team. The more the merrier. What about you?"

"I don't know. Two. Three."

"Three," I chuckle, wrapping a piece of her hair around my finger, "what's one more?"

She's saved from answering—more like I'm saved from hearing her answer—by a soft knock on the door.

"Mr. McCallister? Ms. Hughes?"

With a groan, I rise from the bed and stretch my arms above my head before opening the door. The staff member who escorted us to our room stands there waiting.

"Hey, what's up?" If my father heard me speak so casually to one of the staff, he'd be pissed.

"Your parents are requesting your presence for dinner on the upper deck at six this evening."

"Okay, thanks."

He nods and walks down the hall. Closing the door, I dive back into bed.

"Dinner in three hours with my 'rents," I relay to Vanessa, crooking my elbow over my eyes. "That gives us enough time for a nap and shower."

"I think I'm too hyped to nap."

"Trust me," I lower my arm, "you're going to need it."

DESPITE VANESSA NOT BELIEVING ME, I wake up two hours later to her body curled against mine. We both have a bad habit of octopusing one another in our sleep. Not that I'm complaining. The feel of her breasts against my chest is worth it.

Nudging her lightly, I brush my lips against the top of her head. "Van, we need to get up."

"Vuttamizit."

"What was that?" I laugh, knowing exactly what she's saying but hoping to hear her ask in her cute sleepy voice again.

"What time is it?"

Ah, disappointment, my old friend.

She slowly blinks her big blue eyes open. "Five 'til five. We need to get moving."

"Ugh. I didn't even think I was sleepy." She sits up, scrubbing a hand over her face. There are red lines on her left cheek, imprints left behind from my shirt.

"You can shower first."

"It's okay."

"I insist, ladies first."

She bites her lip, lids lowering. "Teddy?"

Please ask me to kiss you. Please let me roll your body beneath mine and peel the clothes from your body. Please—

"If I'm going to shower first, you're going to have to stop touching me."

308

"What?"

I realize then that my hand is under the back of her shirt, my fingers playing with the band of her bra. Apparently, I'm not fully awake either.

"Fuck." I yank my hand away. "Shit, I didn't mean to grope you, Van."

"It's okay." She looks down, trying to hide her pink cheeks from me. "I know you didn't mean to."

The way she says it I don't think she means it like "Oh I know it was an accident and you wouldn't purposely paw me," but more like, "I know you wouldn't mean to touch *me*."

She's already climbing off the bed, and when I call after her, she hesitates to turn back to me. When she finally does, I have to swallow down words that might scare her, ones that speak of feelings I shouldn't have. Lust? That she'll understand. But love? It would send her running for the hills. The last thing she wants to hear is that I've fallen that hard for her.

"I want you," I tell her, my voice still deeper than normal from a heavy sleep. "I want you in all the ways a man wants a woman. Don't try to diminish this. I'm attracted to *you*, Vanessa."

She's quiet, but I can see I've made her nervous in the way her tongue slides out to moisten her lips. "I-I have to clean m-myself. Wash myself. Shower!" The slam of the bathroom door is the exclamation point on the end of her spiel.

I lay back onto the fluffy pillows and glare at my right hand. "It's just you and me, dude."

THIRTY

Vanessa

GREECE.

I, Vanessa Ann Hughes, am in Greece.

A country rich with history and beauty and bursting with life.

When Teddy suggested we explore the city, I was more than game, plus after last night's cold shoulder dinner where only his mom and I spoke, trying to fill the awkward silence, the last place I wanted to be was on the yacht and risk the chance of running into his father.

Teddy holds his hand out to me after he hops out of the small boat that he drove from the yacht to here—yeah, there's a boat inside a boat, in fact there was more than this one *plus* several jet skis. I can't imagine having enough money to own a basic boat, and Teddy's father not only owns one of those, but several, a mega yacht, jet skis, a private plane, and God knows what else.

It's more than a little horrifying thinking about one person having control of so much wealth.

"You act like you know where you're going." The palm of his hand is warm in mine, a bit rough, but it feels nice.

"That's because I do. It's a little café about a ten-minute walk from here. It's my favorite."

"Where all have you traveled?" I blurt incredulously. I can't imagine living a life where I've been to a place like Greece so many times that I have a favorite café to visit.

"Too many to name."

"Wow."

We grow quiet on the walk, mostly because I can't stop staring around me at the bright white buildings and the bustle of life on the island. We pass a chaotic fish market where it seems like everyone is yelling to be heard. I don't understand a word they say, but I'm certainly fascinated.

We continue along, eventually turning down a narrow street where Teddy tugs me inside a building. The café is tiny, with only two tables, but the scent of coffee and pastries permeates the air, making my stomach growl. We skipped out on breakfast, choosing to come straight here.

"What would you like?"

I look at the menu that's very much in Greek, not English. "Um ... something like I usually get back home ... I guess."

He laughs. "Do you trust me?"

"Yes." The answer rolls off my tongue effortlessly, and

I realize it's true. Over the past few months, I've come to trust him more than anyone.

He steps up to order, my jaw dropping when he starts speaking Greek.

What the fuck? It seems there's still a lot I don't know about my fake boyfriend.

Looking behind him, he chuckles at my open-mouthed expression, and my stomach churns with … oh no.

Oh. Fucking. No.

I cannot, under any circumstances, catch feelings for this man.

Not him, not him, please not him.

I know pleading is futile, because somehow, slowly, gradually, one second at a time, I've started to fall for this man in all the ways that matter. Sure, he's good looking, but there's so much more to him than that.

And he just spoke Greek like a fucking pro, and that might be the most attractive thing I've ever seen.

"What?" he asks innocently, the brim of his baseball cap shielding me from the intensity of his eyes.

"N-Nothing."

"Lies." He unleashes that carefree grin on me, and my stomach does the weird flippy thing again. *Not cool feelings, stop this right now!* "I know you well enough now that I can sense when you're hiding something."

"Just grateful to be in such a beautiful country," I lie.

He doesn't buy it one bit, but lets it drop when our order is ready. He says something in Greek that I assume is the equivalent of thank you, and then we sit down at one of the tables.

He passes me the glass with cold coffee and some kind of foam. "Try one." He points to one of the two matching pastries on the plate.

I do as he says, surprised at how yummy it is. It's savory but somehow sweet at the same time. I've never tasted anything like it. "That's incredible."

"Now the coffee," he coaxes, enjoying this based on the upturned tilt of his lips.

I take a sip, my eyes widening. "Wow, this is so much better than back home."

"See, I know what you like."

For some reason his words make me blush. Ducking my head, I study the depths of coffee like it's the most fascinating thing in the world.

My skin prickles all over when he touches his index finger beneath my chin, forcing me to raise my head. "It's okay, you know?"

"What's okay?" I rack my brain, trying to figure out what he's talking about.

I nearly cower away from the intensity of his green eyes, but somehow I manage to hold his gaze.

"That you want me."

"I don't—"

Thumb on my chin, he holds me in place. "Don't lie. Not to me."

My breath catches in my throat.

I am so fucked.

———

AFTER EXPLORING the city for several hours, and sticking my toes in the ocean, we go back to the yacht to relax a little before enduring dinner with his dad. Easy going, carefree Teddy grows tenser with each passing hour that brings us closer to the meal.

I hate that one single person, his own parent at that, can fill such an otherwise happy person with so much dread. It's not right, and he deserves more.

"You wanna go to the pool?" He hooks his thumbs into the back of his tee and yanks it over his head.

"The ... pool? You mean the ocean?"

He rifles through the dresser drawer where he unpacked his things—unlike me who hasn't bothered and is living out of my suitcase.

Holding up a pair of swim shorts, he shakes his head. "There's a pool on the yacht."

"Is there a shopping mall too? Perhaps a bowling alley?"

"A bowling alley would've been a good idea, but no."

"It must be nice to be rich."

He freezes, looking at the bright green shorts with white stripes clasped in his hands. "I'd take being poor and surrounded by people who care about me any day."

"Teddy—"

"But money, or lack of, guarantees nothing in life. I mean, you grew up differently than I did and look at how your sister has treated you. If there's any knowledge I wish I could impart on the world, it's that people, the ones we love, matter more than any of this shit." He waves his hand, indicating all of the luxury encasing us.

I don't know what makes me do it, maybe I'm feeling weak, or maybe this attraction to him is just too big to ignore, but I stand on my tiptoes and press my mouth to his. It's barely a kiss, more of a glide of my lips, but he growls low in his throat, and his hand goes to the back of my neck holding me there as he deepens it.

Kissing Teddy is like standing in the pouring rain—exhilarating, raw, and somehow melancholic at the same time because I know at the end of the semester, I'll be saying goodbye to this, to *him*.

Then why don't you enjoy everything he has to offer while you can? My mind taunts me.

My body sinks into his and he holds me steady. Teddy is my pillar in so many ways. I didn't even realize until now how I've come to rely on him. He seems like someone you shouldn't be able to count on, but it's the complete opposite. He's the person that would drop anything to be there for the ones he cares about.

Standing on my tiptoes I deepen the kiss, moaning when his tongue tangles with mine. I gasp when he grabs me under the ass and lifts me easily until my legs twine around his hips. I want to scream that I'm too heavy and to put me down, but clearly, he's not having any trouble holding me, so I keep my mouth shut.

"God, I could kiss you forever," he murmurs, peppering small kisses on and around my mouth. He dives back in, giving me a long, deep kiss. My pussy clenches in response to his words and the feel of his growing erection pressing into me.

I want to blame my hormones for this lapse in judgment. It's been too long since I've had sex, and I'd be attracted to anyone. But it's not true. I don't want to admit it to myself, but I want Teddy.

My back is pressed into the wall, and he uses his hips to hold me in place, taking both my hands in his and pinning them above my head. He kisses my neck, sucking on the skin hard enough to leave behind a mark.

"Been dying to kiss you again." He skims his lips over my collarbone.

"Why haven't you?" I sound breathless and moany, and I would cringe at myself if I wasn't so turned on right now.

"Waiting." Kiss to my jaw. "For you." He kisses the corner of my mouth. "To make the." Another kiss to the other corner of my mouth. "First move." He punctuates that statement by kissing me fully on the lips, his tongue seeking the seam of mine.

I open willingly for him. I don't think I've ever been kissed this passionately, like I'm his entire world and he's trying his hardest to prove it to me with every touch of our lips. His erection pushes into me, and I moan at the feel of it.

"I want to fuck you," he confesses, a tad breathless which is the biggest turn on ever. "Fast. Slow. Hard. All of it. Then I want to do it all over again, every day for the rest of my life. I want to make love to you slowly until you beg me to let you come. I want to take you fast and hard because we both can't fucking stand waiting. I want you in so many ways, Vanessa, and not just sex."

His confession should freak me out. It should send me

running off this boat and straight into the ocean. But I hear his sincerity, I feel it in the way he holds me.

"You weren't supposed to fall for me."

Brilliant green eyes hold me captive. "Too fucking bad. You're mine."

Possessive terms like *you're mine* used to be one hell of a turn off for me, but coming from Teddy, I've changed my mind. I know he isn't trying to control me.

"You're fucking gorgeous," he continues as my head falls back against the wall, my hands still caged in his. I nearly fall apart when he kisses the exposed swells of my breasts. I had no idea when I put on the fitted tank this morning that it would serve such a good purpose, but here we are.

"Teddy? Vanessa? Are you back?"

The door rattles and we both startle like we've been caught doing something wrong. We were both so lost in the moment we didn't even notice a knock at the door.

Teddy sets me down slowly, his chest rising and falling rapidly as he struggles to regain his breath. I'm equally as winded. We stare at each other, both knowing that something's changed in this moment, something we can't come back from. His eyes hold a promise of *later*.

Bending, he scoops up his fallen swim trunks, holding them in front of his obvious erection so he can open the door to face his mom.

Running my fingers through my hair, I try to smooth it down so it's not a tangled mess that screams, *"I almost let your son fuck me against the wall."*

"Hey, Mom," he says in greeting.

"Hi." She smiles, looking for me over his shoulder. I give an awkward wave when she spots me. "I wanted to see if you and Vanessa wanted to join me for tea."

"Sorry, no can do, Mom. We're headed up to the pool."

"Oh." I hate how disappointed she sounds. "Another time, then. Enjoy your pool time."

Her high heels clack down the hall, because even on vacation she's wearing stilettos.

Teddy closes the door, leaning his head against the thick wood. "Cock-blocked by my fucking mother."

I throw my head back and laugh.

The look he gives me says he thinks this is anything but funny.

Side-stepping him, I rifle through my luggage pulling out the hot pink bikini I bought for this trip.

Never have I worn a bikini—at least not a true one that exposes so much skin. Even the swimsuit Teddy bought me for lessons was more full coverage—a tankini I guess you'd call it.

Despite my lack of swimming, I have spent summers on the lake or by the pool, and I always opted for a swimsuit that covered as much skin as possible. Not this time. I'm embracing my curves, stretch marks, and cellulite. Those things don't define me and they're not imperfections like some people think. They're a story, a road map woven into my very skin.

Shutting myself in the bathroom, I take a moment to gather myself after our intense makeout session. When I look at myself in the mirror, I find that my eyes are a shade darker than normal and have a glazed quality to them. My hair? That's a complete and utter mess. My lips are red and deliciously swollen. My face is a bit red too from the rough scratch of his stubble, and sure enough there's already a hickey forming on my neck that will be nearly impossible to cover up. Hopefully my concealer will do a good enough job when it comes time for dinner. The last thing I want is his father commenting on it. Ick.

After I've changed, I open the door to find Teddy lounging on the bed looking at his phone in all his tanned skinned, muscular glory, and I have to bite my lip to not moan at the sight of him.

I've never been able to deny that he's hot.

He looks up from his phone quickly and then back down before he does a double take, staring hard at every inch of my body. In the past, I would've felt nervous under such blatant scrutiny because I don't do well with attention but having Teddy's undivided attention makes me feel good.

He falls dramatically into the pillows, covering his eyes with the crook of his elbow. "You're trying to kill me. You really are."

The giggle that erupts from me sounds girlish and foreign to my ears.

"Hurry up. I thought we were going swimming."

He sits up, pointing to his crotch. "You want me to go swimming with a hard-on?"

"Don't be such a baby." I gather my hair back into a messy knot and tie it off. "You didn't teach me to swim for nothing did you?"

He groans, rising from the bed. "Guess not." I shiver

as he steps up beside me, skimming his finger lightly down my arm. "I hope you plan on letting me remove this later." He toys with one of the thin straps tied around my back.

My throat is suddenly dry, my heart pounding in my ears.

"No, I'm capable of taking it off myself."

He grins, leaning in so his mouth presses against my ear with every word he speaks. "You and me Vanessa. It's happening. What just happened proves it. Stop denying yourself what you want."

"And what is it I want?"

Green eyes twinkle. "Me."

THIRTY-ONE

Teddy

"LOOK! I'M TOUCHING A FISH!" VANESSA SQUEALS,
holding up the slimy and squirmy fish she caught so I can
take a photo before she releases it back into the ocean.

I don't know what possessed me to take her fishing,
but I'm glad I did. The local fisherman captaining the boat
chuckles in amusement at Vanessa as she leans over the
boat to put the fish back in the water. I can't help myself,
checking out the curve of her ass in a pair of cut off denim
shorts.

"I think all the fish are far more attracted to you than
me," I comment, eyeing my fishing pole with disdain.

"What can I say? I'm a natural fisher-woman."

The boat bobs on the rocking water, and Vanessa
starts to lose her balance. Gripping her arm, I hold her

steady so she doesn't fall overboard. Despite her swim lessons and the life jacket strapped firmly around her body, you can never be too careful.

"Careful, Van." I release her and she settles down in her seat beside me.

"Thanks for that."

"Don't mention it." My eyes zero in on her glossy pink lips, picturing her mouth wrapped around my cock.

It's been three whole days since we made-out in the room. Three days of dancing around the inevitable while our chemistry grows to damn near combustible levels.

I'm not leaving Greece until I have Vanessa in every imaginable way.

She bumps her elbow against my arm, her smile damn near infectious. Dark sunglasses hide her eyes from view, but I have a feeling laughter would be reflected in them.

"Do you want me to help you catch one?"

"I'm doing fine on my own."

"Whatever you say." She props her legs up on an upturned bucket. "I'm having way better luck than you are."

"You're a natural."

"Forget PR work, I'm just going to fish for the rest of my days."

"Can't say I'd blame you. Not with a view like this." Clearing my throat, I say, "I know we got suckered into this, but thank you for coming with me."

"Are you kidding me? This is Greece. I should be the one thanking you. Besides, we've only had to deal with your dad for dinners, so it hasn't been a big deal."

And thank God for that. He's been too wrapped up with work and trying to secure the purchase of some massive hotel in Abu Dhabi to pay us much mind. That doesn't mean we're in the clear though. He can always find an opportunity to torture me whenever he sees fit.

"Teddy! Your pole!" Vanessa's shriek of surprise brings me back to reality and I grab ahold of it, reeling in whatever is on the line. It puts up a massive fight and we're both certain I've caught something huge only for a tiny, six-inch fish to be caught on the end. The boat's captain has a big laugh over my catch. I do to, since I'm a good sport.

After Vanessa snaps a picture of me with the little guy, I let him go.

Dinner time is approaching, so I tell the captain we need to head back.

Vanessa lets out a dreamy sigh and my eyebrow rises. "What was that sound for?"

"It's kind of sexy hearing you speak Greek." The way her cheeks turn pink I have a feeling she finds it more appealing than the words *kind of* portray.

"There are other languages I'm far more fluent in."

"Like what?" She gives me a narrowed eyed look like she expects me to say something cheesy about language between the sheets.

"Well," I look out at the waves as we glide over them, "Spanish for one. French and Italian. German. Japanese and Chinese. Those are just the ones I'm fluent in. Obviously, I speak a fair bit of Greek. I know a decent amount of Korean. A tiny bit of Russian. Some Hindi too."

She lowers her sunglasses, eyes narrowed in speculation. "You're dead serious, aren't you?"

I laugh, not at all offended. "Why does everyone always doubt me? It's not some line when I say I have a genius level IQ. And—" I can't stop myself from reaching over and drawing my finger around her bare knee. "I happen to have a fondness for linguistics."

"You are the most fascinating person I've ever met."

"And that's the best compliment I've ever received."

Back on land, we hop on the moped I rented for the day. It's worth every penny for the simple fact that it forces Vanessa to hold on, pressed firmly against my back.

She lets out a shrill shriek as I speed down the streets, heading in the direction of where the yacht is docked off a different part of the island.

When we get off the moped, Vanessa removes her helmet shaking her hair free. I'm hit once again with a rush of desire. I've been good for way too long. I want her in every possible way, and I know she feels the same.

"What are you smiling about?" Her laughter carries on the wind. She reaches up, trying to keep her hair from flying in her face, but it's a futile attempt.

"Nothing."

Lie.

"Liar."

I grin, shoving my hands into the pockets of my board shorts. "Just admiring the view."

"You were staring at me."

"Like I said," my smile grows bigger, "admiring the view."

She turns away from my scrutiny like it embarrasses her. Closing the distance between us, I wrap my hand around her wrist, and with the fingers of my other hand, I lift her chin. "Don't hide from me." She opens her mouth to protest, but I don't give her the chance to speak.

She moans at the first touch of our lips. If I had any lingering doubts about whether or not she wants this, that sound alone erases those fears. Her hands splay across my stomach, the heat of her skin seeping into mine even through the cotton of my shirt. She presses up on her tiptoes, trying to get closer to me. I love how fucking eager she is for me.

"You want me," I growl against her lips. "Now admit it to me." Stubborn girl that she is, she tries to ignore my request, but I'm not having it. I'm not letting her avoid this. Grabbing her elbows, I force her back, and she mewls in protest at the loss of contact. "Tell me what I want to hear, Vanessa."

Hooded eyes hazy with lust flutter up at me. "No."

"So fucking defiant." Lowering my voice to a whisper, I say, "I should spank you for it."

Her tiny gasp sends blood rushing to my dick.

I give her a long, slow kiss and step away. "You will be mine. In every possible way."

When she doesn't protest, I know she's finally realized what I've known for a while. We're inevitable.

MY DAD PLACES his napkin on his plate, his signal that he's finished with dinner. He stands, smoothing his hand down his pressed shirt. "Son, I'd like to speak with you in my office."

Yeah, my dad has an office on his fucking yacht.

"I'm still eating my dessert." I didn't used to balk him this much, it's never been worth it, but something about Vanessa makes me feel strong enough to defy him every chance I get.

It's funny, seeing as how I'm a man now and far bigger than him—able to lay him flat without a blink if I wanted —but there's something about standing in front of your abuser that makes you cower and forget how strong you actually are. Abusers have this strange sort of power over you that renders you frozen, locked in a different time.

"Now."

I give my chocolate torte a forlorn look and push my chair back from the table.

Vanessa sends a sympathetic look my way, her eyes following me out of the room.

My father says nothing as I trail after him, his back stiff and shoulders straight. Onto the elevator we go— yeah, there's an elevator—and not a single word is spoken on the ride.

The doors open, and he marches down the hall, expecting and knowing that I'll follow.

I feel like I'm being led to my death—but that's how I usually feel with anything involving this man. There's a constant cloud of gloom and doom that follows him. As hard as it was growing up away at school my entire life,

I'm fucking thankful for it, because if I had constantly lived under this man's rule, I'm afraid I might've turned out exactly like him.

Sure, I've done things I'm not proud of, but at least I have a sense of humor, and I *care* about people. I have true friends who are like family. And I even have Vanessa.

He unlocks the door to his office, and steps aside to let me in first. Bastard keeps it locked unless he's in it, afraid of the staff snooping through his documents.

He slams the door closed behind him when he enters, and it takes everything in me to not physically wince.

He moves behind his desk, head lowered with his hands on his hips.

"What are you doing, son?"

I fucking hate it when he calls me son. It implies a level of care, of respect, of what our dynamics should be — but it's nothing but another way for him to belittle me and a reminder of the fact that I don't truly have a dad.

"I'm not sure what you mean, sir."

I'm not prepared for his backhanded slap. It comes out of nowhere, rocking my head to the side. I'm too shocked to even feel the sting.

"You know what I'm talking about." *I really don't.* "The girl has to go. She's from a low-class family that has nothing to offer our name. There is no future for you there and frankly, I'm not sold on the two of you." I keep my mouth shut for now, not wanting to incur his wrath a second time. As it is, I'm trying to stop myself from grabbing him by the shirt and tossing him against the wall.

Eyes narrowed, he says, "She's not your usual type and that makes me suspicious."

"Suspicious?" This time I can't stay quiet.

"It'd be an easy lie to tell." He picks up a paperweight from his desk, turning it in his pale fingers—sickly white despite the Greek sun. "And someone like her," disgust drips from his words, "would be an easy target and all too agreeable. Just look at her. I'm sure having someone like you on her arm raises her social status, and who wouldn't want that."

"You have no idea what you're talking about," I grit out, each word grating on my throat.

"Do you think I'm stupid?" He slams the paperweight down on the desk hard enough to leave a dent in the expensive wood. In an eerily calm voice, eyes devoid of any emotion, he says, "Keep playing your little games. Just remember, though, I always win, and I always get what I want." Ice crawls down my spine. "Now get the fuck out of my office."

I don't have to be told twice.

THIRTY-TWO

Vanessa

TEDDY DOESN'T COME BACK TO THE DINING ROOM after he leaves with his father. He's not in the room either, and as I sit on the bed waiting and time continues to pass, I grow more worried.

I mean, I don't *think* his dad is dumb enough to kill him and toss his body into the ocean, but who knows.

I already changed out of my dress I wore for dinner and into a pair of blue cotton shorts and an over-sized t-shirt, so I shove my feet into my flip-flops as I go in search of him.

He isn't in the library, or in the kitchen stuffing his face with more food. Nor is he at the pool.

I don't know what makes me do it, but I eye a ladder that leads up to a small deck and take a deep breath before

I grab a rung. I *hate* heights, but I don't think about it right now. When I top the ladder, I find Teddy lying in a pile of blankets on his back, arms behind his head as he looks up at the starry sky. Somehow, my body knew I'd find him here.

"Are you okay?" I ask, crawling over to him—too nervous to stand up here despite the railing surrounding us.

"Yeah." But he turns his head, and already I see a bruise forming on his cheek.

I feel sick at the sight of it. "Teddy." His name falls from my lips sadly.

"It's no biggie. Come here." He scoots over, making room for me on his mountain of blankets.

I want to ask him about the bruise, what went on with his dad, but I know he doesn't want to talk about it. Lying down beside him, I turn to my side and lay my head on his chest. His heart is a steady rhythmic beat against my ear.

He wraps his arm around me, lazily stroking the bare skin of my arm. Goosebumps rise from his touch, my nipples pebbling against the fabric of my shirt.

"Cold?" he asks when I shiver, his arms automatically tightening around me.

"Yes," I lie, because it's easier to agree than to admit how much I want him. "You're still in your clothes." I close my eyes, wincing at my phrasing, but his laughter makes my blunder worthwhile. "You know what I mean." I pluck at a button on his dress shirt. "You're all fancy and stuff."

"If you wanted me to take my shirt off, all you had to do is ask."

He sits up, bringing my body with him. I pull away as he makes swift work of the buttons and discards the shirt on the deck before lying back down and tugging me with him so I return to my former position.

His bare skin is warm against the side of my face. I trace a circle around his nipple, and he groans low in his throat. "Careful, Vanessa, you might get more than you're bargaining for."

He keeps his eyes firmly on the night sky above us — filled with more stars than I've ever seen before.

There's a light smattering of chest hair between his pecs, and I tweak one of the hairs, making him jolt. He glares at me, but his grimace quickly snuffs out when I speak. "Maybe I am bargaining for it."

His sensual lips part, eyes searching mine for any sign of dishonesty.

He rises up over me, lust swimming in his gaze. "What are you saying, Van?"

I moisten my lips with a swipe of my tongue. Gliding one hand up his smooth chest, I wrap my fingers around the back of his neck and tug him closer, closing the distance between us until our lips almost touch.

"I want you. I want *this*."

He doesn't respond with words. He closes the infinitesimal space between our mouths, angling my head back as his tongue finds mine. He kisses me slowly, thoroughly. He takes his time, imprinting himself on my lips so they'll never forget the taste and feel of him. Teddy wants to ruin me for any guy that comes after him, and it scares me to realize that he's already been successful.

His hands tangle in my hair, focused on kissing me. It surprises me that he isn't hurrying this along, afraid I might change my mind. But no, Teddy is intent on savoring this—*me*. He worships my mouth thoroughly before moving to my neck.

He tugs the collar of my shirt down. "I love seeing you all marked up by me." My skin is still speckled with hickeys from our intense make-out session.

"Teddy—"

"Don't rush me," he growls the command, moving down my body. "Do you have any idea how long I've waited to taste you?" His eyes are twin green flames in the dark of the night. He grabs my shorts, shimmying them down my hips and off my body. "No panties? Color me intrigued, Ms. Hughes."

"I'm in my pjs." My treacherous voice is breathless. "Of course I'm not wearing underwear."

"All the more fun for me."

He lowers to his stomach on the deck, forcing my thighs to spread to accommodate his wide shoulders. I cry out at the first swipe of his tongue against my pussy, my hips lifting off the deck. He loops his arms around my legs, holding me in place. It quickly becomes apparent that all my previous experiences with oral were lacking. Clearly all the practice Teddy's had fucking around has been worth it because he's definitely learned a thing or two.

I gasp, crying out. My fingers tighten in his hair,

holding him against me. "Yes! Just like that! Do that again!" I've never been so loud or so bossy, but with Teddy, I feel comfortable enough to be vocal. He swirls his tongue around, sucking at my clit like I wanted. "I'm so close." It's a statement, but I'm practically begging. My orgasm flutters around the corners of my eyes, my vision nearly blacking out.

When he curls a finger into me, the orgasm shatters through my body, and a string of words flies out of my mouth that my brain can't even decipher, but from his soft chuckle against me he must find my ramblings amusing.

As I come down from my high, a shiver courses through me from the feel of two of his fingers lazily stroking me.

He grins, his lips with moist from my juices. "Think I can make you come again like that?" I can't find my voice, but he doesn't appear to have a problem with that. "I know I can. And then I'm going to make you come all over my cock while you scream my name for everyone to hear you."

My jaw drops, a cry of pleasure slipping out when he covers me with his mouth again.

I don't think it's possible for me to come again so quickly and so forcefully, but apparently Teddy is a magician because he pulls one hell of an act when I fall apart, legs shaking.

He kisses my inner thighs before paying special attention to my stomach. An area I'm normally insecure about, he worships, reminding me that my entire being is beautiful—not only one part.

333

Lifting my arms so he can rid me of my shirt, I marvel at the lust in his eyes as he takes in my breasts.

"You're so fucking gorgeous." He grabs my boobs, testing the weight in his palms. They're large enough that not even Teddy's big hands can fully cover them. He dips his head down, sucking on one nipple and then giving the other the same attention.

I push at his shoulder, and he gives me a betrayed look as he stops sucking on my breasts.

"I want you naked," I say by way of explanation.

His boyish smile makes my stomach dip with affection. I never expected to develop feelings for Teddy, and even though I don't quite understand them yet, it feels like a pretty big deal.

"Just admit it, you've wanted to see me naked ever since you checked me out in the admin building."

Rolling my eyes, I protest, "I didn't check you—"

He presses his index finger to my lips. "Don't lie to me, especially not after I made you come twice with just my tongue and fingers."

He shucks off his pants and palms himself over his boxer-briefs. My mouth waters at the vision of his dick straining against the fabric. I've already seen him naked, and I'm reminded of the conversation we had that time.

Monster truck.

He chuckles, still stroking himself. His boxer-briefs lower with the movement, revealing the head of his cock beaded with pre-cum.

His eyes are hooded with lust watching me as I watch him. "You want this?"

He squeezes his cock, and I whimper. "Yes."

Leaning back on his elbows, he arches a brow. "Show me."

Crawling over to him, I rake my nails down his abs, relishing when he shivers from my touch. I lick my lips in anticipation. In the past I was never too eager to give a guy a blowjob. It never appealed to me and felt more like an obligation than anything else. But with Teddy I crave the taste of him, curious to see how he fills my mouth.

He helps me remove his underwear, and then he's completely bare before me. His cock juts out proudly from his body, reaching his naval. The four-leaf clover tattoo on his hipbone begs for my attention. I trace my finger over the shape of it before using the same finger to trace the scar on his stomach. He shivers at my touch, still reclined on his elbows so he can watch everything I do.

"You haven't even put your mouth on me, and I already feel like I'm going to blow my load," he confesses, voice shaky.

I laugh at that, wrapping my hand around his cock. He's thick and warm, and I find myself fascinated by the thick vein on the underside of his dick. I press my thumb against it and let go.

"Woman, you're killing me," he groans, sounding pained.

Looking up at him, I bite my lip to hide my growing smile. "We can't have that, can we? Especially not before we get to the fun part."

"By fun part—oh *fuck*." Whatever he was going to say is cut off when I take him into my mouth.

His head falls back, eyes drifting closed. I can't help but watch him as I lick and suck, relishing in the way his long lashes fan against his cheeks with slow blinks, how his mouth is parted, and his chest rises and falls with each heavy breath.

Reaching down, he gathers my hair back away from my face so he can watch as I take him in my mouth. I go as deep as I can, gagging on his length and pull away, wiping my mouth.

"Fuck, you're so hot," he practically purrs, making me feel like a goddess. I stroke him with my hand, dipping my head back down, but he tugs on my hair, stopping me. "As much as I'd love to come in that pretty mouth of yours," he rubs his thumb over my swollen bottom lip for emphasis, "I'd rather be inside you."

I nod my head in agreement—apparently a little too excitedly because he chuckles in amusement. He reaches for his pants and pulls out a condom wrapper.

Arching a brow, I narrow my eyes in accusation. "Why are there condoms in your pocket?"

Grinning, he rips the foil open. "Like a good boy scout, I like to be prepared at all times. I knew this was going to happen with us eventually, so I started keeping them on me. Relax."

"You knew, huh?" I watch as he sheaths himself with the condom, stroking himself once. Twice.

He reaches for my hips, pulling me up his body. "Babe, with chemistry like ours, it wasn't a matter of *if* but *when*. It took you longer to see that than me." His hold on my hips tightens, fingers flexing. It looks like he's fighting every ounce of self-control he possesses. "Now," he practically begs, "ride me."

Reaching between us, I grip his cock and lower myself onto him.

We moan in unison, the sound filled with both pleasure and relief.

"You feel better than I imagined," he confesses, rocking my hips against him.

I push his hands away, and he smirks. "Put your hands on my chest," I command, and he does as I ask eagerly, cupping my boobs in his big hands. It feels better on top with him holding my chest. Guys might love to look at big boobs, but that doesn't mean they're comfortable for the one that actually has them strapped to their chest. I rock against him, my clit rubbing against his pelvis. Tiny little moans escape me.

"Fuck, Van. You look so gorgeous on top of me."

I *feel* gorgeous.

Lowering until our chests are pressed together, I rock back while kissing and sucking on his neck. His hands grip my ass, urging me faster. Sweat dampens our skin. I feel my orgasm building.

"I'm almost there," I pant, my mouth pressed to his jaw. I can feel the crescendo rising, my breath nothing but a gasp at this point. My whole body tightens, and I cry out when the orgasm hits and then just keeps going. "Oh my God!" My nails rake into the skin of his chest. "It's not stopping."

I nearly lose my mind when Teddy flips me over, pounding into me so that just as my orgasm is starting to fade, another goes off, exploding against me. My legs shake uncontrollably, my eyes squeezed shut from the intensity.

"Holy fuck," he groans, rubbing his thumb over my clit. "You're squeezing my dick so tight."

I couldn't help it if I wanted to.

Sex has never been like this for me before. I'm not saying it's been *bad* every time, but average seems like an apt description. With Teddy it's downright explosive.

He throws his head back, hips rolling against mine with his thumb still rubbing that bundle of nerves. He keeps a steady pace, and I'm shocked when I feel myself starting to come again.

"Yes! Yes! Oh my God, *yes!* Don't stop! Right there!" I realize I'm begging, completely wanton, but I can't bring myself to care, not when that delicious high is in reach.

We fall apart at the same time, my whole body trembling uncontrollably. I'm suddenly very glad he switched our positions because if he hadn't, I'm pretty sure I would've fallen off. Teddy moans through his own release, the sounds of pleasure he makes turning me on all over again because he's feeling this way because of *me*. It's a powerful, intoxicating feeling.

Teddy burrows his face into my neck, peppering kisses all over my sweat damp skin. "Vanessa," he murmurs my name in a way that says so many other things, things he knows I'm not ready to hear.

Rolling off my body, he removes the condom and ties it off. He moves to lay back down beside me as I sit up.

"I should go ... clean up."

"Not yet." He wraps his hands around my wrist. "Stay here a bit longer."

I nod my head in agreement, allowing him to tug me back against his side, our naked forms curled together beneath the night sky.

THIRTY-THREE

Teddy

IF SOMEONE TOLD ME THAT WHILE I WAS IN GREECE, I'D be waking up one morning to the delicious sensation of Vanessa's mouth wrapped around my dick, I would've been certain they were lying, too afraid to get my hopes up for such a thing.

Rubbing sleep from my eyes, I groan at the vision that is a naked Vanessa between my thighs. We had sex *three* times last night, but apparently it wasn't enough for her. I never would've taken Vanessa for someone so sexually voracious, but I should've known better.

She hums as she works her hand and mouth over my cock.

"Fuck, babe," I groan, my voice deep and scratchy from sleep. I gather her hair away from her face so I can see her better. "I fucking love your mouth, and I love fucking your mouth." She laughs and the action of it around my cock is mind-blowing. "Holy shit!" I can't hold myself back, and I blow my load right into her mouth. She takes it all though, and after she's swallowed, she gives me an innocent look that's ruined by the evil twinkle in her eyes. "Come here." I crook a finger, encouraging her to climb up my body. She doesn't have to be told twice. "Sit on my face," I command. Now, she chooses to hesitate.

"Teddy," she says my name softly, hesitantly. "Are you sure?"

"Why wouldn't I be?" I narrow my eyes, not sure where she's coming from.

"I mean, my thighs are kind of big and—"

"Fuck that shit, don't worry about me, if I tell you to sit on my face, it's because I fucking want you too. Now give me that pussy."

She hesitates only a second longer before she does as I asked. I loop my arms around her thighs, holding her steady. My nose presses against her clit and I swipe my tongue against her core. She cries out, and I hear her hands slam into the headboard above me. Hopefully she grabs onto it, because she's going to need something to hold on to since I plan on staying here a while.

I had sex with a girl one time who wasn't into oral— and that's fine if it's not your thing—but her reasoning was she was embarrassed about how she'd taste.

Like what the fuck does that mean?

I know it's not going to taste like a pineapple or strawberries or whatever the fuck else. A pussy tastes like a pussy, just the way I like it.

"Oh God, Teddy," Vanessa cries out above me. I can already feel myself growing hard again from the taste of her and the little sounds she makes. It doesn't take much to turn me on where Vanessa's involved. She could read a fudge recipe to me, and I'd get hard.

I lap at her juices, holding on tighter to her when her legs tremble.

"I'm almost there ... so close ... *yes*." She goes off, griding her pussy into my face, and I take everything she gives me.

Guiding her back down onto the bed, I swipe a condom from the table and put it on in record time. Lifting her hips, I enter her from behind. Her pussy squeezes my cock and I bow over her back. "Fuck, babe." I reach for her boob, tweaking a nipple which makes her shriek. "Keep squeezing my cock like that, and I'm not going to last long."

"I like it when you can't control yourself." She wiggles her ass against me, meeting me thrust for thrust.

I spank her ass, and she cries out in surprise. That cry quickly turns into a long, drawn-out moan. "You like that?" It's a rhetorical question. I know her body backward and forwards, inside out now. "You like it when I spank you?" I do it again and she moans. "I like seeing my handprints on your ass."

"Oh God," she moans.

She also likes it when I talk dirty, but she won't admit it.

Throwing my head back, I pump into her, fucking her hard. She takes everything I have to give and then some. Fast, slow, hard, or soft, Vanessa doesn't care, and I love her for that. She wants it all, not just something basic.

I pull another orgasm from her before I pull out of her and rip the condom off. It only takes a few strokes of my cock before I come all over backside, relishing in the image of dirtying her up.

"Fuck," I growl. "That's hot."

Vanessa collapses onto her stomach on the covers, breathing rapidly as she struggles to regain composure. Slipping from the bed, I clean myself up in the bathroom and grab a washcloth, dampening it with warm water. She looks at me with wide, surprised eyes as I clean her up.

"You came all over me and now you're cleaning me up?" She turns her head back, watching me as I wipe the cloth over her.

"What can I say? I'm a gentleman. A filthy one, but a gentleman nonetheless."

When she doesn't roll her eyes at me, I know I've fucked her so thoroughly there's no sass left in her for the moment. As soon as she regains her energy it'll return.

Bending, I kiss her naked shoulder.

"I don't want to go home," she admits quietly. "I love it here."

We board the plane in just a few hours, and I'm not looking forward to it either. Despite my father's presence aboard the yacht, this has been the most enjoyable vacation I've ever had, and I know it's all due to the woman lying in my bed.

"Me either. But duty calls." More like school calls, but whatever. At least we're nearing graduation. "What do you want to do today?" I climb into bed beside her after tossing the cloth in the hamper. We're lying the wrong way, but who cares.

"Whatever you want and then…"

"And then?" I prompt, wondering what she's thinking when her face turns a bright red color.

"And then I was thinking when we're on the plane…"

"Yeah?"

She traces a finger over my chest, playing with one of the stray hairs there. "Well, I don't think I'd mind it so much if we joined the mile high club."

"Yeah?" I cup her cheek, leaning in to kiss her.

"Yeah," she echoes.

I knew there was a reason this girl was placed in my path, and it's because she's fucking perfect for me in every possible way.

THIRTY-FOUR

Vanessa

TEDDY WON'T STOP KISSING ME WHEN HE DROPS ME OFF at my dorm.

"I have to go," I laugh, trying to dodge him before we get caught up and I decide to drag him up to my room. Not that I think he'd complain, but Danika is probably back, and I really do need to get settled and ready for class in the morning.

"Are you sure you don't need help getting these bags back up to your room?" He gives me my favorite smile of his, the naughty boy one that says he knows he can get away with whatever he wants.

I look down at the ground where all of my stuff sits. Yes, I need his help. Am I going to accept it? No. Why? Because if it's this difficult to resist his advances out here, it'll be damn near impossible with my bed only a few feet away.

"I can handle it. Besides," I place my hands on his lower stomach, giving him a light shove away from me, "you need to go check on Jude and make sure he didn't get an STD while he was away."

Teddy gives a groan, but he knows I'm right. "I'll see you later?"

"You aren't sick of me yet?"

"Never," he growls, swooping in for a kiss. "All right, all right. I'm going," he laughs, backing toward his car when I give him another shove.

Somehow, I manage to gather up all of my stuff, and thanks to the help of a girl that lives in my dorm, I get inside and onto the elevator without dropping anything.

Entering my room, I find Danika must've only recently arrived too since some of her things are strewn around the shared living space.

She walks out of her room, and I'm surprised by the big smile she gives me. "Hey, how was Greece?"

"Spectacular."

I'm aware I'm beaming from ear to ear, and while the trip has a little to do with it, it's mostly due to my traveling companion.

"You're definitely glowing," she affirms, looking me over.

"So are you." She got one hell of a tan at whatever beach she went to. "I wish it lasted longer, but at least graduation is soon."

Speaking of, I didn't do one lick of studying while I

was gone. I need to crack open a textbook and get some reading in tonight so I'm not completely lost tomorrow.

Dragging my stuff into my bedroom, I get to work unpacking. Once everything is put away, I breathe a sigh of relief that the room is back in order.

Danika pokes her head into my open room. "You wanna go out tonight?"

I blink at her, taken off guard by the question. We're not friends, so she's never asked me to hang out before. "Where?"

She shrugs. "Harvey's." I must be giving her a weird look, because she steps into my room and lowers her arms from her chest. "Look, I know we haven't been friends, and that's on me. I had a shitty roommate the first two years who I thought was my friend, but it turns out she was nothing but a liar and manipulator, so I knew whoever I got paired with for junior and senior year I was going to keep at a distance. I realize now that wasn't fair to you, and I'm sorry. I know we're about to graduate, but I'd like to try to make amends." I give her a blank, bug-eyed stare that has her moving awkwardly from foot to foot. "Look, you don't have to it's just that—"

"No, no. I'm in," I rush to say. "It's just that this isn't all on you. I haven't made much, well any, effort to be your friend either. I mean, if I'm being honest, I don't have any friends here ... until now."

Because Teddy and Jude, they are my friends now. Sure, it's not a lot, but it counts. It's kind of sad how I've kept myself at a distance from everyone the whole time I've been here. Time's been an issue since I work a lot on top of school, but the past few months are proof that I could've made room for people in my life. I just didn't want to.

"I guess we're both making progress then. Should we leave at seven?"

"Sounds good."

———

"DON'T BE surprised when Teddy pops out from somewhere," I warn Danika, smoothing my skirt down. "I told him we were having a girls night and not to crash, but he never listens."

Touching up her red lipstick she eyes me over her compact. "He has hot friends he always travels with, so I'll forgive him." Snapping it closed, she puts her lipstick away and gives her hair one final fluff. "I need a free margarita."

"They're free tonight?" I ask way too enthusiastically because I can't say no to my favorite drink.

"They are when someone else is buying them." She winks and I give her a slow clap for that one.

Inside a country song is blasting across the speakers, my head automatically bobbing along.

We've barely walked a few feet through the door when an arm sweeps around, and I'm tugged into a familiar chest. "I missed you."

"You just saw me this afternoon." My arms wrap around Teddy's neck, from the corner of my eye Danika smiles at us.

"Still long enough for me to miss you." He ducks down, kissing me quickly before we get carried away. Clearing his throat, he turns to my roommate. "Nice to see you, Danika."

"Likewise." She tries not to laugh. "Are you trying to steal my date?"

"No, you were. This one's always mine." He smiles at me and my stupid heart flips over. "Come on," he jerks his head in the opposite direction, "we already have a table."

"Who is we?" Danika asks cautiously, gripping her wristlet to her chest like she needs to protect it from someone.

"Everyone." Teddy guides me along and Danika is forced to follow or give up on the idea of us hanging out.

When we approach the table Jude hoots and stands up, throwing off the girl who was all over him. He doesn't seem to notice the loss of her presence as he steals me from Teddy, hugging me tightly. "There's my girl."

"Your girl? *Your girl?* That's mine, get your own." Teddy fake pouts at his best friend.

"Ah, not yet. I'm not ready to settle down. Maybe next year, but not likely." He releases me and tosses a wink at someone I can't see.

"Someone will come your way and change your whole world," I promise him.

He chuckles, but a dark look passes over his face. "I doubt it."

He turns away before I can say more or question him about it.

"Babe, sit down." Teddy tugs me to the booth where

349

everyone else waits. Danika hesitates but follows, sitting beside me on the end.

"Hey, guys," I greet everyone, not feeling nearly as awkward as I used to. I don't know if it's because what Teddy and I have has grown into more or if time has made me feel more a part of the group versus an outsider.

"You look amazing," Rory gushes, reaching up to adjust her glasses on her nose. "Mascen said you guys were going to Greece. I'd be jealous, but this one took me to London." She pokes his cheek and while he glowers like he's mad, his eyes tell a completely different story— one that makes it clear he plans on devouring her later.

"Thanks. Greece was amazing." I smile up at Teddy, and when he returns mine with one of his, I feel the lurch, the dip, the *shift*—whatever you want to call it. The one where you know deep down that something monumental has changed. It's like my cells have been shaken up and realigned and they all say the same thing.

I'm in love with Teddy McCallister.

How … what … when the fuck did this happen?

I never intended for this to happen. Feelings lead to heartbreak, and falling for Teddy is the biggest risk I've ever taken. Even though he's proved over and over that his feelings are genuine, it doesn't mean this whole thing won't blow up in my face.

"What's wrong?" Teddy smooths his thumb over my cheek like he's trying to get rid of whatever expression has overtaken my face.

"Nothing," I rush to say, perhaps too quickly based on the way his brows scrunch together. "Just happy to be here." I press a kiss to his jaw, and he relaxes, seeming appeased by this.

Drinks and appetizers are delivered to the table, ordered before Danika and I arrived, but I'm not surprised Teddy went ahead and got a margarita for the two of us.

Danika picks up her glass with a look that says, *I told you so.* We clink our glasses together.

———

FLUSHED FROM A FEW DRINKS, I drag Teddy onto the dance floor by his shirt. Cheers ring up around at the display. A remix of Taylor Swift's Love Story plays at a deafening level, made worse by the drunk college kids — myself included — singing at the top of our lungs.

I shout lyrics at Teddy about Romeo throwing pebbles and kneeling on the ground.

He goes along with it, singing along. I have to admit I'm impressed he knows every single lyric. Then again, this is Teddy, so I shouldn't be surprised. He's a man of many talents.

"Did you mean it?"

"Huh?" He turns his ear toward me.

"Did you mean it?" I yell again. "In Greece. When you said you want me in all the ways that a man wants a woman, did you mean you want me for keeps?"

He hears me this time. Heated green eyes make my core clench. He cups my cheek, thumb rubbing over my bottom lip. "I've wanted you for real for … *God*. Months now. I've been waiting for you to catch up." His mouth is a hard press to mine. Demanding. Insistent. I open for him, his tongue sweeping inside my mouth and staking claim.

Behind those boyish smiles, and twinkling eyes, and sexual comments, there's a man who just wants to love a woman, and that woman is *me*.

I've never seen myself as particularly lucky, but I can't help but think that Lady Luck's guiding hand put us in each other's paths.

I saw the shift in Teddy, how his feelings grew real, and I ignored them. Pushed him away. Insisted on keeping this arrangement as it should be. But my heart didn't get that memo.

As Taylor Swift croons, I smile up at him, our own love story being written around us.

THIRTY-FIVE

Teddy

"WE SHOULD TAKE MY CAR."

I guffaw at Mascen's absurd suggestion. "Why would we take that?" I point at his bronze-colored Land Rover behemoth. "When we have this?" I move my hands to encompass my sleek, sexy cobalt blue Porsche.

We have an away game today, and normally we'd be on the bus with our teammates, but the two of us had to stay behind for an interview with a local magazine. Thank fuck Coach was the one who mis-scheduled the interview or we would've had hell to pay. As it is, with the interview done, we're stuck road-tripping it together to our game. True, we could drive separately but that doesn't make much sense, and time will go by faster if I have Mascen to annoy.

"Because," Mascen intones, pinching his brow, "your car *screams* mid-life crisis, insecure, and most importantly small peepee."

"Did I seriously hear you use the word *peepee*?"

He holds up a hand to silence me. "Whereas my beautiful Rover here says one thing and one thing only."

"And what's that?" I challenge, arms crossed over my chest.

"Big. Cock."

"Do you want to compare sizes right now because I'm happy to whip it out and prove you wrong?"

"Keep your pants on McCallister. I see enough of that thing in the locker room."

I smirk. "It's huge, isn't it? Nothing small about it. You can't miss it."

He throws his arms up in the air and curses under his breath. "Forget it. You drive."

"Yes!" I jump up and down in victory.

"Get in the car," he commands in a booming tone, like a parent. "We're going to be late."

"Yes, sir."

I slide behind the wheel, put the address in my phone, crank up some tunes and we're on our way.

————————

"WE'RE GOING THE WRONG WAY."

I swing my head forcefully in Mascen's direction, surprised when I don't get whiplash. "No, we're not. I put the address in and everything." I point down at my phone in the cupholder that's been spitting out directions for the last hour and a half of our six-hour trip.

"I'm telling you, we're going in the wrong direction. We should've headed east and we're going west."

"How would you know?" I sound defensive, but how can I not? Everyone uses their phone's these days, and Mascen's over here acting like Dora the fucking Explorer with a trusty map—only this one seems to be in his head.

"Common sense, dumb ass." He starts pointing at signs and spewing out words that make no sense to me, but finally I agree that he's right, and I've put in the wrong location.

Coming off the highway, I fill up with gas while Christopher Columbus—fitting since that dude was as big of an asshole as Mascen—figures out the new course.

"You want anything?" I poke my head in the car at him, desperate for some snacks.

"Just some water ... maybe a sandwich if they don't look like shit."

I rap my knuckles against the hood of the car and take off for the store, gathering the goods.

When I return, Mascen has a map up on his phone and starts rattling off what we need to do.

"Time's going to be tight," he warns, buckling in.

"Don't worry, I'll get us there no problem."

———————

LIE.

Not an intentional one, but who could've predicted

we'd get stuck in traffic—a complete standstill—because of an accident.

Mascen is a jittery mess beside me. "This wouldn't have fucking happened if you'd let me drive. Then we wouldn't have gone in the wrong direction for too long."

"It's not my fault you didn't realize it sooner," I defend. "Besides, at least we're not the ones in the accident."

Mascen's eyes flash at me, the kind of spark that screams murder. "You're about to be in a bloody accident if you don't shut your mouth."

"You're stressed, sweetie, so I won't take anything you say to heart. Promise." I pout my lips at him.

"I have never wanted to punch another human being more than I want to hit you."

I sigh at this, gripping the wheel. "You're not the only one." The teasing light-hearted tone leaves me, a world-weary weight settling upon me.

"What's that mean?" His question is a cutting demand as I crawl forward an inch.

"Nothing. Forget I said anything."

"No," he insists in a very un-Mascen-like way. "Tell me. You meant something by it."

I don't say anything, and Mascen isn't the type to push too hard, so silence fills the car.

Until I decide to rip the Band-Aid off and put it out there. "My dad hits me."

My heartbeat pounds in my ears. Vanessa was the first person I ever shared the truth with. Now there's one more person in the world who knows.

"Fuck," Mascen curses into the silence of the car. "Seriously, man?"

"Yeah."

"Wow," he mutters, shaking his head. "Shit. I don't know what to say. Sorry seems weak."

"You don't have to say anything." I stare straight ahead. "It's not your fault my father is a manipulative, abusive asshole. That's on him."

"Is it shitty to say I never would've known? You're always so fucking bright unlike me. I haven't had the best relationship with my dad, but I know he wouldn't lay a hand on me or my siblings. He's a good man, we just butt heads."

I glance at Mascen, allowing the car to crawl forward another inch. "That's because you guys are too similar."

"Trust me, we're not." He snorts like the idea is ludicrous.

"Maybe not in obvious ways, but what do I know? I've only met your dad a few times."

He must decide to change the subject, because out of nowhere he says, "You and Vanessa looked cozy the other night."

I know he means at Harvey's. We definitely were heavier on the PDA than we've ever been, because now it's different. Before I was always hesitant to push her for too much beyond the role I had bribed her to play.

"Things changed with us."

"In Greece?"

"Yeah." I lean around the steering wheel, trying to see

if there are blue lights in the distance, but nothing. Apparently, we're still far from the crash site.

"You slept with her." It doesn't escape my notice that he framed it as a statement.

"I don't kiss and tell."

"Since when?" he accuses with an amused uptick of his mouth.

Glowering at him, I bite out between my teeth, "Since Vanessa."

He throws his head back and laughs, clapping his hands. "You've got it bad."

"You're one to talk," I grumble under my breath. "Look at you and Rory."

Where Cole and Zoey are a peaceful, humble sort of love, the one Mascen and Rory shares is a loud cacophony. I don't know what that makes Vanessa and me.

"Yeah, yeah," he chants, dismissing my words. "I know."

A look crosses over his face, one of stupid carefree love. It's funny to see on his normally rigid face. But I guess that's what love does to us—turns us into fools.

Silence fills the car for a good long while, the car barely crawling forward.

Mascen grows more agitated by the second, his knee bouncing so hard the whole car shakes. "We're going to miss the fucking game. I told Coach to cancel the stupid interview, but he wouldn't listen and now look." He points an angry finger at the unmoving traffic. "This is insane."

"I can't make it go faster." He levels me with a glare

and reaches for the handle. "What are you doing?" I'm aware I sound like a panicked child being abandoned by his parent, but I don't care.

"Walking."

"You can't walk all the way there!"

He leans back in the car. "I can try." He slams the door shut.

I quickly roll down my window, sticking my head out so I can yell after him. "Come back, Sweetums! I'm sorry! We can work this out! I promise to do that tongue thing you like later!"

He gives me the finger over his shoulder.

We don't make it to our game.

THIRTY-SIX

Vanessa

I'M SUPPOSED TO BE WORKING ON MY FINAL TERM PAPER for one of my many public relations courses—for this paper we were each given a scenario and have to lay out in explicit detail how we would handle this particular mishap—but it's kind of impossible to type with Teddy's head in my lap, despite my computer propped on a pillow.

Forgetting my paper for the moment, I brush my fingers through his soft brown hair.

"It was a disaster. We didn't even make it to the game. Mascen's pissed, Coach is pissed, and fuck it, I'm pissed too. We only have a few games left this year and then it's over. Onto … onto whatever it is that's next."

"Have you thought more about what you want to do?" I pick up the plastic bag from the bed, plucking a snickerdoodle cookie from it. Apparently once Teddy got back to campus after the disastrous attempt to get to the game, he started stress baking.

He's quiet, unusual for him. I continue to run my fingers through his hair and his eyes grow heavy. Just when I'm certain he's fallen asleep he says, "I have some idea, but it's going to sound crazy."

"Teddy," I stifle a laugh, "you're already the craziest person I know, so it would take a lot to surprise me."

He wiggles on my bed, adjusting his head in my lap. He looks up at me, green eyes bright with excitement, and his jaw stubbled with several days' worth of scruff. "I think I want to move to New York City and buy a food truck but focus on pastries and sweets. Mostly cookies, obviously. Just like you suggested. The more I think about it the more I like the idea."

"I think that sounds amazing." I beam down at him, brushing his hair off his forehead which I then kiss. "I'm brilliant, after all, so why wouldn't you listen to me?"

Reaching up, he grabs a piece of my hair twirling it around his finger. "I know you've mentioned doing PR in the city before, and I thought you might want to live with me." He clears his throat. "You know ... more economical."

Shocked doesn't even begin to cover how I feel. Yes, what Teddy and I have has morphed into more, but we haven't even said I love you yet, and he's talking about moving in after graduation? The idea should scare me more than it does, but I can see it working.

"Maybe," I hedge, not wanting to commit to anything since I don't even have any job prospects lined up.

His warm hand cups my cheek, gently tugging my chin down to look at him. "Let me make something clear to you. I don't want this to end after we walk across the stage."

"Why? Why me?"

"I'm not following."

I sigh and he sits up, turning to face me. "I mean, you could've had any girl you wanted at any point in time. What changed? Why am I different?"

"You're different because you're you." I start to tell him that's not a good enough answer for me, but he goes on. "You see me for me. You've never looked at me with dollar signs in your eyes. You haven't used me to climb the social ladder. If anything, I used you, in the beginning at least. With you I can be my true self. I look at you, and I see everything I didn't know I wanted. A future that actually means something."

"Teddy." My throat closes up with emotion, and I hate myself for showing that vulnerability. But I know he won't judge me for it.

He sets my laptop with the pillow on the floor, his eyes intense and full of promise. He climbs over me, and I lie back.

His mouth descends on mine, the taste of cookie on his lips from one he ate earlier. He kisses me slowly, but deeply. I feel it all the way down to my toes.

He takes his time, undressing me slowly like I'm sort

362

of precious present. And then he hovers above me naked himself but doesn't push inside me.

"Beautiful," he murmurs before capturing a nipple between his teeth with a tender love bite. He licks and sucks his way to my other breast, giving it the same attention.

When he finally sinks inside me, we both exhale a long moan.

He makes love to me slowly, showing me with every movement, every kiss, that what's between us is real. Even if neither of us has said the words, the love is undeniable.

———

WE WAKE up sometime later to the incessant buzzing of Teddy's phone.

Brr. Brr. Brr. It seems to rumble through the whole room.

"Ugh, make it stop," I groan, peeking at the clock. "Shit it's not even nine, and we fell asleep like that?"

"Good sex will do that to you," Teddy says, his voice deep and rumbly as he leans over me and grabs his phone from the pocket of his jeans.

"Don't you mean boring sex?" I don't know why I'm trying to get a rise out of him.

He smirks at me, eyes glancing over the dozen or so love bites all over my chest and shoulders. "If it was bad you would've gotten up and left."

"This is my room."

He shows me his phone screen, that it's his father calling and tells me to be quiet before he answers. "Dad, to what do I owe this pleasure?" His dad's voice rumbles across the line, but I can't hear what he's saying. "Why would I need to go?" Teddy asks him, his lips turning down at the corners with distaste. "Mhmm, yeah. I'm not sure she can go." He eyes me. "Required? Why?" He nods his head some, face wrinkled with displeasure. "Whatever." He winces at something his dad says. "We'll both be there." A heavy sigh. "I said we'd be there. Yup. Goodnight."

He ends the call and tosses his phone to the floor, burying his head into the crook of my neck. He lets out a groan that cuts off when he kisses my neck, and I giggle.

"What was that about?" I massage my fingers into the back of his neck.

Rolling to the side of me, he props his head up on his hand. "Just Daddy Dearest requesting both of our presence at this event in Nashville this Friday. No clue why he waited so long to say something. It sounded like he knew about it for a while. It's black tie."

"Black tie?"

"Formal wear."

I bite my lip, trying to catalogue the clothes Teddy bought for me before. "I think I have a dress that'll work."

"If not, I'll get you something, and don't fight me on it. You shouldn't have to pay for a gown just because my dad decides we need to be some place."

"I don't know how you've dealt with this lifestyle for so long."

"It's all I've known." I detect a hint of sadness in his

tone. "I know other lifestyles exist, but this is my reality." He tilts his chin down, staring at me intently. "I want a different future for myself, for any kids I might have."

Cupping his jaw, I pull him down into a kiss. "You're nothing like I expected."

He glides his big thumb over my bottom lip. "You're not either." Clearing his throat, he lies back down in the bed and tucks me against his chest. "Let's go back to sleep."

I don't argue with that.

I SMELL like a mixture of grease and cheese. It's not a good combination. Especially not when I have to be ready in *two* hours to head to Nashville with Teddy for the event. It's to be held at some rich person's estate.

"Whoa, what's going on?" Danika's voice is laced with concern as she watches me rush past her and into my bedroom. I have to shower the smell of The Burger Palace off me stat and then it's hair, makeup, getting dressed—it all feels like too much.

While I double check that my dress is wrinkle free and grab my stuff for a shower, I quickly fill her in on what's going on since I act like I'm trying to get to a fire.

"I could do your hair," she suggests casually. "Makeup too. I don't mind."

My shocked eyes meet hers. "Are you serious?"

Do I sound as stupidly relieved as I feel?

She shrugs. "I wouldn't offer if I didn't want to. It's no biggie."

"Trust me, it is. I owe you so much for this."

I give her a quick hug, surprising us both, and then I'm locking myself in the bathroom.

Washing my hair and scrubbing my body until there's no trace of restaurant smell left, I then make sure to shave every inch so I'm smooth to the touch. Rich people don't like hair unless it's on their heads.

Drying my body with a towel, I slip on my undergarments and pull a robe on. I don't think there's any point in putting on actual clothes until I have to slip into my dress.

I've barely set foot out of the bathroom when Danika tugs me into her room. She points for me to sit in her desk chair, and she gets to work.

I realize as she blows out my hair before rolling it with these big round curlers that she leaves in my hair that I've never actually been in her space before. Sure, I've seen it in the casual way one glimpses things passing by, but I've never been close enough to truly inspect things.

Her walls are plastered with posters of bands, artists, and others that seem to be of places she's traveled to. On the ceiling she's hung a tapestry of the moon and stars that drapes down a bit, giving a cozy effect. And like my room, she has loads of twinkle lights but where mine are white hers are a purple color giving the space a more vampy feel.

"This is cool," I comment as she secures a roller with a bobby pin. "Your room, I mean."

"Thanks." I see her smile in the reflection of the round mirror she set on her desk. "It's the first time I could really decorate to my liking. My mom has a very contemporary style, so I was never allowed to have my room the way I wanted growing up."

I can't help but frown. My parents aren't perfect, but at least I was allowed to have my room the way I wanted. "That's sucky."

"I got over it."

She finishes putting in the last roller and before she starts my makeup, she asks to see my dress.

"Oh my God, it's stunning." Her jaw drops at the silky cowl neck dress with thin straps in the most beautiful olive-green color I've ever seen.

"Thanks. I didn't even pick it out for myself, but it's exactly what I've chosen."

Either Teddy did one hell of a job describing my personal style to whatever stylist pulled the wardrobe he got me, or else she was intuitive enough to guess.

"What shoes are you wearing with it?" I show her the strappy gold heels. "I have a look in mind, it's a little daring, but I think it would be perfect. Do you trust me?"

I hesitate for only a second. "Yeah, I do."

I'm ushered back to the chair in her room once more where she gets to work. I feel like a blank canvas as she works intently, adding things like foundation and contour and what I worry is a bit too much blush but she insists is just right. I try not to talk while she works, not wanting to distract her from whatever vision she has.

Finished with my makeup she turns the mirror away. "Hey!" I protest, trying to grab it.

"Nope, not yet. You need to see the final product all

together. Let me finish your hair and get your dress on and *then* you can look."

"Fine." I pout, hoping I didn't ruin the lipstick she applied.

Removing my hair from the rollers she brushes out my hair, teasing it in areas. I've never felt so glamourous in all my life and I haven't even seen myself yet.

Danika puts down her brushes and steps away from me, clapping her hands. The girl looks absolutely giddy which isn't a word I ever thought I'd use to describe her.

"Dress time," she declares, spinning the desk chair around and urging me out of it.

Glancing at my phone I see that I have twenty minutes to spare. She's finished in the nick of time. There's a text from Teddy saying he's on his way. No shock there. The boy is shockingly early for everything.

It's an effort not to sneak a peek at myself in the mirror in my bedroom, but I manage to hold strong. The dress slips over my body, the silky material gliding over me like water. The dress *feels* expensive, and I'm glad it came without the tag because I would probably choke if I knew how much it cost. Certainly, more than my tips from The Burger Palace could handle.

"Hurry up!" Danika encourages from outside the door. "I want to see!"

"Almost!" I call back. "Putting the heels on."

Sitting down, I slip my feet into the shoes and make sure the straps are in place. I was worried my thick calves might look like they're suffocating, but it's a perfect fit.

Opening the door, Danika waits right outside of it

with her hands clasped beneath her chin. Her jaw drops as her eyes take me in from head to foot. "Girl, if I was a le-dolla-bean I'd be all over you right now."

"Le-dolla-bean?" I repeat, confusion written on my face.

"It's a Tiktok thing." She twirls her finger through the air. "Now turn. Show me the full picture." I spin and she claps giddily. "So hot, girl. Teddy is going to lose his ever-loving-mind when he sees you, and if he doesn't, I'll slap him upside his head."

"Can I see myself now?"

"Oh! Right!" She drags me into her bedroom. "Close your eyes." I do as she requests while she positions me in front of her full-length mirror. "Okay, open."

I don't have to be told twice. My eyes pop open and I gasp. "That's me?" I blurt, marveling at how the gorgeous creature's lips move in the mirror to match my question. "Holy shit."

My eyes are done in varying shades of green with a hint of black, smoking out the edges. My lips are candy apple red and my face glows from whatever magic she worked. Something glimmers on my cheeks and collar-bone, and she was right about the blush. It's settled into the skin giving me a sun-kissed look and not the clown one I was worried about.

"I told you," she says proudly.

"You did." I touch my hair, the brown nearly black color of it looking shiny and glossy from the blowout, falling in perfectly voluptuous waves down to my breasts.

The dress is the cherry on top—hugging every curve

and extenuating my best assets, aka my boobs. I turn to the side, and then the back, peeking over my shoulder.

Is my body perfect by media standards? No.

But who gives a fuck?

It's perfect for *me*. *I'm* beautiful—in body and soul.

We're all just skin sacks anyway. Each and every one of us. Why should we listen to what some invisible person spits out in an article? How I feel about myself shouldn't be determined by what someone else thinks of me anyway. I'm not saying I haven't had moments of insecurity, but I don't do it nearly as often now that I've realized how others perceive me is on them and has no bearing on me or my life.

I can still be overweight and beautiful at the same time. Beauty is not synonymous with the word skinny.

"Thank you." The words come out sounding a little choked up.

"Don't you dare cry and ruin your makeup," she warns me sternly, quickly passing me a tissue in case any treacherous tears leak out. "And you're welcome." Her smile reflects back at me in the mirror. The knock on the door signals Teddy's arrival. "You ready?"

If I was spending the evening with only Teddy I'd reply with an enthusiastic yes, but that's not the case.

"I have to be."

She squeezes my shoulders. "I'll get the door."

I appreciate her giving me a moment to catch my breath before I have to face my ... well, *boyfriend*.

The low murmur of Teddy's voice is followed by Danika saying, "She'll be out in a second."

Inhaling a deep breath and choosing to focus on the enjoyable part of this evening — *Teddy* — I square my shoulders, chin held high, and step out of Danika's room to meet him.

He smiles as soon as he sees me, that smile quickly turning to a look of lust and wonder. His eyes rake my body like a lover's caress, eyes shining with the promise of what's to come when he takes my dress off. My nipples harden in response, and I pray to God it's not noticeable in my dress. From the smirk that grows on his devilish mouth I'd say luck isn't on my side.

Bowing at the waist, he takes my hand and places a kiss on my knuckles. In a dramatic British accent, he says, "My lady, you are breathtakingly beautiful."

I can't stifle the giggle that escapes me. Playing along, with an even more horrid fake accent I reply with, "Why thank you, kind sir."

Danika fake gags. "Ew, you guys are sickeningly sweet. It's making my teeth ache. Now get out of here." She shoos us closer to the door. "Romeo brought you flowers." She points to a bouquet of pink peonies.

"You brought me flowers?" I beam at him.

I swear he goes red at the ears. "It's not a big deal."

"Mhmm," I hum, wrapping a hand around his wrist and kissing his cheek. "Thank you."

"We really do have to go."

"Right. Bye, Danika!" I call over my shoulder.

I loop my arm through Teddy's, taking careful but sure steps so I don't trip in my heels. A few girls hanging out in the open area of the floor openly gawk as we walk by. For once, I don't feel embarrassed. If I saw a girl leaving the dorm looking like me, I'd stop and stare too.

We're the only ones in the elevator and Teddy immediately pushes me into the wall, a low growl rumbling in his throat when he sweeps his nose against my neck. "This sounds so fucking cliché, but you look ravishing."

I laugh at his cheesy line, the sound cut off when he kisses me. The feel of his mouth on mine is a welcome pressure, but I know I have to stop him. I push gently at his chest.

"Don't mess up my makeup."

He buries his head in my neck. "How do you expect me to keep my hands off you when you're so fucking hot?"

"I don't know but you're going to have to try."

The elevator opens, and he leads me outside to a waiting black Escalade idling in front with a driver.

"You're not driving?"

"Dad sent a car."

"Interesting."

We slip into the back, the doors barely closing before the driver is pulling away.

Teddy reaches down, messing with something I can't see. He sits up holding two shot size bottles of whiskey. "Bottoms up?" I take one of the bottles from him, clinking it against his. I don't normally drink this, but the liquid courage is necessary on a night like this. We down the shots, both wincing from the alcohol. "Burns so good."

Sort of like heartbreak. I don't know what gives me the thought, but I hope it's not an omen for what's to come.

THE DRIVER TAKES us to an elegant estate just past the limits of Nashville. The home is large and stately, an absolute beauty. It rivals the size of the McCallister Manor. Is it crazy to admit that I never knew such vast wealth existed in the world? I mean, obviously I know there are rich people but not *this* level of it.

Teddy waits for the driver to open his door, which is weird as hell—but I know it's what's proper. He slides smoothly out of the vehicle, straightening his tux before extending a hand back inside the vehicle for me. I slip my hand into his rough palm, allowing his fingers to close over the top of my hand.

Heart-pounding, my high-heeled feet make contact with the driveway made of some exotic material I've never seen before. It looks as if there are tiny seashells in it.

Gathering my breath, I smile at my date. His eyes flash with amusement.

"Nervous?"

"What gave me away?"

"You keep looking at your feet for starters," he chuckles, squeezing my hand affectionately.

A blush blooms on my cheeks. "Sorry," I mumble, looking around and taking in the amount of people lingering outside, ones dressed like us, as well as staff directing where we go.

"I like it when you're flustered."

"What exactly is all of this for?" Probably something I should've asked before, but I figured in these situations, the less I know beforehand, the better. It means I can't overly stress.

"The Boudin's," he nods significantly at the house, "are benefactors for many charities. Tonight they're raising money for a new pediatric cancer wing at the hospital."

"Wow, that's amazing."

We're directed to go into the house, where we're then guided to an event space. I can't imagine having so much money that I would need or even want a room like this in my house. But realistically this isn't a house or a home. It's meant for show.

The space is cold.

This isn't a place where laughter echoes off the walls, or kids kick balls around, or you bond on Christmas morning. I could have all the money in the world and I would never want *this*.

I want warmth and kisses in the mornings and a home so full of love it's practically bursting at the seams.

A server passes by us with a tray of champagne flutes. Teddy's hand shoots out, grabbing glasses for each of us. I have to admit, I feel a little better having something to hold in my hand.

Teddy places his hand on my lower back, the heat of him searing me through the fabric of my dress.

"Our table is over here." He tips his head to the left, guiding me along.

I recognize a few faces in the room, not because I know them personally but because I've seen them on magazines and in blockbuster movies.

I try not to openly gawk, not wanting to be *that* person.

Teddy stops at a table, already occupied by a few people including his parents.

"Teddy." His mom beams, standing to kiss his cheeks. "And Vanessa." She hugs me, which is a tad awkward with the champagne in one hand and her son refusing to let me go. Unfazed, she sits back down beside her husband who openly glares.

"You're late."

Teddy looks significantly around at the empty tables slowly filling in. "Doesn't look like it."

"I told you to be here thirty minutes ago."

"Oh, Ed—" Mrs. McCallister tries to soothe her husband, but he's not having it.

"When I tell you to be somewhere at a certain time, I expect you to be able to follow basic instruction, you insolent—"

Someone clears their throat and Mr. McCallister glances up at the looming presence of a large man that has to be over six-foot-five and built like a tank. "Is everything all right here?"

Mr. McCallister flounders, muttering a string of incoherent sentences.

The unnamed man looks to Teddy and there's a wordless exchange. "If there are any problems come find me."

He moves off, checking on another table.

"Who's that?" I whisper under my breath as we finally take our seats.

"The Boudin's son."

375

"He's ... intimidating but not in a mean way, if that makes sense."

Teddy chuckles, brushing a lock of hair over my shoulder. "I call him the gentle giant."

"You know him well."

"We went to the same school. He was a couple grades ahead of me, but with small classes you know everyone."

Any other questions I might have die on my tongue when someone speaks into the microphone at the front of the room, welcoming us for the evening and going over the list of events for the night, starting with dinner, and an auction, as well as other festivities.

The first course is brought out, and I do my best to remember my manners. Teddy helps me along as I still sometimes struggle to use the correct cutlery.

By the time dinner is finished I feel like a jittery mess. Luckily, a band starts playing and people clear from their tables, some to dance, others to mingle, some I'm sure are desperate for a potty break.

Teddy's arm is on the back of my chair, his fingers lazily stroking against me.

"Dance with me?"

"What is it with you and getting me to dance?"

"I like having you in my arms."

"How can I say no to that?"

He stands, taking my hand and tugging me up easily with him. His dad's shrewd gaze follows us all the way to where the gathered crowd is dancing, the burn of his stare not disappearing until we're lost in the crowd.

"Why do you like to dance so much?" Wrapping my

arms around his neck, my fingers curl into his hair tugging lightly at the strands. He smirks, his jaw shadowed with stubble. I love the way he's never perfectly shaven. Slightly unkempt, perfectly Teddy.

"Because dancing doesn't need words. It's all about the feel, rhythm. It's like this secret language."

"Unfortunately for you, I suck at it."

"No one sucks at dancing. You just need the right partner." He winces, watching someone over my shoulder. "Okay, maybe that guy is really bad at it."

He spins me so I can see the man in question. A laugh bursts from me, because the guy is comically bad.

Teddy laughs with me, twirling me in another direction before we draw attention to ourselves or the unfortunate soul that makes me look like a professional dancer.

I don't know how long we linger on the dance floor, but a sheen of sweat sticks to my skin when Teddy finally drags me to the drink bar getting us both much-needed water.

After hydrating there's more dancing, until everyone's called to take our seats for the auction.

In the chaos of everyone trying to find their seats again, Teddy sneaks us out of the room.

I'm aware I'm a smiley happy mess as I gaze up at him, but I don't care. I never realized how good it would feel to not care and just exist.

"Where are we going?" I giggle. I'm not even tipsy, only drunk on the intoxicating feeling of falling, hard and fast, for the man at my side.

"There's a garden," he murmurs, tugging me along

down the massively wide hall. He clearly knows where he's going. His head dips, looking back at me where I hurry to keep up with his long strides in my pointy heels. His eyes are heated, glowing with a promise that sends a shiver racing down my spine. "And I need you."

There's no mistaking the need in which he's referring to.

He locates the door he's searching for, and we enter another large empty room, furniture covered with sheets. He keeps going, and then we're bursting outside into the crisp night air. Crickets sing their nightly song, lightning bugs glowing intermittently as we pass by. He drags me through a literal maze of a garden, green growing high above our heads. Disk lights are implanted in the ground, guiding our way.

"This looks like something that belongs in Italy," I murmur, more to myself than him. He doesn't answer, determined to bring me deeper into the garden to ensure we're alone.

I don't normally think flowers have a strong scent but enveloped in so many, it's *heavenly.*

There's a bench ahead, and Teddy walks faster with renewed energy.

"Have you ever had sex in a garden?"

His question shouldn't catch me off guard since that's clearly been what this whole mission is about, but it does anyway. "No. Never in a public space."

He groans in a way that I know my answer pleases him.

We reach the bench and he shucks off his tux jacket

while I get rid of my shoes. "Fuck, I need to be inside you," he growls, fumbling with his belt. I swear it looks like his hands are shaking. Belt undone, he shoves his hand in his pocket and rips open a condom foil. "Pull your dress up," he commands, undoing his pants enough to pull his cock free and sheath himself with the condom.

I do as he asks, pulling my dress up to my thighs. He sits on the bench and grabs my hips, yanking me onto his lap. I squeal with the sudden movement, my hands landing on his shoulders for support.

His fingers skim up my inner thighs and he hisses between his teeth when he finds me bare and wet.

"You mean to tell me you haven't been wearing panties?"

I shrug casually but my words come out breathless, betraying me. "You can't risk panty lines in a dress like this and I *loathe* thongs."

He groans, dropping his head into my chest. "You're never wearing underwear again."

And with that statement, he grips my bare hips and pulls me down on him.

My head falls back. *"Oh my God,"* I exhale at the intrusion. I feel so full.

I rock my hips against him, his fingers digging bitingly into my ass. Holding his cheeks in my hands, we're forehead to forehead, eye to eye, breath to breath.

It's incredibly intimate despite the location and our mostly dressed state. I've never felt more exposed. Like Teddy can see every bit of me. The good, the bad, the ugly

379

—*all of it*. And he doesn't look afraid. His eyes seem to say *give it to me, give me every part of you*

With that thought, I fall apart, shaking around him.

My muscles clench around his cock and this sets him off. He pounds into me harder, groaning through his own release.

It all happens so fast, but it's the most powerful sex of my life.

I know that no matter what happens between us, I've been irrevocably changed by this moment and given a piece of myself to Teddy that I'll never get back.

When our eyes connect, I know he feels it too, and a tiny piece of him settles in the space where I gave him a part of me.

We put ourselves back together, shooting heated looks and coy smiles as we right our clothes. Back in order, we clasp hands and reluctantly head back to the madness.

We're outside the main room, the auction still in full swing, when I announce, "I need to go pee."

"Oh, right." He rubs his fingers over his forehead like he should've known. "Restrooms are right there." He points me to the door. "I have to go back to the table."

"I'll be there as soon as I'm done."

Slipping into the bathroom, I expect to find a normal one like in any home. Of course, this isn't the case. Marble extends from the floors to the counters, and then up the walls. It's laid out like a public restroom with separate stalls, and there's even a room off of it that's a lounge.

Shaking my head at the ostentatiousness of it, I pass by a few other attendees who stare at me funny for my open gawking and lock myself in a stall. After peeing and cleaning myself up, I straighten my dress and wash my hands. My hair is mussed from our garden tryst. I do my best to bring order to the unruly sections, feeling the tiniest bit bad that I messed up Danika's hard work — but not too bad, because it was entirely worth it.

Mascara is smeared beneath my right eye. Using a tissue from the counter I wipe it away.

Stepping out of the restroom, I bump into someone, immediately mumbling out an apology as the person's hand wraps around my arm to keep me from falling in my heels.

"You and I are going to talk."

My body goes cold at the sound of Mr. McCallister's voice. All of my happy fuzzy feelings from before are erased beneath his shrewd gaze. He yanks me into a room down the hall. It appears to be some sort of meeting space, if the long table and chairs are any indication.

"Sit."

I do as he says, a tad scared of the what the repercussions might be if I disobey.

He pulls out the chair across from me and sits, his hands clasped on top of the table.

"Why are we in here?" I ask, hating that my voice shakes with nerves, betraying my attempt to appear composed.

His eyes narrow on me until they're nothing but tiny slits. "To talk."

"About what?"

"About you staying away from my son."

I sit up straighter, holding my chin in the air in refusal to cower. "That's not going to be possible."

"Oh, I think it is. You *will* break up with him, and you *will* do it in a way that doesn't show my involvement." My heart gallops a wild beat, sweat beginning to bead on my brow. This man is intimidating regardless, but knowing he beats his own son doesn't leave me appreciating being shut in a room with him where no one knows we are. "I've been suspicious of your relations from the start." His eyes peruse my body, not in a way like he's checking me out —*ew*—but as if I'm gunk caked beneath his expensive shoes. "My son doesn't chase after women like you. He prefers models, actresses, not some overweight back-talking bitch from some stupid town called *White Claw*." He sneers the name. "And before you open that wretched mouth of yours, don't you worry missy, I've done my digging—my *lawyers* have done the digging, and don't think we didn't uncover the fact that my son paid off your tuition. I'm far from dumb, young lady, it's obvious to me that something fishy is going on here. What do you have on him?"

"E-Excuse me?" His accusation has me reeling. That wasn't what I was expecting him to say, or where I thought this rant was going.

"Do I really need to repeat myself?"

"I don't understand the question."

He laughs in a way that lacks any humor at all. "My son is reckless without a care in the world or a semi-coherent thought in his head." I open my mouth, ready to protest that none of that is true and he doesn't know

Teddy at all, but he plows ahead. "For him to pay your tuition, I'm assuming you're blackmailing him for something you witnessed that could ruin his reputation, as if it isn't already in shambles. I'm guessing all of this," he waves a hand to encompass my fancy get-up, "is a part of it too. Get him to pretend to be your boyfriend and all kinds of opportunities open up for you." Pursing his lips, he leans toward me but there's still an ocean of distance between us thanks to the size of the table. "Name your price, whatever it is I'll pay it. The only stipulation is you are never to speak to him again."

"I don't want your money."

He throws his head back and laughs. "Everyone wants money."

"I love your son." The words burst from me before I can stop them. They're true, but I can't believe I'm admitting them to his father before I've said them to Teddy himself.

He blinks stoically at me. "Do I look like I care? Whatever farce this is ends, and it ends tonight, or I will ruin you, and my son won't see a cent of his inheritance. He won't look half as appealing when he's destitute."

"Ruin me?" This time I'm the one laughing.

"I wouldn't laugh if I were you, Ms. Hughes. I'm a powerful man. My reach extends to places you can't even imagine. You want to work in PR? Think again. You'll be lucky to get a job at the local McDonalds when I'm done with you."

My chest seizes up with the realization that he won't quit. I won't be leaving this room until I agree to his terms. Tears build up behind my eyes, but I refuse to let them fall. I won't give this psycho the satisfaction of seeing me cry.

"I don't want your money."

"What do you want then?"

"Can I get it in writing?"

His eyes flicker with hesitation. It takes a moment, but he says, "Yes, of course. I'll get my lawyer on the line." He sets his phone on the table between us when his lawyer comes on the speaker. "Now what is it you want?"

I layout my terms, we come to an agreement, and when I shake his hand it's a done deal.

He's oblivious of my heart, shattered at his feet.

THIRTY-SEVEN

Teddy

I KNOW SOMETHING IS WRONG THE SECOND I CATCH Vanessa approaching the table. Her eyes are distant, refusing to meet mine as I silently beg her to look at me. Behind her my father looms and my veins turn to ice.

Vanessa takes her seat beside me, my father beside my mother.

My eyes bounce from the two of them.

"What did he say to you?"

Startled doe eyes flicker up at me for all of a second before she's looking at the tablecloth like it's the most interesting thing she's ever seen. "Who?"

"I'm not stupid." I'm whispering so no one at our table can hear me. "It's obvious he cornered you."

"It's nothing."

385

At least she's not denying it.

Beneath the table I search for her hand, finding it clammy and limp. "Whatever he said, it's not important. He's an angry rich bastard. Don't let him get to you."

"I'm fine." She forces a smile, lips barely twitching, that never reaches her eyes. Reaching up, she tucks a piece of hair behind her ear. When she lowers her hand, she squeezes my knee, but the gesture does nothing to reassure me that she's okay.

At least the night is winding down and we can head home.

There's a fresh glass of champagne in front of Vanessa. Her hand swipes out as soon as she sees it, fingers closing around the stem, and then the liquid is down her throat.

She looks at me with a tiny bit of shame when she notices I've witnessed this. "I love champagne."

"No, you don't."

She likes bottomless margaritas a Harvey's and that's about it.

"You're right, I don't. But it's all I've got."

"We should go somewhere and talk." I watch my father out of the corner of my eye, but he's not looking our way. He's engrossed in a conversation with one of his many business associates.

"I'm fine, really. You worry too much."

Incredulous, I scoff under my breath. "I'm not sure I've ever been told I worry *too much*. Usually, I'm scolded for not worrying enough."

"Hmm." Her quiet hum feels like a spear to my heart, I can sense her slipping away from me, little by little. Everything was fine in the garden, so something happened in the time between when she went to the restroom and returned. Now that I think about it, she was gone longer than I anticipated, but I didn't think about it in the moment since I was caught up in conversation with people.

Clearly, I should've given it more thought. But I can't go back in time and change it now.

The auction finally winds down and after a goodbye to my parents, Vanessa and I leave for the car.

With every passing minute I can feel her putting walls back up around herself to protect against *me*. I grow infuriated after how far we've come, that she'd do this. I finally got her to open up to me, to see that my feelings are real. I can't go back to pretending.

She lets out a startled squeal when I pull her into a hallway for privacy, boxing her against a wall with my arms.

"You were fine in the garden, so tell me, *what the fuck happened?*"

She won't look at me and I fucking hate that. Grabbing her chin, I force her to. My fingers are tight enough on her that she can't look away, but I'm not hurting her. I would *never* hurt her. But even though I hold her head up, it doesn't mean she has to look at me. Her eyes go to the ornate ceiling above us and stay there. But there's no masking the tears in her eyes.

"I can't do this anymore." The words are heavy, laced with tears.

"What do you mean?"

"I don't want to play this game anymore, I know I owe you because of my loans, but I want out. I'll find some other way to repay you, but I can't do this."

I'm fucking flabbergasted at the words coming out of her mouth. I'm hearing them, sure, but they make no sense.

"There hasn't been a fucking deal between us since before Greece and you know it. Besides, I wanted you before that. Stop acting like all of this is make believe."

"But isn't it?" Now she looks at me, fire in her tear-soaked eyes. "Where can we go from here? What will we ever really be? This isn't my life."

"It's not mine either!" I roar, thankful for the privacy of the hall so no one can see me lose my shit. "You know this shit isn't me." I lower my voice back to a normal volume. "And what are you talking about where can we go from here? We just talked about New York City. I told you what I wanted."

"Yeah, what *you* wanted." She shoves a finger into my chest. "But what about what I want?"

"I suggested that because you said that's where you wanted to go!" I'm baffled, completely and utterly baffled, at where all of this is coming from. "You have to know I would follow you anywhere. I ... I love you."

She winces like I've physically slapped her, and now tears spill free from her eyes.

"I never asked for you to follow me. I never asked for any of this."

It feels like she's shoved her hand into my chest,

between my ribcage, and grabbed my heart where it's held between her fist.

"What are you saying?"

"I'm saying, I want this to end ... before either of us gets hurt more."

I clench my jaw, staring at her. Long seconds tick by and neither of us says anything. I keep waiting for her to say this is a joke, but she doesn't.

"You want to break up?"

She laughs humorlessly. "I guess if you can call this entire mess of us a relationship, then yeah, I want to break up."

This isn't how I expected things to go when I finally told a girl I loved her. Maybe this is my punishment for never settling down. The universe finally gives me the girl of my dreams, but apparently, I'm not the man of hers.

Tears track down her cheeks, I wipe them away with my thumbs on her cheeks. I can't let her go, not yet. My throat is starting to close up, but I still manage to say, "I'm always the one who loves too much, who gives everything, and is left with nothing in return."

"T-Teddy." Her chin wobbles.

"It's okay. I'll be okay. I always am." She opens her mouth to speak, and I know instinctively what she's going to say. "Don't say you're sorry," I beg. "I can't hear you say you're sorry. It'll diminish the realness." She chokes out a sob as I release her and take a few steps away. "I'll get you in the car and find my own way home."

"No, d-don't be silly. W-We can share the c-car."

I rub my hand over my lips, contemplating how to say this. "I can't share a car with you right now."

"Are you mad?"

"No." I shake my head forlornly. "I'm not mad, but I am absolutely devastated."

As promised, I escort Vanessa out to the waiting car before getting an Uber for myself. I have to wait thirty minutes, and in that time, I don't manage to feel any better.

The ride back to campus is excruciating. The guy blasts some kind of techno dance music the entire way, while vaping something that smells like watermelon. Who the fuck wants to inhale artificial watermelon? Not me.

By the time he drops me off, I'm having a coughing fit and smell of his nasty watermelon shit.

Trudging up to my dorm, my legs feel like they weigh a hundred pounds each. It's dark and quiet when I enter the suite, but I'm not about to let Jude sleep peacefully while my world is crumbling.

I knock on his door before swinging it open. There are a few condom wrappers on the floor and he's sleeping blissfully on his stomach, bare ass hanging out, clutching his pillow like a life preserver. The dude's even drooling. If I was in a better headspace I'd snap a pic to lord over him, but right now I don't have it in me. At least there's no chick still here so I don't have to deal with that.

"Dude." I grab a towel off the floor and throw it at him. "Get up."

He jolts awake, arms flailing like he's about to ninja fight someone. "What the fuck?" He sees me standing in the doorway, rubbing his eyes to make sure I'm real and not a figment of his imagination. "Teddy?"

"I need a drink and a friend."

He picks up his phone from the floor where it's plugged into an outlet charging. "At four in the morning? You couldn't have waited a few more hours?"

"Vanessa broke up with me."

"For real, for real?"

"For real."

"Fuck." He scrubs his hands down his face. "Fuck, man," he repeats. "I'm sorry." He rolls out of bed and yanks some boxer-briefs on. "You do need a drink and now, so do I."

If there's anyone well-versed in heartbreak, it's Jude. His high school sweetheart, Macy, cheated on him last year with one of his teammates and now those two are dating. I don't know all the shit that went down with them, but I do know they were serious. Jude talked about marrying her. Now he screws the entire campus.

We each grab a drink from the fridge. I pop the top on my Zombie Dust, and we end up sitting on the couch. It's not the smallest couch in the world, but it is when two six-foot-plus guys sit on it together. Our knees touch, but neither of us bothers to move.

"You want to tell me what happened?"

"She broke up with me, there's nothing much else to tell."

"There's always plenty to tell."

"So, there's more to you and Macy than you've told me?"

He takes a long swig of his beer. "Yep." He wipes the back of his hand across his mouth.

"You want to talk about it?"

"Nope."

"We're two sad, pathetic fucks." He takes another drink. I've barely touched mine other than to open it.

"I didn't know it would feel like this."

"What?"

I pick at the label on my bottle, staring ahead at the black screen of the TV that reflects our two forms. "Heartbreak."

"It fucking sucks." He drinks the rest of his beer.

Setting my full beer on the table, I lean back on the couch eyeing him. "You really think so? You don't think eventually you'll meet a girl who changes everything? I mean, I didn't think I would but then Vanessa happened." My heart cracks again at her name.

Why am I doing this to myself?

"I won't let myself go there right now. I don't want to feel that type of pain again. I mean, never say never, but … I'm not ready."

The way he says it, I know he's still hurting from the loss of Macy and that terrifies me. Is this going to be me with Vanessa? Am I going to always hold onto a level of hurt when it comes to her and relationships? Will I compare every woman I meet from here on out to her?

"The first time I had sex with another girl I cried."

"What?" My head swivels to the left to face him so fast I'm surprised something doesn't snap.

He nods like it surprises him too. "Macy and I started

dating when we were freshman in high school. Knew each other before that too. She was my first everything and I wanted her to be the last too. Thought she would be." He pushes his hair back. "So, when I had sex the first time after we broke up, I cried. I never thought I'd have sex with another person and then I was and I didn't even want to. You would think after that, I'd ... I don't know, have taken some time to myself? But it's like I wanted to fuck the memories out of me, to make sex about something other than her. I wanted to make it about the act itself, I guess, like the other person doesn't matter. *Fuck*." He tosses his empty bottle at the trash can and it goes right in. "I sound like such a dick, but it's true."

"Self-preservation makes monsters out of the best of us. Look at me."

"You've never been a bad guy, or a monster. You've taken things too far on occasion, mostly to get laughs out of people, and fucked around, but you've never been mean, or a bully. You care, dude. Not to get cheesy on you, but you're the best friend I could ask for." He slaps a hand down on my shoulder. "Nobody's perfect, though, and no point acting like it."

"I don't want to lose her."

"Clearly, she's going through something. Stay away, but remind her you're always there. Even as a friend."

"You didn't do that with Macy," I accuse.

"Because I didn't want her back. When she cheated on me instead of communicating with me, she broke my trust in a way that can never be repaired between us. I've seen the way Vanessa looks at you, and you her. Honestly, I'm shocked she's ending things. Doesn't seem right. But maybe she's scared."

"Yeah, maybe…"

"Get out of that tux and go to bed."

I smirk at him, feeling a tiny kernel of humor flicker inside me. "I didn't know you wanted to see me naked that bad."

Standing, he rolls his eyes. "I see enough of your dick as it is. *Go to bed.*" He says the last part like a parent exasperated with their child.

He heads to his room while I dump my open beer down the drain, watching it swirl away.

Remind her I'm there.

Closing the door to my room, I head to my desk. I don't bother changing, and I don't go to bed like I should. Pulling out a piece of paper, I start writing.

THIRTY-EIGHT

Vanessa

IF I THOUGHT MY HEART HURT AFTER THE STUNT MY sister and Tristan pulled on me, it has nothing on how I feel now. Whenever movies made it seem like a girl was literally *sick* with heartbreak, curled up in bed, no appetite, I thought it was so dramatic.

I was wrong.

It *is* possible to feel sick with heartbreak, like your whole body is sore with the loss of something vital, my stomach rolling every time I think of the look on Teddy's face when I broke us.

He must hate me. I can't say I blame him.

I did it because I had to, because I couldn't let him lose everything because of me when the whole point of us to begin with was to protect his inheritance.

Danika pokes her head in the door. "Do you need anything before I go to class? Medicine? An ice pack? Orange juice?"

"Orange juice?" I start to tear up, thinking about Teddy and his love for the fruit juice.

"I know it sounds insane, but my brother swears by it when he's sick."

"I'm fine."

"Well, okay." She tucks a strand of hair behind her ear. A few loose pieces frame her face, the rest tied in an intricate braid. "I have to go to class, but I'll text you before I come back to the dorm in case you've changed your mind."

"Thanks."

She gives me a sympathetic look before leaving me to my wallowing.

As pathetic as it is, Teddy is—*was*—my first real relationship. I've had one-night stands and short flings that lasted no longer than a month. And man, if this is what it feels like when it's over, I never want to date again. I'll be an Old Maid with a million cats. Honestly, I don't know why people talk about that in a negative light. Sounds like the dream to me.

Sniffling, I grab a tissue off my nightstand, drying my swollen eyes. How I have any tears left is beyond me.

Across the room, from my Bluetooth speaker, Harry Styles croons about the sign of the times. I decided to forgo using my record player today so I wouldn't have to move from my bed to flip it over and change them.

Because I love to torture myself, I think about Teddy

showing up with Five Guys and eating in my bed. All the times we watched *Beverly Hills 90210*—now that show is ruined for me because I'll only think of him every time I watch it.

Pressing the heels of my hands into my eyes until I see stars, I cry fully—body shaking sobs—because so many things about my life are entwined with Teddy now. Even The Burger Palace reminds me of him. I both hate and love that so much of my life has revolved around him in recent months.

"What are you doing?" I ask myself. "Get yourself together. This is pathetic. He's just a guy."

My pitiful pep-talk does me no good. The tears keep falling and eventually I roll over, cupping my hands beneath my head, and fall back asleep.

"YOU'RE NOT ACTUALLY SICK, are you?"

I crack an eye open to find Danika standing above me, an iced coffee in her outstretched hand and a muffin in the other.

I shake my head, and dammit if my lip doesn't start trembling with renewed tears even after hours of sleep.

"What is it and who do I need to beat up?"

"M-Myself." I sit up, taking the coffee and muffin from her. One sip of coffee and I already feel a tad stronger.

Danika sits on the end of my bed, twisting her body toward me. She utters one command, "Spill," and I do.

Not just about breaking up with Teddy—but all of it,

from how we began, to his father and what a monster he is, to how things changed in Greece, and finally I reveal what happened two nights ago at the party.

"Whoa." She smacks the back of her head against the wall when I finish, rubbing the spot she didn't mean to hit. "That's heavy."

"It's a lot to process," I agree.

"You can say that again." She's flabbergasted, trying to process all the details I've sprung upon her. "But you love him, really love him?"

I swallow a bite of muffin. "So much."

"Then why the fuck did you agree to break up with him? His father sounds like a world class dick. I would never do what he says."

"*Because* I love him, I had to agree. I couldn't stand to see him lose everything. I'm not worth it."

She's quiet for a moment, my comforter scrunched in her hands. "Do you think Teddy would agree with that statement?"

"Why wouldn't he? That's the whole reason this whole thing started."

"It seems like it grew into something ... *real*."

A heavy sigh rattles my chest, shaking from the tears still held inside. "He was a player before me. He'll go back to his old ways and survive."

"But will he? Will *you*?"

My silence is answer enough.

I'm not so sure.

A WEEK PASSES BY, and I avoid every possible place and route I might bump into Teddy on campus. I feel like a shell, barely aware of my classes and putting in the bare minimum effort. Somehow, I manage to keep my grades at a passing level, which is good considering graduation is around the corner. At least then I'll be free of this place, of the memories, of ever seeing Teddy again. If only that thought brought the relief I wish it did. Instead, thinking about how I might never see him again makes me feel even more devastated.

Going through the motions at work, I do the best to get through my shift. My tips are shitty, but I can't even be mad because I know I'm not my typical self and customers think I'm a shitty waitress—which at the moment I am. I've messed up three orders, spilled five drinks, and spilled a basket of fries in one customer's lap, and I've only been here for two hours.

When I come out of the kitchen and spot a dark-haired figure sitting in a booth, my heart trips over itself. But I quickly realize it's not Teddy.

It is someone I know, though.

I approach the table like a grenade is about to go off. Stopping in front of Jude, I say, "Hey, what can I get you to drink?"

"A root beer." I look to the opposite side of the booth and find Cole there. I don't know how I missed him, since he's giant-height, but my brain must've been focused on Jude since from a distance I thought he was Teddy.

"Coke for me, please." Jude flashes his trademark winning smile.

MICALEA SMELTZER

"I'll be right back with those."

My legs feel wooden as I head for the drink fountain and grab their sodas, worried Teddy is going to show up and join them but too scared to ask. *Would* Teddy show up? Possibly try to force me to play along like we're still in a relationship?

No, my conscience informs me emphatically. *Teddy's not vindictive. He wouldn't do that to you.*

Drinks in hand, I carry them to the table and place them in front of the guys. "Do you know what you want to eat?"

Jude takes a sip of his Coke, cringing. "Shit, dude. This is your nasty ass root beer."

Great, now I can add mixing up customer's drinks to the list.

They switch drinks and place orders for food. Before I can walk away, Jude says, "You hurt my friend."

Sucking in my cheeks, I say, "I'm hurting too."

His eyes narrow. "Then why did you break up with him."

"It's none of your business," I snap.

"Teddy is our best friend," Cole interrupts, rubbing a hand over his closely cropped hair. "That means it is our business."

Biting my tongue, I say, "It's complicated."

"We know you were fake-dating him to start with." My jaw falls open at Jude's admission. "In fact," he leans his big body onto the table, hands clasped in a way that makes his muscles stand out, but I'm in such a piss-poor mood I can't even admire the show, "we've known for a

400

while, and we've also known since Teddy spilled those details that he had real feelings for you."

"Things are complicated," I repeat myself, my brain short-circuiting on other things to say.

Cole taps his fingers on the table. "Care to elaborate on this complication you speak of."

"Not really. I'd like to take your orders and move on."

"No offense," Jude begins, and I automatically know I'm going to take offense, "but you look like shit. I can tell you've been crying, and you look sick. Guess what? Teddy looks like shit too. So tell me, why are you both wasting your time being miserable when you could make up and agree this is all a big misunderstanding, a speed bump in the road if you will, and move the fuck on."

"*I can't.*" My hands fist at my sides, I'm vibrating with anger at his pushiness. Cole sits there playing with his straw wrapper.

"Let it go, dude." Cole shakes his head. "This isn't our battle."

Jude sighs heavily. "You're my friend too, Vanessa. Sure, I haven't known you as long as I have Teddy, but I like you, and I fucking hate seeing two of my friends miserable and hurting when they don't have to be. Let me ask you something. Whatever happened to spook you, is it worth losing him?"

With those parting words, they slap money down on the table—way more than enough for the drinks and I guess deciding they don't want to eat after all in my presence. They stride out of The Burger Palace, leaving me standing at the table lingering in a pool of doubt.

I did the right thing.
I think.

THIRTY-NINE

Teddy

IT'S THE LAST GAME OF THE SEASON, THE LAST GAME OF my college career and *I don't care*.

I should be hyped, high on this ending and what comes next, but I'm not because my thoughts are all tied up with Vanessa, mingled with hurt and confusion.

It's a home game, another thing I should be fucking elated over, but I'm not. I'd rather be ending this at an away game so I wouldn't obsess over the possibility of Vanessa showing up. I don't think she will, but I can't help but think *what if*.

I never thought I'd turn into this pathetic fucker over a girl, but here I am.

"Get the fuck out of your head," Mascen scolds, slapping the back of my head in an effort to snap me from where I've drifted off to. "We have a game to win."

"I know, I know." I jerk my pants on.

"Someone put Teddy's hype song on," Murray yells out, hands cupped around his mouth.

I groan, burying my head inside my locker in an effort to disappear. It's ironic since normally I love being the center of attention, but not right now.

'Everywhere I Go' by Hollywood Undead starts to play and I shrink even more.

"Turn it off," I beg Mascen or anyone who hears and decides to have mercy on me.

Mascen's eyes narrow on me and the next thing I know he's grabbing me and dragging me to the showers where it's quiet.

"What the fuck?" He crosses his arms over his chest, leveling me with one of his trademark glares.

"Uh ... am I supposed to respond to that?"

He shakes his head, pinching the bridge of his nose like I'm giving him a headache.

"You need to get yourself together." I start to protest, but he shuts me up with a look that says he's ready to kill me. "I get you're going through shit right now. Fuck, I'd be worse than you if Rory left me, but the team is counting on you. Get through this game and then you can fall apart."

Rubbing a hand over my unshaven jaw, I nod. "Okay. I can do that."

He gives me a sympathetic look, a rare thing from Mascen, and then he surprises me even more when he says, "I'm sorry."

"Let's just win this game."

Pasting on a fake smile, I go back into the locker room and play my part. The one of the goofy, overzealous guy who doesn't have a care in the world.

No one cares that it's a lie.

———————

WE WIN THE GAME, but barely.

After a long-ass shower, I change into my clothes, and all the guys head to Harvey's to celebrate. For once, I'd rather not, but what choice do I have?

We end up at our usual table, the whole team plus friends and a group of girls. Murray has one girl draped over his lap, his tongue down her throat.

That used to be me.

And now I'm sitting here like a sad fuck thinking about how I wish I was celebrating with Vanessa. For a second, I thought I saw her at the game, but when I looked back, I realized it was someone else.

I order a beer. Then when it's gone, I order another drink. And another. Drinking until the room spins and I feel like I might throw up. It's better than pretending all evening I'm fine.

A steel band closes around my body and I jerk against it. "What the fuck?" I look down and realize there's a dark arm wrapped around me. "Cole? My duuuude. What're you doing?"

"Getting you out of here before you pour even more

alcohol into your system and do something you might regret in the morning?"

"Like what?" My feet drag against the floor and somewhere in my brain I register that Cole is dragging me, not because he has to but because my feet won't work. Zoey trails after us and I laugh, calling to her, "Hey, Mom!"

"I don't know, like hook up with another girl."

"I would never!"

"There are lots of things people do when they're drunk that they wouldn't normally do. I'm not going to let that happen."

"It's not like it would matter," I grumble as we exit the building into the cool night air. It feels good against my too-hot skin. "I don't have a girlfriend anymore, remember?"

"Don't make me slap you silly," Zoey scolds, picking something up off the ground.

My shoe. It's my shoe.

Why did my shoe fall off?

"Get the truck unlocked," Cole tells her.

The door squeals in protest at being opened. Zoey climbs in first, taking the middle seat, and Cole shoves me in beside her.

"I'm going to be sick."

"Don't throw up on me!" Zoey shrieks in horror.

Leaning out of the truck, I empty my stomach on the ground. Cole groans, muttering, "At least you missed my shoes."

I don't remember the drive back to their apartment,

but I do remember getting dragged up the stairs and dumped on the couch.

"Sleep it off," Cole commands. He doesn't sound disgusted, just worried. I don't know why. I'm fine.

"Whatever you say, Dad." I kick off my shoe, Zoey still has the other one, and drape a blanket over myself.

"Goodnight." Zoey ruffles my hair as she passes by me.

"Mmm," I hum back.

Cole chuckles from the area of the kitchen.

Crooking my arm over my face, I fall asleep.

"WAKE UP." Zoey shoves what I assume is her foot into my ribs. "Cole's making breakfast."

"Food," I grumble, waking to the smell of bacon. As I become more aware, I realize I have to take a piss. "Ugh." I sit up slowly, head pounding. Cole knows better than to let me fall asleep after a night like that without drinking water and taking an aspirin. Fucker probably just wants me to suffer today.

"Go wash up." Zoey comes into focus, her curly hair pulled up on top of her head. "You smell like a zoo."

"Thanks for the compliment, Mom."

"You're welcome, Fido. Who's a good boy?" She pets the top of my head. I playfully swat her hand away.

My body creaks and groans as I manage to stand and waddle down the hall to relieve myself. I feel loads better having an empty bladder. Grabbing some of Cole's toothpaste, I put some on my finger and swipe it over my teeth before rinsing. It's better than nothing. I steal some of his cologne too, dabbing it on my skin so I won't smell like the zoo Zoey accused me of.

When I leave the bathroom, breakfast is ready. My stomach rumbles with the promise of greasy bacon.

"How are you feeling this morning?" Cole lifts a cup of coffee to his lips, eyeing me over the rim.

"Like death or close to it."

He chuckles. "You were really pouring it in last night."

"Yeah, well," I stir my fork around in my scrambled eggs, "I miss her."

"None of this makes any sense," Zoey says softly, like she doesn't want to startle me, which is unusual for her. Normally she loves to give me shit.

I shrug indifferently, like none of this matters. Taking a drink of orange juice, I go over that night again, pouring over every detail in my mind. I always stop, coming back to the fact of my father trailing behind her. Things were *good* with us, I'm not that oblivious, and I know in my gut he has something to do with this, but if I can't get her to talk to me, what am I supposed to do?

I must say the last part out loud because Zoey gives me an incredulous look. "Jesus, Teddy, I don't know maybe send her flowers or something? Girls really aren't that complicated."

Cole chuckles into his eggs. "You stay out of this," I grumble at him.

He only laughs harder. Jerk.

I leave their apartment and return to my dorm, grabbing another sheet of paper and writing down my thoughts. I feel a little better when I finish writing and fold up the paper, but it still doesn't entirely erase the ache settling into my bones. The only thing that will fix that is getting Vanessa back.

FORTY

Vanessa

MY FEET ACHE FROM BEING ON THEM FOR HOURS working. I've been picking up extra shifts when I can, needing to save every penny I can because I *refuse* to move back to White Claw. I love my parents, but I can't go back there and deal with my sister and Tristan who will no doubt begin popping out kids soon.

I need distance to build my own life and focus on my dreams. Am I going to have enough money to go to New York City? Definitely not, but maybe I can make it work somewhere else and build things up and then get there. Dreams don't come true overnight. They take work.

I sit down for my break with a glass of fresh lemonade and a B.L.T. sandwich with fries. I know I need to eat, I barely ate breakfast, skipped lunch, and it's past dinner-time now, but even looking at food has my stomach rolling.

It's been two weeks since I broke up with Teddy. Stupidly I thought by now I'd feel better, not worse. Every single day I wake up aching all over, my heart heavy in my chest. I did this to myself, I know, but I had no choice. Teddy is too close to gaining access to his inheritance to lose it because of me.

Fixing my ponytail, I glare at the plate of food like it's personally offended me.

"What's wrong with you?" Hailey, one of the other waitresses asks me.

"Haven't been feeling the best."

Her lips purse in speculation. "You're not pregnant, are you?"

"No," I scoff, offended by the suggestion.

She shrugs. "It was just a question. Don't get so pissy." She moves away from me, checking on one of her tables.

Resting my head in my hand, I nibble on the end of a fry. When it goes down okay, I eat another. My classes wrap up this week, with graduation the week after. I should be excited, downright ecstatic, but I feel numb. I hate that such a monumental moment is being ruined for me all because I fell in love. Love is stupid. I should've known the day I returned to campus and couldn't get into my dorm that it was some sort of omen. Clearly, I didn't listen to what the fates were telling me.

A body slides into the booth across from me, and I

jump at the surprise intrusion. Jude places his muscular arms on the table, lacing his fingers together. Lowering my eyes from his stare, I push my plate away. I had no appetite to begin with, and now I really don't have one.

"Haven't seen you in a while, so I thought I would drop by." He picks up my discarded straw wrapper, ripping it into tiny shreds.

"You've gotta stop showing up to my job like this."

He rolls his eyes. "Maybe I really want a burger. Who are you to judge?"

"Tell me why you're here and stop wasting both our time."

He leans back in the booth, draping his right arm along the back. The shiny red vinyl squeaks as he moves. "I guess I'm waiting for one of you to get your head out of your ass and fix this."

"Jude." My shoulders deflate. "Let this go."

"Listen," he leans forward, "I've been through a bad breakup before. Had my heart ripped out of my chest and everything I pictured for a future ruined. Something unforgivable happened, and I knew there was no fixing it, so I guess I have to ask you—is this fixable?"

"It's not like that." I look at the wall beside the booth, there's an old Corvette poster framed there.

"Then what is it?"

Letting my hair out of its ponytail, I smooth it back and refix it. "I can't say."

"Don't be ridiculous, Vanessa."

"Look," I scoot out of the booth and stand, "I like you,

Jude ... as a friend." As if that isn't obvious. "And as a friend, I'm asking you to drop this."

I pick up my uneaten food to get back to work, but he stops me. "Whatever this is, is it worth it?"

I exhale heavily, tears stinging my eyes. "It has to be."

FORTY-ONE

Teddy

"What the fuck is all of this?" Jude enters our suite, looking around at every surface covered in cookies. Cookies on plates, in baggies, on cooling racks, literally everywhere. "How many cookies have you made? Is there a bake-off happening? A charity auction? Explain, I'm begging you." The door closes behind him, his boots landing with a thud a moment later.

"I'm stress-baking," I bite out.

"What are you *this* stressed about?" He picks up a chocolate chip cookie and shoves it in his mouth, crumbs dribbling out of his mouth onto the floor.

"I think my dad has something to do with Vanessa breaking up with me."

"And your solution was to bake cookies?" He swipes

another one—oatmeal raisin this time—he cringes and tosses it in the trash before grabbing chocolate chip.

"You know about my dad." My shoulders hunch, the counter clasped tightly in my hands. Letting all my friends in on the secret of my abusive father was fucking hard. It's still weird thinking about telling them all, but I'm glad they know. "Confronting him is difficult to me—don't get me wrong, I'm going to—but first..." I trail off, motioning to the piles and piles of cookies.

"Wow." His eyes widen. "That's a hell of a lot of stress over one person."

"It's not easy challenging your abuser."

Jude's eyes fill with sympathy. I hate it. I don't want anyone to feel sorry for me. He swipes two more cookies and claps me on the shoulder. "You're stronger than he is. Don't let small men make you feel weak. He's torn you down because he knows you're more than he can ever be."

"Thanks, man." Looking at the mess of cookies, I know I need to stop avoiding this. "Do me a favor and hand these out around campus. I'm going to see my dad."

Jude grins. "Are you sure you don't need company?"

"I can handle this."

———

I LET myself into the house. It's possible he's not even here. For all I know he's flown off to another country for business or he's playing golf with his rich friends. But when I got in my car, this is where I came, as if drawn by a magnet.

I surge through the house like a raging storm. Any staff I pass eyes me speculatively. No doubt they're aware I haven't been called here, and since I don't show up voluntarily, they're probably wondering what the hell is up.

"Teddy?" My mom's high-pitched shriek of my name comes from the tea-room.

Yes, the tea-room. A room specifically for drinking tea. Or at least that's all I've ever seen her do there.

I halt my steps, back tracking to poke my head in the room. "I'm looking for Dad."

"Oh." Her eyes widen, darting above her to where he's probably upstairs in his office. "Why?" She looks scared. Shaky. Like she knows confrontation between him and me is coming and it terrifies her.

I narrow my eyes on her, studying the way even in the summer heat she's wearing long sleeves.

"Roll your sleeves up."

"What?" Her lashes brush her cheeks, stunned by my question. Frustrated, I stalk forward, gently taking her wrist in my hand. "No, no. Teddy, don't," she pleads, but it's useless. I yank up the sleeve of her shirt, revealing a band of bruises on her slender arm in the shape of fingerprints.

Our eyes meet, a wordless communication passing between us.

"Why didn't you ever leave him?"

She swallows, eyes dropping to the floor. "Do you really think a man that powerful would let me *leave?*"

"Fuck." I rub my hand over my face. "I hate him."

416

She smiles sadly, touching her hand to my cheek. "I know."

"Vanessa broke up with me."

"What? No." She looks at me with surprise and disbelief.

"I think he made her."

"I'm sorry."

"I won't let him control my life anymore."

"You don't have to." She lets her hand fall from my face.

"Is he in his office?"

"Mhmm," she hums.

Wrapping my arms around her, I bury my head in her neck. Neither of us has ever spoken a word about the abuse, maybe thinking if we didn't give it voice then it wasn't real. But this has to end.

"I'm going to graduate, Mom. I'll be on my own. Leave him. We can figure it out."

"It's not that simple." I can see her retreating into herself, her body physically curling up as she tries to make herself smaller.

"Okay." My voice is soft, hurt. But I know better than to push this right now. There will be plenty of time later for me to try to convince her to walk away from him.

Leaving her to her tea, I bound upstairs down the long hall and into his office.

He's on the phone when I shove the door open. I can tell it's on the tip of his tongue to yell at whoever has dared to breach his space, but he must see something on my face that stops him from doing that.

"I'm going to have to call you back." He hangs up the phone and stands. Despite working from home, he's dressed in a suit and tie. It's pathetic how far he goes to be in control. "What are you doing here, son?"

"Something tells me you already know."

"Ah." He grins, clearly pleased with himself. "The girl."

Storming forward, I slam my palms down on the table. Items on his desk rattle but he doesn't seem to care. He stands there, coolly amused. "The girl?" I repeat in a mocking tone. "The. Girl? You mean the one I love, the woman who means more to me than my next fucking breath? That one?"

"Don't be dramatic, son. I know she was blackmailing you." He sits down, leaning back in his chair. Calm, cool, collected. Nothing ruffles this man.

"Blackmailing me? What the hell makes you think that?"

His eyes narrow. "I know you paid off her tuition."

If he was anyone else, I'd tell the truth, but I can't do that. "Did it ever occur to you that maybe I love her and wanted to do that?"

His lips turn down in a frown, and I realize that no, this thought didn't cross his mind. He's so fucking jaded his first thought was blackmail.

"If that were the case, she wouldn't have agreed so easily."

"Agreed to what?"

"To go away."

"What did you do to her?" Fear rattles inside me, of what he might've done or said to her.

"Nothing." He can't help but smirk. "I offered her money, but she wouldn't take it."

He tried to pay her to break up with me, and she said no? Then what —

He must see the question on my face, because he reaches into his desk drawer and procures a stack of papers. Flipping to the last page, he shows me a digital signature in Vanessa's handwriting. He closes it back up, holding it out to me. "Take it."

I yank the papers from his hand. A hiss flies out of his mouth, and I hope the fucker got a papercut. I don't look down at them, not caring about the details. They don't matter. The only thing important here is leaving this life behind and convincing Vanessa she matters more than any of this ever could.

"You are out of my life. You won't control me anymore. You can't order people in my life around. You are a small, pathetic man who uses his fists and words to control others, but I'm done being your punching bag. You'll never lay another hand on me again or I *will* talk." His eyes widen with shock like it's never occurred to him that I could speak out on this. "Stay the fuck away from me."

With those parting words, I head out. I shut the door behind me. I don't slam it, there's no point. He doesn't deserve anything from me, not even my anger, because he doesn't mean a thing to me.

FORTY-TWO

Vanessa

WITH AN EXHAUSTED EXHALE OF BREATH, I UPLOAD MY last paper to my Marketing in the Digital World class.

I'm done.

That's it.

College is over ... well, basically.

I still have to wait for final grades to be put in, but I have no doubt I'll pass despite the less than stellar way I've been feeling. Closing my laptop, I shove it aside and stand up to stretch. My body pops and cracks like I'm eighty-two. That's what I get for sitting still too long.

The door to the suite opens and shuts with a click. *"Please* tell me you're down to share a pizza tonight?" Danika practically begs, sounding exhausted. "I'm starving and don't feel like cooking."

"Pizza sounds great." Stepping out of my room, my eyes dart to the stack of letters in her hand. "Jeez, what's all that?"

"It's for you." She holds them out to me. They look like they're all the same size and roughly the same thickness. "They don't say who they're from. I finally dropped by the mail room because I had an Amazon package arrive." She waves the yellow package. "They just have your name on them."

Puzzled, I take them from her. She's right, all they say on them is my name. No dorm address. No stamp. No nothing.

Odd.

She tucks her package underneath her arm. "I'm going to order the pizza. You cool with mushrooms?"

"That's fine," I say distractedly, fixated on the scribble of my name and the handwriting I recognize.

We both head to our rooms. I close my door behind me wanting privacy as I spread the letters onto my bed. My heart feels heavy with hurt and excitement.

I grab one at random and open it carefully, not wanting to rip the edges.

Pulling out the piece of paper, Teddy's scrawl fills the page.

This writing letters thing is weird, but somehow therapeutic. Jude told me to remind you that I'm here, and I figured letters were a good way to do that—not intrusive but something physical you can hold that shows you no matter what, I'm always here for you. But I'm finding that writing these to you makes me feel better. Even if you never read them, I think this is necessary for me.

I know I'm not the best at expressing myself in words. What can I say? I'm a physical kind of guy.

But maybe I should've used my words more to tell you how much I care.

How I love the sound of your laugh, and the way your eyes twinkle when you think I'm funny, and how your mouth curves when you're trying not to smile but you can't help it.

I love the way you tuck your hair behind your ear.

I love when you give me hell because you think I need to be knocked down.

I love lying in your bed, even when you make me listen to Harry Styles.

A giggle bursts free from me at that.

Vanessa, I love YOU. Every little thing that makes up who you are. I hope you know that.

I should've told you sooner.

I don't know what happened to us, but if you ever give me another chance, I'll tell you every second of every day what you mean to me.

Teddy

I don't realize I'm crying until a tear drops onto the paper. "Shit," I curse, not wanting to smear his writing. Setting the letter on the bed I grab a tissue and dry my face. Reading his words hurts, that ache of missing him settling deeper into my chest where it's never entirely gone away in these long as hell weeks.

Once I have my tears under control, I pick up another letter.

This one is short and simple. Three words.

I miss you.

I grab another at random.

I didn't expect to fall for you, but I did.

Little by little. With every new detail I learned about you, I fell harder.

I hope you know that everything with you was real. I wasn't playing you if that's what you think.

I don't know what I did to change what we had. I wish I understood.

— Teddy

I'm greedy now, tearing right into another.

I never knew my chest could hurt like this. There's an ache that's lived there ever since I watched the car drive away with you in it. You ignore my texts. Don't answer my calls.

You're all I can think about — but do you think of me at all?

Maybe I was never as special to you, as you are to me.

— Teddy

My heart breaks more than it already has, thinking about Teddy believing he's not special to me when he's become my everything.

I've been doing a lot of thinking.

So many things don't add up.

We were fine — better than fine.

When I held you in the garden, your body grinding against mine, I saw it in your eyes. The words I said later.

I love you.

You love me — I know you do.

That leaves me with why?

Why would you end it?

Are you scared? Of me? Of feeling too much? Of falling too far?

I'm begging you.

Fall with me.

I'll catch you. Promise.

—Teddy

My fingers shake as I lower the letter. "Oh, Teddy," I sigh aloud. Sniffling, I wipe away the tears on my cheeks. I hate that I hurt him, broke him in such a way. Broke myself too.

I know I was backed into a corner. I did what I had to do. But that doesn't make me feel better.

I'm not giving up on you, Vanessa.

It would be easy to tuck tail and admit defeat. To turn back to parties, drinking, women. But that's not who I am anymore and who I've become is yours.

I'll give you space, for now, but I'm not going down without a fight.

—Teddy

I hurry through the rest of the letters, then reread them.

If I had any doubts about how Teddy really feels about me, there's none left.

His words bleed with truth.

But none of it matters.

I signed a contract. It's a done deal. I'm out of Teddy's life for good.

FORTY-THREE

Teddy

I KEEP PUTTING LETTERS IN VANESSA'S DORM MAILBOX. I have no fucking clue if she's even getting them, but it makes me feel better to know that they're there for her. I start sending flowers every day too—wanting her to know she's always on my mind, that I haven't stopped thinking about her even if I haven't seen her in person.

As much as I've wanted to show up at her door, I haven't.

I read and reread the contract she signed with my father, stunned to learn that she only agreed to breakup with me if my father guaranteed I was allowed my share of the family company on top of my inheritance from my grandfather—both to be given to me as soon as I walk across the stage and graduate.

She knew I was going to walk away from the family company, but Vanessa thought I deserved what I'd rightfully earned, so she made sure I'm to get it. I could throttle her if I didn't love her so damn much. She means more to me than my family's various businesses. I don't want it. Not any parts of it.

But I couldn't throw her sacrifice away, so after pouring over the papers, I knew I had to wait until after graduation. The way the document is worded, there's nothing that says we can *never* get back together—not that I'd listen anyway if that were the case—so after my diploma is in my hand, I'm getting my girl ... and then selling off the shares I'll get of the McCallister empire.

My father will fucking *love* that—curse my name and hers, but he can't stop me from doing what I want with my half of everything. Guess he should've read the fine print better.

"Dude, are you ready?"

Jude appears in the doorway of my room. He'll graduate next year, but he's going to be in the stands since he has so many friends graduating.

"Yeah, yeah, yeah," I chant, sticking my cap on my head and giving him a goofy grin. "I'm ready."

Ready to get my girl back. The diploma is a small bonus compared to that.

———————

THE GRADUATING class this year is massive. We're seated on the turf of the football stadium, the stands filled with family and friends. I'm sweating in unmentionable places as speech after speech is given. I start to nod off at one point and the chick next to me rams her elbow into my ribs. I don't know whether to be grateful or annoyed.

When names finally start being called, I grumble out a, "Thank fuck," earning me a glare from the girl. "What?" I ask innocently.

She rolls her eyes in answer.

When Cole's name is called, I cheer loudly, whistling to get his attention. He marches across the stage and accepts his diploma with a grin. The guy is joining the NBA, but he still wanted to finish school.

Murray is the next friend to walk.

Then it's Vanessa's turn. I yell so loudly that I'll probably go hoarse. She looks out into the sea of graduates, but I know she can't see me. I can't wait for this to be over so I can hunt her down, say what I have to say, and kiss the fuck out of her.

The row I'm in stands, making our way to the stage.

Then my name is being called, and after four fucking years, all my friends are about to learn my actual name. The one I loathe more than anything. The same name as my father's, passed down for generations but one I *won't* be passing down to my son if I have one.

"Edmund Olivier Arthur McCallister."

Edmund. Fucking *Edmund*. What kind of name is that anyway? I'll forever be grateful my mom started calling me Teddy—and not Eddie—when I was young. Teddy is a whole lot cooler than *Edmund*.

Edmund doesn't slay dragons, he *is* the dragon—and not the good kind either.

Teddy ... well, hopefully he gets the girl.

I take my diploma, enduring the rest of the graduation. When I toss my cap off, I have only one goal in mind, finding Vanessa, but I know it'll be nearly impossible in this crowd.

I move through the crowd, toward where the H's were seated hoping she hasn't made a mad dash for the exit. Murray intercepts me, throwing an arm around my shoulders.

"Edmund?" He shakes me and I laugh. "Your name is fucking Edmund? Dude, how have you kept this shit under wraps for so long?"

I laugh, extracting myself from his grip. "Money talks, my friend. Take this for now." I shove my diploma holder at him.

"Where are you going?" He calls after me as I slip away.

"I gotta find Vanessa," I yell back, the crowd swallowing me.

I'm not sure I'll find her, it seems like an impossible task, but then I spot her curly dark hair cascading down her back, the loose gown unable to hide her curves.

Marching up to her, I grab her hand. She gasps at my touch, her eyes wide with surprise.

"Teddy?"

Taking her cheeks in my hands, her skin smooth and soft against my palms, I kiss her like I've been dreaming about for weeks.

Mine, my blood seems to shout through my system as I kiss her.

She kisses me back, her body melting into mine.

My girl.

"Y-You can't do that," she stutters when I release her mouth. "We broke up."

"Babe, I know."

"If you know then why are you kissing me?"

"No," I laugh, "I mean I know why. What you did. What my father made you do."

"*Okay*," she drawls, "then you know I signed a contract, and we can't be together."

"Unfortunately for my dad, he must've been in a hurry, because the way it's worded nothing is preventing us from being together now that we've graduated, and do you really think I would've let that stop me anyway?"

"But—"

I place my forefinger over her full lips. "You mean more to me than anything, Van. I would give everything up for you, don't you get it? Loving you is the greatest thing I've ever done. I'm not going to let that go easily."

I let my finger drop, taking in every inch of her face and committing it to memory. I didn't realize it standing in the admin building the first time I saw her, but this girl is *the* girl. There's no one else for me. One day I'm going to get down on one knee and ask her to marry me, I'm going to wait at the end of an aisle for her, and then if the fates allow it, we'll have kids. The idea of a child that looks like the both of us fills me with a feeling I've never experienced before. But those things can all come in time, right now I need her to come back to me.

I take her face between my hands again, afraid if I don't keep touching her, she'll vanish. "I would've shown up at your dorm the second I realized what my dad made you do, but I didn't want your sacrifice to mean nothing. There's nothing he can do now to stop me from getting my inheritance from my grandfather, or the portion of the family businesses you secured me, and he definitely can't stop me from getting you."

"I can't believe this." She blinks up at me, tears filling her blue eyes. "I got your letters," she admits, biting her lip. "I love them."

"What do you say, Van? You want to try out this thing called life with me? For real this time? No agreements, nothing standing in our way. Just you and me?"

A single tear falls from her right eye. I swipe it away with my thumb. I hope she never cries because of me ever again, at least not sad tears. Sniffling, she nods enthusiastically, throwing her arms around my shoulders. I catch her, holding onto her and burying my head into her neck. Inhaling her scent, I feel grounded like … like I'm *home* and I realize I've never understood before what that word truly means, but that's what Vanessa is for me.

"I love you."

My body warms at her words. I've been waiting so fucking long to hear her say that. "Say it again," I beg, not caring if I sound pathetic.

"I love you, I love you, I love you … Edmund."

I groan, chuckling against her. "Don't go and ruin it for me."

"I can't believe your name is *Edmund*."

"I can't either."

She pulls away enough to see my face. "I really thought it was Theodore and you were just messing with all of us."

Throwing my head back with laughter, I say, "No, definitely not. You know you didn't actually give me an answer."

She laughs and I feel that sound through my entire body. It's only been a few weeks since I've seen her, held her, but it feels like years. "I thought 'I love you' was answer enough."

"I want to hear it, Van," I plead.

She smiles, reaching up to trace her finger over the side of my jaw, over my chin, and then around my lips. "I want to be yours. For real this time. No take backs."

"No take backs."

I kiss her again, silently vowing to kiss her every single day for the rest of our lives. She deserves nothing but the best, and that's what I'm going to be.

EPILOGUE

Six Years Later
Vanessa

WALKING DOWN THE BUSTLING BROOKLYN STREETS, I can't stop smiling to myself. I'm sure to anyone glancing my way as they pass by I look like I've lost my mind, but I'm so happy I can't keep my smile contained.

My life is as close to perfect as one can get.

I have my dream job in Manhattan, working PR for a book publisher. I've been married to the love of my life for the past four years. We have a beautiful three-bedroom apartment that's spacious for the city. Shortly after we graduated, just like he said he would Teddy sold his shares in his family's business. Well, all but five-percent. I think there was a part of him that couldn't fully part with what he always thought he'd have and that's fine. Now, he owns a cookie food truck that's become a hot spot throughout the area. And our relationship is solid. He's my rock, my best friend, my lover.

Teddy McCallister is everything I didn't know I wanted and everything I needed.

Walking up the steps to our building, envelope clutched to my chest, I take a breath to calm my excited nerves.

Teddy and I have been trying to get pregnant for two years now. After no luck, we finally got pregnant six months ago but it ended in a miscarriage at eight weeks. It was devastating for both of us and having to tell everyone we lost the baby was the worst kind of torture.

This time around, when I missed my period and took a test, I didn't even tell Teddy. Not because I didn't want to, but I saw how much it upset and stressed him after we lost our first baby, so I wanted to wait until I went to the doctor and got everything checked out. Sure, anything could still happen, but my doctor is optimistic so I'm choosing to focus on that.

Letting myself into the apartment, I'm met with my husband yelling after our pug—he surprised me with a puppy a year after we moved to the city, all because he remembered me telling him in the truck stop when we were first getting to know each other that I had always wanted a pug.

Teddy doesn't forget a thing.

Closing the door behind me, I kick off my flats. Heels are in my bag, but I refuse to walk around the city in them, only slipping them on when I reach my office.

"Penny! Stop stealing my socks! This is why I don't have any matching ones."

He runs past me after the pudgy little pug, a hot pink sock with pizza slices on them clasped in her mouth.

I laugh at them, setting my bag down. My fingers flex around the envelope, excitement pulsing through my blood.

"Babe," I call out. "Forget about the sock right now."

"But—"

"Please." I pout my bottom lip.

Penny wiggles her chubby butt beneath the couch, tail wagging victoriously.

He follows me into the kitchen, grabbing orange juice from the fridge and taking a drink. "How'd your doctor's appointment go?"

I told him I wasn't feeling great and had an appointment since I knew I'd be later than normal getting home from work.

Sitting at the counter—we don't have room for a table —I slide the envelope across it. He eyes it, then me, a question lingering there.

"Take it." I bite my lip, suppressing my smile.

He places his hand on it, hesitating. "You're not sick-sick, are you?" The worry in his tone gives a tug on my heart.

"Not in that way, promise."

He opens the envelope, pulling out the ultrasound that shows the tiny little bean living inside me. His eyes grow large, lips parted as he looks from it to me and back again.

"You're pregnant?" I burst into tears, nodding enthusiastically. "We're having a baby?"

"Yes," I gasp out. "It's still early but … yes." He pulls me off the stool, hugging me so tightly I can hardly breathe. He buries his face into my hair, his body shaking. "Babe? Are you crying?"

"Of course, I'm crying." He doesn't sound the least bit ashamed. "We've been waiting so long for this." He holds my face tenderly between his hands, kissing me reverently. Then he drops to his knees, putting his hands on my stomach and kissing it through the fabric of my dress. "Hi, baby. I'm your daddy. You better hang tight in there and grow strong, because your mommy and I want to meet you so bad."

I can't help it when I start crying. I wish I could blame it on hormones, but it's not that. Not getting pregnant was hard, losing our baby was torture, now we hang in the balance of being thrilled at being pregnant but terrified of what could happen.

"Don't cry, Van." He looks up at me from his knelt position. "The baby told me it's here to stay. It can't wait to meet you."

"You think so?"

"I know so." He stands, kissing me again and doing his best to erase my fears.

He wraps his arms around me, holding me, supporting me. "This baby is so lucky to have you for its daddy."

"We're the lucky ones, Van."

I curl my fingers around his neck, tears coming anew. "You're right."

Placing my head against his chest, his heart thumps steadily against my ear. Who would've thought that Teddy McCallister would become my whole world and now we're going to have a baby.

I used to a dream of a life like this.

The reality is even better.

WANT EVEN MORE **Teddy and Vanessa?** Check out this bonus epilogue and find out what happens next.

HAVEN'T READ **Mascen and Rory's book yet?** Read it now.

WANT to know more about **Cole and Zoey?** Read it now.

WHAT'S COMING NEXT in The Boys series?
   Good Guys Don't Lie (Cree's Book)
   Broken Boys Can't Love (Jude's Book)
   More information coming soon.

ALSO BY MICALEA SMELTZER

Outsider Series

Outsider

Insider

Fighter

Avenger

Second Chances Standalone Series

Unraveling

Undeniable

Trace + Olivia Series

Finding Olivia

Chasing Olivia

Tempting Rowan

Saving Tatum

Trace + Olivia Box Set

Willow Creek Series

Last To Know

Never Too Late

In Your Heart

Take A Chance

Willow Creek Box Set

Always Too Late Short Story

Willow Creek Bonus Content

Home For Christmas

Light in the Dark Series

Rae of Sunshine

When Stars Collide

Dark Hearts

When Constellations Form

Broken Hearts

Stars & Constellations Bundle

The Us Series

The Road That Leads To Us

The Lies That Define Us

The Game That Break Us

Wild Collision

The Wild Series

Wild Collision

Wild Flame

The Boys Series

Bad Boys Break Hearts

Nice Guys Don't Win

Real Players Never Lose

Good Guys Don't Lie (Cree's book, coming soon)

Broken Boys Can't Love (Jude's book, coming soon)

Standalones

Beauty in the Ashes

Bring Me Back

The Other Side of Tomorrow

Jump (A 90s novella)

Desperately Seeking Roommate

Desperately Seeking Landlord

Whatever Happens

Sweet Dandelion

Say When

ACKNOWLEDGMENTS

The hardest part of writing any book is the acknowledgments. I'm always afraid I'm going to leave someone out.

Life's been crazy lately and writing this book was a welcome distraction. Teddy is so much fun to write and I love Vanessa too.

So much more goes into a book than just writing it, though.

That's where I have to thank Emily Wittig for the amazing cover and for being one of my best friends. When I say I don't know what I'd do without you, I truly mean that. I think we're meant to be in each other's lives for the long haul.

Thank you to my friends for keeping me distracted and not working too much. God knows without you guys I'd just work non-stop.

A big thank you to my lovely beta readers who were

an absolute godsend with this book since I was running behind. Each of you is a treasure and I can't thank you enough.

The biggest thank you, of course, goes out to YOU. Thank you for reading my books and allowing me to live out my dream. I hope I can keep bringing you more stories.